RAGE KING

BOOK 1

AARON CRASH

BLACK FORGE BOOKS

Rage King is a work of fiction. Names, characters, places, and incidents either are the product of the author's imagination or are used fictitiously. Any resemblance to actual persons living or dead, events, or locales is entirely coincidental.

Copyright © 2022 by Aaron Crash and Black Forge Books
All rights reserved.

No part of this publication may be reproduced, distributed, or transmitted in any form or by any means, including photocopying, recording, or other electronic or mechanical methods, without the prior written permission of the publisher, except in the case of brief quotations embodied in critical reviews and certain other noncommercial uses permitted by copyright law. For permission requests, email the publisher, subject line "Attention: Permissions Coordinator," at the email address below.
JStrode@ShadowAlleyPress.com

For this certain Adam I know.

CHAPTER ONE

Colton Henry Holliday turned around slowly as Jimbo Bunker and his goons approached. He put himself between the three men and Gillian, squaring his shoulders, already knowing that this was gonna be bad.

"So, Colt, you want to tell us who this is? Is she your girlfriend?" Jimbo asked.

Benny smirked. "Yeah, Colton, is she your girlfriend?"

Baxter echoed him. "Is she your girlfriend, Colton?"

It would have almost been comical if Jimbo wasn't Colton's boss, and wasn't so much of an asshole he needed two *more* assholes to handle the overflow.

Colt answered the question in a controlled voice. "She's a girl. She's my friend. But, no, she's not my girlfriend."

Gillian Croft was speechless. Gilly was cute in a nerdy girl way—brown hair in a ponytail, thick-framed black glasses, and startling blue eyes. They were the kind of eyes that seemed to get bluer the longer you looked into them. She hugged a textbook to her chest. They had a statistics class together at Metro State University. She was just dropping off the book for him, and he was going to give her his notes. He'd made copies. It shouldn't have been a big deal.

Gilly handed him the textbook. "Uh, here it is, Colt. I'll just go."

Jimbo laughed. "Don't hurry off. You're kind of cute. I mean, you'd need to do something with your hair. And come on, you don't need the glasses. Get contact lenses."

Colt pointed at Jimbo. "That's enough. You're done."

"Am I, Holliday?" Jimbo grinned. He was a thirty-something douchebag with bad teeth and bad breath. He worked out his arms only, so his whole body was bicep. He had the skinniest legs in the warehouse. "Or are you done? One more strike against you, just one, and you're fired. Then what happens?"

Colt knew what would happen.

Life could piss you off in any number of ways. In some ways, it felt like anger was a byproduct of breathing. That could've destroyed Colt's life, but unlike his father, he'd learned to control his temper. It was why he wasn't removing the teeth of the smirking son of a bitch in front of him. So he stood in the warehouse his grandfather had bought. The warehouse—the whole company—should've been Colt's. But that hadn't happened. Nothing happened like it should've.

Without another word, he escorted Gilly out of the warehouse. The January day was cold even though the sun was out. In the distance was Denver International Airport.

Gilly looked pale. "Do you think I need contacts? I mean, I like the glasses."

"I like the glasses too." Colt really liked them. He really liked Gilly. Which is why he didn't tell her she looked like the actress Zooey Deschanel. He'd just watched *Elf* over the Christmas holiday. He'd had to work straight through Christmas Eve and Christmas, but he didn't have anyone except Will Ferrell to spend it with, so working wasn't an issue.

He'd just wished management would've asked him and hadn't just assumed he'd work it.

Colt motioned for Gilly to take the lead as she walked down

the cement steps. The vans were all out on deliveries, so it was easy to get to her car—a really old Prius.

She saw him looking. "I'm not a hippie or anything. It's my parents'. It's their old car. I'll buy a new one once I graduate, or I hope I will. You know, it's the American dream. Get a job, get a car payment. Sign up for too many streaming services. Am I rambling? It feels like I'm rambling."

"You're fine."

It was either the cold or the embarrassment, but her chest reddened.

Colt wasn't about to get caught staring at her chest. He kept his eyes on her face. He'd done enough looking at her body in class.

Gilly was that rare beautiful girl who didn't know she was beautiful. She kept to herself. Colt figured she had a boyfriend, but he hadn't had the courage to ask her out. It was stupid. His whole life was stupid.

He was going to fucking change that.

Colt drew a hand through his own brown hair. "Sorry about that asshole. I never would've had you drop off the book if I'd known you'd have to deal with Jimbo and his henchmen."

"It's fine." She raised an eyebrow. "But are you going to be okay? I think the minute you use the word 'henchmen' it's a toxic work environment."

"You have no idea."

"I know it's not my place, and that I shouldn't say anything, but." She cut herself off. "No, I'm not going to say anything." That blush crept to her face. She turned abruptly around and opened her car door. She went to get in, but then spun back to him. "Okay, just this one thing. Don't stay in bad places. I've been in bad places before. And I didn't stay there. I'm glad I left. It's hard, I know, and now I'm definitely rambling. I'm gonna go now."

"It's just a long story, Gilly."

She waited for more. Her black glasses somehow made her eyes bluer.

"Maybe you and me could have coffee sometime." There, he'd done it. He asked her out. Coffee wasn't dinner. But it wasn't nothing either.

She actually winced. "Or talk after class? I'm funny about dating. Not that you asked me out. It was just coffee. Dinner would've been a date. Drinking coffee is what friends do, or at least that's what happens in New York in the 1990s. With that *Friends* reference, I'm going to excuse myself. Let's just talk after class. Or before. I don't know. I'm going to quit embarrassing myself. Bye."

Before he could say a word, she got in her car and drove off.

That was when he realized he hadn't given her his notes. That had been the deal. He liked writing on a legal tablet; it slowed down his head, and he wasn't good at typing anyway. He'd made copies. He'd just have to scan them and send them to her.

Colt closed his eyes.

He could almost hear Aunt Jewel's voice. *At least you didn't hit that asshole. You still have your job. Just another year of torture, Colt. You can do anything for a year except for, you know, actual torture.*

One of the vans pulled up. It was funny. If you looked closely, you could see the old logo of New Eden Import/Export underneath the newly painted Unlimited Shipping & Post logo. They were just another division of USP. It wasn't a family business anymore. It was just some nameless, faceless corporation, and Colt was just a cog in the machine.

There wasn't even any upper management on site. They had a district manager that came by every once in a while to make sure Jimbo wasn't actively murdering employees. No one stood up to him. No one talked shit about him either—not to his face and not to corporate.

Colt knew why. Jimbo worked at the Denver facility for one reason whether he knew it or not.

"Fuck my life," Colt whispered. But Aunt Jewel was right, or at least the memory of her was—she'd been dead a year. On the day she'd died, Colt had taken a sledgehammer to his dirtbag father's old truck rusting in the backyard of his house. His father had always wanted to fix it up, but that was just one of Ike Holliday's many fantasies.

Hard to work on a truck when you were locked up.

Colt had beat that truck until his hands bled. He should've at least put on gloves. But the damage had been done—to the truck, to his hands, to his heart.

Standing in the cold sunlight of the January day, he swore he wouldn't make a big deal about Gilly turning him down. It stung. But he'd be fine. It was better this way. Now he knew where he stood. Or at least that's what he kept telling himself.

The reality was, Colt needed to get out more. The more women you talked to, the better your chances of sparking something, and the less it stung when you got rejected. And rejection was just part of the game.

He marched back into the warehouse, and right into Jimbo and his henchmen. Andy, who worked in the back office, hurried back from break. He kept his eyes down. As did a few of the drivers who came in early to clock in.

No one wanted to cross Jimbo. Not even Phyllis and Marcy, who weren't afraid of much. They were also warehouse employees, and both were funny and hard-working. Both needed their jobs in the worst possible way.

Colt knew if he could just get back to his forklift, he'd be fine. Jimbo wouldn't talk smack about Gilly, and Colt wouldn't punch him in the face. He just had to get to his forklift.

But Jimbo, Benny, and Baxter blocked the entire aisle.

Colt returned Jimbo's glare. "I need to get back to my forklift."

"Yeah, you do." Jimbo shifted to the side.

Colt walked by them, stepping over Baxter's foot when it came by to trip him.

"Next time clock out, Holliday, when you want to talk to your girlfriend," Jimbo snapped at him "We got a new van just in. Careful, bro. This stuff came from the Middle East. It's fragile."

Colt was always careful.

Back in the day, New Eden Import/Export had the best reputation in the business. It was how Grandpa Walt had built up such a great client base—from the Denver Museum of Natural History to the tech center to the various colleges around—people knew they could trust New Eden not to wreck their stuff.

Colt drove the forklift over to the main dock doors where the back of the van was open. His forklift beeped as he backed up to make sure his forks were aligned with the pallet of wooden boxes. They looked dusty, and they were stamped as antiques. Yellow straps secured them to the pallet. The interior of that van seemed darker than normal, almost as if there was black smoke back there.

"Okay," he said to himself. "This shipment does look old and important."

Jimbo and his henchmen were watching.

"Should we unload them by hand?" Colt asked.

"No, dipshit. Just grab them. They go in the way back. Special delivery to some place up off I-25, in Firestone. Not a regular customer."

"Why didn't the van just take them up there?" Colt asked.

"USP policy. We scan them here, and then we'll send them out tomorrow. They went through customs a bit faster than we expected." Jimbo shook his head. "Why am I even telling you this? Your job is to move shit, Holliday. So move shit."

Colt wanted to comment on the stupidity. Actually, he wanted to drive his forklift into those fuckers.

Instead of getting angry, he thought about something Aunt Jewel used to say: *Don't get mad and don't get even, get out of town and find a beach somewhere where the bitches and the bastards can't find you.* Aunt Jewel had made it to Hawaii once, but most of the time, she'd settle for Chatfield Reservoir's beach. She'd supplied her own umbrella drinks.

Just thinking about his aunt made him feel better. He carefully eased the tips of his forks into the slots on the pallet. He made sure they were seated.

At the very last minute, Colt saw two wooden boxes teeter on the edge. Someone had undone one of the straps, just enough for those boxes to come loose.

Two guesses who that could've been? That was the trouble with working with morons—

they did moronic things. And then everyone had to clean up their messes.

Aunt Jewel had a name for morons—useless motherfuckers. Or UMFs. The world was full of them.

Colt knew if he tried to overcorrect, he might dump the entire stack of boxes.

Instead, he gritted his teeth and watched in slow motion as first one box fell, then the other.

Crunch. Something inside the wooden crate broke.

Colt watched in wonder as red smoke boiled out of the box. The crate burst into flames.

That red smoke—fire, it had to be fire, right?—struck Colt, right in the chest. Right in his heart.

At first, Colt was surprised, and then he was pissed. Some asshole had filled the wooden boxes with something flammable. That wouldn't have been a problem if some other asshole hadn't screwed up the straps.

A fury beyond what even Colt had known before filled him.

A deep, powerful voice filled his head. *Free? No. But it's a cage I can enjoy. You have such anger in your heart. I will show you what we can do with that rage.*

For a brief second, Colt felt like he had some control over his temper, but then something strong and dark took control.

Reality seemed to break apart. He was only dimly aware of his actions after that, and they seemed impossible. Like in a dream, he tore apart the forklift with his bare hands and started throwing the parts at Jimbo, Baxter, and Benny.

The blond girl with the red lips came later.

Funny. He didn't feel the fire. He only felt the rage.

That fury consumed him, and he lost consciousness.

CHAPTER TWO

C olt came to in the field behind the warehouse.
He thought he saw Gilly's Prius driving away, but that couldn't be. She'd left.

Ha. Maybe she'd come back to take him up on his offer for coffee. Probably not.

Colt sat half-naked in the field between the parking lot and I-70. He felt weird in ways he couldn't explain. First, there'd been that voice.

Then there'd been the dream of utter destruction.

Strange—he could feel the highway like never before. It felt like I-70 was throbbing. The traffic in both directions was completely stopped.

All the drivers were gaping at the fire engine battling the fire engulfing the delivery van and the opening of the warehouse. Other fire engines were racing down the street in a wail of sirens. And there were three ambulances, as well as police cars.

Colt looked down. He was shirtless. His shoes were gone. His socks were gone. It looked like the bottom of his pants had been burned off. He looked at his hands, and they were black, covered in soot.

He didn't know what had happened, but he had to clock out.

Or check in. Or do something. What does someone do when their workplace was currently on fire?

He looked around and couldn't find his clothes.

He walked shirtless up to a row of people. He recognized a few drivers, a few other warehouse guys, and there were Phyllis and Marcy, standing with Andy.

Phyllis looked like the woman from *The Office*. She found it funny. Marcy had long black hair with square bangs. Both of them were a pair, all right, and swore that they would be retiring in twenty years, whether they could afford to or not! Marcy was married, and her family had a ton of medical bills. She needed the job. Phyllis dated a whole bunch after a series of bad husbands. She was working hard to make sure her four kids had the best opportunities, and so far, they were doing pretty well. Phyllis also needed the USP job, and if all went well, next year she would get a big promotion. It was just one of the reasons Colt had to stay at the terrible job.

Phyllis had known him since middle school. She'd literally watched him grow up.

When she saw him, the big woman ran over and grabbed him. "Colt! Colt's not dead! I can't tell you how relieved I am!"

Colt was suddenly wrapped up in a big lady hug.

"Thank goodness!" Marcy burst out. "I didn't want to lose anyone I actually liked."

Andy scowled. "Ouch, Marcy. It's too soon."

"Not really." Phyllis stepped back. "Oh, Colt, what happened?"

Colt didn't answer. He was speechless.

Three body bags, on three stretchers, were being loaded into three different ambulances. Those were the bodies of Jimbo, Benny, and Baxter.

Colt felt chilled. "What the hell happened to them?"

Marcy shrugged. "Like we know. Phyllis and I were in the back shelves. Andy was in the office. The floor was basically clear.

Except for you and those bastards. Can I speak ill of the dead? Oh, I just did."

Colt stood there with his mouth gaping. "So Jimbo and his henchmen are dead?"

"So fucking dead," Phyllis said.

"Language!" Andy admonished. He was pale. "There was an explosion. It killed them. It must've thrown you."

Andy could be a pain sometimes, but all in all, he was a good guy. He was taking care of a sick mother with the help of his father. Colt could respect that.

Marcy nodded. "You're lucky to be alive, Colt. You were at ground zero. Jameson is flying in as we speak. To clean up this mess it seems."

Jameson Astor was the district manager. He'd be taking over because, well, Jimbo, Benny, and Baxter all seemed to be dead. That seemed so surreal. What the hell?

It was the voice. It had to be the voice. Had it thrown chunks of the forklift at those guys? It seemed impossible. But what was in that crate?

Colt was given a blanket by an EMT guy. He'd not even felt the cold.

He had to answer a bunch of questions. The police, the fire chief, and then Jameson, who showed up to fill out all the forms and to cover USP's ass.

Colt couldn't tell them much. He talked about the box, the fire, and then he said he got knocked out. He left out the red smoke, the strange voice, and his memories of decimating the forklift.

He also didn't mention the blond girl with the red lipstick. She'd touched his arm. He'd stared into her face. Who was she?

He figured she was a dream. Like the voice. Like the forklift. The warehouse had security cameras everywhere. Jameson and the authorities would be checking them to see what might have happened. If Colt had accidently killed his boss and his asshole henchmen, it would be on the tape. Should he be nervous? Colt found himself strangely calm.

He had his souvenir emergency blanket. One of the firefighters found one of his half-burned shoes. It looked like someone had put a stick of dynamite in it.

Other than the van, none of the other cars had exploded.

After being questioned, Colt was free to go. He went to his truck, a two-door Ford truck with the extended cab. When he slammed the door, he'd never felt so tired in his life. Good thing it was only a mile to his house.

He pulled into his driveway. He lived in one of the few houses in the industrial parts of North Denver. There were machine shops and warehouses and mechanics all around his little blue house. His house backed up to the light rail that led to the airport. To the right was Sir Car-A-Lot, a used car place owned by Franklin D. Schmidt. It was a dumb name, and Schmidt poisoned TV by having the worst commercials possible.

The used car salesman had hated Grandpa Walt, had hated Colt's father, and now he hated Colt. He was not a happy neighbor.

Grandpa Walt had been there before the used car lot. Colt's grandfather had just wanted to live close to his business. He probably should've bought a bigger place. But Grandpa Walt basically only did two things—work to improve his business and play video games. Even though he was older, Grandpa Walt had been hooked ever since the first time he played Pong. An Atari 2600 followed.

The house was just two stories of tiny rooms. Most were full of boxes from Colt's family. Funny thing about funerals—they didn't give you much motivation to go through the deceased's stuff.

Colt's Uncle Elam had taken all of his things. That was basically the only thing that Uncle Elam had done to help them out.

Colt's father, Ike, had pawned pretty much everything he'd ever owned. Not a lot was left. As for Colt's mother, she'd bounced in and out of his life so much she hadn't been able to leave much of her shit in the Holliday family home.

Yes, the little blue house was small, but hey, at least it was paid for. And with housing prices booming, Colt was pretty happy to be a homeowner.

He went through the front door, put his wallet and his keys on the table in the little dusty living room, and went into the kitchen to grab chicken from the fridge. He was starving. He stood at the sink, eating. The southern windows overlooked the back porch and the yellow back lawn, where his father's old truck lay on flat tires.

He could see the hammer marks.

Even a year later, Colt was still pissed that Aunt Jewel had died. She went from complaining about her lower back to her grave in a week.

Worst fucking week of Colt's life.

Colt's room was off to the side of the kitchen. He had a door that led to the back porch. His room was messy, but it wasn't like the stacks of boxes in the second-story rooms. At some point, he'd have to go through the three rooms above. It wouldn't be that night—his mind was still reeling from everything that had happened that day.

Colt put on sweats and a New Eden hoodie and returned to the kitchen. He popped open a beer and watched the light rail train rattle past his backyard. To the right, he could see a few of Denver's skyscrapers.

Jimbo, Benny, and Baxter were dead.

Colt might've killed them, but how? He knew how to fight, but three against one? No.

On the other side was I-70, and while he couldn't see the traffic, or hear it, somehow he could still feel it. How could that be?

He didn't know.

Most likely, he'd lost control. But no, that's not what happened. He knew that fuck-it feeling of giving in to his rage. He hadn't made the decision to explode. Something had done the exploding for him.

He distinctly remembered ripping apart the forklift's cage. The metal felt like it had been made of Play-doh. Then he flung the cage at Jimbo, or at least part of it. Colt remembered pulling off the steering wheel. The metal had squealed, and he'd smelled the hot engine. Oil had leaked onto the floor.

It probably ignited. That explained the fire. His clothes had been burned, but he didn't have a mark on him. It didn't make sense.

The doorbell rang.

Colt had no idea who it could be. Unless Jameson Astor wanted to ask him more questions. Colt had his own questions. Like what was the security video going to show? What had been in the crates? Who had sent them? And who would've picked them up in Firestone?

Lastly, who was the blond girl with the bright red lipstick?

The doorbell rang again, and then someone knocked.

Maybe the blond girl had come to give him answers. Wouldn't that be nice?

Colt peeked through the peephole and saw some random woman walking back to her car.

Colt opened the door. "Hey. Why'd you ring my doorbell?"

The woman turned. She was dressed like a soccer mom in a down coat, jeans, and black UGG boots with shiny buckles. When she spoke, her breath came out in clouds. "Uh, I'm just the Food-Wheel girl, dropping off your Denver Biscuit Company." She pointed to a bag on Colt's porch.

"I didn't order anything."

The woman glanced at her phone. She had short hair with frosted tips. There was a tattoo on one of her hands. Her lipstick wasn't a bright red, more like a soft peach color. "Says here that Julie Holliday wanted this delivered to you. She left instructions to ring the doorbell and knock."

"She's been dead a year."

"Not my problem." The soccer mom winced. "That came out wrong. Sorry for your loss. I really don't know. The credit card worked. Don't know what else to say." She paused for a second. "Maybe this is one last thank you."

"Maybe." Colt found himself smiling at her.

She smiled back.

He'd always done well with older women, which wasn't a surprise given the bar he frequented and the age of his best friend.

The FoodWheel woman went to get in her car but then shouted, "Don't one-star me, dude. Just wait to leave the review after you eat your biscuit. That shit is good."

Colt knew how good the Denver Biscuit Company was. It had been Aunt Jewel's favorite. Her real name had been Julie, but Colt hadn't been able to say Julie, and so her name became Jewel. She loved it.

And she loved a good mystery. This was just the kind of thing that Jewel would do.

Colt opened the bag in his kitchen. There were two boxes. Both were the Strawberry Shortcake Biscuit—a big pile of biscuit, strawberries, strawberry sauce, and whipped cream.

Colt checked his credit cards for a charge. Nothing.

"What the hell?" he asked his empty house of boxes and memories.

A sudden sound made him jump. "Not in hell yet, Colt. Are you trying to curse me or something?"

It was Aunt Jewel's voice, coming from the living room.

His weird day was only getting weirder.

CHAPTER THREE

"Aunt Jewel?" Colt called from the kitchen. His heart was beating fast. He felt tingles across his skin. "You died."

"Yeah, kidney cancer. Monday, I have back pain. Friday, I'm dead. That sucked. But you know that. You were there for every minute of every day. You know, that damn job is going to kill you. You should quit."

"I can't, Jewel." He sighed. "You know that."

"Hey, I've not been around for a bit. What was the deal again?"

"When Uncle Elam sold the company out from under us, he made a deal that they couldn't shut down the warehouse as long as a Holliday was working there. Well, I'm the Holliday working there. At least for another year. Then Phyllis has her ten-year anniversary, and she joins the quote unquote family as the Holliday in question. Then I can leave."

Jewel laughed. "Oh, right. We had that old thing about our employees being family. Is that going to hold up in court?"

Colt put his beer bottle to his forehead. He was feeling hot, feverish almost. He was trying to get a grip on his emotions. "Jewel. Why are we talking about this? Shouldn't we be talking about you being dead? Or me being crazy? I think I got possessed by a demon today."

Actually, now that he thought about it, that made perfect sense.

"Well, that sounds exciting. Turn down the lights in there. We can talk while I watch you eat that biscuit, since I can't eat anything anymore."

"Then why buy two?"

"Habit, mostly. But you'll want that second one for breakfast. You love to have something sweet first thing in the morning."

"Why do I have to dim the lights?" Colt asked.

"I'm a damn ghost, Colt. Ghosts don't like light. It's why you don't see us around in the day. And it's why we like it around 3:15 a.m."

"Like *The Amityville Horror*?"

"Kinda. I figured I'd visit early and not wake you up. I didn't want to completely scare the shit out of you."

Colt turned off the lights. His sweat felt cold.

The streetlights and the Sir Car-A-Lot security lamps gave Colt plenty of light. It was dark enough for the ghost of Aunt Jewel to come creeping out of his living room. She wore her old terry cloth bathrobe and her pink fuzzy slippers. Of course, she'd have on her equally fuzzy PJs.

She sat with a sigh in a chair at his little kitchen table. "Let me tell you, being dead is pretty cool. I get to always wear comfy clothes. And my sense of smell is amazing. All of my senses are turned up to like eleven. Those biscuits smell so good. Feel free to dig in."

Colt took two big steps back. He was pressed against the back door. "Uh, Jewel, so, why not haunt me right away?"

"You needed time. I needed time. This was a big adjustment. I would've waited another year, for when you were free from that terrible job, and then I might've visited you in a dream or something. But no, today happened, and everything has changed.

Trippy, huh? You've completely changed. I felt it right away, which is why I ordered the FoodWheel."

Colt squeezed an eye shut. "Do you know what happened?"

"Yeah," she said. "You lost your shit. I'm impressed it took a year before you tried to kill Jimbo and the Bs."

Benny and Baxter. The Bs. Colt had forgotten Jewel had nicknamed them right away.

"No, Jewel. The part where the box fell, and the fire started. Then I heard this voice, talking about being freed, or being caged, or something. Then I think I blacked out. I might've actually killed them."

"You didn't kill anyone. You wouldn't. It's not your fault." Jewel motioned to the food bag in front of her. "If you don't eat your biscuit while it's still warmish, we didn't raise you right."

Colt shook his head. "I'm not hungry. I mean, there's a ghost in my kitchen. And I might've ripped apart one of our forklifts and used it as a murder weapon."

"It wasn't our forklift. And USP can afford to replace it. And if you ask me, it's nice when bad shit happens to shitty people." She grinned. Her face was the same, just paler. She had the same gap-toothed smile, and her brown hair was a bit on the wild side. Just like always. Just the same. Aunt Jewel.

"Should I feel bad?" Colt asked. He didn't. He was relieved that he'd never have to deal with Jimbo and the Bs again.

Jewel shook her head. "No. You shouldn't feel bad. From the very beginning, Jimbo was brought in to get us to quit so they could close down the warehouse. He was a corporate enforcer. A bad egg. The USP executives knew what they were doing. They didn't realize we were tougher than their goons."

"Jameson felt bad about it, I think," Colt said.

"Fuck Jameson." Jewel sighed. "Don't be the angsty hero, Colt. It's not a good look. You didn't murder them. Whatever this new thing inside you is what did the actual murdering. So let's move on."

Colt laughed. "Damn. I am so glad I don't have to be the angsty fucking hero. Yeah, let's move on. So what happened to me?"

"Like I know!" Aunt Jewel said loudly. "All I know for sure is that there's this new power inside you. It's given you supernatural powers, which is how you can see me. I'm getting flashes of today, though. Call it ghost ESP. Though I'm basically limited to sticking close to this house, I can sometimes see what happens to people I love. That box fell, and you red hulked out. Can I say that? Is that verb trademarked?"

Colt couldn't believe he was talking to his favorite aunt. She was so great, and she could always make him laugh. "I don't know, Jewel. Then what happened?"

"Well, you changed. You had red skin, huge muscles, and you had fire instead of hair. That was the mysterious entity now connected to your soul. The rage beast took out its anger on that poor forklift and threw pieces of it at Jimbo and the Bs. They, uh, didn't survive. After that, you decided to beat the shit out of a van. And you did. You did beat the shit out of a van. Damndest thing I ever saw. You do have some anger issues. Like your dad."

"Don't remind me." Colt touched his hair. "My hair was on fire?"

"Yeah. And you split out of your clothes. Grew all these muscles, and you had these enormous hands. Made for good fists."

"Did you see a blond girl with bright red lipstick?" he asked.

"Oh, yeah. She was in the shadows, wearing a big coat, big hat, sunglasses. I'm betting she was a vampire. She was dressed for shade."

Colt cocked his head. "Wait. Vampires?"

Jewel sighed. "Grandpa Walt never wanted you to know. Hell, he didn't want me to know. There's not just humans on this rock, kiddo. There's this whole underground society, and in some cases, I mean that literally. Underground. Whatever happened to you must have something to do with the Monstra."

"Vampires are real. Well, if ghosts are real, I guess that makes sense." Only it didn't. Colt was pretty sure he'd had a brain aneurysm, and all of this was a hallucination. "But Grandpa knew?"

"So did my least favorite brother. Wait. I hated both my brothers. Elam and Ike. Bad news. The good news is that I like you."

"Good enough to haunt me, Jewel. That's love."

"You aren't wrong."

"What did the blond vampire do?"

Jewel shrugged. "She went to help you, or something, but you were still a literal rage monster at that point. She calmed you down and took off. Oh, and your friend from school was there. Gilly. She drove back."

"To get my notes." Colt had no memory of that. He'd gotten blackout drunk a few times in his life, and this felt like that. Total loss of time and memory.

"Gilly drove away quick, kiddo. But that was when you were still throwing forklifts at people. I think I have the order right. I can't really leave this house. It's not a complete *Beetlejuice* situation. I can extend feelers like. Especially now that you're channeling so much power."

Colt pushed his fists against his eyes. "What stopped me finally?"

"The vampire," Jewel said. "When you saw her, you stopped punching the van. By that time, it was on fire anyway."

Colt had to sit down. And yeah, he was hungry. It wasn't like the brain aneurysm would get worse if he ate the biscuit. He didn't even bother with a fork. He just dove in with his fingers. He'd have to talk with Gilly about all this.

A thought struck him. "Gilly is okay, right? Do the vampires and monsters kill people who see them?"

"That's a complicated question. And it's Monstra, or Leyfolk, but not monsters. They hate to be called monsters. There are two main camps who want to keep the Monstra a secret. The Monstra themselves have the Umbra Alliance. They want to make sure no one knows about them. As for us humans, we have the Brightest Light. Those are basically monster hunters. Like in those Larry Correia books. Both sides can get a little, oh, what's the word? Excitable."

"You guys were never going to tell me about this?" Colt took a big flaky bit of biscuit and smeared it through strawberry sauce. He topped it off with a bunch of whipped cream and popped it into his mouth.

"Grandpa Walt wanted you to have a normal life. Whatever that means."

The truth hit Colt hard. Whatever had happened that day had changed him. Maybe forever. "I can feel I-70. How can that be? Like, I know exactly where it is."

"The Ley Lines." Jewel nodded. "I can feel them too. I mean, I couldn't when I was alive. But dead? Oh, yeah. The Ley Lines are also known as Gaia Lines. They fuel supernatural creatures."

"Creatures plural?" Colt asked. "Like vampires, werewolves, what else?"

"Not sure, nephew," Jewel said. "Grandpa Walt wasn't too excited that his kids knew the little we knew. There are definitely vampires and werewolves. Look, this is tiring me out. I haven't expended this much Gaia since, well, ever. Gaia is what powers the supernatural entities. Like me. I'm such an entity now. Despite that fact, I gotta go ghost nap. Just don't make any rash decisions. And for now, don't get angry. There might not be a vampire around to help you get your shit together."

"Wait, Jewel. I need to know more. You can't just leave me."

"Grandpa had a box in his room. It would probably have something—"

In mid-sentence, his aunt faded away. She left behind an empty chair and darkness.

Colt was stuck with sticky fingers and a world of questions. He wasn't suffering from a traumatic brain injury. No, he was now part of a supernatural world that seemed impossible.

His entire life had suddenly changed.

He'd felt that before. And every other time, it pissed him off like nothing else. He couldn't afford that. If he gave into that fuck-it feeling, he might turn red and smash his house to bits.

At least Jewel had given him something to do—find his grandfather's box. That wouldn't be easy, given the state of the house. Grandpa Walt had been a great guy, but he'd also been a hoarder.

Colt figured he'd go up to his grandfather's room, but he didn't think he'd find anything. He didn't have the energy to search much, but he'd give it a try.

Colt found himself standing in the doorway of his grandfather's room. The bed was swamped by stuff. There was a ton of old video game systems stacked in front of the bed, blocking the TV mounted on the wall. There was a whole collection of Atari games, from the 2600 to the 5200. Mixed in were ColecoVision and Intellivision consoles. Moving up a layer? A Sega Genesis and the original Nintendo, followed by PlayStations, Xboxes, Nintendo Wii, and lastly, a Nintendo Switch on top.

Colt had bought a PlayStation 5 in memory of his grandfather, and it was in the living room below. He'd also bought a gaming laptop because Grandpa Walt loved those indie games that were PC only. Still, Colt would come and switch out the gaming systems every once in a while.

Seeing those gaming systems brought back so many memories of hanging out with his grandfather, who was so patient, so determined, in both his life and in his games.

Colt felt something, a little bit of Gaia energy, maybe, to his left.

He looked down, and jammed between a bank box and the wall was a snow globe of Mile High Stadium—proudly proclaiming it was home to the Denver Broncos. Back then, though, the Denver Bears, a minor league baseball team, had played at the stadium as well.

For some reason, Colt had always loved snow globes. He liked how there was this mysterious snowy world inside the glass orb.

Colt picked up the snow globe, thinking he'd take it downstairs and put it on the kitchen table.

The minute he touched it, however, the thing glowed with a bright red light.

Colt felt a warmth in his belly, and he realized his belly was glowing red under his shirt. Then every inch of his skin started to glow. An instant later, the light was gone, and the orb itself turned from red to green.

He had the impression he'd just been scanned in some way.

Inside, instead of seeing Mile High Stadium, Colt saw a figure appear, a huge man with red skin and massive muscles. Yellow flames flickered on his scalp.

"Jewel?" Colt called out loudly.

His aunt didn't answer him.

Holding the glowing sphere, he backed out of his grandfather's room and into the hallway. The bathroom was up ahead. Jewel's room was across the way. Narrows steps led back downstairs.

"Okay, demon, are you going to tell me what's going on?"

The little figure inside the snow globe stood on what looked like sand, or dust, with a few plants. The snow inside glowed green, which clashed with the red demon's appearance. The monstrous figure wore a leather battle skirt but didn't have any other clothes. He stood there, looking forward, hardly moving, until he folded his arms across his chest.

"Are you going to talk to me?"

The figure simply stared straight ahead.

A second later, words appeared in the glass of what was called a Gaia Orb.

<<<>>>

Gaia Orb for Urgu-Uku
Gaia Force Level: 0

Rune Genesis Status: Green (Go)
Body Progression:

- Unknown

Gaia Abilities:

- Strength I
- Invulnerability I

Special Gaia Mutations:

- Unknown

<<<>>>

Colt read through the list of stats. The Gaia Orb had scanned him, and now it was compiling information on him. But the damn guy wasn't saying a word.

Colt felt a flash of anger. "Hey, asshole. You possessed me and used my body to kill people. The least you can do is talk to me." He smelled the sharp scent of hair beginning to burn. His hair? He wasn't sure.

The deep, powerful voice returned in Colt's head while the figure in the orb looked up at him. *What do we have to discuss? You do not want your home destroyed. There is no blood to spill. What you see is the work of an Augmenter. It seems your grandfather wasn't the man you thought he was, since he had such a device in his possession. Now, unless you want to revel in the destruction of your city, leave me be.*

The monstrous figure then returned to staring straight forward. Green flakes continued to spin around him as he stood there on the desert floor.

Colt sat on the top step, staring at his stats in the globe.

Grandpa Walt did seem to have his secrets, but for someone who loved video games, having a way to track progress would seem natural. So that explained why Grandpa Walt would have the Gaia Orb.

However, the demon inside Colt couldn't give a shit about what was happening. His name seemed to be Urgu-Uku. But he couldn't be Level 0. Who started at Level 0 anyway?

Maybe that was a good thing. As Colt progressed, stats would get unlocked. One of the sections made perfect sense—Gaia Abilities. He had something called Strength I, which meant there was probably a Strength II and Strength III. Invulnerability would probably work the same way. Colt was reminded of how enchanted items worked in Minecraft.

He was glad he had both because strength without invulnerability wasn't a good idea. You might be able to rip apart metal, but if your body couldn't handle all that force, you'd wind up with shredded skin and shattered bones.

Colt had definite questions. What were Special Gaia Mutations? If Gaia powered the Monstra, what kind of mutations could he expect?

The Body Progression section was another mystery. That might refer to his human form. Or it might be the demonic form he'd taken when he'd ripped apart the forklift.

Lastly, he wasn't sure about his Rune Genesis Status. It said it was green, as in "go," and that was probably why the Gaia Orb was glowing green.

What did that mean? Go where?

Colt put the orb against his forehead. He smiled. He wasn't going to be an angsty hero. He'd figure things out, with or without the entity inside of him.

Aunt Jewel was an entity now. So was he.

Like her, he needed sleep.

He took the Gaia Orb into his room and fell asleep, watching the green snow drifting around the sphere. It had been the strangest day of his life, but it had also been the best.

He'd gotten to talk with his Aunt Jewel again. And it seemed his grandfather, besides being a successful businessman, might also have been some kind of wizard.

Colt liked the idea of being the grandson of a sorcerer even with the fire-headed demon inside him.

CHAPTER FOUR

The next day at work, Colt wasn't surprised when Jameson said that the security cameras only showed static. Was that because of the Umbra Alliance or the Brightest Light? Or was it just the supernatural energy that had erupted from the box that fell off the pallet?

Colt did go over to the van, which they'd hauled to the side. He could see massive knuckle marks in the parts of the metal that hadn't melted. He really had punched the van into submission.

He spent the day going through their inventory, scanning packages and trying to salvage what they could. There were some tears over Jimbo and the Bs, but on the whole, the warehouse was more relaxed.

Jameson seemed shocked and saddened by what had happened. At the same time, Jewel would say he should save his tears. He'd let Jimbo terrorize the warehouse.

The pallet that had caused the problem, the one with the bad strap and the two lost wooden boxes, was gone. Jameson assumed it had been destroyed in the fire.

Colt wasn't so sure. He had the idea the remaining boxes might've ended up in Firestone, off I-25, after all. The computer records didn't say there was a delivery, but that didn't mean that the blond vampire hadn't grabbed the pallet. Or maybe someone else had.

And why had Gilly driven back? Could she have taken them?

He got the address to where the destroyed shipment was supposed to have been sent—it was an address in Firestone, just off I-25. From a quick search on the internet, there wasn't much there, just an old gas station. The contents of the shipment were described as "Antiquities of a sensitive nature." Whatever that meant.

Colt would have to go up to Firestone to check out that gas station himself. Not that night—he had class, and he wanted to ask Gilly about what she might've seen. He'd been texting her, but she wasn't answering him, which made him wonder if he'd see her at class tonight. Taking a single class a semester meant he wouldn't get a degree until he was in his sixties. It seemed pointless. It was another thing that pissed him off. His plan had been to take over the family business. That hadn't happened. Uncle Elam was to blame. End of story. But it wasn't the end of Colt's life. Once Phyllis could take over the warehouse, he could quit, finish his degree quick, and figure out something else to do with his life.

Or maybe not. Things had fundamentally changed.

And that was good.

After work, Colt drove his truck to Metro State University. He parked off campus and walked the half-mile in. Like before, he could feel I-70, but now he also added I-25 into the mix. It was a strange feeling to be so connected to these Ley Lines. He was surprised that they were even real. Even stranger? Why did they correspond to the American freeway system?

Just another mystery.

Metro was a good school. There were a lot of different kinds of students running the gamut of ages, so being twenty-five wasn't a big deal. Gilly was four years younger. Was that why she didn't want to date him? Maybe.

He slid into his class and glanced around at the college students. He didn't have a lot in common with most of them.

There was one old guy who was taking statistics for fun, both the fall semester and the spring semester. It was a year-long class.

Now that Colt knew that not everyone was human, he wondered if the old guy was a vampire. Or a werewolf. Or a serial killer. Weren't all vampires serial killers?

Gilly entered the classroom, took one look at Colt, and then spun. She nearly ran out of the room.

Colt felt his jaws clamp shut in anger. He started to feel lightheaded. He smelled burning hair again. Was this going to trigger the rage that might destroy another forklift? He had to breathe. He had to count to ten.

Mostly, he thought of all the funny shit that Aunt Jewel would say. She'd talk about Jameson being named after whiskey because he'd start off smooth but then make you want to puke by the end of the day. Jameson. The walking hangover.

He was fine if Gilly didn't want to breathe the same air as him, but he needed to know what she'd seen. He needed to know if she knew about the Monstra and all the other crazy stuff he'd learned from the friendly ghost who bought him a strawberry shortcake biscuit the night before.

And yeah, for breakfast, that biscuit was heaven.

Colt was still angry, though. But then his new friend showed up.

After her! Did you not smell her? Did you not see her beauty? The only time destruction fails to excite is when lust consumes the rage. Surrendering to lust is just as sweet as surrendering to the rage.

"So are you ready to talk now?" Colt whispered to the thing inside him.

I am not here for banter or jests. I have always been a laconic god. After her, fool!

Laconic god? What did that mean?

Colt got up from his seat and gathered his stuff.

The professor gave him a perplexed look. "We were just about to get started, but now you're leaving, Mr. Holliday. Something I said? Or something I didn't say?"

"There's a fifty percent chance this has nothing to do with your class, Professor."

That made the teacher laugh.

Colt hurried out of the lecture hall to chase down Gilly. She'd made it outside and was heading for the parking garage. It was starting to snow a bit. It wasn't dark exactly, because of streetlamps on the walking path, but it was definitely gloomy.

"Gilly!" he shouted. "Wait. I need to talk with you."

He was so relieved when she stopped. She was in her long coat, a cute scarf, a cute beanie. Her hair was pulled back in a ponytail. Her glasses were a bit foggy.

"Uh, Colt, hey. I, uh, I'm having a day. And a night. And a life. Sorry I didn't answer your texts. I have an excuse, but it's crazy, so, so crazy. You'd never believe…"

Her voice died.

Then her eyes flashed blue, several shades brighter than usual.

She whipped off her glasses and swept off her beanie. She stuffed both into the pockets of her coat. Were her fingernails glowing blue as well? Or was that some kind of new nail polish?

She gave him a smile that almost melted his underwear. "Greetings, Urgu-Uku. Seeing you again, just the sight of you, takes my breath away. Now you are close. I can smell you. But it's not enough. I need to feel your heat."

Gilly's voice had totally changed. Her words didn't have their normal musical lilt. The new voice had an accent, and it was deeper and more powerful.

Gilly, or whatever was possessing Gilly, took his hand and pulled him into the space between some juniper bushes and the building. It was dark and private.

Then she bent close and sniffed. "Yes, your smell. I thought it would be lost forever, my love, my lust. We can find somewhere. We can enjoy our flesh as never before. How young this little vixen is. How imaginative, yet so inhibited."

Colt wasn't sure he liked being sniffed, not even by a girl he'd just asked out the day before. The rejection had stung.

This felt even more awkward somehow. And Urgu wasn't saying a word.

Then Gilly, or whoever was riding shotgun in her soul, grabbed him. One hand went around his neck. The other grabbed his ass.

The otherworldly woman's voice was ragged. "I cannot wait. I want to smell your spit on my skin. I want to drink from your mouth. I am thirsty for you, my Rage King. Your goddess is wet for you, my eternal love. I long to feel your stiff cock inside me once more."

Then she was kissing him, his neck, his cheek, his mouth.

But he wasn't kissing her back. How could he? This wasn't Gilly. This wasn't the adorable, awkward, nerdy Gilly who rambled when she was nervous.

Those blue eyes gazed into his. "Please, kiss me, my love, my god. Please. Your goddess needs her god. I need it like this young body needs breath."

Colt saw that need. Whoever this goddess was inside Gilly, it was pretty clear that if he didn't kiss her, she might fall to pieces. And yet, he knew that Gilly probably wouldn't be too excited to get such a kiss.

Colt loved the feel of the woman pressing up against him. Her coat had split, and she was straddling his leg, pressing her center against his thigh. He could feel her breasts pushed up against him. Her eyes were so blue. Her cheeks were rosy. Her mouth hung open.

"She wants it," the woman whispered. "Gilly desires your kiss. As I desire it. But truly, her need is keener. Such imagination. Such inhibitions."

That was all Colt needed to hear. He took the goddess's delicate head in both of his hands. Her skin was warm. Her hair was soft. He inhaled her perfume. Then he pressed his lips against hers.

She moaned. She rubbed herself on his leg. She was nearly sobbing when she offered him her tongue. He dropped a hand to her ass, and grabbed it, and they were pushing their bodies against each other.

He couldn't help but rub his stiff cock against her.

It was too much. It wasn't enough.

He could smell the kiss, which was what she wanted. She'd wanted to smell his spit on her skin. And he could smell hers on his. Her tongue was soft, wet, and so inquisitive. He loved touching it with his own tongue.

Then she was sucking on it. And she took his hand from her head and shoved it inside her coat. He was cupping one soft tit, kissing her, rubbing against her, just as she was rubbing against him.

She pushed her head against his chest. She had both of her hands around him, grabbing his butt and holding him in just the right position.

He already knew what she was doing, but the otherworldly presence inside Gilly wanted to tell him, in no uncertain terms, what she wanted. "I am so very close to my joy, my love. So. Very. Close. This girl does like her rubbing, just as I did, oh so long ago. I can feel you, my love. I can feel your hard cock against me. I want it. I want your hard cock in my wet cunt."

Then she was whimpering as she stiffened in his arms. Despite the cold and the snow, both of them were sweating. He loved how much heat they were generating in their little love nest behind some juniper bushes. He smelled the pine scent. He smelled the snow. He smelled her.

He'd never felt so alive. It was more than that. Like how he felt the freeways, he also felt the goddess's orgasm, and it nearly made him climax. It was like his soul was throbbing along with hers. They felt connected, and suddenly, his left arm was tingling. Then again, his entire body felt like it had been plugged into a nuclear power plant.

The otherworldly woman smiled. "Yes, my joy. I had memories of such joy, but those memories were nothing compared to the music a hot, young body can make. You don't know you are Urgu-Uku, do you?"

Colt was speechless.

She kissed his neck. And smiled slyly. "Oh, perhaps you do know something after all. What is your name, boy child?"

"Colt," he said. "And let's not call me a boy child. This whole young body thing is kinda creepy. It's not working for me."

"I'm Zeh-Gaba. I'm timeless. Even the oldest woman alive is but a child to me. However, I will respect your wishes, Colt of Denver. For this is Denver, correct? I've looked through the eyes of Gillian Hermione Croft."

Colt couldn't stop himself from laughing. "Hermione. Like Harry Potter?"

Zeh-Gaba obviously had no idea what that was.

She simply hugged him harder.

He eased her back. "Who is Urgu-Uku?"

"The god of rage and destruction. He is the Rage King, and he is inside you."

Colt touched his chest. "A god. A laconic god. What does that mean?"

Zeh-Gaba appeared perplexed. "This is a school, is it not? Do they not teach English vocabulary? A god is a powerful divine entity. Laconic means someone who says very little. My Urgu never liked inane prattle. He only liked destruction and fucking."

Colt had to take a moment. Okay. He was possessed by a god, and Gilly was possessed by a goddess. But how did Zeh-Gaba get into her?

Then he knew. "Okay, Zeh-Gaba, you were in the second box that fell. And that's when you found Gilly, right? What are you the goddess of?"

Those blue eyes lost some of their intensity. Her fingernails weren't blue anymore, just short clipped normal nails.

Gilly's hands were shaking when she pulled her glasses out of her coat and slipped them on. "Uh, hi, Colt. So, this is going to kill me because I am so darn embarrassed. Capital 'S,' Colt. Capital 'D.' Capital 'E.' So. Dang. Embarrassed."

"Dang or darn?" he asked. He held up a hand. "Don't answer that. I want to know if you really wanted to kiss me, or else I'm going to feel like a piece of shit."

She smiled, turned purple, turned, turned back around. And put back on her beanie. "Yes. I wanted to kiss you. But we're not going to talk about that. And we're not going to date. We are going to figure this out as friends. I can't do the whole dating thing. So, what we did was, uh, what we did. But no more. Okay?"

Colt remembered what the goddess of whatever had said. Gilly was both imaginative and inhibited. That certainly was an interesting combination.

Colt looked into Gilly's eyes. Or tried to. Her glasses had steamed up. "You and I need to talk," he said.

CHAPTER FIVE

Colt slid behind the wheel of his truck.

Gilly was beyond embarrassed by their kissing in the bushes. She wanted to talk off campus. They decided to meet at the White Spot Cafe on Colfax. They drove there separately. That was Gilly's idea. She needed time to compose herself. Colt also thought she might need to change her underwear. He'd had a long-term girlfriend for three years—Pamela Emory. Pam had talked about such things after a long night of making out.

Pam had been great. Until she'd taken a spoon to Colt's heart. Why a spoon? Because it hurt more. In the end, hooking up with older women at the Sons of Italy hall had been a far better deal. But even that had slowed down in the past year.

So Gilly needed a moment. Colt did too. How did he feel about the kiss?

Well, if that was their first kiss, then their first date just might kill him. He certainly didn't feel like a god. That was kind of disappointing.

He had to decide how much to tell Gilly. He didn't want to put her life in danger. At the same time, how could he talk about gods and goddesses without mentioning vampires, werewolves, and Ley Lines?

He had to tell her. And he had to warn her.

Colt was lost in his thoughts when some asshole nearly side-swiped him. Colt smacked the horn and swerved. He smelled hair burning and his vision reddened. His heart hammered in his chest.

The clueless asshole had been drifting between lanes. After nearly hitting Colt, the asshole kept right on going, as clueless as ever.

Urgu's voice wasn't far behind. *Let us hunt down that automobile and tear it in two. We can do the same to the driver. There will be blood, and there will be gasoline.*

"Not today, Urgu." Colt focused on his breathing. He remembered Aunt Jewel talking about how Denver traffic was like a gladiatorial arena full of toddlers and the elderly.

Driving was going to be rough. And Rage King inside of him wanted to come out and play.

But why, Colton Henry Holliday?

"Colt is fine. How do you know about automobiles and gasoline?

You know, so I know. Why is it not time to revel in destruction?

"I'm pretty sure if I let you out, you'd rip your way out of my truck, and I like it too much to ruin it."

Very well, Colton. I will bide my time until we can unleash our anger again.

Colt was oddly looking forward to it. He parked and walked through the cold and snow.

In the diner, he found Gilly already at a booth. He sat down in the seat across from her. She had two coffee mugs in front of her. She shoved one at him. "This is coffee. Coffee is not a date. Right?"

"Right." Colt sipped his cup of joe. The White Spot was famous for having coffee that could peel the paint off a Studebaker. Swing shift cops went there at 3 a.m. to get jacked up on caffeine. Some even won the "Gold Cup award."

Gilly had taken off her coat and beanie, but she kept her scarf on.

Colt set his mug on the worn table. "We're not on a date, Gilly. You've established that. Is it me? You don't have to answer that, but how can I *not* take that personally?"

Gilly didn't answer. She slopped cream into her coffee, then shook about five packs of sugar like they were maracas. She systematically ripped one open at a time. "No, Colt, it's not you. It's me." She sighed at herself. "That sounds like the worst cliché ever. Let's not talk about me and dating. It never goes well. Not that I've dated a bunch. And that kiss? Oh boy, we are not talking about that kiss. But I'm talking about it, aren't I?" She pointed to her mouth. "Mouth. No talk of kissing. Even the word mouth sounds…erotic. But I didn't just say the word erotic. No, I didn't. Because why would I? I'm already dying of embarrassment. Oh, Gilly, you've done it now!"

In a rush of words, she poured the sugar packs into her cup. She then looked him in the eye. "Let me be clear. Let me slow down and speak clearly. What in the freak is going on?"

"You don't curse." Colt sipped. "Haven't I heard you curse in class?"

"I try not to curse," Gilly said. "I like clear, concise language. Not that you would know that because you've only ever seen me ramble. Because I'm nervous. Because we're not talking about that. Okay. You're going to explain why I kind of remember grabbing you and kissing you. Or did you kiss me?"

"You kissed me," Colt said. "But we're not talking about that."

Gilly blew out a breath. "And why did I do that?"

"Because I'm possessed by the god of rage. And you're possessed by the goddess of…something. She left before I got the whole story."

"Or I kicked that witch out of me." Gilly held up a hand. "Excuse me. Not a witch. A goddess. Of something. So that was the blue fire that came out of that box. It came bursting out of your warehouse. I went back for your notes. I felt this…I felt…

we're not going to talk about what I felt. But I had to get out of there. There was a fire. Was that you?"

He nodded. "Yeah. I punched a van. To death. After I ripped apart a forklift. Actually, I didn't…the god of rage did. I guess the god of rage has fire for hair. I don't see it."

"Like Ghost Rider?" Gilly asked.

"Who?"

"Comic book. Flaming skull. Never mind." She blew on her coffee. "So what are we going to do?"

Colt toyed with his mug. "At this point, we need to gather information."

Gilly brightened. "Research? I love research! I can get on board with that."

"Gilly, what if this research was dangerous?"

Her smile dimmed. "You mean paper cuts? Dust that messes with my asthma? Or do you mean like reading forbidden texts that will drive me insane?"

"That last one." Colt shook his head. "I don't want you to get hurt."

"I was joking. But now you're scaring me. Why are you freaked out?"

"Besides being possessed by an ancient murderous god of rage?"

"Right."

Colt puffed out his cheeks and then let the breath out slowly. "Fine. My dead aunt visited me last night. I mean, as a ghost. Somehow, she ordered biscuits for me."

"Denver Biscuit Company?" Gilly asked loudly.

"Yeah."

"I'm loving your aunt right now." Gilly was far more comfortable with banter than she was with talking about kissing, dating, and all that. "So, gods are real. Ghosts are real. Are there fairy princesses? Angels? Demons? Cat girls? Werewolves?"

"Werewolves are real. I haven't seen them, but Aunt Jewel said that there were vampires and werewolves. Also, Ley Lines are real."

"Because I can feel the Mousetrap in my teeth!" She looked relieved. "Can you feel I-70 and I-25?"

"Those are Ley Lines. Or Gaia Lines maybe. I don't know how it works. Aunt Jewel said it was hard for her to stick around. I guess it takes some kind of energy." Colt paused. "So yesterday, did you see—"

Gilly cut him off. "What about alternate realities? Like the multiverse? What if in some over version of Denver the White Spot closed down at some point? Or never even existed at all?"

"I don't know. But, Gilly, yesterday did you see—"

The door opened and four girls came in, talking loudly, giggling, probably a little drunk. Colt recognized them from school. The four Metro students sat in the booth next to them. The blondest of the blondes pointed her key fob at a Cadillac Escalade and locked her doors with a flash and beep.

Gilly turned pale.

The blondest of the blondes snickered. "I didn't know the White Spot was so porn friendly. You know someone shot porn here. It's so porn-y."

Gilly got up. "I'll pay. Let's just go."

"But we haven't finished our coffee."

Another of the girls chattered on. "The real problem with porn is all those girls sleep around, and they get all these weird diseases."

Gilly was up and almost running to the counter. She'd left behind her beanie.

Colt picked it up and stopped by the table.

All the pretty women looked up at him.

The blondest of the blondes gave him the fakest, most innocent smile he'd ever seen. "You heard us talking, didn't you? Do you know *anything* about Gilly?"

Another less blond girl rolled her eyes. "Of course he doesn't. Or he wouldn't be with her."

From a third. "No, he's way too cute for someone like her. Why is he wasting his time?

That brought a storm of giggles.

"What about Gilly?" Colt asked.

Shrugs all around, but the silence spoke volumes.

Colt hated the smug looks on their pretty faces. He smelled burning hair. He clenched his hands into fists.

We should've destroyed the automobile of the man who cut you off. Or should we destroy this restaurant and relish the fear of these petty women?

Colt didn't respond to that. He kept his focus on the petty women. "So this is some mean girl middle school bullshit right here. I like Gilly. Leave her alone. Leave me alone. And quit talking shit."

"Okay, Colt." The blondest of the blondes giggled.

The others laughed. "Who names their kid after a baby horse?"

"Or maybe it's after the gun?"

"He seems old. How old are you, Colt? Gilly might have daddy issues on top of all her other issues."

It was clear that if Colt stayed, he would end up disemboweling the White Spot if not the four girls. He turned on his heel and stomped to the door.

Those four girls weren't going to give him any real information. But they might be the reason why Gilly didn't want to date anyone from their school.

Colt smelled rubber burning, along with his hair, and he realized his shoes were smoking.

We know their vehicle. Let us smash it to bits.

Colt gave it some serious thought, but he had the idea that Urgu was trying to trick him. Give a god of rage an inch, and he'll destroy a mile.

Colt took in a deep breath. Aunt Jewel always said that girls were far meaner than boys. Boys might punch you in the face, but girls would punch you in the heart. If they were feeling nice. If they wanted to be cruel, they'd cut off your balls and send them home to your mother in a mason jar. She'd been very specific about the mason jar.

Thinking of Jewel took most of the heat out of his anger.

He met Gilly outside and gave her the beanie.

The snow had stopped. They'd only gotten maybe a quarter of an inch of snow. It still made driving home just a bit more treacherous.

"Friends of yours?" Colt asked with a smile.

Gilly closed her eyes. "Yeah. Sure. We're so close." She gave him a miserable look. "That was sarcasm. I went to high school with two of them. Was friends with one. But I don't even want to say her name. It's a long story, and we have far cooler stuff to talk about."

They stood there not talking for several long seconds. Their breaths puffed out in the cold. The temperature had dropped fifteen degrees since they'd made out behind the bushes.

Gilly stuffed her hands into her coat. "Let's talk in my car. I'm sorry about the coffee. We could get a Starbucks. I'll pay."

"I'm okay. Let's just talk more. I still have a ton of questions. I'll drive."

He got into the driver's seat and Gilly rode shotgun.

It was slick getting out of the parking lot, but Colt was a Colorado native. He knew how to drive in the ice and snow.

They went east on Colfax, by the capitol, Capitol Hill Books, the Cathedral, and some concert venues. There was a collection of homeless people, some new rich people in the neighborhood, and other people from downtown. Despite the cold, people were out.

A beat-up minivan wove in and out of traffic. It slid through a light in front of them before careening to the side of the road. A rough-looking guy barreled out the side door and marched into a liquor store while the driver waited.

Driver probably wasn't the right term. It wasn't some soccer mom. It was some asshole who thought he was too important to drive safely.

Colt drove past him. The asshole gave both him and Gilly a dirty look.

Urgu had something to say about that. *There is a term. Road rage. I like this term. We can do road rage and destroy Denver until there is no traffic. Everyone will be happier.*

Yeah. Traffic was a definite trigger for Colt.

He focused on being with Gilly. The heater blasted and cleared the windshield. He asked his first question. "Did you see a girl with red lipstick yesterday? She might've been wearing a coat and a—"

"Big hat. Big sunglasses. Short blond hair." Gilly nodded. "Yeah. She was there. I saw her near this pallet of boxes. She was really pretty." She abruptly stopped talking.

"But she was mostly covered up, right?" Colt asked.

Gilly swallowed hard. "Yeah. But. I could just tell she was pretty. Just from her mouth. She had these perfect bow-shaped lips. So red." Gilly blushed.

Colt could read her like a book. She was so pretty, even with the severe ponytail and the glasses. And she smelled so good. He was so glad they'd kissed. From what the mean girls said, Gilly had a bad reputation, but how could that be?

Gilly's mouth fell open. "That girl was a vampire. That's why she had those bright red lips. I dare you to tell me differently. I double-dog dare you!"

"Yeah, I think so." Colt thought for a minute. "My boss, er, my new boss thinks the pallet of boxes burned up in the fire. I wasn't a hundred precent sure about that. I think our vampire friend might've grabbed them. There is no record they were delivered, but I have the address in Firestone. I was going to head up there tomorrow night."

"Wow. Vampires." Gilly shot him a big grin.

Colt told her all he knew about the Monstra, Ley Lines, the Umbra Alliance, and the Brightest Light.

Gilly listened closely. "The Brightest Light are the monster hunters, right?"

"Right."

Gilly shook her head. "This is so amazing. I'm not even sure I want to go back to being normal. Maybe having this goddess around might not be so bad. If we can control our powers, maybe we can do all sorts of things."

Colt stopped at a light. He glanced up at the rearview mirror and got mad all over again.

Gilly turned to see what was going on. "Darn. That minivan guy is going too fast."

Colt turned to see that same beat-up minivan slide toward them. It nearly bumped them. The guy behind the wheel saw Colt looking, and gave him the finger. The other men with him were laughing. That fucking car was packed with assholes.

"Did you see that?" Gilly asked.

Colt did. He smelled the stench of burning hair. He'd hated the look of that driver and his shitty minivan the first time he'd gone sliding through a light. Now, he'd almost rear-ended him.

This fool has put our love in jeopardy, Colton. Let us end this menace.

Colt tried to stop himself, but he knew he wasn't going to be able to. He surrendered to that fuck-it feeling and slid headfirst into fury.

He left his truck with the keys dangling in the ignition.

"Where are you going?" Gilly asked.

Colt heard Urgu speak through him. "There is a minivan that needs a thrashing."

CHAPTER SIX

This time, Colt felt the change. His insides burned. He could smell his hair burn off his head. His body ripped through his shirt and his coat, and exploded out of his shoes.

He stalked forward on feet that melted the snow covering the road.

He looked down at his huge hands, and he saw his skin was a dark red. His hands were huge. And on his left arm, which had tingled when he'd felt Gilly's—or the goddess's—orgasm, a complex rune glowed a bright crimson.

Then it was hard for Colt to think. Because he wasn't exactly Colton Henry Holliday anymore. He was Urgu-Uku, and yes, he knew Zeh-Gaba. He knew every inch of her. The woman in the black glasses wasn't her. And yet, it was her.

Steam rose off his red body. Snowflakes sizzled on his skin. Colt punched the minivan, right in the passenger side door. It rolled to its side.

Colt watched as dirty people with greasy clothes and grimy beards climbed out the top. Colt could feel Urgu's urge to murder —if he punched them, they would pop like water skins full of blood.

Colt knew that the sigil on his arm was the only thing keeping Urgu from murdering every single person on Colfax. Colt wasn't in control, not at all, but he was able to direct Urgu's rage at the minivan. Colt hated minivans.

Urgu grabbed the chassis. The metal parted like butter, and he hurled a big chunk of the minivan through the window of a nearby shop. He pulled off the wheels. He pulled out the engine. The mechanism was hot, but it didn't hurt his hands. The heat actually felt good in the chill night.

"Colt!" Gilly was calling out to him, but she wasn't just Gilly. She was Urgu's love, Zeh-Gaba.

Colt could feel himself pick up the carcass of the minivan. Not everyone had gotten out. The driver who had flipped him off was still behind the wheel, caught in the seatbelt.

Colt knew that Urgu was grinning as he shook the shit out of the minivan. He then dropped it back onto the street.

The Rage King pulled off the door and flung it behind him. He was about to pull the driver out, which would've broken bones, surely, when someone touched him.

Colt was losing consciousness, but he managed to hold on, just a bit longer.

He turned. There was a pretty woman there, not just any woman, but Zeh-Gaba. On her left arm glowed the same sigil that was on his arm. His was a dark red. Hers was a bright blue. She was saying something, but Colt was having a hard time hearing it.

Urgu had more and more control.

The woman hosting Zeh-Gaba grabbed Urgu's massive red arm. "We need to go! This can't be good. The Umbra Alliance, or the Brightest Light, or whatever, isn't going to happy that you're publicly beating up traffic. Come on, Colt. Come back to me."

This woman was beautiful. As beautiful as Zeh-Gaba had been, so very long ago.

But Urgu couldn't remember what had happened between them, so Colt couldn't either. Something had happened, something bad.

The minivan driver had unclipped himself and scurried out of the minivan. He had a weapon. Colt felt Urgu rifling through his mind for the word—a shotgun. A sawed-off shotgun.

Urgu thought it wouldn't make a very good saw, which made Colt laugh.

Ah, to be hosting an ancient god.

The driver fired the shotgun, and Colt felt the blast hit his chest. It stung, yes, because he only had Invulnerability I, but it was enough to leave his skin undamaged.

Urgu laughed at how ineffectual the weapon was. Colt was just relieved.

"Fuck you!" the driver screamed. "And fuck your bitch." He worked the action on the shotgun and aimed the weapon at Zeh-Gaba. He pulled the trigger.

It would be the last thing he would ever do.

Colt wasn't able to stop Urgu from bringing his fist down onto the man's skull. The results were not conclusive. Did Urgu smash in the driver's skull? Or did he ram the man's head into his thorax? Either way, the man was headless. He fell with a squelching sound onto the pavement.

Urgu laughed because the Rage King loved to kill as much as he liked to destroy. After all these millennia trapped, he was finally getting to shed blood and smash things. He was Urgu-Uku, the god of rage and destruction.

Gilly staggered back, but no, no such simple weapon would be able to hurt her. For inside her was Zeh-Gaba. What was that rune on her forearm? It was strange.

It didn't matter. Nothing mattered except destruction.

Colt realized that Urgu wasn't strong enough to truly destroy the city yet. No, he needed more of the Gaia Unum, the Gaia Force. Once the Rage King had that, he would tear apart the city and rejoice in the chaos and murder.

Unless Colt could learn how to control all of that unchained power.

For now, though, it wasn't possible. Colt lost himself in the rage.

He was gone.

And only Urgu-Uku remained.

CHAPTER SEVEN

Colt found himself sitting on a curb, eye level with his truck.
He wasn't the Rage King anymore. He was just a guy, getting cold. He climbed inside his truck while Gilly drove. The cab was warm, and it smelled like Gilly's perfume and pine trees.

Colt had a vague memory of some asshole firing his shotgun at Gilly. "Did that guy shoot you?"

Gilly squinted one eye closed. "I think so. My coat is basically ruined, and I've been pulling little BBs out of my pants. Wait. That didn't come out right. To be clear, they were in the waistband. But yeah. Do you remember what you did?"

"What did I do?"

"You killed that guy. I mean, you can't live after getting your head squashed. Then you waged war against a McDonald's and liquor store. They lost. Nobody else died, so that's good."

Colt felt a flash of that old anger. "Yeah. But he shot you. After he shot me. Fucker. After nearly hitting us. Fuck him."

Gilly's mouth fell open. "No guilt?"

"He was an asshole driver, and he shot you." Colt paused to really think about it. Then he nodded. "You know, my Aunt Jewel used to say some useless motherfuckers were just cluttering up the planet with their DNA. Well, not anymore. In my defense, right before I felt Urgu take over, I swore I wouldn't go around killing random people. I definitely had some control. My arm. There was a rune on my arm."

Then he remembered—on the Gaia Orb, there was a Rune Genesis Status. He was dying to get home to see if anything had changed.

Gilly glanced at him. "I have a rune on my arm as well. But yours is red and mine is blue. Are we connected?"

"I think so, Gilly." Colt touched his left forearm. It was just his normal skin. "I know you don't want to talk about it, but when we—when you had your moment—I felt the tingle on my arm. I think that's what did it. It was the rune that helped me have control, at least for a bit, before Urgu took over."

Gilly was the color of a plum. "When I had my moment? Didn't the goddess say something about her joy? I don't know. It was like I was riding shotgun in my own head. Was it like that for you?"

"Kind of." Colt frowned. "It's like blacking out, mostly. I don't remember much. But the rune helped. How did you lure me away? And do you think anyone saw us?"

"They had to, right? Security cameras, or whatever. And everyone has a phone with a camera. Colfax is never not busy, so I bet you're going to be all over the news."

Colt didn't think he would be. Something told him that there were forces who were desperate to keep the existence of the paranormal a secret.

"You know, Gilly, my family knew about the Monstra. My grandfather, and my aunt, probably my dad and uncle. Aunt Jewel mentioned something about a box. I found one thing, but I bet there's more. I'll look tonight. But we have to be careful. I don't know how dangerous the Umbra Alliance and the Brightest Light are, and I really don't want to find out."

Gilly actually laughed a little. "I'd dare them to mess with you.

Holy cow, you broke that minivan like it was nothing. And I can't believe I got shot. Clearly, I did. Am I bulletproof now? How would I even test that?"

Would Colt's Gaia Orb work for her? Or would she have to get her own? More questions.

He risked taking her hand and squeezing it. "I don't want you to get hurt. I have to control this thing inside me. Or get rid of it."

"Do I want to get rid of Zeh-Gaba?" Gilly whispered the question. It was more for herself than for him. Then her face hardened. "We need to get a better understanding about all of this. For the time being, I'll be careful. And I'll see what we missed as far as class goes tonight. I don't want to get behind, you know, in school." Then she rolled her eyes. "After like actual murder tonight, school just doesn't seem so important." She sighed.

The murder bothered her. It probably should.

The weird thing was, it didn't bother Colt. Mr. Shotgun decided he didn't want to live anymore the minute he pulled the trigger. Like Aunt Jewel said, Colt wasn't going to be the angsty fucking hero. He'd always be an eye-for-an-eye and a tooth-for-a-tooth kind of guy when it came to crime and punishment. Would Mr. Shotgun have felt bad if he'd blown Gilly away? Maybe. Maybe not. From the look of that guy and his cronies, Colt didn't think they'd be getting good citizen awards anytime soon.

Gilly pulled into the White Spot.

Traffic was backed up going east on Colfax—the flashing lights were visible in the distance. Police, fire, and medical vehicles were there, cleaning up Colt's mess. Well, it was really Urgu's mess. If Colt hadn't had that little bit of control, there would've been a lot more corpses for them to bag.

"Keep in touch." Colt looked into her blue eyes. "It's not a romance thing. I'm not hitting on you. We just need to watch each other's backs until we can figure all of this out."

Gilly didn't look away. She searched his face. "Right. We'll stay in touch."

And Colt felt the pull to kiss her. There was this energy

between them—he could feel it. And he had the idea she felt it too.

She said no dating, and he was going to respect that. At the same time, he felt his pants get uncomfortably tight. He wanted her.

But he broke eye contact and cleared his throat. "Right. We'll stay in touch." He'd repeated her exact words.

Gilly's eyes flashed a brighter blue. Her voice was deeper and had an accent. "Oh, I'll be keeping in touch all right. I'll be touching my pussy all night, thinking about your big fucking cock." She slammed her hands over her mouth. Her eyes couldn't be wider, but they were back to being their normal blue.

"Did I just say that?"

Colt nodded. "I'm afraid so."

Her blue eyes brightened again. Her voice changed back to the goddess's. "And I'm afraid you might have a small dick. Tell me you're hung like a Babylonian stallion. Tell me, stud. Tell me you'll stretch out this little slut's virgin cunny until we both scream in ecstasy."

Gilly squeezed her eyes shut. "That's not me. You have to believe me. Yeah, I can't go around with this goddess person inside me. Even that sounds wrong. Like she's in me."

Her voice changed. "Like you want his big fuck stick in you."

More shock on Gilly's face. "This is terrible. I'm gonna go now. And yeah, text me. I'll stop her from texting you back anything, you know, inappropriate. At least I'll try."

She got out the driver's side. Colt got out the passenger's side. He was immediately freezing, and his toes felt like they might fall off.

The four mean girls were still in the White Spot.

They were pointing and laughing at him. He was an easy target. He was shirtless and his pants had been burned off at the knees.

Gilly hurried off to her car.

He got into his truck and wondered why some people were so

fucked up. Why did those four girls want to torment Gilly? What kind of history did Gilly have?

The questions didn't end there.

Why didn't his pants burn off completely? If he had fire for hair, wouldn't his pubic hair ignite as well? That didn't seem to be the case.

Colt got on I-25, and he felt himself relax. Being on the actual freeway felt good. The power seemed to leak up from the asphalt and into his cells. He felt the energy rejuvenate him. Urgu thought of it as Gaia Unum, otherwise known as Gaia Force. Getting on I-70, there was a subtle shift in power. His body continued to drink in the energy.

He drove into the driveway of his house just as his phone vibrated in his pocket.

He kept the engine running while he checked it. There was a text from Gilly.

> hey, tonight was weird. scary. exciting. i got shot. then i said all that…so embarrassing! but hey, i just wanted to text you that i got home okay. so far, no government agents lol

He answered her.

> Cool. I got the text. Sleep well. Call me if anything weird happens.

Colt had to wonder how much she had to edit that last message. He might have a rage monster inside him, but it seemed that Gilly had a lust monster.

Hmm. Was Zeh-Gaba the goddess of lust? That made sense. But in the end, Gilly was right. They had to gather more information.

> i will.

And then Colt saw the message from FoodWheel. His order would get there in ten minutes. It was more Denver Biscuit Company. This time, it was the Franklin, which was buttermilk fried chicken, bacon, and cheddar cheese on a delicious biscuit covered in sausage gravy.

That was thanks to Aunt Jewel again. Add another question to the list. How was she paying for his FoodWheel deliveries?

Inside his house, there was no sign of the ghost. He turned on some lights and turned up the heat before popping open a beer. He drank half of it while he put on some warmer clothes. That was two pairs of pants he'd lost. While he waited for his order, he turned on the TV.

The local news said that Alonzo Packard had been killed on Colfax. The victim was wanted for a variety of crimes, and local authorities thought it might be a gang-related killing. Or there might be a possible vigilante on the loose. His accomplices were still at large.

One of the cops mentioned that no one got any video footage —all of the cameras in the vicinity had malfunctioned at the same time. A McDonald's and a liquor store had also been destroyed.

That made Colt grab his laptop. He did a quick search. Alonzo Packard might've been a beloved member of Aurora's methamphetamine community, but his wife must be glad he was dead. It seemed her fingers got tired dialing 911 to report him for domestic abuse.

Colt texted Gilly the results of his search. He didn't get a response.

Was that because she was busy? Or did she just assume he was trying to justify murdering someone? But Colt hadn't murdered anyone. That was all Urgu's doing. If Colt hadn't been able to influence the god of rage, there would have been a lot more people dead.

He wasn't going to freak out about Gilly not responding. She was at least bulletproof now. Who knew what other powers she might have?

When Colt's food got there, it was the same delivery woman as the night before. She smiled. "Can't get enough of the biscuits! How was the strawberry shortcake?"

"Delicious. Hey, is it the same person who bought me the food?"

"Yeah. Julie Holliday. I have no idea how she's doing it, but your aunt must really love you to send you food from beyond the grave. It's sweet. If a little weird. Or are you messing with me?"

"Not messing with you." Colt felt a wave of emotion grab him. "My aunt did love me a lot."

The MILF with frosted tips and the tattoo on her hand gave him a nice smile. "It's good to be loved." She kept eye contact a bit longer than normal.

Colt felt the tension in the air, so much so the woman blushed. Then she was marching back through the snow to her car.

Colt waved. "Drive safe. It's snowing cats and dogs."

"Meow!" The woman laughed. She made a scratching motion with her long fingernails. Could she be a Monstra? Vampire? Werewolf? What else was there?

Colt collected his food and went back inside. Then it was biscuits, gravy, chicken, and bacon, while he watched more of the news. There was no mention of his green truck or a giant red demon with flames for hair.

It seemed like he, Urgu, Gilly, and Zeh-Gaba—all four of them—were in the clear.

After dinner, he went to his room and grabbed the Gaia Orb.

It immediately flashed yellow this time, and the tiny figure of the god of rage stood there, arms crossed.

<<<>>>

Gaia Orb for Urgu-Uku
Gaia Force Level: 1 (New! Update Ability?)
Rune Genesis Status: Yellow (Caution)
Body Progression:

- Unknown

Gaia Abilities:

- Strength I
- Invulnerability I

Special Gaia Mutations:

- Unknown

<<<>>>

Colt saw that he could update one of his abilities, but there was no menu option of what to choose. And there was no information on the Yellow (Caution) Rune Genesis Status.

He had an interface to his powers, but he had no idea how to use it. It was interesting that he had levelled. Could it have something do with the sigil on his left forearm? It seemed so.

But how could Colt know? And what would Gilly's Gaia Orb show?

Then a thought struck Colt. Maybe Grandpa Walt had a manual for the orb. He walked up the steps to his grandfather's room. On the right were all the gaming consoles and boxes of cartridges as well as manuals. Colt went through old *Super Mario Brothers'* manuals, *Metroid*, *Altered Beast*, some *Castlevania*, *Shadow of the Ninja*, and the list went on and on.

Grandpa Walt probably wouldn't have put his Gaia Orb documentation in with his video games. He probably would have had his own special place for all his sorcery stuff. Or what had Urgu called him? An Augmenter?

But where to find the special place?

Colt opened one crate and found a stack of old *National Geographic* magazines. Was there a clue in them? There was no way to know. He wasn't feeling up to the task. The mysteries of the hidden Monstra world might be in that hoarder's paradise, but it was going to take days to find them. If Aunt Jewel bought him biscuits a second night in a row, she might come back and give him a hint to where the important stuff was.

What Colt really needed was a good long walk to clear his head. And maybe a few shots to help him muddy it up again. Yeah, he needed out of the house. The closest bar wasn't actually a bar at all. It was the Sons of Italy Community Center, but they had a liquor license and a nice little watering hole.

Grandpa Walt had been an American mutt, but he'd married Annamaria Smaldone, who was a fullblood Italian. It was just one more reason why Grandpa Walt had settled in North Denver, so Grandma Marie could be close to her family. Back then, there was no Rino district, otherwise known as the River North Art District —it was just the Italian part of town.

Colt hadn't kept up with all of his relatives, but he'd become a fixture of the Sons of Italy Community Center. That was where his closest friend was, a guy thirty years older than Colt, Ernesto Corlino. Or just Ernie.

The Sons of Italy basically catered to all the Italians and machinists in the area. At one point, there was talk of starting an actual bar called the Center Punch, but that was just a bunch of drunks talking shit.

The Sons of Italy, or just the Sons, was a good enough bar for most people. And it was just down the street from a local grocery story, Yantorno's, which mostly sold Italian products. If you wanted fish for Christmas Eve, or pizzelles for Christmas Day, it was the place to go.

Colt would walk to the bar, get some drinks, walk home, and hopefully Aunt Jewel would show up to help him find Grandpa Walt's box o' mysteries.

Colt put on his grandfather's big coat and crunched through the snow. He'd be scraping ice in the morning. He'd have to allow some time for that.

At least he wouldn't have to clear the ice off the cars in the Sir

Car-A-Lot. Franklin D. Schmidt could take care of that. The neon tried to buzz in the cold, but failed. The cartoonish King Arthur just looked sad covered in snow.

Colt thought the snow was over, but new big fluffy snowflakes drifted down from the dark sky like cotton balls. It was wetter than normal, especially since it was January. Generally the wet snow fell in March, Denver's snowiest month.

It was just under a mile to the Sons. The windows of the main hall were dark, but to the side was the bar. There was a glowing Budweiser sign in the window, and lights that lit up a big Italian flag.

Inside, the bar looked warm and cozy. It wasn't as crowded as normal since a lot of people stayed home because of the snowstorm.

Colt pushed open the door.

The bartender, his buddy Ernie, waved at him. "There he is. Come on in, Colt."

Ernie was short and dark-skinned. He might as well have walked off the last plane that landed from Rome. Ernie had white hair balding into a widow's peak.

Colt's eyes went to the back of the place. There was the normal rows of faces at the bar itself. But in the corner there was someone in a fedora with a cane propped up next to him.

Colt felt his left forearm tingle.

At some point, he'd be talking to the guy in the hat with the cane. He could feel it.

First, though, Colt was going to have a drink.

CHAPTER EIGHT

Colt didn't go to talk to the guy in the corner right away. He sat at the bar next to Bob Scarpetti. Holly Milano was down the way with her friend Dena and her brother Dwayne.

Ernie gave Colt a smile. "We heard about the fire at the warehouse. We were worried. I sent you a text."

"Did you?" Colt asked. "Because I don't think I got a text."

Ernie looked guilty. "Tried to text. Uh, you're going to have to show me how to do it again."

"You're fifty, Ernie. Most fifty-year-olds can text."

Bob, a bearded mailman, nodded. "Yeah, Ernie, get with the times." Bob then turned on Colt. "But you, young man, needed to let us know you were okay. After all the shit that's happened the last few years, we worry."

Colt felt the love. "I'm just fine. Give me a shot of Ancient Age and Budweiser on tap."

Ernie laughed. "In other words, the good stuff."

Colt slammed the shot and felt the heat warm him almost instantly. After the day he'd had, it was a little bit of heaven. He then sipped his beer. "Hey, Ernie, what's with the guy in the corner?"

Ernie shrugged. "He came in, ordered a glass of the best wine we had, and then sat in the corner. I don't think he's Italian. And he's not a machinist, not dressed like that."

Bob leaned in close. "Actually, he asked about you, Colt."

Holly, Dena, and Dwayne nodded.

Ernie rolled his eyes. "And there you have it. Trying to keep secrets at the Sons is basically impossible because we're all unapologetic gossips."

"Guess I better go talk to him." Colt felt a quick flash of anger, but he had to let that shit go. He didn't want to destroy the Sons of Italy. Not only was it the closest bar, but they had pancake breakfasts, pasta bars, and fish fries during Lent. It was basically a second home to him—third if you counted the warehouse where he worked.

Colt forced himself to have an attitude change. Aunt Jewel liked to say if you're having a bad day, you could start it over at any time because it was morning somewhere.

Colt had wanted a break from the supernatural shit, but that wasn't going to be the case that night. Might as well lean into it.

He crossed the room and sat down at the corner table. "So, I like the hat. And the cane."

"Thank you." The man had a goatee streaked with gray. It was the only imperfection. Smooth brown skin. Black eyebrows. Green eyes that seemed somehow serpentine. Colt noticed that he had actual diamond cufflinks keeping his sleeves closed on his black shirt. A red velvet vest covered the shirt. That included a golden watch chain.

This guy must've been from out of town. And probably from another time completely. He looked like he'd stepped out of a picture of 1890s London.

The cane's handle had a goat's head made of silver. He adjusted his fedora.

Colt resisted the urge to check his shoes for spats. "I heard you were asking around for me."

The mystery man smiled. His teeth were straight and white.

Maybe a bit too white. "I had high hopes you'd come in tonight. You've been busy the last couple of days."

Colt touched the condensation on his beer and drew a little circle on the table. "Yeah, I've been busy. Let's cut to the chase. Why do you want to talk to me?"

The mystery man gripped his wineglass between his finger and thumb. He swirled the wine around. "I think you know the basic subject of our conversation. As for who I am, you can call me Mr. Gentleman. I represent certain parties that are concerned about your indiscretions."

"Mr. Gentleman?" Colt asked.

"My name isn't important. You are a stranger in a strange new land, Mr. Holliday. It's important that certain realities are kept from the humans. We're not sure what you are, but you and your lady friend need to follow our rules. That includes avoiding cameras and large-scale displays of power in public. So far, there have been two in the last two days."

Colt sipped his beer. "So are you from the Umbra Alliance or the Brightest Light?"

"If I were from the Brightest Light, you would be dead already. As it is, some of their hunters will be sniffing around town for the next few weeks. It's imperative you keep a low profile."

Colt didn't like this guy or his weird name. "I just have work and school. That shouldn't be a problem. So, you're with the Umbra Alliance. Thank you for not killing me. You're right. I am new to your world."

"Which rarely happens," Mr. Gentleman said quietly. "You are a real mystery. What are you?"

"I work in a warehouse. I'm a student. Sometimes I get mad and bad shit happens. What are you?"

Mr. Gentleman looked mildly amused. "I deal in problems. Some I fix. Some I cause. If you are wise, you will not see me again."

"Did you know my grandfather?" Colt asked.

Mr. Gentleman swirled his wine more. Had he drunk any of it?

"Walter Holliday worked with us when we needed certain items imported discreetly. Yes, I knew your grandfather. I am sorry for your loss. He didn't know me. I'm fairly certain that no human alive knows me. And no one knows my true name."

That was an interesting distinction. *No human alive…*

Colt drained half his beer. "So let me get this straight. I stay hidden. No more property damage. And you leave me alone. Is that right?"

"That is correct. If you fail again, you'll see me again, and our interaction won't be as pleasant."

"Sounds like a threat." Colt didn't think this guy would be able to do a thing against him, not when he had the power of the god of rage and destruction. However, he was new to the Monstraverse. He didn't mind risking himself, but he wouldn't risk Gilly.

"It's not a threat," Mr. Gentleman said. "It's a friendly warning. But you'll only get one, Colton Henry Holliday. For your sake, for the sake of your family, stay hidden. All of us know how difficult that can be. But just because something is difficult does not mean it's impossible."

"Why do we need to stay hidden?" Colt asked.

Mr. Gentleman's smile was arrogant. "I'm rarely asked that question anymore. The humans are very good at procreating. Nine months and they have a new baby. For some of us, that might take nine years. Or ninety. Or nine hundred. It was less important when the humans had fewer effective weapons. But splitting the atom did change things, didn't it? So we remain hidden to be safe. So we can continue to drink from Gaia's bounty."

"But you do have some magic, right? It's why there's no video of the warehouse fire or what happened tonight on Colfax."

"You are correct, Mr. Holliday. And perhaps one day, we might have enough power to remove humans from the world entirely. Or at least put them on short leashes. For now, however, we remain in the shadows."

"The Umbra Alliance. Umbra is another word for shadow."

"You are correct." Mr. Gentleman's hand went to a vest pocket. He slid a golden coin across the table. "This will more than pay for the wine. Stay careful. Stay hidden. Stay alive."

"Aren't you going to drink your wine?" Colt asked.

Mr. Gentleman's next smile showed fangs. "I don't drink… wine. Isn't that the line?" A second later the fangs were gone.

The mystery man rose and moved across the floor. He did have spats on his two-tone shoes. He tipped his hat at the gawkers sitting at the bar.

"What was that all about?" Ernie asked. He touched his chest and winced in pain.

What was that about? Ernie was the rare bartender who didn't drink, didn't smoke, and just enjoyed the company of his patrons. The Sons didn't really cater to hardcore alcoholics. It was a far more friendly place. And Ernie wasn't shy about cutting people off.

The old guy was in shape. Why was he touching his chest? He was pale, without a doubt.

Colt sat down at the bar. "It was just a friend of my grandfather's from out of town. He'd just heard and wanted to offer his condolences." It was a good cover story.

Though Grandpa Walt had died five years ago, people were still coming out of the woodwork, surprised at his passing. Walt had known a ton of people. And monsters it seemed.

"He come from some kinda costume party?" Bob asked.

"Something like that," Colt said. "You feeling okay, Ernie?"

The little man nodded. "Sure. Just a touch of indigestion. Had a spicy meatball tonight."

"You still seeing that big woman?" Bob asked.

"Naw," Ernie said. "She's allergic to cats. Gotta find myself another crazy cat lady. Then it will be true love forever."

Everyone laughed.

Colt kept an eye on Ernie, but he seemed fine. Just to make

sure they could keep in touch, Colt taught him how to text again. He wasn't very confident that this lesson would take.

They all talked about nothing for another hour, just friendly talk. Colt limited himself to one more shot, and then walked home. The snow crunched under his boots. More snowflakes drifted down. The grit and grease of the machine shops, warehouses, and parking lots were covered in a pristine layer of white.

He was comfortably buzzed, and oddly at peace with the direction his life had taken. Even encountering Mr. Gentleman didn't feel that surprising. If Colt had been a part of the Umbra Alliance, he might've done the same thing.

Colt figured he had two options. He could try to get rid of the god inside of him. Or he could learn how to control it.

He flexed his left hand. That rune had given him a few minutes of control. Could he expand on that sigil? Or could he get another one?

Someone texted him on the walk home. It was probably Ernie, practicing.

Once he got onto his porch, he checked. The text was from Gilly. She couldn't sleep and wanted to talk.

Colt thought that was a great idea. But then he looked up and saw Aunt Jewel's face in the living room window. She motioned him inside.

He had a moment of tingles and fear. Seeing his dead aunt was still kind of a surprise.

She might have to wait a minute.

Colt wanted to take care of the living first, and that meant making sure that Gilly was okay.

CHAPTER NINE

When Colt opened the door, his aunt was gone.
"Jewel?" he called.
No one answered him.
"Come on, Jewel. Don't mess with me."
But was she messing with him? He didn't know. This whole ghost thing was new to them both. He called Gilly. "Hey."
"Hey, Colt. I'm just freaked out. I can't sleep. I can't study. I don't know if it's the ancient goddess of whatever inside of me. Or if it's the fact that I witnessed my first murder. Good thing that guy was an asshole, right?" She didn't wait for him to answer. "I'm rambling. I know. I know. Can we meet somewhere? I feel alone. My parents are here, but I can't tell them what's going on. I love 'em, but they are mayonnaise. This is far too spicy for them, and I'd be afraid they'd find a facility for me."
Colt wasn't sure what to say. It was bad out there. He didn't know how fucking Priuses did in the snow, but he didn't think it would be safe for her. "I could come and pick you up. We could drive around."
"Did you find anything from your grandfather? There was a box, right?"
"Does a box of *National Geographics* count?"

"Probably not. But we don't know, do we?"

"You're not wrong." He sighed. "I did find this magical snow globe. Don't laugh. I'd like for you take a look at it. Also, there's the Firestone address I was going to check out tomorrow night. I still don't know where those crates wound up."

"Maybe the blond vampire took them." Gilly laughed. "Oh, God, I can't believe I'm talking about vampires unironically. I can't make you drive in these conditions. It's not like I'm from California. I'm a Colorado girl. I can drive in the snow."

"Good thing. Us natives have to stick together." Colt walked from the living room down a short hallway and into the kitchen. The microwave said it was a little after ten. It felt so much later.

"Listen, Gilly. I talked with someone who might be an actual vampire at this bar I sometimes drink at. He's from the Umbra Alliance. Long story short, he told us to keep a low profile, or we'd be sorry."

"This probably isn't good, right? Clearly, we don't want to find ourselves on the wrong side of something called the Umbra Alliance."

"Clearly."

He heard her sigh. "So, Colt, there's no easy way to ask this, but can I come over? I'm feeling weird being alone, not that I am with Zeh-Gaba around. Anyway, I think it'd be fun, and it would definitely get my mind off all the weirdness, and it wouldn't be a date. We wouldn't be doing anything together. Just going through your grandfather's stuff to find some kind of clue about all this."

"Gotta admit. My pulse is racing. Why do you think I haven't attacked the boxes stacked in my house? It's just too exciting."

"Ha, ha. I'm so laughing," she said with faux seriousness. "Give me your address. I'll be right over." Then her sigh came over his phone. "Oh my goodness. I just invited myself over to your house. In a snowstorm. After we, uh, kissed today. And there was, um, joy."

That made Colt chuckle. "There was joy. It's fine, Gilly. We're in this mess together."

He texted her his address and then wandered through the house looking for Jewel, but she was nowhere to be seen.

He ended up making popcorn using Aunt Jewel's air popper. He melted a ton of butter and salted it down. Jewel said that it was physically impossible to add too much butter or salt to your popcorn. Worst-case scenario, you make buttered popcorn balls, or you have to eat your popcorn with a spoon. Either way, it was a win/win scenario.

It was a little after eleven when Gilly parked out front. A good eight inches covered the ground. The plows had already gone, removing the snow and treating the roads. They weren't bad.

Gilly marched up to his door. He invited her in. He loved the wet smell of her wool coat and her perfume. Her cheeks were red from the cold. Her glasses immediately fogged up. She cleaned them with a little cloth. "So you live really close to where you work. That's convenient."

"Totally convenient. My grandfather bought the house when he started his business. I made popcorn. I have beer and water, unfortunately. Maybe tea."

"Tea," Gilly said. "Any god-level events after the Colfax wreck?"

"Nope. How about you? Did the goddess show up?"

She frowned. "I don't think so." She glanced at the living room and grinned. "I thought this might be a hoarder type of situation. But I can see carpet."

"And the really old sofas. Hoarder central is upstairs." Colt motioned to the staircase leading up.

She followed him to the kitchen.

He turned. "I keep things pretty clean down here. Fairly. My room is off to the right."

It was odd seeing Gilly in his kitchen. It was like worlds were colliding.

He got Aunt Jewel's kettle on the stove. He thought about cracking open a bottle of Bud, but he'd had enough beer that night. He filled a glass with water.

Gilly stood near the sink. She gazed out the back window at the world of white beyond. The husk of his worthless dad's old truck lay like a buried animal in the backyard.

"Good choice to stand there. That's where I stand." Colt leaned against the fridge.

"It's nice. You can kind of see Denver. And you're close to I-70. I can feel that. That's the light rail track, right?"

"It makes it easy to get to the airport. The nearest station is about a mile away. It's not a bad walk. Too bad I never go anywhere."

"I've been to California," Gilly offered. "And Florida. Disney stuff. I was super into Disney during my formative years."

"Favorite Disney princess?" Colt asked.

"That's a very personal question." Gilly munched popcorn. "You must have one."

Colt risked a joke. "Ariel is super hot."

Gilly rolled her eyes. "Of course you'd like the redhead who can't talk. Sheesh. Typical guy response. I always liked Belle. I loved books, and I kinda liked how the Beast could be…dangerous, but still sweet. To her. I know, it's cliché. Why are we talking about this?"

"You went to Disneyland and/or World. Travel."

Gilly squinted. "Right. Travel. I've also been to Las Vegas. It was for this speech and debate tournament. I was in forensics in high school. It was this special thing. But I haven't been out of the country." She looked at him. "But you've been on a plane, right?"

Colt shook his head. "Nope. It's funny. I've been dealing with international packages all my life, right? We've gotten shipments from pretty much every country on Earth. Definitely every continent. Even Antarctica. When my grandfather had the business, he had this big world map full of pins. If we got a package from, like, South Africa or Malawi or Paraguay, he'd put a pin in the country. I used to eat lunch and stare at that map and dream about being able to just ship myself there. I'd find a box, curl up inside, and then bam, be sent off to Australia, or South Africa, or Ireland."

Gilly stared at him, a soft look on her face.

It was Colt's turn to feel shy. "Why are we talking about this?"

The tea kettle whistled, and Colt snapped off the gas. "So I have green tea, something called Sleepy Time tea, or cinnamon death."

"Nuh-uh. You don't have cinnamon death."

"Cinnamon apple. Excuse me."

"I'll take the cinnamon death please."

He got her one of Aunt Jewel's mugs. The one that said "Asshole Repellant—Just Add Caffeine." He put the tea bag in and poured the water.

When Gilly saw the cup, she grinned. "That was my problem at the White Spot. I needed more caffeine to deal with those mean girls."

"You want to talk about them?" Colt walked over and ate with her, standing there next to the sink with the snow falling outside.

Gilly gave him a miserable look, then remembered that they really didn't know each other despite all the weird things happening. "Clearly, I'm the victim of many a vicious rumor. If I'm Belle —not that I think I'm that pretty—then Amanda Buckman would be my Gaston."

It took Colt a minute to remember who that was. Mostly, he'd complained when Aunt Jewel insisted on watching a—yuck— princess movie. However, he wasn't kidding about Ariel. He'd liked that mermaid right away.

"So, Amanda Buckman."

Gilly tried to laugh it off, but she looked haunted. "Yeah. Amanda Buckman. We went to high school together. When she followed me to college, it felt like I'd been followed by my own personal demon. It's a long story. I have a goddess in me. You're the Rage King. Let's just shelve the Amanda Buckman drama. Someday, you can dare me to tell you, and I will. Just not tonight."

"Not tonight," Colt agreed. "It's going to be rough enough for me. There's a reason why I haven't tackled those boxes."

"Yeah. Tell me."

It was Colt's turn to look away. "Do you know why I've never been on an airplane or taken a vacation? It was Grandpa Walt. His business was everything to him. He poured his heart and soul into it. My grandmother died fairly young, in her fifties, just a big ol' heart attack."

"Sorry."

"What do your parents do for a living?" Colt asked.

Gilly held her tea to her chest. She was done eating popcorn. "My dad works at a big insurance company. My mom is an executive admin for a tech company in the DTC. See? Mayonnaise."

"They might be painfully normal, but they got vacations and stability. We never had that. You have your Amanda Buckman story. I have my parents. I don't want to go into that. We're talking about the boxes."

They stood there in awkward silence for a second.

Colt then decided to share his story. "You know, Gilly, I really thought I'd just take over the business. Then Grandpa Walt died. Heart attack out of nowhere. Lightning struck twice. Three years later, my evil uncle sells New Eden to Unlimited Shipping & Post. There was this contract that required at least one member of the Holliday family to work there or USP could close it down. Long story short, there's this woman, Phyllis, who will take over my spot next year. So I'm stuck. I could leave, but then a lot of good people would lose their jobs. I can't do that to them. So another year. Then? I don't know. I have my truck, and I'll have the house, and I don't need much." He motioned above him. "I have a whole cupboard full of tea. What more does a guy need?"

"Probably a lot more," Gilly said softly. "So the boxes are your family's dreams. The ones that didn't come true."

Colt felt those words hard. They made him tear up. He wasn't going to show this girl that side of him. He felt the old anger hit—at the heart attacks, his worthless father, his absentee mother, and Uncle Elam. He wanted to slam his glass down or throw it against the wall.

RAGE KING

Urgu was listening. *If we destroyed the house, we could destroy those memories. You could start anew, baptized in fire and blood.*

Of course Urgu wouldn't give a shit about Colt's little blue house.

He remembered what Aunt Jewel used to say. *When life gives you lemons, trade them in for limes, salt, and some tequila. You'll thank me.*

Colt laughed a little. "Okay. So. Enough drama and trauma, Gilly. Let me show you something."

He went into his room, grabbed the Gaia Orb, and returned. It was still full of the yellow flakes surrounding the Rage King. He gave it to Gilly, and the minute she touched it, the god was gone, as were the golden sparkles. It returned to showing Mile High Stadium in a snowstorm.

"Go Broncos!" Gilly said in wonder.

Handing it back to Colt, the figure of Urgu-Uku reappeared. Along with the stats. Gilly read through them.

Colt regarded the orb. "My grandfather loved video games. I think he made this."

"But it's all pretty cryptic. Even down to the Rune Genesis Status. Yellow as in caution. We need an instruction manual."

"My thinking exactly," Colt said. "I bet there is one, but finding it isn't going to be easy. Let me show you what we're up against."

He led her upstairs to Boxville, U.S.A.

Gilly winced. "It's, uh, not so bad. I saw this one episode of *Hoarders* where this woman hoarded cats. It was bad. She didn't have a working toilet. You can imagine how that worked out."

"I would never willingly watch that show," Colt said.

Gilly picked up the box of *National Geographics*. "So I can throw these out?"

Colt nodded. "Yeah. You won't believe the reason why I've kept them for so long."

Gilly's eyes turned a brighter blue. Her voice changed. "You liked looking at all the titties, didn't you?"

69

She dropped the box to cover her mouth with both hands. When her eyes changed back, she lowered her hand. "That was the goddess. That wasn't me. I mean, I was thinking it. Because there was nudity in the old *National Geographics*. But you had access to the internet, right?"

"Not at home," Colt admitted. "Not for a long time. And Aunt Jewel always threw away my magazines."

Jewel's voice made him jump. "I did. I wanted you to get out of your room and date actual girls. And for the record, we got internet so Grandpa could play World of Warcraft."

From the sound of it, Jewel's voice came from her room, which was packed with her stuff.

"Is someone here?" Gilly asked, standing in a pile of old magazines.

"Hi, dear. I'm Colt's dead aunt. This is as awkward for me as it is for you. Being a ghost is kind of embarrassing."

Gilly was pale. "How much did you hear?"

"Most of it, dear. But I understand the basic situation. It's not your fault. Colt, what was that comic book movie with Tom Hardy and that gooey black demon thing in him?"

"*Venom*." Colt turned off the hallway light and pushed open the door to his aunt's room. "Jewel, where have you been? I saw you in the living room when I got home from the bar."

Her shape was near the window, in the back of the room, on the other side of more cardboard boxes. Jewel raised a ghostly hand. "Hi, Gilly. It's nice to meet you."

"Hello, Ms. Holliday. Or should I call you Jewel? Or your ghostliness? I ramble when I'm nervous. Like now. I don't know what to call you. Should I call you auntie?"

"You can. You don't necessarily need to be formal with the dead. Sorry, Colt, showing up like this takes more Gaia Force than I got. It's rough. I don't have much time."

"It's okay, Jewel. I'm glad you got to meet Gilly." Colt glanced down. One of the magazines had opened to show a beautiful

African woman who was very topless. He bent down and closed it, and started loading the box back up.

Jewel got down to business. "Okay, you two, I think I know where this box is. But I do like the idea of you going through the boxes. Gilly was right. These are our family's dreams. But you two can dream new dreams. Let these old ones go."

Colt closed his eyes and felt his jaws get tight. He wanted those old dreams. He wanted to run New Eden with Jewel and keep his old customers happy while getting new ones. He wanted his whole life to be different.

He smelled his hair burning, which meant he had to let that shit go. "Where's the box, Jewel?"

"It's near his nightstand on the other side of the room."

Of course it was on the other side of the room. He had to crawl across boxes, across the bed, to get to the other side. Instead of a nightstand, Grandpa Walt had a chunky gunmetal filing cabinet there. It was rough getting over there, but Colt did get a nice view of the street in front of his house. More snow was falling. He wasn't sure if Gilly should drive home or not.

The thought was nice, but he had to make sure she didn't feel strange about sleeping over. That wasn't going to be easy. Gilly went from normal to awkward in 2.8 seconds.

Next to the filing cabinet, Colt saw a crate that was like the ones he'd seen on the pallet. He lifted it up and dragged it back to the hallway. He set it on the box of magazines. The crate had a wooden lid on hinges. Opening it, Colt saw it was full of doorknobs.

"Doorknobs, Jewel?" he asked.

But the ghost was gone.

Gilly's grin was adorable. "Well, we didn't think this was going to be easy, right?"

CHAPTER TEN

In the morning, Colt woke with a start.

He heard someone rustling around in the kitchen. The smell of coffee followed. His first thought was that it was Aunt Jewel, but no, she couldn't be making coffee. She had a hard time just showing up to whisper from the shadows.

Then he realized it was Gilly.

She'd spent the night. He'd fixed her up in the living room, where there was the world's most comfortable couch. He'd given her sheets and a thick quilt, and then left her to her own devices. She'd used the bathroom upstairs.

They'd stayed up late into the night, sifting through Grandpa Walt's stuff. The only thing they found of interest was the wooden box full of doorknobs. Some were made of simple brass. Others were made of crystal. There were white ones, clear ones, some green, and some red. The stems were interesting as well—octagon ends, hexagon ends, circles, and squares.

Gilly thought they might be able to cast spells using the doorknobs, but neither of them were wizards. Gilly tried to summon Zeh-Gaba to ask her, but the goddess was feeling shy.

Colt thought he might have a way to summon her, but there was no way he was going to suggest that he and Gilly get into a big talk about sex. However, just like Colt was taken over by Urgu-Uku when he got mad, he thought Gilly might lose control when she thought about sex.

But he wasn't going to bring it up. Things weren't desperate just yet. He might change his mind if he destroyed a Denver skyscraper. He just couldn't get mad. Which meant he shouldn't do any driving at all. Or deal with people. Or go to work.

He didn't have a choice about that last one. It was a little after seven. Good thing the warehouse was so close. He'd easily get to work by eight.

Colt smelled bacon frying. If he hadn't liked Gilly before that morning, he certainly did then.

He rolled out of bed, went to the bathroom, and combed his hair. He brushed his teeth and hurried to get dressed for work. He came out of his room to see her putting the bacon on a paper towel covering a plate. "Good morning, Colt. Where did you get the name Colt?"

"Both my grandmother and grandfather liked country music. So I was named Colton Henry Holliday, after the gun, after Hank Williams, and, of course, after Doc Holliday. Grandpa said he was a distant relative. My mom and dad could give a shit about what they named me. But we're not talking about them. Like we're not talking about Amanda Buckman."

"Thanks goodness!" Gilly looked washed and clean. Her hair was still a little wet.

"You showered. I didn't get you a towel. I'm sorry."

"Auntie Jewel came back after we went to bed. She showed me where the extra towels were. And there is a ton of soap and shampoo in the bathroom upstairs. She pointed it out. She's so funny. Was she that funny when she was alive?"

"Yeah," Colt said, feeling a bit sad. "She was the best. I love her haunting the house. It's weird, but it's at least one nice thing to come out of this shit show."

Gilly looked at him for a long time.

He found himself staring into her eyes.

Time seemed to stop.

It was like they were a couple, on the edge of marriage, and he felt so connected to her. The nice thing? He could see she felt the same thing for him.

She glanced down. "Yeah, this is a total train wreck for the most part, but there are some good things about it." Her voice was low. She had a wistful smile on her face.

Colt wasn't sure he believed her. "What is our end game here? Do we want to get rid of Urgu and Zeh-Gaba?"

She couldn't hold his gaze. "I think so. You can't go around punching minivans. And I can't just say the dirty things I have on my mind all the time." She winced. "It's mostly Zeh-Gaba. Not that I don't think about sex…it's just…complicated. But I'm going to stop talking now. Let's eat breakfast. You sit down."

"I can't have you serve me."

Her eyes flashed a bright blue. "We can role-play," she growled. "You can be the handsome college student. I'll be the slutty middle-aged waitress. You can eat bacon while Mommy sucks your cock."

Gilly closed her eyes. "That wasn't me. That definitely wasn't me." She touched the sigil. "It tingles. I'm wondering how we can get more control. If we could, then, well, I like being bulletproof. Just sit down. We won't role-play."

"I am kind of a college student, so I wouldn't be playing against type." Colt sat down.

Gilly brought him food and then sat down to eat with him. Coffee, eggs, bacon, and toast. "Next time, I'll bring my waffle maker over. I have a recipe where you add actual bacon grease. I set some aside."

Colt's heart swelled. That meant she was planning on coming back. Having someone else—someone who had a pulse—in the house felt good. "I'm going to take you up on that, Gilly. I can make some awesome French toast. Best of your life. Guaranteed."

"Big talk. You might be the Rage King, but I am the queen of breakfast."

That made Colt laugh.

After their meal, he insisted on her leaving the dishes. He'd do them once he got home that night. She teased him about him having a wild Friday night. Was it Friday night already? It seemed like it had been so much longer.

After the last couple of days, Colt looked forward to having a quiet night, but that wasn't going to happen. He was going to drive up to Firestone to investigate the address where the shipment of boxes should've ended up. From his searching, it was just a derelict gas station. Or maybe something else was there.

Gilly let the issue of the dishes go. She did insist on helping him shovel the walks. It didn't make much sense since he didn't have neighbors, but old habits died hard. Grandpa Walt always insisted on clearing the driveway and sidewalks of snow. He said he wanted to avoid a lawsuit.

Aunt Jewel said that the stray dogs wouldn't be able to hire very good lawyers.

Colt paused to watch Gilly working, wearing that cute hat and scarf, with matching gloves she'd pulled out of her Prius. He had to wonder how much of her sexual side was the ancient goddess, and how much was her own natural desire. He might never know.

He liked Gilly. She was that rare combination of pretty and funny and adorable. Hot girls like Amanda Buckman knew they were hot. Gilly, though, seemed too awkward to know she could win a beauty pageant easily.

It did make him curious about her past.

He thought about her while he scraped the ice off her windows as the car warmed up.

They left at the same time.

The roads weren't bad, and it wasn't long before Colt was caught up in his workday. Over his lunch break, he rechecked the address where the pallet of boxes should've shipped to. The name on the shipment was Abraham Jacobs.

Colt wrote down Abe's address, and then texted Gilly.

I should've asked you this morning. But I was going to drive up to Firestone after work tonight. Traffic on I-25 is going to suck.

i wanna go! can i tag along?

That surprised Colt. He had to take a minute to think about how to respond. He didn't know how dangerous it might be, and he didn't want to seem too eager.

Then he shrugged. He liked Gilly. And with the runes on their arms, they were connected.

Yeah. You should totally come. I can pick you up. But aren't you tired of me yet?

no! not tired of you! and no! I'll drive to you! what time?

Colt got off work at 5:00 pm. He'd meet her out in the warehouse's parking lot.

After that, all he could do was look at the clock, which made the minutes crawl. He had to force himself not to keep checking the time. He avoided Jameson, kept to himself, and got through the day.

At 5:00, he left the warehouse and met Gilly, just getting out of her car.

Colt felt his phone buzz. Who would be calling him?

He'd gotten a lot of bad news over the phone, and so he steeled himself instinctively, especially when he saw the name of the caller. Ernie Corlino.

Colt answered it, while at the same time putting up an index finger. "Hold up, Gilly. I have to get this. Hey, Ernie, what's up?"

"Hey, Colt. Tried to text but not sure I did it right."

"Did you hit send?"

There was a moment of silence. Then, "Damn. Anyway, Colt. Remember last night when I was having chest pains. Yeah, yeah,

yeah, I tried to hide it. And failed. But look, it really was just indigestion. I'm feeling great. Too bad my old Aunt Sophia had the heart attack. I'm on my way to Denver Health right now."

Colt was taken back to all the shitty calls about heart attacks he'd received over the years. He was so glad this one was going differently. "Dammit, Ernie. You scared the shit out of me. If you and your Aunt Sophia need me, I'll drive over to the hospital right now. I remember her cannoli."

Ernie laughed. "Hold up, partner. They're only doing immediate family, and I guess nephews count. Anyway, I need you to go take care of my animals. Luna is gonna cover my shift. Some other people from the Sons are setting up a schedule to go and play with my pups and kittens. If you can handle it tonight, we have the weekend covered."

"Sure, Ernie. No problem."

"There's a key under the mat."

"That's not very good security, Ernie," Colt said.

"Don't mother me, pal. I know, I know. But I figure if someone is so hard up that they'd want to steal from me, they have way bigger problems than I do. Later, Colt. And thanks again."

Colt hung up the phone.

Gilly touched his arm. "I'm sorry. It sounded like bad news."

Colt took a deep breath. "Actually, it's bad news for my buddy Ernie. His Aunt Sophia had a heart attack, and he's helping her out. Which means he needs us to help him. Do you mind if we go and take care of Ernie's animals before we head out?"

"Cats and dogs? Or snakes and spiders?" Gilly squeezed his arm. "Doesn't matter. Let's go."

Colt was disappointed that they couldn't go on their quest just yet. However, he did like Ernie's pets. And he knew Gilly would like them as well.

CHAPTER ELEVEN

Colt risked road rage to drive over to Ernie's place.
Urgu had definite opinions, but Colt was able to ignore him.

Colt took it slow and ignored people who didn't use their turn signals. Gilly sat next to him, trying to keep him calm by going off on rambles.

Ernie lived about fifteen minutes away, in a section of Denver called Globeville. He had a little house with a well-kept lawn and a back garage that housed his Harley-Davidson. Ernie's Cadillac wasn't in the driveway.

Colt found the key under the mat. When he unlocked the door, he heard a storm of puppies charge the door.

Gilly looked nervous.

Colt tried to reassure her. "He has pit bulls, but they're sweet. It's the cats you have to worry about."

When he opened the door, Bugs and Daffy gave him a few barks and growls until they caught his scent. Then the two big dogs tried to lick him to death. Bugs was gray and white, while Daffy was mostly black with a little white on his chest.

Colt pushed them back. The pups happily went over to Gilly,

leaning their bodies against her legs. They whined until she bent down to give them lots of pets and scratches.

Colt moved further into the house. It was only a couple of bedrooms, a couple of bathrooms, and a living room and kitchen.

In the kitchen, the cats scattered.

He called to the dogs. "Bugs! Daffy! Let's have you go outside, and then I'll feed you!"

The big dogs stampeded the kitchen, nails clicking and clacking. He opened the door, and they went racing into the backyard in well-worn tracks.

Colt got their food and poured it into their bowls. That brought out the two cats, Bluto and Olive. Bluto was completely black, with a ton of hair hanging off his chin like a beard. Olive was long, skinny, and completely white. She looked at him warily.

Bluto gave him a glare and a hiss.

Then the weirdest thing happened.

When Gilly entered the kitchen, both cats leapt down to purr and rub her legs. "I thought you said we had to be careful with the cats!"

"Those cats hate everyone! Including Ernie. He jokes that they give him a complex. But they clearly love you!"

Gilly gave him an adorable smile. "Because they have such good taste." She paused and frowned. "If you need to visit Ernie's aunt, I'd understand. Heck, I'd even go with you to support your friend."

Colt went into the fridge and got out the cat food. "Ernie said that he was doing okay. He has this huge Italian family, and a lot of them are pretty old. Let's just say this isn't the first time he's had to rush off to the hospital. He'll have at least five cousins with him."

"That sounds like so much fun. I wish I had a big family. It might be less mayonnaise and more marinara."

Colt laughed. He let in the dogs, and they gulped down the food and slurped up water in seconds.

The cats had retreated to the counters, where they gazed down at the dogs like they were uncouth ruffians.

The dogs got Gilly to play fetch with them in the living room while the cats ate.

Bluto gave Colt another hiss before he started eating.

It only took about half an hour, but it was enough that when Colt and Gilly were back on the road, the traffic on I-25 was twice as bad.

Gilly smiled at him. "It's so sweet you helped your friend."

"I love Ernie. My whole family did. It's like he was all of our best friend, and really, it's the least I can do. Those dogs are great."

They sat in traffic. However, being on the freeway felt oddly good. He liked how Gilly added a different smell to the cab of his truck.

When they finally did start moving, Colt kept having to hit windshield wipers from the melted spray from the asphalt. The heat blasted out. They chatted about this and that until Colt got off at the right exit.

"Abraham Jacobs. Biblical." Gilly leaned forward. "Do you think that's Mr. Gentleman's real name? And what's with this Mr. Gentleman anyway? Talk about an anime name."

That made Colt chuckle. "From what he said, Mr. Gentleman didn't seem to know about what's going on with us. He just wanted to make sure we kept a low profile. Or else."

"I can't believe that I'm being threatened by an international supernatural organization. Me. Gillian Croft. That wasn't on my agenda this week."

"Zeh-Gaba said something interesting." Colt made a turn down the frontage road that ran parallel to I-25.

"What?" Gillian motioned to her squinched-up face. "I'm wincing. This is a preemptive wince."

"Gillian Hermione Croft. I know your middle name."

"Never repeat it to anyone!"

"Your secret is safe with me." Colt checked the GPS on his phone. This was the right place.

Gilly sighed. "I'm just glad she didn't go into detail about, oh, I don't know. Anal sex or something."

"So you're into that?" Colt asked.

Gilly gritted her teeth even as she blushed. "Would a girl with a middle name of Hermione be into anal?"

Colt smiled at her. "It's the quiet ones you have to watch out for. Come on."

He got out of his truck and crunched through the snow. They were in the parking lot of a derelict gas station. It was just farmlands around them. The only sign of civilization was the highway.

Gilly followed him, looking doubtfully at the plywood covering the windows of the building. The pumps were there, but the canopies covering them were gone. The old Conoco sign was broken and weatherworn.

One streetlight was still working, giving them a dim light in the otherwise complete darkness.

Colt cupped his hands on the glass and peered inside. There were some old dusty shelves, and the refrigerator cases were intact, but everything looked like it was a million years old. He reached out with his new Gaia senses to see if he could feel anything inside the old gas station, but the only thing he felt was the freeway.

"This can't be right," he murmured. "This really is just an old gas station. It looks like it's been out of commission for years and years."

"Let's go around back, Colt. Isn't there something about deliveries being made in the rear." Gilly's eyes turned a bright blue, and she grabbed her left arm. Her fingernails also took on a blue hue. A look of shock painted her face.

Colt tried to make things less awkward. "I know. Deliveries in the rear. You don't need to say another word."

Gilly stood stiffly, fists clenched at her sides and her eyes squeezed shut. Her voice was normal. "Okay. Okay. She's trying to come out. She's trying to come. She might come. She wants to come."

"She's not being very subtle," Colt said.

"Subtlety is not Zeh-Gaba's strong point. But she can help us, I think. But I'm not completely convinced she's on our side."

They still didn't know what kind of goddess Zeh-Gaba was. She might be the goddess of death.

Gilly blinked, and her eyes were back to being their normal blue color. "That was a lot. But I controlled her. This gives me hope."

"That gives me some hope as well. Let's check around back."

Behind the gas station they found a little brick shack, basically a single room with a pot-bellied stove. The chimney rose from the shingles. Split pine logs were stacked up outside. There was nothing else back there. The asphalt of the parking lot soon gave way to weeds.

Colt knocked on the door.

No one answered.

He tried the knob. It turned in his hand.

Pushing, the door creaked open.

Gilly used her phone as a flashlight. There was a little couch, a little desk, and some blankets. An old square TV was mounted on the back wall far enough from the stove so the heat wouldn't bother it.

There were some old papers on the desk.

Colt stomped his boots to get the snow off. Then he walked across the wooden floor. He pulled out his own phone so he had some light.

The papers were just financial records from the Conoco and a bill of sale. There wasn't anything remotely interesting there. Colt saw that Abraham Jacobs was the new owner of the Conoco. That was it. He couldn't help but feel disappointed.

He'd hoped to find the blond woman with the bright red lips. She might know what happened that day, and how Colt and Gilly might remove the gods from their souls. Or the blond woman might know how they could control them better, and why they had runes on their arms.

Gilly closed the door and locked it. "From the look on your face, it's pretty clear that those papers aren't the written confession of a vampire ordering ancient statues from Mesopotamia. Nothing on Urgu-Uku. Nothing on Zeh-Gaba."

Colt sighed. "Nothing. Unless the ancient gods were looking to buy a gas station. What were gas prices in Sumer five thousand years ago?"

Gilly laughed. It sounded like she was nervous. "I think I might be able to help. But that means I'll have to trust you. And that we would have to get sexual with each other. I want to, Colt. It's just…I'm afraid."

Colt saw where this was going. "If we get sexual, Zeh-Gaba will come out to play. I can ask her more questions. Is that right?"

"That's right." Her eyes were wide. She looked torn.

He tried his best to comfort her. "I like you, Gilly. And you can trust me. I don't know what happened with Amanda Buckman, and you don't have to tell me, but I loved kissing you. I mean, it wasn't you, it was Zeh-Gaba. I know I'll like kissing you more."

In the dim light of their phones, they looked into each other's faces.

Colt could feel the connection. He could feel the heat between them.

Looking into her eyes felt like coming home. He'd never felt so comfortable around a beautiful girl like that before.

"I'm going to let her come into me," Gilly said quietly. "She's going to want to do all sorts of things. Promise me we won't, you know, go all the way. If that happens, I want it to be me, and not her."

"I understand." Colt then watched as Gillian Hermione Croft became someone else.

Someone who wouldn't be satisfied with just kissing this time.

CHAPTER TWELVE

Zeh-Gaba ripped off Gilly's glasses and threw them on the desk. She then pulled off her hat and scarves and tossed them there. She stripped off her coat.

Gilly's eyes gleamed a bright blue. As did the rune on her arm. Her voice also showed the change. "I am glad the girl decided to embrace her passion. She is such an inhibited little thing."

"Hey, Zeh, do we want to talk here? Or should we go back to my place?"

The goddess winced and grabbed her arm. "She is strong, this Gillian woman. She wants to do it here. The door is locked. The parking lot is deserted. No one would dare interrupt us."

Colt felt the sexual tension in the air. He found himself speechless.

The goddess girl smiled. "This place is powerful with Gaia Unum. I can feel the Gaia Force in the Ley Lines near us. You can feel it too. It feeds us like nothing else."

She circled an arm around his neck and gazed up at him. "She touched herself, last night, before she went to sleep. Gillian was alone. She thought of you and your cock."

Speaking of which, Colt was painfully hard. "Let's just keep this between you and me. Or should I say me, you, and Urgu-Uku."

"The Rage King is a simple god, one of rage and destruction. Five thousand years ago, he and I were so much in love. We kept each other sane. Until the First Cage. But let's not talk about that."

Colt was having trouble thinking. First, he couldn't get the image of Gilly masturbating on his couch out of his mind. Secondly, he loved the feel of Gilly's tits pushing up against him. She smelled so good.

It took all of his willpower to gently pull away from her. "If we're going to do anything with each other, let's get things warm in here first. It's really fucking cold."

"It won't be, Colton Holliday. Once we start fucking."

Colt went to the stove. Whoever used the shack knew how to start a fire. There was paper and kindling, ready for a match. He found one and got it lit. He made sure the flue was open.

The blast of heat felt good.

He turned to face the goddess. She had unbuttoned her shirt to show her cleavage and bra. Her ponytail was undone. Moisture gleamed like diamonds in her dark hair.

"Gilly likes showing you her body like this." She drew a hand down the open shirt and brushed the swell of her breast with the back of her hand. "All of her thoughts have been of you."

Colt fed a few split logs into the fire. He turned and took off his coat. "I've been thinking about her as well. But business first, Zeh. How did you and Urgu keep each other sane?"

She lifted her arm. "The runes of power kept us both under control when we walked the world in our own bodies. The runes leashed us. For he would've destroyed the world in his fashion. I would've destroyed it in mine."

"Back when you were gods walking the Earth?" Colt asked.

Gilly's eyes filled with tears. "Back when we ruled the Earth. When we were adored. Before the First Cage. Like I said, I will say no more of that."

"What are you the goddess of?"

"What do you think?"

Gilly's body started to sway. Those tears were gone. The shirt was undone. She took it off and tossed it onto the desk. She then scooped her breasts out of the bra.

For the first time, Colt was seeing Gilly's tits. She had pink nipples rising out of puffy pink areolas. She cupped them. "I am the goddess of lust. My breath is the fire of eternal love, a fire that would destroy the world with unbridled passion, jealousy, and hate, for isn't hate just as powerful as love?"

"I don't understand the specifics," Colt said. "I can feel that Gilly and I have some kind of connection, and that the rune on my arm helped me keep Urgu in check. At least initially. But how can I increase that control?"

Zeh-Gaba came up to him and took his hand. "It would be easier for me to show you. Oh, so the girl wants to come out to play. I will let her. I know that to enjoy my own lust, I must surrender to hers. It is the same with Urgu's anger. For him to relish his rage, you must enjoy it as well. Thus we are all connected. And henceforth, we're all symbiotic."

A second later, Zeh-Gaba was gone. Gilly stood there, her eyes their normal blue color.

Colt expected her to cover herself up, but she didn't. Instead, she dropped her bra onto her cast-off coat.

She smiled shyly. "I think I know how this works. This time, it's your joy we need."

She put his hand on her exposed breast. Her skin was so soft and supple.

The fire was heating the little shack, but so were their hot bodies, wanting release.

Colt felt his cock harden. Just like Gilly's nipple was hardening in his palm.

He cupped her other tit and then leaned forward to kiss her. He was feeling her up when his lips found hers. Hungry, horny, she moaned as they kissed. She'd talked about him getting his joy, but it seemed like she was going to get hers as well.

She offered him her tongue, and he tasted it. He licked her tongue and then sucked on her lips. He couldn't resist. He sucked on her neck and then knelt before her. He was tall enough that kneeling, he was tit level with her. He sucked on her tit. Her nipple was so hard in his mouth. He licked her nipple like he'd licked her tongue.

He took his mouth off her to look at how wet and swollen her nipple was now. She was staring down at him. He glanced up.

She didn't look away. Her voice was breathy. "Now the other one. She's getting jealous."

He licked across the valley of her breasts to her other nipple. This one hardened in his mouth as well. He smelled her body heating up. She was perfume and musk and a deeper, more animal smell. He kissed his way down her belly, but she grabbed his head.

"I got my joy last time, Colt. It's your turn, silly."

Colt so wanted to set her down on the couch, take off her pants, and taste her.

But this wasn't just about sex for them. Oddly enough, it was about gaining more control over the entities that possessed them.

He stood up.

Gilly pushed him onto the couch. "That fire is really heating this room up."

She bent and undid her shoes. When she did, Colt got a view of those wonderful breasts dangling.

With her shoes off, she undid her jeans and pushed them down over her hips until she could step out of them. She drew her panties up higher above her hips. He could see she hadn't shaved completely; she had some pubic hair, but none was showing. "Don't get any ideas, young man. Remember, this is your joy."

"I hope you'll get some joy of your own," Colt whispered.

Gilly laughed. "Maybe. But this is for you."

She pulled his boots off and then got between his legs. She put her hands on his bulge. "Oh, it feels so big. I can't believe I'm going to get to see it. I heard what Zeh said about me, you know, touching myself, and thinking about you. I was kinda shocked. And kinda turned on. Really turned on if you want to know the truth. You don't think I'm too weird or perverted, do you?"

There was only one answer to that question. "Of course not. It's hot."

She bent and inhaled. "I've dreamed about smelling you like this. Okay, I know this is weird and perverted. But I can't help it. I can feel Zeh in me. She's goading me on. She says you won't care. She says you like it when I'm weird and perverted."

He reached for her head, but she grabbed his hand.

"Just be patient, mister. It's going to happen."

"What's going to happen, Gilly?"

"What do you think?"

"I want to hear you say it."

Gilly's blue eyes gleamed. "I'm going to suck your cock."

Colt wasn't sure if that was her or Zeh, but it seemed like both. She undid the button on his jeans. And then unzipped him. His cock was throbbing at this point. It wanted to be free.

Colt raised his hips.

Gilly laughed again. "Someone is getting a little too excited, I think. That's okay. I'm dying to see your cock. To feel it. To suck it."

She pulled his pants and underwear off. His cock was there, right there, in front of the girl from his statistics class.

Her hands went around it. Her fingers were soft and warm. She gripped him hard. "It's so hard. Cocks are so cool. Can I suck on it, Colt? Can I suck on your cock?"

He couldn't believe how dirty this innocent girl was talking. "Yeah, Gilly, suck my cock."

She took her hand off his sex and bent forward. She licked up his thigh until she got to his balls. He felt her horny little tongue on his ball sack, and then she was licking up his shaft and right up to his helmet.

Her hand went back around his cock, and she squeezed. A

little pre-cum bubbled out of his piss slit. She licked it off. "You taste good. Are you going to give me more cum, Colt?"

"If you keep this up, I'll have to."

"I hope so." She leaned down and sucked his sex into her mouth. It was the warmest, wettest, softest place his cock had ever been. She didn't stop; she went down, deep, until he hit the back of her throat.

She choked a little and then came off him.

Spit covered her chin, covered the shaft of his sex, and even dribbled down onto his balls. She could easily jerk him off. "I don't know what I like doing better. Jerking you off or sucking on you. I like looking at your cock. You're so hard. But I love it in my mouth, too. I love taking you deep. It's weird, but I like it in me. It just feels so hot. Like I'm fucking you with my throat."

Again, he had the idea that it was both Gilly and Zeh there, talking dirty.

She went down on him again, and again took him into the back of her throat. This time, she didn't gag. She drew back, stroked him, then sucked on him.

Her other hand was between her legs. She still had her underwear on, but she must've been touching herself. He watched the motion of her arm. He watched her pretty face concentrating on sucking him.

She had this perfect motion. He didn't need to thrust forward. He didn't need to do anything but feel her sucking on him. She loved it. It was clear she loved sucking his cock, gagging on it, jerking him off, desperate for his cum.

Before he knew it, he was on the edge. Right before he came, she pulled her mouth off him. She grinned at him, face gleaming. "I keep tasting your pre-cum, but I want the real thing. Don't worry. I want you to come in my mouth. I want to swallow it."

Before he could say a word, she was back on him, stroking him, sucking on him, harder and harder and harder.

Her hand felt as perfect as her mouth.

It was easy to let himself. The waves of ecstasy hit him hard, over and over, as he felt the sensations fill his mind and his body.

But there was more to it than that. That orgasm seemed to be coming from the same new part of him that could feel I-25 outside. It was like he had a core of energy in his belly, and that was the nexus of his power. At the same time, he could feel energy flowing through all parts of him and extending out. He knew no one was around. They were alone, in this shack, with her tits out and her hand buried between her legs.

His right arm tingled, glowing red. The existing sigil on her left forearm glowed blue.

New runes were appearing, but she still wasn't stopping. She was swallowing his cum. She was moaning while he came, moaning like she was coming.

The orgasm was too intense, and he felt his heart tremble. He had to be careful with her. He had to be careful, or the sex just might kill him. He realized this was what the Rune Genesis Status was referring to from his Gaia Orb. Green meant go. Yellow meant caution. And he'd been at yellow the night before.

Gilly's arm was still glowing as she leaned forward, resting her face on his thigh. He touched her hair, watching her, as she rubbed herself.

Colt was worried that if she came too, it might rupture something between them, but at the same time, he didn't want her to stop. She was masturbating right in front of him, playing with her pussy in that little shack like she'd played with it on his couch the night before.

She was unbelievable.

"Uh, uh, uh." Gilly made little grunting noises. And he felt her orgasm, in his core, in his arms, in his cock. It was like he was coming again as well.

Her body was a mass of pleasure and stress until she sagged against him, and then she let out a long breath. "Well, that was intense."

She held up her right arm, the new rune glowing blue. "The

more we have sex, the more control we should have. But we have to be careful. That's what the Rune Genesis Status means. If we do it too much, we could break our Gaia Cores. That's what gives us our power. Humans don't have them, but then, we're not humans anymore. We're something else." She gazed into his face. "Can you feel that?"

"I can," Colt said.

Gilly climbed up onto his lap, her face buried in the side of his neck. "I hope that wasn't too much. I know I'm weird and perverted. It's just, I lose control. And with Zeh in my head, urging me on, I think I'm even more perverted."

"I love that you're perverted." That was only part of the story for Colt.

The rest?

He was beginning to love every part of her.

It had only been a couple of days, but it was beginning to feel hard to imagine a life without Gilly around. And it wouldn't be a life that Colt wanted.

CHAPTER THIRTEEN

It was funny. The longer they sat in the little shack behind the gas station, the more Colt wanted to be there. It was this little warm space, tucked away from the world. The shack just felt good for some reason. Was it because of I-25 and the Ley Line that ran underneath it? That could be.

Colt didn't want to leave. He used FoodWheel to order dinner from the Lazy Dog Bar & Grill. They had chicken wings, onion rings, and something called fried deviled eggs. Gilly insisted they couldn't be totally unhealthy, so she made them get Brussel sprouts as well, which had bacon so it wouldn't be a total waste of money.

While they waited, Colt went through the papers again. He found that the gas station had changed hands any number of times, but it was pretty clear the owners never really had plans to open it back up.

That was strange. It was definitely part of the mystery.

Colt got more wood for their fire. He also went back to the gas station, checking the back door. The doorknob was loose, but he was able to turn it. It seemed this Abraham Jacobs didn't believe in locks. The back door just led into a utility closet that led to the main store.

Colt was there to flag down the FoodWheel driver, who wasn't a hot soccer mom, just some guy who was a little nervous delivering to an old gas station.

Colt and Gilly ate in the shack, talking and laughing, and it felt perfect.

After dinner, they kissed more, but both of them had started to get tired. Not physically. It was more like the new parts of themselves were exhausted. They were curious to see if they had more control over the gods inside them, but Colt wasn't sure how to test that. The old gas station was probably a good enough place to test out his powers, but at the same time, he was worried he might rush over into traffic and start tossing cars around on I-25. Bashing in semis on a major freeway would be hard to hide, so Colt didn't want to risk it. He'd taken Mr. Gentleman's threat to heart, though he didn't know if the vampire could really hurt the Rage King.

Colt also wanted to get home to check the Gaia Orb. He seriously thought about carrying it around with him, but if it broke, it wasn't like he had a way to get another one.

Colt doused the fire, and they left the shack as they'd found it. Colt put their trash in the back of his truck.

They were soon zooming down the highway. Colt handed Gilly his phone. "Hey, check if Ernie texted me. It would be very surprising if he did."

Gilly checked. "Ernie is a genius! He figured out texting! Aunt Sophia is gonna need a big surgery, but Ernie is back at home with his puppies and kitties. He thanked you."

"Text him back that it wasn't a problem."

Gilly typed with her thumbs. "I'm going to blow his mind with emojis. It's a brave new world, Ernie."

Colt laughed.

After she sent the text, they lapsed into silence.

Colt sighed. "Well, tonight was a bust. I mean, as far as trying to find the blond woman with the red lips. Or Abraham Jacobs."

"Don't be a Negative Nelly, mister." Gilly massaged her right arm. "Tonight was awesome. Not only did we make progress on the sex front, while we were kissing, during that second round, I felt like I had more power over Zeh. She'd suggest I say something super dirty, and I was able to resist her. Let's hope the next time you lose your temper, you'll be able to stop the Rage King from destroying Denver."

"Let's hope. Tonight was amazing. I didn't mean it like that. It's just..." He searched for the right words. "I'm worried about whoever was expecting that shipment of boxes. Eventually, they're going to come looking for the boxes. They might've been destroyed in the fire, but I don't think they were, and I want to get to them before they get to us."

"Well, that's a scary thought." Gilly was quiet for a while. "Let's put a pin in that conversation. I'm pretty tired."

He drove them to the warehouse, where he kissed Gilly one more time and watched her drive away. He had to remind himself that she was bulletproof and that she could take care of herself. Still, he didn't like the idea of her being too far away from him.

Even more depressing, she wouldn't be there in the morning.

He was reminded of that fact when he returned home to their breakfast dishes piled in the sink.

The whole night seemed like a dream. That shack. Gilly giving him joy. The whole encounter.

He'd left the Gaia Orb on the kitchen table. He picked it up, but this time, the snowflakes were blood red, which matched the demon god's skin. He read through his stats again.

<<<>>>

Gaia Orb for Urgu-Uku
Gaia Force Level: 2 (Two New Updates Available. Update Abilities?)
Rune Genesis Status: Red (Stop)
Body Progression:

- Unknown

Gaia Abilities:

- Strength I
- Invulnerability I

Special Gaia Mutations:

- Unknown

<<<>>>

So he had two new updates, but he had no way to use them. The Body Progression, Gaia Abilities, and Special Gaia Mutations were all the same. He set the Gaia Orb back on the table.

It was near midnight when he found the motivation to clean the kitchen.

He got lucky because Aunt Jewel showed up to keep him company.

"Hey, lover boy!" Jewel's ghost called from the other room. "Dim the lights so I can sit at the table."

"No problem, Jewel."

Jewel appeared at the table, in her normal spot. "So, how did things go with Gilly tonight?"

"Like I'm going to kiss and tell. Even though you're a ghost, you're still my aunt." Colt wiped the bacon out of the pan with a paper towel. He noticed the little bowl of grease that Gilly had set aside. He was dying to try her waffles.

"Fine, fine, fine. And just so you know, I'm not going to be haunting you during your sexy times. I might've been a perv in life, but I was never that much of a perv. I've regained my virginity in death. I am very pure now. Not having a body helps with that."

Colt squeezed his eyes shut. "These are all things I don't want to be talking about. We went to the shipping address in Firestone. It was this abandoned gas station. No one was there."

"Any doors missing a doorknob?"

Colt stopped washing. "Now that you mention it, the doorknob on the back door was loose. I opened the door, and it was just this wrecked convenience store. You don't think that Grandpa Walt's doorknobs might change things, do you?"

Jewel chuckled. "While me and Pop were alive, he never wanted to talk about the Monstra more than he needed to. I would ask all these questions, and he'd say even knowing about them put us in danger. He was convinced the Umbra Alliance was quick to remove anyone who might be a security risk. Then you had the Brightest Light, who weren't above torture to find Monstra so they could kill them."

"Did you meet any monster hunters?" Colt asked.

"Hard to say. Like I said, your grandfather kept us sheltered. I will say, I met some pretty weird people. Some of them could've been vampires."

Colt grabbed a kitchen towel to dry the pan. "So, Jewel, if I did get rid of Urgu-Uku, if I were human again, we probably couldn't talk like this, right?"

"Right. You'd be human. I'd still stick around, though, to watch over you. Maybe you'd have a dream or two about me, but it wouldn't be like this." Jewel's face was hard to make out in the darkness, but he could see she was frowning. "You can't ruin your life for some dead lady, Colt. I lived my life, and I'm grateful for it, like I'm grateful for you. And it makes me proud that you didn't just walk away from USP the minute I kicked the bucket. You'll finish off the contract, you won't let USP close down the warehouse, and you'll go on with your life. You have a house in Denver, bought and paid for. Just that has put you way ahead of most folks. More than that, you're a good man, Colton Holliday, and that will get you far in life."

Colt remembered how hard all the death had been. He realized something. "How come Grandpa Walt isn't around? He's a ghost now, right?"

Jewel chuckled. "Dad put everything he had into his life. And he was in his seventies when he died. He'd done his bit, and he went off to his great reward. For me? That reward can wait. I didn't feel like I was done yet. So here I am, ghosting it up! Seeing you with an actual girl again warms my heart, kiddo."

"I've been with girls before."

"Oh, do you mean those women from the Sons of Italy? Or Pam? Ugh, you mean Pam. She was a long time ago and not worth the effort. I like the FoodWheel MILF more than I liked Pam. But look, I'm sorry you got your heart broken. But hearts heal. We both know that."

Colt shook his head. "Sometimes hearts don't heal, Jewel." He put away the dishes. "If Gilly wasn't so great, I wouldn't be risking my heart again, I don't think. Then there's this weird connection we have. Not just us. Urgu and Zeh have this connection as well. I can feel it."

He stopped to touch where his right forearm tingled. "Gilly thinks that I might have more control over the Rage King next time I get pissed off. I hope so."

"Well, I didn't want to say anything that might get you mad, Colt, but we've had some people keeping tabs on our little house."

"What do you mean?"

Jewel flicked out a thumb. "Go out into the living room. Through the front window, across the street, there's a motor home. You probably didn't even notice it, but it showed up last night. There are some guys in it, three guys I've seen so far. One's this big, bald giant, the second is a tall, razor-thin guy, and the last one is short and fat. They are taking turns watching our house."

Colt felt his heart sink. He walked quickly down the hallway and into the front room. Through the window, he saw the Winnebago. He had missed it. Then again, it wasn't in the direction he normally travelled to drive home.

"Should I go and punch it?" he asked. "I haven't punched a motor home yet."

Jewel appeared behind him in her favorite chair. "That is one option. There's no one around, and it might be worth seeing how much control you have over everyone's favorite god of rage and destruction. On the other hand, let's get back to the subject of doorknobs. I'm thinking you might want to know more about whoever might be in that motor home first. Before you start punching Winnebagos."

"Doorknobs." Colt sighed. "You'd think I'd get magical keys. No, I get doorknobs. If those guys are watching me, do you think they're watching Gilly? And what are they waiting for? Who are they working with?"

"All good questions, kiddo. I'm pretty sure you'll get back to punching large vehicles, recreational or otherwise, at some point. For now, let's have you gather more information. They could be waiting to see if everyone's favorite surviving Holliday does indeed have a god inside him. I wouldn't let anyone in on that secret until we have more information."

Colt was pretty sure the blond woman with the red lipstick would have that information. Or Abraham Jacobs. Either way, he'd be making another trip back to the Firestone gas station to see if Grandpa Walt's doorknobs were magic or not.

And if those guys in the Winnebago came calling, Colt would unleash the god of rage on them. Bringing him out wouldn't be a problem.

The fact that he had people spying on him pissed him off like nothing else.

Then he thought about someone hurting Gilly. He smelled burning hair.

Yes, Colton, there is a special satisfaction to murdering those who would murder you. Let us go enjoy the damage we could do to the bus house. Let us wreak havoc on the Winnebago.

Colt was tempted, but he wanted to be strategic.

Besides, Jewel was there to lower his temperature and make

him laugh. "Aren't you glad to have your dead aunt still around? Don't answer that. Everyone likes dead aunts. It's like peanut butter and chocolate."

Colt laughed and felt better. He'd been so tired before, but now he figured sleeping would be basically impossible. He'd still have to try. He had a big day tomorrow.

He saw Gilly had texted him, and he texted her back. That immediately made him feel better.

In the end, sleep did come easy. It was the dreams that were hard.

CHAPTER FOURTEEN

Colt went to sleep texting Gilly, and he woke up texting her. He'd had the strangest dream, and he couldn't wait to tell her about it. It seemed she was having strange dreams as well.

Gilly said she was okay, and she didn't think anyone was spying on her.

Colt shuffled out of his room and into the cold, empty house. Aunt Jewel wouldn't be around—it was hard enough for ghosts to appear at night in the dark. It was even harder for them to manifest during the day. From his limited understanding, it seemed that ghosts used the Gaia Force to keep their shape.

Gilly had some stuff to do that day so she couldn't meet him until that night. She'd drive over to his house, and they'd return to the Firestone gas station together. If nothing else, they'd go back to the shack, have another fire, fool around, and do another FoodWheel order from the Lazy Dog.

They couldn't go all the way, not yet. His Rune Genesis Status was red. Gilly, too, was feeling the aftereffects of what they'd done the night before. He traced the skin on his right forearm. He couldn't see the rune, but he could still somehow feel it.

He checked on the Winnebago. Both the RV and the spies were gone. Was that a good sign?

He did some homework, did some cleaning, and went through another one of his grandfather's boxes. This one was full of old clothes, which he set aside to donate. He then realized that Aunt Jewel could help him go through her room.

Colt couldn't help but feel like he was starting a new life. A lot of the stuff in the house was just relics of a future that could never be. He had a new future to consider.

There was no guarantee that he would be able to remove the Rage King from his soul. What would that mean? He wasn't sure. He hoped the blond woman with the red lipstick would be able to tell him more.

At one point Colt saw the filing cabinet on the other side of the room. It was locked. Could there be more secrets inside? Would that be where the manual for the Gaia Orb was? He thought that it was a definite possibility. He'd just have to empty out the room to get to it.

Later that evening, Gilly showed up at the house. Opening the door, he couldn't stop himself from hugging her and kissing her cheek. "So glad you're back."

"Glad to be here. My parents were very understanding about me sleeping over. They hardly said a word, though I think my dad just lost a few years of his life over it. And my mother is somewhat grayer."

Colt grabbed his keys, and they got in his truck and once more drove up I-25 to Firestone. The old Conoco seemed like it was just the same.

Colt didn't even bother going up to the front door. He drove around to the back.

"What was this dream you had?" Gilly asked. She was wearing a dress with thick tights and low-heel boots.

Colt parked and turned toward her. "I destroyed a temple. Or at least I think it was Urgu that did it. I had this sense of being him, and it was like one of his memories. I walked through this city. I remember the name. It was called Jemdet Nasr. There were people throwing javelins at me, a few bigger spears, some arrows. Nothing hurt me. I marched up to the temple and started destroying walls until the whole thing collapsed. If anyone came close to me, I killed them."

"Jemdet Nasr and Uruk were Sumerian cities like five thousand years ago." Gilly's chest reddened. "I had dreams too. But there's no way I can talk about them."

"Sex dreams?" Colt asked.

Gilly nodded and adjusted her glasses. "Sex dreams. Huge sex dreams. Like, at an oasis in the desert. It was probably Sumer. I think I saw some icons to Ishtar there. She was an ancient goddess of sex and fertility. And the goddess of war. She had wings and this huge bow and a quiver of magical arrows. There were all these women there. It was a harem, and things happened, but we are not going into detail."

She glanced at him, coloring. "I'm bi. Or I think I am. Not that it matters, since you're a boy, but you should probably know. And we're moving on to another subject. We both had crazy dreams, which are probably the memories of the divine entities that are possessing our souls. Okay. That was a sentence I never thought I'd ever say out loud."

A clear mental image of a Sumerian Gilly filled Colt's head. He could picture her walking down the steps of a desert goddess temple, palm trees all around. There would be women lounging on the marble deck surrounding a pond with pristine blue waters. Gilly would be in a tunic and sandals, carrying a bow, with a quiver on her back.

She was powerful and beautiful, and the women couldn't resist her.

Colt knew he was seeing Gilly's goddess form five thousand years ago. His dick got hard picturing her being ravished by any number of women of all different ages, races, and sizes.

"What's wrong, Colt?"

He needed to lie, but nothing came to mind. "I'm picturing

you at the oasis. It's like I'm remembering it. I bet you if we both drew the temple of Ishtar there, our drawings would be exactly the same."

"I'd want to draw this dark-skinned woman with big tits and a hairy pussy," Gilly growled in her Zeh-Gaba voice. "We sixty-nined until I came on her face."

Gilly cleared her throat. "Zeh would like me to pass on that Ishtar was one of her old names. The ancient gods and goddesses had many names. Some of them historians remember, some they don't. But you get the point."

"I get it." Colt shook the crate of doorknobs. "Are you ready? I can't imagine we'll find anything, but we can try."

Gilly fanned her face. "Yes, sorry. Just the memory of the dream has me a little flustered. I'm sorry your dream wasn't as nice."

Colt didn't say it, but the most troubling part of the dream was that he enjoyed punching the heads off the Sumerian warriors that came charging up to him. And he loved the screams of fear and shouts of horror. He had the idea that he started with the temple, but he didn't stop until he'd torn the entire town apart. There was a word, "raze," that meant you destroyed a city until no two stones were stacked. He was pretty sure he'd levelled Jemdet Nasr, and enjoyed every minute of the chaos and destruction.

"Well, Colt Holliday, let's see what your grandfather's door-knobs can do."

They left the truck and slammed the doors.

Except for the drone of the highway, the night was quiet. The winter smells of the plains filled the air. That included the wet asphalt from the snowmelt. Colorado was nice. If it snowed, the snow wasn't around for long.

Colt carried the box of doorknobs under his arm to the back door.

Gilly jiggled the existing doorknob in the back door, and before she knew it, she'd pulled it out. She glanced at it. "Uh-oh. I hope I didn't break anything. Give me some light, Colt."

He fished his phone out and shone it on the end of the doorknob. It was hexagon shaped, with a little line of metal across one of the ridges.

He knelt down on the cold asphalt and shone his light in the box. He brushed around some of the doorknobs and soon found one that had the hexagon shape, but this one had two ridges. It took a bit longer for him to find the right one.

He pulled it out, and it was your typical old-fashioned white crystal knob.

Colt inserted the stem into the empty hole on the door. "There's no way that this is going to work."

Oh, how wrong he was. The crystal knob was glowing, casting a supernatural light across the ground.

"This is not happening," he whispered.

But it was.

He turned the doorknob, which was growing warmer in his hand. He pushed open the door, and it wasn't just an old utility closet or an old gas station. It was something completely different.

CHAPTER FIFTEEN

Colt stood in front of the magic doorway.

Gilly pressed against him, and he felt how warm her body was against the chill night.

Colt was looking down wood steps that hadn't been there the night before. Against the wall were hissing gas lamps. The light threw a warm glow on the old wood of the stairs.

Colt couldn't help but close the door and take out his doorknob, which immediately stopped glowing. He put in the old doorknob. Again, it was a loose fit in the slot. The door opened to reveal the dusty, dirty inside of the old gas station.

"It's all in the knob!" Gilly snorted. "That's what she said."

Colt put the crystal doorknob back in and reopened the door. The wooden stairs and the lamps reappeared. The walls were wood paneling. Down farther, there was red velvet wallpaper.

Colt felt the hairs on the back of his neck lift. "I think we found the exact place where the package was going to be delivered. The question is, do we go down those stairs?"

"You bet we do!" Gilly said with some excitement. "A secret doorway to another world? Pinch me, I'm dreaming!"

"Maybe later," Colt said with a grin.

He led the way down. The stairs squeaked underfoot. The

velvet wallpaper was soft and smooth with age. The whole place seemed so ancient. And who used gas lamps anymore? They gave off some warmth, which helped in the chill air. That staircase seemed far damper and colder than the winter night.

The staircase descended to what seemed like the lobby of a hotel or a waiting room. Red carpet covered the floor. Red and gold wallpaper was above wood wainscotting. There were some lamps glowing on tables, but not many. Most of the room was dark, including a bar top of polished wood and a brass railing. Across the way were two double doors—a grand entrance,

but an entrance to what?

The place smelled like dust and spice, a musky incense.

It took a second for Colt to realize there were men sitting on the back couches across from the bar. They were in dark clothes, wearing three-piece suits. Their eyes were a gleaming silver color.

One of them stood up. He was a big, bald giant. This had to be one of the RV spies that Aunt Jewel mentioned. Now that Colt's eyes were adjusting, he could see the other two matched her description. A tall, razor-thin man with a scraggly beard. And a short fat man with long hair and a moustache.

The bald giant walked out in front of them, blocking their way to the doors. Those silver eyes didn't look right. Then the giant opened his mouth. His canines were long and sharp. They would be perfect for opening a throat so he could guzzle down blood. "What do we have here? You two are in the wrong place. But at the right time. Me and the boys are hungry." He had a slight German accent.

"Colt," Gilly hissed.

Colt glanced over at where the thin man and the short man had been. They weren't there. They were behind them now.

Gilly whirled, keeping her back against his.

Colt felt the adrenaline hit. He could feel that thin line between fear and anger. He could slip into that fury if he needed to. It was an interesting feeling. It was the sensation of standing on a cliff above murky water. To jump was dangerous but not necessarily deadly.

"We're looking for Abraham Jacobs," Colt said. "I would suggest you find something else to eat."

The bald giant took a few steps closer. "I don't know who Abraham Jacobs is. But I do know you and your girl there. We watched you. But you know that. So, are you as dangerous as the Meister says?"

"And who is the Meister?" Colt asked. He found himself having trouble looking away from the bald giant's eyes.

The giant chuckled. "You are new to this world. You even left your doorknob out there. Mr. Isaac is not going to like that."

Colt didn't even bother to ask who Mr. Isaac was. "Gilly, you need to run back up those steps."

She wasn't responding.

Colt knew why. Those silver eyes had hypnotized her.

The bald giant was approaching, and Colt couldn't move. This was some kind of predatory hypnosis thing. These three were vampires, and they could freeze their prey so they wouldn't be able to move. Not even when the vampires ripped their throats out.

"And the Meister said you would be trouble." The bald giant had a sneer on his face. "You're not trouble. You are dinner, liebling."

Colt fucking hated that self-satisfied smile. The rage hit him all at once. The stench of burning hair filled his nose. The runes on his forearms glowed a bright red, both of them, and Colt didn't even bother with his shirt and coat. Those burst into flames as he started getting bigger. Urgu was silent. The god didn't need to say a word because it was finally time for violence again.

That smirk was gone from the bald German.

Colt stormed forward and drove his fist into the man's face. He didn't use his full strength, no, because if he killed the German, he wouldn't be able to get any information out of him.

Colt wanted to know if the Meister and Mr. Isaac were the same person.

The giant staggered back, his face bloody.

Colt turned to see Gilly on the floor. The thin man was at her neck, while the stubby man had pulled up her dress and pulled down her tights. He was going for the big artery in her thigh.

Colt felt rage like he'd never felt before. It felt so fucking good. He grabbed a sofa and hurled it. The sofa struck the thin man and knocked him sprawling. Colt took three big steps and kicked the stubby, long-haired man into the wall. There was the satisfying crunch of ribs snapping.

The room was full of smoke from his burned-off clothes and from the flames rising from his scalp.

Colt wasn't cold anymore. He was rather comfortable now. And with the two runes on his forearms gleaming, he had far more control over the rage god than he'd ever had before. He caught sight of himself in a mirror. It was his face, but bigger, and yes, instead of hair, flames topped his skull. He was a muscled juggernaut of red skin with twin runes glowing on his arms. He still had pants on, so he was right—his pubes didn't burn like the hair on his scalp.

Colt picked up Gilly in his left arm. She hardly weighed a thing. She was blinking her eyes, coming around from that strange hypnotic spell that the vampires had put her under. Vampires. They were actual vampires.

Gunshots sounded in the room, and he turned to see the German giant with a pistol, unloading the clip.

The bullets only tickled Colt. He strode forward and tried to grab the German, but the man was quick. He ducked back.

Smoke swirled around him for a second, but that smoke soon turned into two figures—the thin man and the stubby man. Both attacked him.

Even holding Gilly, it was easy to backhand the thin man, caving in half his face.

Then Colt kneed the stubby man in his already broken ribs.

The stubby man fell to the ground, most of the bones of his thorax broken.

Colt finished off the attack by ramming his head into the German's face. Not only was the German's face bloody from Colt's initial punch, but now he was burned as well. Lucky the giant was bald, or his hair would've caught fire.

The double doors were thrown open. Men and women in uniforms rushed. They had silver eyes and fangs. These were vampires, but what were those uniforms? They looked like something a constable might wear back when Colorado was a territory. With them were tall, thin figures, very beautiful, with long pointed ears.

Holy shit, those were elves.

The graceful figures were dressed like maids and butlers. They had old-fashioned fire extinguishers, the kind you pumped. The elves used them to put out the fires that Colt had started.

Colt realized that if he wanted to find the blond woman with the red lipstick, he needed to get out of that room, but it was getting harder and harder to control the Rage King.

Urgu's voice was so loud in his head. *Let us bathe this room in blood. Let us behead, disembowel, dismember every single one of our enemies! Let us leave behind nothing but ruin and sorrow!*

The thought of pulling vampires apart was appealing, but Colt was able to retain control of himself. He didn't bother to explain how indiscriminate murder might bring more trouble down upon himself and Gilly.

He rammed his way through the crowd and right through the double doors. He was on a platform, facing a narrow canyon, with walkways, houses, and businesses lining both sides of the strange crack in the ground. The canyon was narrow, probably a quarter-mile wide but at least a mile deep, and who knew how long? All the buildings in the crack were old-fashioned, like Victorian buildings from the 19th century. More gas lamps provided light. There was a gondola-like sky train crossing on suspended cables. The train led to a vast mansion made up of balconies, fountains, and big rooms with ornate windows.

That seemed to be the underground city's palace.

Glancing up, Cold could see the night sky somehow, but it was probably a mile away. He got a sense of the gas station above, but more importantly, I-25 was above them, and cars raced over a see-through highway. Golden light rushed in a torrent under the cars. That had to be the Gaia Unum that fed the gods inside them.

It truly was an underground world of mystery.

To the right were brass gates blocking their way. To the left was a building built into the rock of this strange world. An art deco sign above it said it was Firestone Alley's Constabulary. That explained the cops.

Colt struggled to keep control. Urgu-Uku wanted to bust through those brass gates, grab a car from the sky train, and hurl it at the mansion far below. It would be fun to see those ornate windows shatter.

Colt had a better idea.

He took Gilly and leapt over the edge. He fell with buildings whirring past him.

Fear not. Such a fall will not kill us, and I will ensure your pretty girl's safety.

Colt wasn't worried. Even as they fell, he got a better look at the mansion, its balconies, fountains, and pools. There seemed to be a party going on. It reminded Colt of the party from *The Great Gatsby* movie.

Colt slammed through another balcony. He hardly felt a thing. And then he hit the bottom, which was a murky channel of sludgy water with rough brick shacks and rock houses next to a concrete ditch.

There was a narrow cave that Colt made wider with a punch. Rock debris went flying.

He hustled back there, trying to get control.

Gilly was struggling against him. The runes on her forearms were glowing. She was saying something, but Colt couldn't figure out what it was. He couldn't think. He was just so pissed off. On a tide of red fury, he was whisked off into unconsciousness as Urgu-Uku took over.

Now, that we've seen the city, we can destroy it. None shall escape our murderous fury! It will burn! It will burn! It will burn!

Some time later, Colt woke up. He didn't smell a city burning, but he did smell laundry. A lot of laundry.

CHAPTER SIXTEEN

Colt lay in a pile of sheets.

There was a little blue man with a wrinkled face, pointed ears, and a big mess of white hair on his head. That hair was as thick as his white goatee. He wore a pair of tiny overalls. Goggles hung from his neck. A pair of leather gloves were tucked in his belt. "Well, now. The mister is awake, missy. And his hair ain't burning. He seems quite a bit smaller, if ye don't mind me sayin'."

Colt pulled himself up. He was surrounded by vast machines chugging away with the familiar sound of a washing machine gurgling laundry. In other places, industrial dryers rattled as they spun loads dry. A collection of the blue people were busy with a hissing, steaming machine, working on men's shirts. Others were folding women's underwear. It was a hive of activity. Most of the blue men kept their eyes on their own business. The women looked similar to the men, except the women didn't have beards, goatees or otherwise.

The little guy near Colt and Gilly frowned. "We don't get many of the Uttuku here. Sorry, missy, in yer human tongue, that would be a demon. Yer probably not a demon. Too pretty. I'd say ye were one of the Annukai."

"What are the Annukai?" Gilly sat on a little wooden chair. She sipped from a dark bottle with a strange homemade label.

"Angels, miss. Yer as pretty as one."

She blushed and smiled.

Colt let out a breath. "So, then, what are you, captain?"

"Not a captain," the little blue man said. "I'm a Tomte gnome, one of the Order of the Forge. Ye two are strangers here. Aye, but maybe not so strange. Yer Walt's kid, or that's what I heard."

"I am," Colt agreed. "Colt Holliday."

"And I'm Barnard Bafflestone, but either Barney or Bafflestone would be fine. Yer grandpa was a good one. He would come here every so often. He'd be delivering packages back before…back when." The gnome's eyes filled with tears. He wiped them away with a sweep of his leather gloves. He put them on. "Back when I wasn't in this garn laundry room. Back before Vincent Isaac took over Firestone Alley. And everything changed."

Gilly frowned. "You're going to have to go slow with us, Mr. Bafflestone. We're new to your world."

The gnome chuckled. "Oh, I'll bet. Walt wouldn't've said a garn word about us Leyfolk. He wanted a part of our magic. I wonder if that particular dream ever came true."

Colt didn't know whether to be pissed off at his grandfather or grateful. Colt had gotten to live a relatively normal life, and there had been no secret organization out to kill him for knowing things he shouldn't. "My grandfather might've created something, something called a Gaia Orb."

Bafflestone turned a bit pale. He sat there, blinking.

Colt wasn't sure what that meant. He glanced at Gilly. "So, uh, last thing I knew the Rage King wanted to destroy the entire city. I'm assuming that didn't happen."

Gilly nodded. "That's right. Me and Zeh talked tall, red, and fire-topped out of destroying everything. He might be the Rage King, but he's a sucker for a pretty face."

Bafflestone leapt up and grabbed Colt's arm. "Walt done did it! It was an idea I had, but garn, I never thought we could track the Gaia so closely. I have to see that orb! By the Order of the Forge, I have to see that orb!" The Tomte let go of him. "Well, now I, uh, seem to have lost control of muh-self."

"It's fine. If we ever get out of here, I'll bring the orb around. But what do you mean the Order of the Forge?" Colt asked.

"The Monstra races are divided into different orders. Us Tomte build things. Why, I helped update Firestone Alley back in the day. I worked with Silas Church, an alpha vampire. He was kind, you know, for being a part of the Order of the Night. He was one of Felix Mudd's originals. Couldn't compete against Vincent Isaac. Vincent Isaac killed Silas about a hundred years ago. Took power. Brought in the Lyra elves to take over engineering and services. Kept the old Tomte like me around, just to maintain things."

"We saw the elves," Gilly said. "What is their order?"

"Order of the Song. They like music and such things. But they can also engineer. Sure they can. But not as well as us Tomte." Bafflestone hooked a thumb at his chest.

Colt was feeling better. "That big bald German guy mentioned a Mr. Isaac. Is he also the Meister?"

"Aye," the gnome agreed. "If ye met Otto, then ye must've met Warren and Sodd as well. Warren is the skinny one. Sodd is the stubby one."

"We did," Colt said. "How did I get here?"

"Cave brought you here, friendo," Bafflestone said. "Girl talked the garn demon out of ye. But she said that it tweren't a demon. Twas a god. That's hard to believe. My bet is still on the Order of the Damned, or the Order of the Adored. That's the order for the demons and the angels. But we covered that."

Colt wasn't too sure Gilly should've told the gnome about the gods possessing them. However, it was too late now. Bafflestone was obviously interested in them.

"Have you heard of humans being possessed by gods?" Colt asked.

Bafflestone thought for a minute, hand on his beard. "Only in stories."

"Is there a chance we might go back to being human?" Colt asked.

Bafflestone shook his head. "Not likely. That change would be permanent, except for, well, except for special cases. I'd have to do more research. I'd do it for ye, if ye promise to show me the Gaia Orb, but really, I'd do it anyways since I always liked Walt. Speaking of yer gramps, I'm trying to remember something about him. But the old noggin isn't what it used to be."

Colt found himself oddly at peace with his fate. With the second rune, he had so much more control. He didn't think Bafflestone would know how the runes worked, but if the little blue man was as smart as he said, he might be able to really help them, especially with the Gaia Orb.

Bafflestone snapped his fingers. "We retrieved yer grandfather's doorknob. Ye don't just leave it up there. Lucky we had a Tomte tooler doing some maintenance near there." From his pocket, he gave them back the white crystal doorknob with the hexagon stem.

"Thanks." Colt put the knob in his pocket.

Gilly's eyes were bright. It was clear she was loving this. "But back to the Leyfolk. How many different orders are there?"

"Twelve known orders," Bafflestone said. "Aye, wish we could talk more, but I have to get back to work. Can't lose my work. Been here too long to find another place in another Gaia Town. The missy was saying ye were looking for someone. Blond hair. Red lipstick. Probably a vampire 'cause she was wearing old-fashioned clothes."

Colt glanced at Gilly.

She shrugged. "Well, she was. That hair wasn't right, and her clothes were like something out of the 1930s. And she wore a hat. Like not a hat anyone has worn for a long time. Do you remember the hat?"

"Maybe. But I was pretty out of it. I'd never been possessed by an ancient god before."

Bafflestone frowned and scratched his goatee. "Garn, I can't stop thinking about a real-life Gaia Orb. I had my theories. We Tomte are good at such things. Twas the Tomte that figured out how to generate electricity using the Gaia Force. That was back when I was but a little blue squirt."

"How old are you?" Gilly asked.

Bafflestone grinned, showing even white teeth. "Two hundred and thirty-five years old. Grew up on I-35 in Kansas. Moved west to make a name for myself. I did for a bit."

"So those lamps are running on electricity generated from Gaia?" Colt asked.

"Yep. I worked on some gauges to keep track of the wattage, which gave me an idea for the Gaia Orb in the first place. Everyone laughed at me 'cept for Walt. Now, most Gaia Towns have electricity 'cause of me."

Colt had to shake his head. He'd seen it before. Sometimes talented people were wasted because of grudges, politics, or just bad luck.

The gnome continued. "I've kept track of that human tech. Getting better and better all the time, mister. But for now, let's talk about yer blond vampire. I know her, I think. She's trouble. She only recently got out of prison. I don't like her. No one does much. Her name's Eliza Bennet, and she works for Vincent Isaac. He's having a party, and she might be there, but I doubt it. Like I said, she's despised. She keeps to her room in Isaac's palace."

Colt remembered the *Great Gatsby* party he'd seen above, in that mansion with the balconies, fountains, and swimming pools. "Can you get us to her room?"

Bafflestone glanced over at the other Tomte gnomes handling the piles of laundry. They were pointing at their wrists, frowning at him.

"Yeah, yeah, don't get your garn panties in a twist." Bafflestone fixed his goggles into place over his eyes. They made his eyes look huge. "They hate it when I don't work. Even though I was head engineer, that don't mean much now that we're on laundry detail. I can get ye to the palace. I can tell ye where her room is. But you'll need a disguise. Word of intruders has even reached our blue ears."

Bafflestone called over to the other gnomes. "We'll need sizes of clothes for these two. Trust me on this. And, Belinda, come and do this girl's hair up. She'll lose the glasses. That should work. As for fire-top here, no one is gonna know who he is."

"Why are you helping us?" Gilly asked.

Colt had that same question.

Bafflestone shrugged. "Oh, boredom mostly. And to mess with that garn Vincent Isaac. Won't never forgive him for throwing me and my people down here. He said the elves were prettier. Taller definitely. Us Tomte might be smaller, but we're also smarter." Bafflestone then regarded them. "And if ye both are gods, well, I'd like a god on my side for once. Aye, ye might decide to take over the Alley, and then ye'll know who to put in charge of engineering. Right?"

"Right you are," Colt said. "Though we don't have any plans to try to take anything over. We don't even really know what's happened to us, or what our future might look like."

Bafflestone chuckled. "Oh, I would imagine ye'll figure that out. Yer Walt's grandson. Can't imagine ye'd have a bad head on your shoulders."

Colt didn't mention his father.

Gilly glanced over at the crowd of Tomte workers. "Are any of the other gnomes going to tell Vincent Isaac about us being down here?"

"Nope. I'll tell 'em not to. They won't. We all hate Isaac. The more difficult ye make that asshole's life, the more we'll like ye." The gnome pulled his leather gloves tighter. "Let's get ye up top. Lucky for ye, I know all the secret back ladders and back ways. Now for disguises."

Colt's head was spinning, but he soon found himself being dressed by a half-dozen blue women. The men wore overalls, but the women wore drab work shirts tucked into denim slacks. Both sexes had black boots.

They braided Gilly's hair and gave her a revealing dress—men wouldn't recognize her because they'd be too busy looking at her cleavage. The outfit came with a scarf, a hat, and sexy stockings. They found stylish black boots for her.

Bafflestone made a joke about vampires complaining about lost laundry. It wouldn't be the first time.

Colt found himself in a three-piece suit that included a cravat. He'd have preferred a shoestring tie, but oh well. He also had a hat. They found black shoes for him. The shoes were a bit too small, but he wasn't going to complain. He had his disguise.

Colt thought about leaving and coming back when the heat had died down, but Bafflestone assured them that with the party raging, there wouldn't be a better time to try to talk with Eliza Bennet. The gnome didn't tell them why he didn't like her or what she'd done to be imprisoned. He didn't want to talk about it.

Colt saw that Bafflestone was being diplomatic. If Colt was friends with this Eliza Bennet, it would be rude for the gnome to talk bad about her.

Clearly, Bafflestone saw Colt and Gilly as potential allies in his quest to regain power in Firestone Alley.

Bafflestone gave Colt and Gilly a backstory. "So ye two are human, all right, but ye'll tell anyone who asks that yer bloodbonded to the Knight family. Marcus Knight is a powerful alpha vampire who lives up in Plainsong City. That's a Gaia Town off of I-80, just east of Cheyenne, Wyoming. Mostly it's the werewolves that own that Ley Line, but Marcus managed to make peace with 'em."

"What's bloodbonded?" Gilly asked.

Bafflestone shrugged. "Humans can become a part of a vampire family by letting the vamps feed off 'em. I guess some humans just like walking around as snacks for a particular family. I never understood it, but I guess it feels good. People'll do a lot just to feel good. Most of the humans among the Leyfolk are bloodbonded. But not all. Like Walt wasn't."

Bafflestone led them to the back of the laundry cave, to a big round iron grate. On the other side was a ladder that led up to some laundry chutes, and then out to the front walkway.

Colt had to stop himself from gaping. He went to the polished wooden railing to look down to see how far they'd come up. He couldn't see the ditch at the bottom, but he did get a glimpse of a park on the other side, lots of strange luminescent grass, and the glitter of a few otherworldly trees, all under the ever-present streetlamps, which were powered by the throbbing Gaia Force around them.

Being in Firestone Alley felt good in some strange way. It was the same as how he'd felt when he'd been on I-25. He just felt at home.

Bafflestone saw his awe. "Aye, Firestone Alley is a pretty something to consider. And ye've only seen a small part. Normally, we'd take the elevators, but we don't want to draw attention to ourselves."

The Tomte gnome led them up more ladders, through another maintenance tunnel, and up a spiral staircase. The steps took them to the laundry room in the back of the palace.

Bafflestone pointed at the back door. "That's going to take ye through a linen closet and into the party. Keep going straight. Don't go to the right. Stay left, and ye'll find a staircase outside that will lead ye up to Eliza Bennett's room." He paused. "Ye both look garn good, if I do say so myself. If ye ever need me, mister and missy, just send a letter to my private address."

From a pocket, he gave them a card that had a Firestone Alley address under the name Walter Wondergear.

"That's Walter as in Walt. Like your grandfather. Mail will take a day. Or, if you mention that name to the right person, I'll hear about it sooner. Ye two be careful. Something tells me this is the start of a beautiful relationship. Don't forget old Barney when ye get up top now. I betcha I can help with the Gaia Orb."

Colt was pretty sure that was the truth. With Bafflestone's help, he just might be able to upgrade his abilities.

Bafflestone gave them a little salute, turned, and then started back down the ladders. For being so small, he was quick on the rungs.

Gilly surprised Colt by putting her arms around him. "Well, now, Mr. Holliday. You ready to take me to the party of a lifetime?"

Colt grinned. "In a secret underground city? Surrounded by vampires?"

"And elves," Gilly said. "The Order of the Song."

"You keeping track?"

"You bet I am."

Colt took in a deep breath. "Let's not gawk. We have to be cool."

"Like flippin' ice." Gilly kissed him, and he kissed her back. He couldn't help but grab her ass in the dress. He realized at some point she'd taken off her underwear.

Now that was true commitment to a disguise.

Colt just hoped it would work. If not, he'd unleash the beast. Do enough damage, and someone would bring him the blond girl with the red lipstick, gift-wrapped, on a silver platter.

CHAPTER SEVENTEEN

The first door led to a vast room full of sheets, towels, and even some curtains, all stacked on shelves. The next door brought them into a hallway with a loud, steaming kitchen on the left.

Colt glanced inside to see elves making appetizers and uncorking wine bottles. Other elves, the Order of the Song, carried trays out the front door. The pointed ears were a little hard to get used to, but other than that, the elves were all so beautiful and full of light.

"Okay," Gilly said. "We're bloodbonded, remember? Bafflestone said that Marcus Knight isn't here, so there's no danger of being caught."

"Right." Colt pushed open a door into a dark room, and it was too late to simply close it.

The main party was up ahead, through an archway. This was some kind of martini bar, with low lights, soft music, and a gleaming bar where some guy with black hair served up drinks. Some of the bottles held alcohol. Others clearly held blood.

Speaking of blood—low leather couches filled the room. On every couch, there was a half-naked human. Vampire couples, or threesomes, drank from the bloodbonded humans, either from their throats, wrists, or thighs.

Colt tried not to stare, but he saw one woman with her shapely legs spread. She was rubbing her pussy while a girl vampire drank from her thigh.

Another woman was on her back, watching as a male vampire kissed a female vampire, both sharing a bloody kiss. The male then went back to the woman, holding her naked tit while he feasted at her throat.

One man had his slacks pulled down so his pale ass was showing as he thrust into a woman. He sucked on her neck while he fucked her. From the look of it, she liked the feel of him drinking from her as much as she liked the sex.

It was something out of a movie.

There were soft sighs, orgasmic cries, and quiet laughter.

Colt had a lot of questions about how vampirism actually worked. Were the humans at the orgy being turned into new vampires? Were crosses a problem for the vamps? Did they have to sleep in coffins? What was their stance on sunlight? Being underground, that might not be a problem.

He then remembered that Gilly had said the blond girl with the red lipstick had been covered in a big coat and a wide-brimmed hat.

Colt took Gilly's hand and led her through the couches and out through the archway. They went over a little wooden bridge with clear water running underneath.

A tall man with wide shoulders stood at the top of the bridge. Everything he wore was gray, from his shoes to his gray gloves. Iron gray hair topped his head. He had a perfectly unlined face— no wrinkles— even when he smiled. "Did you have fun in The Playroom?"

Colt turned to see that the room they'd just left was called The Playroom. Stage lights flashed on another art deco sign. It was like a vampiric version of the video game *Bioshock*, one of Grandpa Walt's favorites.

People were dressed up like it was the first half of the twentieth century. Everyone had hats on.

Gilly went on a ramble. "We're bloodbonded with Marcus Knight. He wouldn't want us playing with anyone else. You know, because we're bloodbonded. But no sex. It's just the blood. You know. Because vampires are a thing. Why wouldn't they be a thing?"

Colt laughed, like it was all just a joke. "Come on, honey, you're drunk. Good evening, sir."

Colt escorted Gilly off the bridge and into the heart of the party. The balcony had a polished wood floor and a wooden railing with brass fittings.

A fountain, bubbling with champagne, dominated the center of the balcony.

The place was packed. A huge band, like something from the 1930s and '40s, played on a stage. Glenn Miller, or Tommy Dorsey, would've fit right in.

Currently, they were playing the crowd favorite "In the Mood." People danced in front of the stage.

There were a ton of people, and it would be easy to fit in now that they were out of The Playroom.

The vampires looked human enough, until the flickering lights caught their eyes in a certain light and they turned silver. Or when someone exposed their fangs, though it seemed like they did it on purpose. Nonetheless, they could pass outside of Firestone Alley.

The elves had their ears, though. And there were other Monstra at the party. Thick-bodied dog people that were human in every respect except they had the faces of various dog breeds. One bulldog-faced man was talking with two tall women with the heads of collies.

There were cat women there as well, wearing evening gowns to show cleavage covered in short fur. A few cat men stood with them, diamonds winking from their ears. One old cat man wore glasses.

Several people were smoking—tobacco from the scent, but Colt did catch the odor of marijuana as well. The partygoers wore their fair share of perfume and cologne, and there was the odd smell of coal smoke or wood smoke from below them.

Colt glanced up. There was the ghostly image of I-25 above, like a spectral highway. Colt looked closer. There was a faint golden energy underneath the shadowy cars zooming north and south. That was the Gaia Force. That was the Ley Line. It was this beautiful, twisting maelstrom of power.

Colt knew they couldn't still be on Earth. This had to be some kind of pocket dimension. Otherwise, the humans would know about the long crack that extended from Firestone all the way into Longmont.

"I don't think we're in Kansas anymore, Toto," Gilly breathed. She sighed. "I'm the worst spy ever. I totally went off. I talk when I'm nervous. You know I ramble, and spies don't ramble. But when Zeh-Gaba saw that orgy back there, she had all sorts of ideas. I had to fight her, or we never would have gotten out of there. Your average goddess of lust adores a good orgy. Who knew?"

"Uh, probably everyone." Colt laughed.

He and Gilly walked through the party, grabbed a couple of champagne glasses, and then went to the railing. Across the way were the twinkling of the Gaia lamps on balconies and in windows. Colt saw more shops, and farther down, another park.

Colt sipped his champagne. It was fine. He'd never been much of a wine guy.

But he and Gilly followed the railing to the left. That took them closer to the stage and to the people who were dancing there.

Gilly gulped down her champagne. "Uh, I need another one. I'm so frickin' nervous. Bafflestone said not to go to the right. That was the orgy room. Clearly. Then we needed to look to the left. Stairs, right?"

"Stairs to the left." Colt pointed. "Not to the right."

"Such the comedian. Leave the jokes to the professionals." Gilly plucked another glass off an elven waiter's tray.

The band finished with a big blast of brass.

The same man that had talked to them on the bridge approached the microphone. "Are you all having a good time tonight, my friends?"

The crowd let out a yell.

A dog man in a tuxedo growled next to Colt and Gilly. "This is why we're really here. To watch Vincent Isaac eat a snack. To remind us that he's in charge, and if we cross him, we'll end up as dessert."

Colt felt a shiver run down his spine. They'd actually run into the alpha vampire in charge of Firestone Alley.

It made Colt suddenly feel exposed.

Gilly whispered, "Oh, dang. Clearly, I picked the wrong guy to lose it with." She then laughed a little. "We came here looking for Abraham Jacobs, right? But in the Bible, the fathers of the church were Abraham, Isaac, and Jacob. I think we know who ordered that shipment."

Colt knew she was right. That was why Isaac had sent his goons to spy on them.

Colt thought about making a run to the staircase. But if they didn't make a stir, they'd just be lost in the crowd of the big party. Colt didn't want the Rage King killing any of the dog or cat people.

Isaac raised his hands. Diamond cufflinks winked on his wrists. His eyes turned silver. "There's a human among us who is not bloodbonded."

Vincent Isaac's eyes seem to find Colt's.

In that second, Colt found this sneaking around stupid, and he felt an anger fill him. It seemed that the vampire lord had known Colt and Gilly had been at his party all along.

Urgu actually laughed. *If he calls us out, we shall turn this Gaia Town into a butcher shop. There will be so much blood, we shall drown those of the Order of the Night in the gore. They shall not drink. But we shall drink the violence down to the lees.*

Colt whispered to Gilly, "Urgu is talking shit."

"Keep a lid on him!" Gilly was a tense ball of nerves. That pissed Colt off more than anything. He didn't want her being afraid. Ever. Of anything.

He smelled his hair about to catch fire.

You think this city is pretty, Colton. I see it already in flames. Let us revel in the rage.

Colt knew that the runes on his forearms were burning bright. Luckily, both his shirt and his jacket covered them. Still, Colt kinda liked the idea of people screaming in terror, and he could reduce Vincent Isaac's mansion to a collection of sticks, corpses, and broken glass.

Gilly grabbed his arm. "Keep your temper, darling. We don't want to do anything we'll regret."

Her presence calmed him. He took a deep breath. Those runes were helping him keep Urgu down, but it wasn't easy.

Isaac tugged off his gray gloves. "Bring the human to me."

A woman was marched forward.

Colt recognized her from The Playroom. She'd been having sex while getting her blood drained. There was a red splotch on the side of her neck.

Isaac grabbed her hand. "Yes, she is fresh from fucking, and her joy is in her juices. Her lover couldn't turn her. But I can. Would you like to join the Order of the Night?"

"More than anything," the woman said.

Isaac had her captured in his silver gaze. Colt could see how hypnotized she was.

"And what if I desire your heart's blood, lovely?" the vampire lord asked her.

She said something, but no one could hear her.

Isaac shoved the microphone into her face.

She blinked. "Then I would give it to you. I would serve you. Even in death."

"He's gonna kill her," the dog man growled. "The vamps like the heart's blood the best. It gives them the most Gaia. Still, he's doing this 'cause he's a murderous asshole. I wish Silas Church was still in charge. Those were the good ol' days."

Colt was thankful for the running commentary.

"Then I will let you serve me," Isaac said with a booming laugh.

He gave the microphone to a servant, and then he took the girl in his arms. She let out a muffled scream as Isaac bite into her throat. Then she writhed against him, not fighting him but wanting to rub herself on him.

She grew more and more pale until her skin turned gray.

Isaac dropped her lifeless body onto the stage. The slumping sound echoed across the balcony. "We all shall drink tonight! I gave her what she wanted—servitude to me and to the Changku Ley Line forever. Is this not what you all want?"

"Changku Ley Line," Gilly mused. "I bet that's another name for I-25."

The crowd didn't pause. They applauded and shouted, though Colt saw it was more out of fear than adoration. They were doing what Vincent Isaac wanted because if they didn't, they too might end up drained and gray on that stage.

The growling dog man next to them didn't say a word. The elven servants weren't applauding him either.

Colt saw a little path open in the crowd, and he eased Gilly down it.

Isaac kept on talking. "I rule the Changku, but there are other Ley Lines, and my empire will grow. I have plans to increase my power exponentially. All will bow before me when I am done. I will transcend the Order of the Night to embrace the power of a god. I will remember who my friends are when I find the Fate Blade."

For some reason, that made Colt stop. What was the Fate Blade?

Gilly gasped at what Vincent Isaac said next.

"There are intruders at this party that are probably listening right now. I will find you. And I will purify you on the Fate Blade. You will not stand in the way of our ultimate victory!"

Our victory? That meant *his* victory. It was the Vincent Isaac Show, and you were either in the audience or you were dead.

Vincent Isaac left the stage, and the band started again.

Colt wanted Gilly to go up the stairs first so he could have her back. He kept expecting to be grabbed by one of the Monstra, but Bafflestone's disguises seemed to have worked.

The stairs wrapped around the main building and led up to another door at the top of the palace. Pushing that door open, they were shown a hallway of doors. Most were open, so Colt and Gilly could peek inside.

One, though, was closed. Colt opened it. It was a nice, big room, with windows that looked down on the party balcony. It had nice views of the champagne fountain as well as the swimming pools.

Gilly saw the note on the desk.

They read it together.

Dear Vincent,

You won't find it. You won't hurt them. You won't get what you want, and your plans will amount to nothing. Don't try to find me. You'll die if you do.

Yours Truly,

Elizabeth Anne Bennett

Gilly turned to him. "Why do I think that Vince isn't going to take this news very well? Someone is going to get eaten, and not in the good way."

Gilly's eyes flashed blue, and her nails glowed. She squeezed them shut. "Zeh-Gaba has definite opinions about that, but I'm keeping her quiet for now. How do we get out of here?"

Colt grinned. "Watching Vince swagger around was pissing

me off. We could go back there, I could unleash the beast, and I could bash our way out of here."

"Not very subtle. Come on. I have a plan. When in doubt, act stupid."

Gilly's plan worked.

They wandered the palace until servants found them. When Gilly insisted they were just lost, clueless party guests, an elven waiter showed them the way to the exit—the big bronze gates across the way from the Firestone Alley police force.

The constables opened the gates and let them leave. Vampires and elves were still cleaning up the entry room from the fight before.

Colt wondered if Isaac's vampire goons—Otto, Warren, and Sodd—would be able to heal the damage he'd dealt. That was just one of the questions he had.

Where was Eliza Bennett? And what was this Fate Blade?

Colt and Gilly found themselves out under the stars. He inhaled the smell of the sagebrush and cold. They'd made it out with their lives.

"Well, that was certainly an interesting first date," Gilly said.

Colt had a problem with that. "I think the White Spot was our first date, right?"

"Actually, the shack was probably our first date, though are we going to tell our kids that? No. Let's stick with Vincent Isaac's murder party being our first date."

Colt wasn't going to argue.

Was Gilly thinking about kids? They'd only really gotten to know each other in the last three days. Nevertheless, he could feel the connection he had with her.

Getting into his truck felt so surreal after their adventure together. And he still had the box of doorknobs, including the crystal doorknob that Bafflestone had retrieved for him. Were there other Gaia Towns like Firestone Alley? Yes, Bafflestone had mentioned one—Plainsong City, on I-80 outside of Cheyenne. What was that place like?

Arriving back at home, Colt drove past Sir Car-A-Lot and pulled into his driveway.

That was when he noticed that his house was dark.

Gilly went to get out, but he stopped her. "Wait. I have a timer on the living room lamp. It should be on."

Then he saw the shadow of someone in his house.

"Did you see that?" Gilly whispered.

"Yeah," Colt said. "And I think I know who it might be."

CHAPTER EIGHTEEN

Colt wasn't going to go through the front door of his house. If he was wrong about who was in there, he didn't want to make himself a target. He had some control over the Rage King, but not that much.

Gilly stayed in the truck.

Colt went through the back gate, knowing just how to pull down on the door to stop the hinges from squeaking. He left it half-open. On the back porch, he saw his aunt sitting in the darkness.

"Hey, Jewel!" Colt whispered.

"Hey, kiddo," Jewel replied. "You got a visitor."

"Blond girl? Red lipstick?"

"Yeah. And I thought vampires had to be invited in."

Colt let out a relieved sigh.

Jewel smiled. "Hey, do you want me to order FoodWheel? Most places are closed, but there's an all-night pizza place I know of. It'd be pricy."

"How can you order food when you're dead?" Colt asked.

"Grandpa Walt had this thing set up for us before he died. I didn't quite get it when I was alive, but as we've seen, Pop was a secret Augmenter. After I died, I had this weird access to an account that has a bit of money in it. Don't ask too many questions. It's secret ghost stuff. Like I can't tell you about the afterlife. And don't ask about God. That gets complicated quick."

Colt walked onto the porch. "Where is the blonde now?"

"In the living room, looking at your truck and shitting bricks. I'd hurry and put the poor girl out of her misery."

Colt found the extra key he kept in a crack on the floor. It wasn't the most secure spot, but at least it wasn't under the welcome mat like Ernie's had been.

Colt wasn't too worried about burglars. He didn't have that much to steal. Besides, one look at the hoarder's nest upstairs, and most intruders would take off running.

He went through the back door. Jewel had already vanished.

Colt called into the house. "Hey! I'm coming in. Don't attack me or anything. Pretty sure I'd kill you and destroy the house, and that would suck."

The vampire suddenly appeared by the front door in the hallway next to the living room. She wore a hat with a little veil attached. Fancy lady gloves covered her hands. She had a green wool dress and black stockings. Those were old clothes from a hundred years ago.

For being a vampire, Eliza Bennet looked prim and proper.

Colt raised his hands. "We were just in Firestone Alley, looking for you."

"I left. I came here. I didn't have anywhere else to go. Not really." Her voice was tentative. "Perhaps I should've come sooner, but no one knew what to make of you."

Colt heard a strange accent there. It was kind of British, but not really. Then he realized what it was. She sounded like an old movie from the 1930s. That was a Mid-Atlantic or a Transatlantic accent.

Colt got his phone out of his pocket. "I'm going to text my friend waiting in the truck. We wanted to make sure you weren't here to kill us."

"I'm not. I swear it." She plucked her hat off her head.

Colt loved how the blond vampire talked. He sent Gilly a text to come on in.

Then Colt walked quickly down the hallway. "If you could back up into the living room, I want to make sure my friend gets inside safely."

"Of course. I do apologize for being so bold as to come into your home. Perhaps I should've waited outside."

"How did you get in?" Colt unlocked the front door.

He was close enough to notice other things about her. She had dark brown eyes, accented by her makeup. She definitely had a certain allure.

A quizzical smile was on her face. "You really don't know? How can you not know?"

"I'm new to the Monstraverse."

"No one on Earth calls it that." Eliza frowned. "This was a mistake. I should go."

But right then, Gilly opened the door and shuffled inside. "We've got to turn up the heat. It's freezing in here." Then she noticed the vampire in the green wool suit standing in his living room. "Oh, hello. Let me guess. Elizabeth Bennet. Of course you know what my first question is going to be."

"Yes. I'm a vampire." The way she said it, she seemed ashamed.

Gilly smiled softly. "No. We know that. But were you named after the *Pride and Prejudice* character?"

"No. Bennet is my married name. However, my father did read a great deal. My mother never."

Colt noticed she said those words, "father and mother," like "faathah" and "mothah."

She continued talking. "But Father mostly read nonfiction. He tried to keep up on the scientific discoveries of his day. He's dead. My parents are long dead." She paused. "I would imagine you'll want my whole story. I'll tell you the germane parts, but there are some things I would like to keep to myself. Not to be impolite, but mine is a long, tragic story." Her smile was as sad as it was wistful.

"Can I turn up the heat, Colt?" Gilly asked.

"Sure. And we might want to have some coffee. It looks like it's going to be a late night."

"Would you like some coffee?" Gilly asked the vampire. "Or did I hear you say something about leaving?"

"Should I leave?" Eliza asked. "You are never going to trust me. And you probably shouldn't."

Gilly sighed. "No, you shouldn't go. We need you." She walked quickly down the hallway. Her heels clacked on the floor. They were still in the clothes Bafflestone had stolen for them.

"How did you get inside?" Colt asked.

The blond vampire seemed embarrassed. "Vampires can turn into smoke. Those with a great deal of power can exist like that for a long while. I can't. I chose propriety over power."

Colt found her answer odd, but rather charming. "Is that why no one in Firestone Alley seems to like you very much?"

The vampire reddened. "There's a reason for that. Several reasons, actually. However, they have to do with my standing among the Monstra. As for your typical run-of-the-mill human being? Everyone I was ever close to is dead. Let's consider that a tabula rasa, shall we?"

Colt could've listened to that accent all day long. "Sit. Please. Let's not have you leave just yet. We've actually been looking for you. We need to know what you know."

"Of course you do." Eliza sat on the very edge of the couch.

She seemed unmoved by the cold. Was she the classic undead corpse of vampire lore? It didn't seem like it. She gave off a pleasant smell, not quite a perfume, but almost. She had such big, brown eyes, so expressive. But so far, they hadn't shown the silver glint Colt had seen before. She wasn't trying to use her hypnotic powers on him. Other than that magnetic voice of hers.

Colt heard the heater kick on. Gilly worked in the kitchen.

That made Colt pause. "Are you hungry? Can you eat?"

Eliza looked pained. "No. I cannot eat in the traditional sense. I've lost a great deal, but perhaps that is one of the hardest losses I've had to endure. Liquids are fine on my rather delicate system. But of course, I now require a rather uncomfortable beverage. But I feasted a few days ago. I will not need to eat for a few more."

From the kitchen, Colt heard Gilly curse. "No, Zeh, I'm not saying that. Not everything is about oral sex."

Eliza's eyes widened. "Golly. What's that about?"

"That's a long story." Before Colt talked about the gods inside himself and Gilly, he wanted to get all the information he could from the vampire. "You were there this past Wednesday. Both Gilly and I saw you. If you want to start over with humans, let's talk about that day."

"It was…it was my great rebellion." Eliza waved her hand in a flourish. "I was going to defy my lord and master, and yes, I was risking imprisonment again, but I would rather die free than live enslaved."

"Enslaved to who?" Colt asked.

Gilly called from the kitchen, "Wait for me, guys. She shouldn't have to repeat her story twice."

"Is she your wife?" Eliza asked.

"No. She's my, uh, friend." Colt had almost said girlfriend. That was probably the truth, but he and Gilly hadn't really talked about it. They were too busy exploring strange new worlds—you know, meeting blue gnomes and drinking elven champagne and watching a vampire lord kill some random woman.

"Perhaps she's more than a friend? You two would make a swell couple, all right. Why else would she be at the warehouse?"

"We go to college together."

"College, eh? An education is a powerful thing. I came to Denver to be a teacher, actually. It was a…different time."

Colt thought about asking when she was born. Then he remembered that you never asked a woman her age.

Gilly came back with one of Aunt Jewel's ornate serving trays. One thing about living with pack rats—their stuff was sometimes very useful. Gilly had made little graham cracker sandwiches with the strawberry jelly from his fridge. She had three cups of coffee along with a sugar bowl and matching creamer. Again, that was Aunt Jewel's stuff.

"Hey, Jewel, are you around?" Colt asked.

"Just listening…" Her voice drifted down. "Don't mind me."

Eliza glanced all around. "And who was that?"

"My Aunt Jewel," Colt said. "She's a ghost. But that's probably been the least weird thing that has happened to me since Wednesday. Are ghosts normal?"

The vampire shook her head. "No, but they aren't unheard of. Most people merge with the Gaia when they die, or so we think. Ghosts are relatively special."

"Hear that?" Jewel's disembodied laughter floated around them. "I'm relatively special."

Eliza paled. "I didn't mean any offense."

"She's not offended," Colt said. "Just amused."

"Aunt Jewel is wonderful." Gilly curtsied. "I'm Gilly, by the way. We haven't officially met. And this is Colt Holliday. We know about you because, well, we went looking for you. We made a friend in Firestone Alley, quite by accident."

Eliza shook her head. "No. If you made a friend in Firestone Alley, you also made a deal, whether you know it or not. Vincent Isaac has made it so there are no true friends in the Alley. All the friendships are by necessity transactional. Who was it?"

Colt shrugged. "Our new friend would probably want to keep a low profile. Let's just say he was an old friend of family."

Gilly poured cream into her coffee. "And he was up front about wanting to curry favor with a god and a goddess. We liked him, he liked us, and I think we're good there."

"You're no Dumb Dora, keeping your contacts a secret. But I'm safe. You can't know that. You might never believe it. That's all fine, dear. That's just swell." But from the bitterness in her voice, it was clear she didn't think it was swell at all.

Eliza picked up the coffee. "I must say, I never lost my taste for coffee. So, if you'll excuse me, I'll drink it black. And I'll tell you about my great rebellion. That shipment that fell off the pallet? Yes, I saw that. I saw everything. You wouldn't have seen me, but I was there. I took what was left."

Colt snapped his fingers. "Thought so."

The vampire half-smiled. "The boxes are safe. They were on their way to Vincent Isaac, but I knew that if he got his hands on those statues, it would be all over. For the Alley. For the Leyfolk in the Leyworld. That's what us creatures of the night call the Monstraverse, as you so drolly put it."

"Drolly?" Gilly wrinkled her nose. "I've heard the word. What does that mean?"

Eliza was quick with the answer. "Curious or unusual in a way that provokes dry amusement." Yes, the vampire had clearly been a teacher at some point.

Colt got them back on track. "So you know about Urgu-Uku and Zeh-Gaba?"

"The old gods. Yes, and I know they were rediscovered in an ancient temple as far back as America's first war in Iraq. Another American war. I naively thought that the Great War was the war to end all wars. Too bad removing the kaiser didn't remove the violent tendencies of mankind."

It was like Eliza was discussing current events.

"The kaiser?" Gilly then caught on. "Oh, the kaiser. World War I. I'm a little slow. I'm sorry."

"I don't believe you are slow at all, darling. Not one bit." Eliza sipped her coffee. "And you're in college. I would imagine the Great War still gets some attention."

"You'd be surprised," Colt said quietly. He changed subjects. "You watched me rage out then."

"I did. And it wasn't long before Vincent heard about it. He was beside himself. To lose the shipment was one thing. But to lose all the other statues? That was a blow to his manhood. I enjoyed watching that. However, I could never let my amusement show. And now, alas and alack, my little wingding is over. That's a party in modern parlance. He put two-and-two together, my disappearance and the accident, and so I was forced to run."

"But you left him a note," Colt said.

"A warning, yes. And to let him know I know his plans. How is having the gods inside you?" the vampire asked.

Gilly's eyes turned a bright blue. "I like having things inside me." She clapped her hands over her mouth.

Colt shrugged. "It's been interesting. Do you know if it's permanent or not?"

The vampire gazed into his eyes. "It is permanent. I did some research on this, and those gods are now bound to your souls. Your lives will never be the same again. I'm very sorry."

Gilly's voice returned to normal. "I kinda figured. But it's nice to know."

Colt was happy just to have some answers.

Eliza motioned at them with her coffee cup. "The gods are new to being hosted, so I would imagine it's been strange. From my reading, even if you died, your essences would remain intermingled. You'd return to the Gaia Unum together. But there's something else that could happen to you."

She paused dramatically.

"What else could happen?" Gilly asked in a breathy voice.

"If either of you are purified on the Fate Blade, then you would die, and the spirits of the gods inside of you could find new hosts. That is what Vincent is planning to do. First, though, he has to find the Fate Blade."

Colt couldn't help but smile. "I can only imagine how pissed Vincent was when he realized a stupid accident had robbed him of hosting a god."

"It wasn't an accident," Eliza said carefully. "I undid the straps. I was going to steal away the crates one at a time. But then you interrupted me. I'm so very sorry."

"It was still an accident," Colt maintained. "You didn't plan on the boxes falling and breaking. And here I thought Jimbo or his henchmen had fucked up. Guess not."

Gilly frowned. "Vincent wouldn't have been able to control the gods, though, right? Or did he know about the runes?"

At first, Eliza looked surprised. Then she blushed. "So that part is true. Have you experienced the, uh, more physical aspects of rune creation? I can scarcely believe the stories about that are true."

Gilly clamped her mouth closed. Her forearms and fingernails glowed blue.

Colt laughed a little. "Gilly is trying not to tell you in great detail about the physical aspects of rune creation."

Gilly nodded her head so hard that her glasses nearly fell off her face.

Eliza's smile was both amused and troubled. "Yes, well, that aspect of the dynamic is one of the reasons why I fled. Vincent and I have a long relationship, and it's been platonic, but I knew that would change. I knew he would insist that I...we...but I couldn't. Not after. Everything." She laughed a little. "And this, my friends, is where I must beg you for some privacy. I will say this. I want to help you. I want to stop Vincent Isaac. I want things to be different for the Leyfolk. But that is what I've always wanted. And why I'm so hated."

Her laugh was bitter.

The vampire set her coffee on the table. "But let's talk about my many sins against the Monstra at another time, shall we? The sun will be rising soon. I don't suppose you have a basement I could borrow? The sun is literal murder on my skin."

CHAPTER NINETEEN

Colt was surprised that the entire night had passed so quickly. Then again, he'd crossed into another world. That did distract a person.

He and Gilly chatted more with Eliza, but Colt knew that they weren't going to get much more out of her that night. At one point, Colt picked up the Gaia Orb, but nothing had changed. He was still second level with two updates he couldn't use, and his Rune Genesis Status was red. Not that he really understood what all that meant. There was hope, though. Bafflestone seemed to know all about the orb.

He asked Eliza, and she had no idea.

Did Colt trust her? Not really. But she seemed so sad and scared that he couldn't kick her out. He did have a basement, but like everywhere else, it was full of boxes. He moved enough cardboard so she could put a chair down there. According to her, she could sleep sitting up. They would talk more once the sun set that night.

Colt was just glad that it was a Sunday. He would not be comfortable leaving a vampire in his basement while he went to work.

While he got Eliza settled, Gilly cleaned up their late-night snack—her graham cracker and jelly sandwiches had been strangely good.

Colt tromped up the stairs and stood in the kitchen. They were just in time. The sun was rising.

Gilly set a wet plate in the drying rack. "I don't want to go home. Can I sleep on your couch? I mean, I know it's a lot, and we've spent a ton of time together, and I do have homework, but…but I'm rambling. So much rambling." She closed her eyes and leaned against the kitchen counter. "This is a lot. You know, we can't just do normal life until we find this Fate Blade thing. I won't feel safe away from you. Did I just say that out loud? Oh, Gilly, pull yourself together. The ramble is bad tonight. Then again, it's morning, and I haven't slept. So sleep is on the agenda."

"Right," Colt agreed. He went over and took Gilly's hand. "I love having you here. The house felt so empty when I woke up yesterday and you weren't here. Now I'm rambling."

"That is the worst ramble I've ever heard." Gilly pulled him close and rested her face against him. He felt her glasses poke into his chest. "I don't want your house to feel empty, so I'll stay. With the vampire sleeping in the basement. Sitting up. On a kitchen chair. So that's not weird."

"It is. Kinda. A little. Do you trust her?"

"Speaking of weird, I weirdly do. She didn't try to attack us when we first walked in. And she knows about our god abilities. I think we should give her a chance, Colt."

"I do too." Colt kissed her. It felt so right, being in the kitchen, feeling her and smelling her. She tasted so good as well. She was such an angel in his life.

He realized her forearms were glowing.

She stepped back. "The, uh, goddess is getting really loud. We should stop. I need some time to just figure things out, you know? I'm being difficult, and I'm so sorry. Can you be patient?"

"I can be patient, Gilly. And I'm still feeling the aftereffects of the last rune."

Gilly gave him a little smile. "When we enjoyed the more physical aspects of rune creation."

Colt nodded. "Yeah. When I got my joy."

Gilly kissed him again. Then they set up her bed in the living room. Closing the drapes, it was dark enough for her to sleep.

Colt found himself in his room, stripping out of the old-fashioned clothes that Bafflestone had given him. He crawled into bed, and it felt so good to just lie there. He had two women in his house. Three if you counted his aunt.

Colt was about to drift off when he heard his door open. He was up in a flash, his covers down. If Eliza was coming for his blood, she'd have another thing coming.

The runes on his arms glowed red. He could smell burning hair.

Urgu piped up. *And I thought you were drifting off to sleep, Colton. But now we can bring our wrath upon this small home and the automobiles next door. Throwing those automobiles would be very satisfying. We could toss the train off its track. We could sow fire and destruction. Yes. Yes.*

But then Colt saw Gilly. She'd stripped down to a blouse and panties. His eyes went right to her plump legs.

Urgu took notice. *Yes, my love has chosen such a fine vessel. She is so young and plump and full of life's juices. Perhaps our fury can wait while we revel in our lust.*

Colt did like the idea of reveling in lust, but he was also curious to see if he'd get a new rune. He was still trying to figure out the specifics.

Gilly crossed the room. "Zeh was pretty insistent that I not, you know, get my joy alone. And if your house felt empty without me around, well, that living room felt empty without you. Do you mind?"

Like Colt was going to mind.

He threw open his covers. He felt the cold hit him.

Gilly took off her glasses and put them on his nightstand. She then got in bed with him. He only had a twin, so they were close.

Right next to each other. He was warm now, and he loved having Gilly so close to him.

He lay on his side.

She lay on her back.

"How can I help you with your joy?" he asked.

"Kiss me," she whispered.

Colt so wanted to kiss her, but business first. "Just a second. Urgu? What do you know about the Gaia Orb and our Rune Genesis Status?"

There was no response.

Gilly pulled him down to kiss her.

And he did. He loved smelling Gilly. He loved tasting her. And he reached down and undid one of the buttons on her shirt. He eased a hand inside and felt the soft skin of her full chest. Her nipples hardened in his hand.

Gilly stopped kissing him, and she licked his neck. "Zeh says the Rage King never talked very much. He wouldn't care about the Gaia Orb, or anything really, except fighting and fucking. He was a simple thing. The orb did say you were at red. So, let's just see what happens if one of us gets our joy. Do you mind?"

"Not at all," Colt said.

He loved how excited Gilly was—her body was vibrating with sexual energy as she rubbed herself. He kissed her again. At first, she was too turned on to kiss him back, but he waited until she growled and sucked on his tongue. He felt how urgently she was touching herself, and it made him so hard.

He kissed her once more, then moved down to suck on her neck. He couldn't help but straddle her leg and rub his cock against her thigh.

He undid more buttons and licked down her chest to her cleavage. With her blouse completely unbuttoned, Colt peeled it open, and then he caught one of her stiff pink nipples in his mouth. God, she smelled so good. She felt so good, so warm, in his mouth.

The blanket was down, and the cold air hit Colt's back. It felt good compared to Gilly's hot body.

Actually, he wanted to feel her skin on his.

He peeled off his T-shirt.

And Gilly reached down to cup his bulge—there was no hiding an erection in sweatpants. Her hand felt so good on him.

Colt looked down at her. "With my Rune Genesis Status being red, going all the way is probably not a good idea. But maybe I could do to you what you did to me last night?"

Gilly looked gorgeous, lying on her back, her breasts exposed.

He could smell her excitement.

Gilly smiled. "Do you want to eat my pussy, Colt? I want you to eat my pussy. I just don't know if that's going to damage our Gaia Cores. I just don't know. It might be okay. Oh, I want it. I can't help but want it."

She kicked off the covers. Then she drew her legs up, got her panties off, and tossed them onto the floor. She spread her legs. He was seeing all of her. She had a tangle of dark pubic hair, but her clit was well defined, right at the top of her pink slit. Her lips were swollen and wet.

Colt got on top of her, kissing her, pressing his sex against hers. There was only the thin fabric of his sweatpants separating them. It was like he could feel every part of her, warm and wet and ready for him.

Colt kissed his way down her body and sucked on both of her nipples, which made her shudder. Then he was licking around her belly button. She was such a goddess. In Gilly's case, literally.

Then he had his nose in her pubic hair. She smelled so good.

She put her hands gently on his head.

That was when Colt found her stiff clit. He gave it a little lick, which made Gilly gasp. But he wanted more of her. He wanted just a bit more. He slid his tongue down between her lips until he found her tight hole. He pushed his tongue inside of her. His entire world had become this beautiful girl's open sex.

"My clit, Colt. Do my clit. Suck on me, and I'll come."

He could feel that. They were so connected. He licked back up her opening until he took her clit into his mouth. He sucked, licked, sucked, until her hands on his head became insistent.

"Oh, I can't, oh, I'm gonna. Oh. Oh. Oh." And then Gilly was pushed over the edge.

Colt felt her hole open and close to match the spasms of ecstasy wracking her body. And he felt both of his runes tingling. They were glowing red. Hers was glowing blue. But they weren't creating new runes. He could feel the channels of power opening a bit more, though, as their connection grew. And he could feel the strain he'd put on his own Gaia Core. Their sex and the runes were definitely connected.

The minute she was done, Gilly slipped out of the bed and got on her knees. "It's your turn. I felt how hard you are. I know you're horny. I know you want to come."

She pulled his sweats and underwear down.

Then Colt was back in her mouth. She stroked his shaft and sucked on the head of his dick. She was so insistent. She was so focused. It was clear she wanted to drink him down again.

And he was going to let her. He grabbed her head to hold her steady, and she let out a moan.

She couldn't talk dirty, not with her mouth full.

He warned her, "I'm coming, Gilly. I'm coming."

She sucked on him harder. It was clear she wanted his cum.

Again, his runes glowed red. Her runes glowed blue.

Colt was suddenly over the edge, feeling those intense waves of bliss as everything melted into heaven. This was a joy, without a doubt. He felt his load leave him. Every time the pleasure seized him, his cock spasmed, filling her mouth. She drank him down, moaning to match him.

Again, he felt the Gaia from his core reverberate through his body, and while the orgasm felt good, it also hurt a bit, because of the strain. There was a reason why his Rune Genesis Status was red. They definitely had to be careful, but the quick oral sex also proved that they had some wiggle room.

Colt found himself back in bed, naked now, with a naked Gilly holding him close. He'd never felt so tired and relaxed. He couldn't relax too much. Vincent Isaac would be coming after them.

But at that moment, Colt couldn't have them running off. They needed to sleep. Besides, their guest in the basement probably wouldn't want to leave in the daylight.

Colt felt Gilly drop off to sleep. Her breathing changed, she was resting peacefully, and all was right with the world. He was so glad she'd stayed over, and he was even more glad she'd found her way into his bed.

It all felt so perfect.

He'd been so alone.

Now he wasn't.

But there were forces in the world coming after him. He had to protect his home and his friends. Good thing he had the god of rage and destruction in him. And he was pretty sure that after the joy they shared that morning, he would have even more control.

Only time would tell.

CHAPTER TWENTY

Colt woke up. He'd heard a noise.

It wasn't like Vincent Isaac didn't know where he was at that moment. The vampire lord knew exactly where he lived. Colt lay there for a second but didn't hear anything more. It was enough to bring him wide awake, though.

Gilly slept on. Colt listened to her breath. He loved how she held him while she slept.

It was cold in his house, though, and he'd have to get up and turn on the heat, or they might freeze. What about the vampire in his basement? He couldn't imagine a creature of the night getting chilly.

It was a little after noon. Colt knew he was done sleeping, so he slipped out of bed. Gilly sighed and shifted. She fell back asleep in seconds.

Colt padded out of his bedroom. The floor was freezing on his feet. He went to the thermostat and cranked it up to seventy. The windows were covered in ice. At some point, he needed to replace them. He'd save a fortune on his heating bills.

He put on the coffee and considered the door that led to the basement. Should he check on Eliza? He pictured her sitting in a chair, eyes open but sleeping. It was a creepy image to consider.

Would opening the door hurt her? How sensitive was she to daylight?

It was a bright, cold January Sunday. He'd leave her alone until the sun set.

Sipping coffee, Colt got his phone and saw he had a text from Ernie. His Aunt Sophia was still alive, but she was going to be in the hospital another week, at least. Dena and Dwayne from the Sons of Italy were scheduled to watch Ernie's dogs that day.

Colt was proud of his buddy Ernie. He'd learned to text. You could teach an old dog new tricks after all.

Colt stuck his phone in his pocket, got a fresh cup of coffee, and then climbed the stairs to his grandfather's room. If Grandpa Walt had a doorknob to Firestone Alley, could he have information on the Fate Blade?

It was worth checking.

There were a few boxes of old books that were all digital at this point. He went through them quickly. Nothing of note. A lot of paperbacks from the '70s. A few Mack Bolan novels. Nothing rare. Nothing that might tell them where the Fate Blade might be. Or some badly needed Gaia Orb documentation. Maybe a book on being possessed by an ancient god?

Colt believed both Eliza and Bafflestone—Urgu-Uku was part of his soul now.

But what if they were wrong?

What if Colt were purified on the Fate Blade and he didn't die? Vincent Isaac would get the god, and Colt could go back to his regular old life. Work another year for United Shipping & Post, fulfill the contract, and then move on with his life.

But Colt wasn't about to just forget about the secret world he'd found. He couldn't pretend there weren't vampires, werewolves, blue-skinned gnomes, platinum-haired elves, or the cat people and dog people he'd seen.

Colt knew his old life was over. And to be honest? He was loving this new life. As long as he could control the Rage King inside him. With more runes, that seemed completely possible.

Colt carried the boxes downstairs and put them in the living room. Then he was back working in the bedroom. He cleared a path to the bed.

He was looking at an intimidating box full of papers when Gilly walked up the creaky steps. She was wearing a button-up shirt she must've grabbed from his closet. And she'd found a pair of wool socks. She looked like a million dollars. Colt wasn't sure he'd ever seen anything sexier in his life.

"Good morning, Colt. You want to do FoodWheel? Or do you want to try my waffle recipe?" She regarded the room. "But do you think we can find a waffle iron?"

Colt laughed. "I know where one is. Don't worry about that. Do you want to go through the trouble, though?"

Gilly shrugged. "It's not like we have much else to do. We have to wait until the sun goes down. But then what are we going to do?"

"We need to find this Fate Blade. That should be our number one priority." Colt opened a file folder and saw it held some old tax document from the '80s. It could definitely be thrown away. He didn't need most of the documents relating to New Eden. He'd keep some relating to its founding and to the buyout.

The best thing about waiting thirty years to go through your papers? You could toss most everything. Time had a way of clarifying something's importance.

"Because we want to stay like this." Gilly found a seat on the bed. She sat cross-legged with her back against the headboard. "This whole thing about being purified, well, I've been thinking about that. I don't think I want to be purified. Having Zeh-Gaba inside me—" She rolled her eyes. "That is never going to not sound strange. Being possessed by the goddess of lust is rather freeing. It makes me rethink some things."

"Things relating to Amanda Buckman and those girls?" Colt asked.

Gilly looked pained. "Exactly that."

"If you want to tell me, I'll listen," Colt said.

Colt sat on the edge of the bed. He grabbed one of Gilly's feet and rubbed it.

Gilly put her coffee on the gunmetal filing cabinet Grandpa Walt had used as a nightstand. It was near where Colt found the wooden crate of doorknobs.

She sighed. "We've known each for a bit now, Colt, but since Wednesday, we've kinda connected on this whole other level. Am I wrong?"

"You're not wrong." He paused. "On the first day of class, I noticed you right away. You were so cute. I had to wonder why you weren't with someone."

"I had something bad happen to me. Zeh is chatty with me. In my head. I don't think Urgu talks to you much, does he?"

Colt shook his head. "No. He just waits for me to get pissed off, then suggests murder and destruction, before taking over completely."

Gilly chuckled. "Yeah, Zeh says he was never really talkative. She still loved him. She loved his brute strength. I guess I can understand that. Remember our embarrassing *Beauty and the Beast* conversation?"

"You liked the Beast."

"And I wanted to be Belle." Gilly sighed. "My senior year in high school. This is like three years ago, so it wasn't that long, but it feels like forever ago. You know?"

Colt understood how time could flash by so fast, or crawl by so slowly. He knew how that felt. The death of a loved one had that same feeling.

"My best friend was this girl, Madeline Kelley. Maddy for short. We were tight since middle school. You know, like how some girls can become too close. I don't know if boys have that."

Colt didn't think so. He'd had some friends, but they always kept a bit of distance. Actually, the guy he felt the closest to was Ernie, though he was thirty years older than Colt.

Gilly continued. "Well, this new boy shows up, and he's cute and kinda dumb, and it all just happens, but he and Maddy start dating. His name is Jack Walsh. It doesn't matter. I don't know why I need to say their names. It's like I want you to understand me."

Colt could see how this was for her. He kept rubbing her feet. "Growing up is hard. And people can be so fucked up."

"You aren't wrong." Gilly bit her lip.

Colt wanted to help. "Speaking of names. How does Amanda Buckman fit in to all this?"

"She was friends with Maddy. I mean, it was kind of a *Mean Girls* thing. I was always the dorky schoolgirl. Maddy, though, got some social status points from being friends with Amanda. It was a one blonde to rule them all kind of thing."

"Got the reference. Funny." Colt still wasn't understanding all this. But he just waited and made sure he listened to every word.

"One crazy night, me, Maddy, and Jack hooked up at this party. It started with this kind of dare. I was going to watch Maddy and Jack because they thought I wouldn't. I mean, I was super uncomfortable about this whole sex thing. I'm pretty sure my parents had sex only the one time, to have me. I was an only child. Have I mentioned how much I hate being an only child?"

"Yes. If you came from a big family, you'd have been less mayonnaise and more marinara."

"Funny. I'm funny. But yeah, I always wanted to be part of this big, huge family."

Colt smiled. "I had some of that too. For most of my life it was just Grandpa Walt, Aunt Jewel, and me. And this house. Just the three of us. Four, if you count this little blue house, which I kinda do. I thought with a bigger family, there would be more fun. That's probably not always the case."

"Probably not. But you understand." Gilly got a determined look on her face. She wasn't going to stop until she told him everything. "Like I said. It was a dare. Jack didn't think I would do it. Maddy, I think, knew I would. She kinda knew me better than I knew myself. Maddy was wild. I wasn't. Or at least, I wasn't wild when I was around other people. But we're gonna kind of pretend I didn't say that." Gilly blushed. She got quiet.

Colt remembered how she'd been scared he'd think she was weird and perverted. That couldn't be further from the truth. He found this wild side of her exciting.

Colt had to fill the silence. "So the three of you had that night together. Then what happened?"

Gilly's face was blank. "It's funny. It's not like I had actual sex. But we did basically everything else. Jack and me. Maddy and me. I felt okay with it. After that night, I actually thought we'd all become a throuple or something. I saw Maddy in a new light. We'd be friends with super huge benefits. We'd share Jack."

"Sounds like that didn't happen," Colt said.

Gilly shook her head sadly. There were tears in her eyes. "No. It didn't happen. Maddy kind of dropped me. Amanda started all these rumors about me. Zeh thinks Amanda was jealous that she didn't get that wild night. Maybe. I've heard that before. That all these prissy, self-righteous people get all pissed off that the degenerates are having more sex than they are. Jack started calling me, thinking I was this slutty girl. Other guys started hitting on me. It was terrible. I kind of went into a shell, which is why I didn't want to date anyone ever again. And how messed up was it that I ended up at a college with Amanda? She was in the perfect position to spread those rumors all over again. Zeh suggested we send Urgu to her house. That would probably make her stop. To be honest? I don't care."

But it sounded like she did.

Colt remembered how Amanda and those four girls had been so fucking smug. It was like they knew they could kick Gilly as much as they wanted, and she couldn't kick them back.

Colt smelled a bit of burning hair. *There was the woman's automobile, the Cadillac Escalade in your parlance. We could throw it through a skyscraper. We both would enjoy that.*

Right then, Colt seriously considered it. It would be fun to throw the big SUV into a building.

Gilly saw the rage starting, so she nudged him playfully with her foot. "Easy, Urgu. I can fight my own battles."

The runes on his arms dimmed. "It's just so fucked up."

Gilly nodded. "Sex is complicated. I've learned that. I just hate the fact that I'm twenty-one years old, and my entire sexual history is a threesome. And what you and I have been doing." Her playful kick turned into a caress. "Zeh finds me hilarious. I'm part virgin. Part slut. Mostly virgin, though. But not for long, I don't think. If we're going to have these gods inside us, we're going to need to control them. Every time we do something, it feels more powerful. And I had another dream this morning. You don't happen to have a bow and arrow, do you?"

"We might have one in the basement," Colt said. "Actually, yeah, I know we do. Again, that just reinforces my family's bad hoarding habits. Save everything, and the minute someone asks for something, and you have it, then you can justify keeping everything forever."

Gilly laughed and crossed the bed.

Colt found himself holding her and kissing her gently. "You don't think any less of me, do you? For doing that stuff with Jack and Maddy?" she asked.

Colt kissed her. "Kinda jealous of Jack. But seriously. No. I get it. You were feeling unsure of yourself, you let yourself be vulnerable, and then there was all this shitty fallout."

"So much fallout." Gilly snuggled into his chest. "Zeh, though, gave me some perspective. Like five thousand years of perspective. Sex is weird. People are weird. And it's better just to just say, 'Yeah, I'm weird and perverted. If you don't like that then get the heck out of my face."

"Heck?"

"Just because I'm possessed by an ancient goddess of lust and fertility doesn't mean I have to curse like a sailor."

Colt found himself kissing Gilly for a long time, and the kiss became more intense. Then he remembered he was on his grandfather's bed. There was no way he'd ever feel comfortable doing anything on that bed. He was going to clear out the boxes and buy a new bed.

Gilly giggled and sighed. "You know, my asthma should be going crazy in this house with all the dust and, uh, boxes and stuff. But it's not. I can feel that my breathing is so much better. It's the goddess, I know it. I need a Gaia Orb of my own."

"You do. Maybe there's another one in my grandfather's secret files." He crawled across the bed to the little gunmetal filing cabinet. Both doors were locked. Well, he knew this wasn't going to be easy, right?

CHAPTER TWENTY-ONE

While Gilly made waffles, Colt searched for a key that might open his grandfather's filing cabinet.

Colt went through the keys hanging on the kitchen hooks, but no, those belonged to him and Aunt Jewel alone. He went to the kitchen junk drawer. He tried to get it open, but it was too stuffed with plastic bags, tools, flashlights, and Chinese food menus. Why did they even keep those around? It was why God invented FoodWheel.

He had to take everything out of the drawer to rummage around in it. "You know, if you really wanted to hide this Fate Blade, you should just put it in a junk drawer."

Gilly lifted the waffle iron lid and transferred a golden waffle onto a plate. "It's one of the universal constants—a junk drawer. Let's eat!"

Colt ate the most delicious waffles of his life, with lots of butter and maple syrup. They were so good! Gilly nearly broke her face smiling as she watched him eat.

They'd just finished when they heard a knock. It was only a few minutes after sunset.

"Do you want to let our vampire in?" Colt asked.

Gilly went to the door that led down to the basement. She opened the door.

Eliza stood there with her hat in her hand. She looked exactly the same as she had the night before. An embarrassed blush colored her cheeks. "Yes. Hello. Is it okay if I join you?"

"Sure, Eliza, come in. Can I get you anything to drink?" Gilly blanched. "I didn't mean I was…I meant something that wasn't…you know. Blood."

Eliza smiled. "I won't need to eat for a few days. You needn't worry. And if you'll excuse me, miss, I'd rather not talk about my…condition."

Both girls were being so awkward.

Colt swooped in. "Do you need some coffee?"

"Yes, I'd love a cup." Eliza moved to sit at the table. She was upright and rigid. "Actually, along with a dry red wine, coffee is a bit of a vice for me. I like cigarettes as well, though I've learned they have fallen out of fashion. I cannot abide this vaping business." The vampire paused. "I try not to smoke too much. To be honest, it always seemed too lascivious. I know, that sounds so droll, after all I've been through. After all the horrific things I've done."

Gilly stood halfway between the table and the kitchen. She had a mystified look on her face. She clearly had no idea how to react to that.

Colt finally found the plastic Tupperware with all the extra keys. "So, Eliza, we can't stay here. Vincent Isaac is going to send people here, and I don't want anyone ruining my house. Do you have any idea where the Fate Blade might be?"

Eliza shook her head. "No, but I'm certain Vincent didn't have it when I left. I spoke with some of the Lyran staff at Vincent's mansion. They believe the Fate Blade is in Firestone Alley, but they aren't sure where. There is a temple in the old part of the city. They think it might be there."

"I wish we could ask Bafflestone," Gilly sighed.

"We should go back there," Colt said. "It's perfect. Vincent

Isaac comes here to look for us, but we're in Firestone Alley. We know where Bafflestone is, and we have his card, as well as his alias. Walter Wondergear."

Eliza looked surprised. "How did you meet Barney Bafflestone? Vincent keeps him hidden away. And isn't the gnome rather cantankerous?"

Colt gestured to Gilly. "I'm fairly certain it was the goddess girl that won him over. He couldn't resist her smile."

"Whatever," Gilly snorted.

Eliza rubbed her coffee cup against her lips. "Bafflestone basically built Firestone Alley. If the Fate Blade is there, he would know where it would be. But he doesn't like me much. None of the Monstra do. If it hadn't been for Vincent…" She cast her eyes down.

Colt saw how torn Eliza was. He wished he could help her in some way. Gilly looked equally worried.

Eliza set her cup on the table. "Golly, but don't I say the most cryptic things? And yet, you let me stay in your house. You needn't have. So, you both deserve the truth." She gripped her cup with both hands. "Very well. Over a hundred years ago, I wanted to expose the Leyfolk to the human world. Everyone thought it would be genocide, even back then, because we'd seen the devastation of the Great War. Say what you will about the vampiric power to heal any wound, but against machine guns and mortar shells, I'm afraid we'd get the raw end of the deal. And the Monstra cannot possibly procreate fast enough, not like regular run-of-the-mill human folk. But I didn't care. I was too angry at my fate. I never wanted to be turned."

Colt saw the pain in her face. Being hated by monsters couldn't have been easy. But now she seemed to regret not only the decision to try to tell the world about the Leyfolk, but her whole life.

"But it's ancient history now, isn't it?" Eliza asked, with tears in her eyes. "Let's maybe change the subject."

"I do have a question," Gilly said uncertainly. "But I don't want to be rude."

"Ask it, darling. I think politeness won't help us much in our current predicament."

"How does vampirism work? If any old vampire bites you and doesn't kill you, do you become a vampire?"

Colt had the same question.

"No," Eliza said. "Only the god of blood and darkness and his alpha vampires can turn humans. Beta vampires cannot. Alas, I cannot. For I am a beta. But vampires can also get children the old-fashioned away. It just takes a very long time. Gamma vampires are immortal, like we all are, but it takes a long time for them to grow into their power."

Colt found all of this fascinating. "So is the god of blood and darkness inside a statue like Urgu and Zeh were?"

"I do not believe so." Eliza glanced down. "But I can't say for sure. Mudd-Ganzer might be alive. I do know he turned Vincent, and so Vincent is an alpha—he's the one who turned me. He won't say how long it's been for him. Vampires do not like to speak of their turning, for the most part. There's a reason for that. There are many reasons, actually."

"Well, she's not giving you much to go on," a disembodied voice said with a sigh.

"Hey, Aunt Jewel," Colt said. "We're just getting a bit more of Eliza's story."

"So I'm hearing. I'm wondering why the Monstra didn't just stake her like a nameless vampire in a Buffy intro fight scene."

Colt chuckled, remembering how Jewel had complained that many a *Buffy the Vampire Slayer* episode began with a fight scene.

Eliza stiffened in her chair. "The Umbra Alliance wanted me dead, I assure you. But Vincent was a swell guy at that moment. He said he'd lock me up, and he did, in his dungeon. It wasn't so bad, actually. I had a movie projector, and every few years, they brought me new reels. But nothing past 1950. I think they forgot about me. I can't tell you how many times I watched *Casablanca*,

Gone with the Wind, The Treasure of the Sierra Madre. Countless. They brought me blood. But no heart's blood, which I am grateful for, however weak it kept me. But I was always weak because I refused to kill."

"To get heart's blood, you have to kill the person." Gilly nodded. "We watched Vincent drain someone. He mentioned something about heart's blood."

Aunt Jewel had a question. "When you say you were kept weak, what does that mean? I'd like a list of vampiric abilities."

Eliza sipped her coffee. Her hand trembled a bit. Colt could see that talking about all this was hard for her.

Eliza listed off their abilities. "We have our hypnotic gaze, the ability to turn into smoke and reconstitute ourselves, speed, strength, the ability to heal most any wound. We can regrow limbs even. And we won't die of natural causes. Silver or wood to the heart will destroy us. As will prolonged exposure to sunlight or decapitation."

"What about garlic?" Gilly asked. "Will garlic bread kill you?"

"Not kill, exactly." Eliza set her cup down and put her hands in her lap. "Garlic damages us, weakens us, perhaps like Superman and kryptonite. I was given comic books while I was imprisoned. It was Vincent, torturing me. I had always looked down on comic books and pulp magazines, until I was starved for reading. Then my opinion changed. I looked for grand themes. I found them."

"How long were you imprisoned?" Colt asked.

"It was to be for a hundred years, but Vincent showed mercy after ninety-five. By that time, most of the Leyfolk had forgotten their grudge. Not all. Not Bafflestone. Vincent trusted me. He gave me a job retrieving blood for Firestone Alley—from hospitals, blood banks, and private donors. There were also humans who wanted to be bloodbonded. I organized that. Vincent saw me as his errant daughter. I guess he was a second, horrible father. And I betrayed him. Because of the ruin he would bring." Eliza sat up straight. "There will be no sparing me this time. Perhaps it's for the best. I am not cut out to be a creature of the night. I find it all so distasteful."

She fell silent.

Gilly broke the silence. "Why did Vince ship those statues? You would've thought he would've had a full contingent of bodyguards escort them on a private jet or whatever."

Eliza smiled sadly. "But then the Leyworld would've known. As it was, they disappeared from a temple, and no one knew where they went to. Vincent used the human world to hide them. If I hadn't stepped in to retrieve them, his plan would've worked perfectly. It was fortunate for the world. Unfortunate for you both."

Gilly waved away her comment. "Oh, it's not so bad."

Eliza picked up her coffee, but then set it down. "And what do you think, Colt?"

He shrugged. "It is what it is. Even with all the danger, destruction, and murder, I've had the best four days of my life."

"It wasn't you who murdered those three men in the warehouse," Eliza said firmly. "It was Urgu-Uku. I know. I was there. So you should not feel guilty."

"I don't," Colt said. "Oddly enough, I'm fine with how things turned out."

Eliza nodded. "Well, good. I have the remaining crates hidden. I haven't gone through the shipment, but I would imagine there are more statues. They are safe. But you two are not. Nor is the world. If Vincent gets the power of Urgu-Uku, I wouldn't be surprised if he tried to overthrow the Umbra Alliance and kill every last one of the Brightest Light's hunters."

"We can't let that happen." Colt turned to call out to the ghost in the living room. "Hey, Jewel, any idea what Grandpa kept in that filing cabinet? Do you think I could find something on the Fate Blade there?"

"I could never find the key. I suppose you could smash it up, but I couldn't even pry it open. It's sealed tight."

It was bad news, but not surprising.

Colt was certain of their next move. "We go back into Firestone Alley, and we make our way to Bafflestone. I'll show him the Gaia Orb, and we'll ask him about the Fate Blade."

"And I'll guard the old homestead," Aunt Jewel said. "I can't do anything, but I can tell you if anyone comes snooping around. Just don't come through the front door. Come to the back porch. If anyone is here, I'll tell you, and you can rip them a new asshole."

Colt smiled. "I can do that. But first, do we have an archery set in the basement?"

"We do. This seems like an odd time to pick up a new hobby, Colt."

"How strange would I look walking around in Firestone Alley with a bow and arrow?" Gilly asked.

Eliza seemed to look upon Gilly with newfound respect. "You'd be a dame with more than your fair share of moxie. I know that much."

Gilly waggled her eyebrows. "I've always wanted to have moxie. So this is a good sign."

Eliza gave her a quizzical smile. "In some ways, that would be a good disguise, and I need a disguise. You two are not known at all down there. But me? I'm public enemy number one. Wouldn't Father be proud?" Her voice came out bitter.

Gilly gazed upon Eliza. "I can help with a disguise. Hey, Jewel, is your makeup still around?"

The ghost chuckled. "You've seen our house, darling. You know we don't throw anything away."

Gilly looked delighted "Then let me get started. I'll need a box of hair dye as well. If you don't mind. Your pretty blond hair definitely makes you stick out."

"Pretty?" Eliza asked, touching her head. "You can't mean that."

Gilly rolled her eyes. "Of course, I do. As a dame with moxie, I wouldn't lie to you." The goddess girl took out her phone. "Colt, I'll text you what we need. You don't mind hitting the store, do you?"

"Not a bit," Colt said. He could hit Yantorno's—it was mostly an Italian market, but it also carried everything else your typical grocery store/drug store carried.

Jewel's voice echoed through the house. "And I'll keep watch. Until we get that Fate Blade, we need to be on high alert. Even then, Vincent Isaac might need to be taken care of in a more permanent way."

Colt was thinking the same thing. And Urgu would definitely like the idea. For a second, Colt thought he might be able to shift into his more monstrous form with full control.

He'd try that, definitely, but not inside his house.

He had to make a trip to the store, and he'd find the archery equipment. Once again, they were going to sneak into Firestone Alley. This time, however, they would have a guide.

CHAPTER TWENTY-TWO

Colt returned from Yantorno's with the hair dye.
Opening the front door, he heard laughter from upstairs. He took a minute to enjoy it.

Then he climbed the stairs. There were several boxes in the hallway near Jewel's room. He peeked inside and saw his aunt sitting in a chair in the shadows. "I had the girls go through some of my stuff. Those boxes can go right into the dumpster. You know, being dead is kinda nice. You can see how much of your stuff isn't stuff at all. It's just crap. Which brings up the age-old question. What is stuff and what is crap?"

Colt laughed. "That's a question our family has had a hard time answering."

Jewel joined him in laughing. "So far, no monsters have come knocking. Go give your vampire girlfriend her hair dye."

"Not my girlfriend."

"You should've heard them talking about you, Colt. It was girl talk at its most interesting."

Colt was mystified by that. Eliza seemed as uncomfortable talking about sex as a 19th century schoolmarm.

Speaking of which…

"No. Be serious, Eliza," Gilly said. "You were a schoolmarm? They called you that?"

The vampire answered, "It was 1885, Gillian. It's why I came to Denver. But yes."

Colt found the two girls in the bathroom. He dropped off the dye. Eliza sat on the toilet in one of Aunt Jewel's old button-down work shirts. Jewel had been on the bigger side. Eliza was very thin and not at all large-chested.

Gilly stood above her, preparing the vampire's hair.

Eliza glanced at the hair dye box nervously. "Have you done this before?"

"Of course," Gilly said. "Most girls have tried to dye their own hair, and lots of women regularly do it because a box of hair dye is so much cheaper than getting it professionally done."

Colt leaned against the door jamb. "You don't mind if I watch?"

Gilly turned. Her eyes were a bright blue. Her voice came out in a seductive growl. "I hope you won't just watch, lover. I want you to fuck us both."

"Golly," Eliza whispered. "That was Zeh-Gaba, wasn't it?"

Gilly glanced down at the blue runes glowing on her arms. "It was. I'm slowly getting better at keeping her under control because of, well, you know…"

"Since you and Colt have been intimate again." Eliza swallowed hard. "I can…tell. There is one ability I didn't, uh, mention. My olfactory senses are especially keen."

"Oh, God," Gilly whispered. Again, the runes on her arms glowed. She was literally biting her lip.

Colt could only imagine what she was struggling not to say.

"It is your…uh…scent, Gillian," Eliza said. "But it's also the blood singing in your veins. For vampires, girls who have been… pleasured…are a delicacy. This is so shameful for me to say. I don't know why I'm saying it."

The vampire's cheeks glowed. Her eyes were bright—not the

silver of her hypnotic ability. No. It was a different kind of sparkle.

Colt had to wonder how that worked with vampires. Was she cold? Was she actually undead? How could he ask about any of that without being rude?

Gilly laughed. "Zeh-Gaba has that effect on people. I find myself saying all sorts of inappropriate things. As we've seen. Or heard, actually, in this case." Gilly applied Vaseline to Eliza's hairline, so the dye wouldn't stain her face. She was going to be dyeing the blond hair a very plain brown.

Gilly had clips, a comb, and a brush so she could do it in sections. Gilly wore the thin plastic gloves she pulled from the box. She squeezed the dye onto Eliza's hair a little at a time, and as she worked the dye into the hair, she piled it up on the Vampire's head, to let the dye sit for a while.

Eliza sat very straight. She had the most perfect posture Colt had ever seen.

"How did you get so good at this, Gilly?" Colt asked. "I thought you were too much of a schoolgirl for this girly stuff."

Gilly shot him a dangerous look over the top of her black-rimmed glasses. "Easy, mister. Schoolgirls are girls too. Growing up, I watched hours upon hours of hair dyeing and makeup tutorials. It's the birthright of every single red-blooded American of the female persuasion."

"You mean the YouTubes?" Eliza said with some excitement. "I've seen the YouTubes. There is much there on the current American culture. But we can't change the conversation just yet. We must talk about my role in helping you both gain more runes. By necessity, it must be of an intimate nature."

Gilly continued working on Eliza's hair. "We can't ask you to do that. Sure, Zeh takes over, and I say these outrageous things, but that's not going to kill anyone."

Eliza gave Colt a meaningful look. "But Colt's condition is a different matter entirely."

"It is," Colt said. He knew that Urgu-Uku would love to tear Denver apart and kill anyone who crossed him.

The vampire then stared straight forward. "Which is why I have to at least try to be intimate with Colt. It's been so long, though. And even then, it brings up such memories. My last love wasn't a man. It was a woman. Alas, both my relationships ended in tragedy. Lucky in cards. Unlucky in love. Or in my case, I never gambled at all. Golly, but I'd imagine I'm unlucky in both."

"I can't ask you to do that," Colt said. "But I have to ask—since we're talking about intimate things. Are you cold? I mean, are you undead?"

From the other room, Jewel laughed. "And there's my nephew, sticking his foot in his mouth. Good job, Colt!"

"Don't eavesdrop, Jewel!" Colt yelled back. "Good ghosts don't eavesdrop."

"Who says I'm a good ghost?"

Gilly laughed. "Oh, aren't we having fun? I can tell you—Eliza has body heat. And she smells divine. I bet that's another vampire power. She smells so good to make it easier to seduce humans."

"Perhaps," Eliza said with a little smile. "But I'm glad you like how I smell. I like how you smell. Golly, I shouldn't have said that."

Gilly kept on with the dyeing. "I'm surprised either one of us can smell a thing with all these chemicals in the air."

Colt wasn't sure what to ask next.

Eliza shot him a side-eye. "As long as I have blood in my veins, my heart beats, I'm completely alive, and yes, I'm fully a woman in all aspects. It's when I don't have blood that I grow cold and pale, and slow down. If I go long enough, well, I'm sure you've seen Boris Karloff in *The Mummy*. I'll look about as good. Boris was handsome, I grant you. But I carry off the withered look better."

"Do you mean Brendan Fraser?" Gilly asked.

Jewel's voice carried in from the other room. "I'm already dead, Gilly. Don't make me feel old as well."

Gilly finished off the dye. They had to wait twenty minutes, and so they chatted more—about movies, the YouTubes, as Eliza called them, but nothing about Eliza being intimate with them. Colt could see how it would give him more power, but he wasn't going to pressure the vampire to do anything.

Besides, watching Eliza with Gilly, she seemed far more comfortable with another woman. It was surprising what Eliza had said about being with a woman. There was a long story there, obviously. Eliza had started teaching school around the age of twenty, and that was in 1885. If she were born in 1865, that meant the vampire was one hundred fifty-seven years old.

Gilly shooed Colt away once Eliza's hair was ready for the rinse. Already, the vampire looked like a different person, and Gilly hadn't even done her makeup yet.

Colt took the boxes from out of the hallway and down to the trash. It took a couple of trips. Then he went into the basement and retrieved an old bow and a quiver of dusty arrows. He also found finger and wrist guards. He brought them up and set them on the kitchen table.

By that time, Gilly was leading Eliza down the steps. She was dressed in Jewel's clothes from when she was a teenager—brown boots, jeans, a maroon wool hunting jacket with a thick shirt underneath. All the clothes looked baggy on her, but it wasn't bad.

She gripped the unstrung bow and slung the quiver over her shoulder. "I'm ready. But if we get in trouble, I'm giving the bow to Gilly."

Gilly couldn't wait. She snatched the weapon out of the vampire's hands.

The goddess girl's eyes glowed blue. As did the runes on her forearms. She strung the bow and grabbed an arrow. "I know of the passions of vampires," she growled. "There was a time when I would ready randy women for the queen. I'd lick their wet little pussies until they came in my face, and then Queen Lilith would drink them, tasting the sex, reveling in the gore, but never the heart's blood. Not with her harem. Queen Lilith didn't mind boys after they drained their balls, but she liked the maidens the best. I would like an arrow, Eliza, if you please."

Mystified, the vampire handed her a feathered shaft. Gilly loosed the arrow. It streaked over Colt's head and struck the door above the lock. It sank deep into the wood there.

Gilly blinked as the goddess left her. "Well. Yes, Zeh had a friend who was queen of the vampires five thousand years ago. And she was very good with a bow and arrow. I'm so sorry, Colt. About your door."

He laughed a little. "It's fine. Let's go while we can.

Gilly handed Eliza the bow back. "Thank you for carrying that. And yes, the goddess of lust happened to be good at archery. Who knew?"

Jewel stood in the shadows of the living room, near the front door. "Okay, you three, I'll be here keeping watch. You be careful, okay?"

"We will, Jewel." Colt waved at his crazy ghost aunt.

Then he and the two girls left the house and got in his truck.

Colt had grabbed the Gaia Orb. His Rune Genesis Status was yellow, whatever that meant. He found a purse that matched Gilly's outfit, and she had it over her shoulder when she insisted on riding in the extended cab, sitting sideways behind Eliza.

The vampire protested but eventually agreed to ride shotgun.

Colt got them back onto the highway, feeling the Gaia energy flow into him. He let out a happy sigh. "Feels good to be back on I-70. You feel that, Gilly?"

"I do, Colt. I do. Hey, Eliza, how do vampires work with Gaia energy?"

Eliza turned to stare out the window at the lights of the city. "We are Monstra, and so we feel the Gaia, and it's the Gaia Unum that allows us to use our powers. But we get the Gaia mostly from blood. Sad to say—it's blood this, and blood that, when you're a soulless bloodsucker." She sighed like her heart might break.

"I don't think you're soulless," Gilly said.

"You haven't seen me hungry," Eliza whispered. "And golly, I hope you never do."

They drove back to the Firestone Conoco, off the side of the highway. Like before, Colt parked in the back near the shack. He turned to see Eliza staring at him. "I didn't force the issue back at the house. But we have to…I have to. You know."

Colt smiled, though he felt bad for the conflicted schoolmarm. "If you can't say it, Eliza, we can't do it."

"We should be intimate," the vampire said at last. "Before we go down there, you and I should at least try. Who knows? It might not be so bad."

"Eliza, please." Gilly's voice died.

Colt didn't know what to say. Even with her hair brown and the maroon lipstick, Eliza was still gorgeous. She knew that another rune might help them. He did too. Even if it was five more minutes of control, it would be worth it.

Still, it felt like a transaction that Eliza wasn't looking forward to. She was clearly pressuring herself.

"We could try the shack again," Gilly said. Suddenly the cab was filled with blue light. "I'm not saying that, Zeh, so just drop it."

Eliza glanced at the shack with wide eyes. "The shack then. It won't be a big deal. I might even have some fun."

They left the truck.

Like before, the shack was empty. It was as they'd left it.

Colt didn't want to start a fire, and it was cold, and suddenly he had Eliza in his arms. She laid her head on his chest.

Gilly stood by, watching with bright eyes. He could feel her lust.

And it made Colt swell. His pants became uncomfortably tight.

Eliza leaned back and stared into his face.

Her eyes were so big, so brown, so fearful. "Just. Just kiss me."

Colt bent and kissed her. She smelled divine, and it was more than perfume, it was the very scent of her skin that made him want to grab her hard. It made him want to follow her anywhere. Her body was so soft and warm.

And yet, he could feel her uncertainty.

And then Eliza staggered back, tears streaming down her face. "I can't. I can't. I had to try, I want to help, but I can't."

She fell to her knees, her face a mask of pain.

Gilly went to her, bent down, and took Eliza in her arms.

Colt had no idea what to do with a crying woman. Dealing with the ancient god of rage felt worlds easier.

At the same time, he couldn't just stand there like an idiot.

He crouched down and held both women to him. It took a while, but Eliza finally stopped sobbing. They stayed with her.

The heartbroken vampire finally laughed a little. "Golly, but this is embarrassing. And I must've made a mess of your makeup, Gillian. I'm so sorry."

Gilly leaned back and caressed Eliza's face. "It's okay. One of the modern-day miracles is waterproof mascara. We can touch you up, and it will be just fine. Us girls with moxie gotta stick together."

Eliza buried her face in Gilly's chest.

Gilly gave Colt a long look.

It said everything. They might have a bloodthirsty vampire with them, but she was a vampire with a wounded heart.

Colt would've done anything to heal this poor women.

First things first? He had to keep her and Gilly safe and alive.

That meant learning more about the Gaia Orb, finding the Fate Blade, and dealing with Vincent Isaac.

If Colt had to tear Firestone Alley apart, he would do it. It wouldn't be the first time the Rage King had destroyed a city, and it wouldn't be the last.

CHAPTER TWENTY-THREE

Colt swapped out the doorknobs in the door so when he shut it, the old worthless knob was there. He pocketed the crystal one. He was in the same outfit he'd worn before—basically a three-piece suit. Gilly was in her party dress, though she was wearing more comfortable shoes. She clutched the purse holding the Gaia Orb. Eliza was wearing Aunt Jewel's hunting clothes, and the vampire held the unstrung bow. The quiver hung off one of her shoulders.

They walked down the steps. The hissing lamps glowed on the red velvet wallpaper.

Colt found himself sweating. He was feeling irritable. Part of him wanted to just get rid of this Vincent Isaac directly. However, Eliza had pointed out that Vincent might already have the Fate Blade. If he did, then Colt might be walking into a trap.

It would be better to face the vampire lord with the Fate Blade in their possession. Then Colt could start throwing punches without worrying. Besides, destroying the city would get in the way of Bafflestone helping them with the Gaia Orb.

They reached the lobby with the double doors. It was still being repaired. New carpet was being laid. There were workers everywhere—mostly tall elves, but some vampire constables as well.

Near the double doors stood two big constables with their arms crossed. At their sides were pistols and nightsticks.

At least Vincent's henchmen—Otto, Warren, and the stubby Sodd—weren't there.

Colt figured they were out in the human world searching for him and his friends. This was the perfect night for them to be sneaking down into the hidden city.

Eliza walked right up to the two constables. She was wearing the finger and wrist guards. She smiled. "Hi, Harry. Jimmy. I'm taking some friends down to Old Town for a little target practice. That won't be a problem, will it?"

The two men glanced at each other, then at Eliza.

It was Harry that spoke first. "Mr. Isaac is wanting us to check everyone who comes in and out. There was trouble in the lobby here. You might know me, girl, but I don't know you."

Eliza put a hand to her chest. "Come on, Harry. At the party? We talked for ten minutes at least. And here I was thinking that you might be interested in a swell dame like me."

Harry shrugged. "You are pretty. What's your name?"

"Ilsa Lund." Her eyes were on Harry. But she subtly lifted her chest a little. She didn't have much there, but it was enough for Harry and Jimmy to glance down.

"Oh, right. Ilsa. And who is with you?"

Eliza pointed. "Rick. And Yvonne. They're bloodbonded to me."

"Lucky them," Harry muttered.

He motioned them through, and Jimmy shouted, "Three going to Old Town!"

Other constables let them through the big bronze gates to the right. Wooden stairs descended to the train platform. Eliza bought them all tickets using gold coins.

They stood at the far end of the platform, away from the other people—a collection of dog men and cat women, a few people that appeared human, and some very fit, very pretty vampire women who kept glancing at Colt. They smiled.

He smiled back. "Why are these vamps being so friendly?" he asked Eliza under his breath.

"You're with two beautiful women," Eliza responded. "One of which is a vampire. That isn't exactly typical down here. They think you're special."

"He is special." Gilly wiped at her forehead. "I've never been so nervous. It's so chilly down here, and yet I can't stop sweating."

"Things will turn out bully for us," Eliza said. "The hard part is over. I'm just glad I knew the constables working the door."

"So there aren't IDs for people?" Colt asked.

Eliza shook her head. "Vincent talked about that a lot. He couldn't get anyone to support them. There are a number of free-thinkers among the Monstra. If you spend enough time on the planet, you understand that power corrupts."

"Should you ever trust the government?" Colt asked.

"Not one run by Vincent Isaac. Surely." Eliza kept her voice down. She sighed. "I'm sorry about what happened in the shack. You see, I'd given up hope of ever feeling…well, now…we don't need to go into all that. We'll find you the Fate Blade, and then we can discuss plans to get Vincent Isaac off our backs. Then I would imagine we'll go our separate ways."

Gilly seized Eliza's arm suddenly. "But, Eliza, we need you. We don't know anything about the Monstraverse—excuse me, the Leyworld. We need a guide. And if we can disguise you, then maybe you can be free of your past."

Eliza shook her head. "It can't happen like that. I wish it could. Tricking two thick-headed constables is one thing, but most people won't be fooled. They'll hate you because they hate me so much. Vincent might've been my only friend, but now that I've betrayed him, he'll never forgive me. I won't have a friend left anywhere."

It was clear to Colt that Eliza was haunted by her relationship with Vincent—the good as well as the bad.

A train car, running along sparkling cables, came to a stop at the platform. The collection of people shuffled onboard. A man in an old-fashioned suit and hat sat with two dark-skinned women. Both were dressed in tight red dresses. Both seemed human, but it was clear they were bloodbonded to the vampire.

Colt remembered something that Eliza had said—the blood of a woman after she orgasmed tasted the best. He would only imagine the night the vampire would be having.

Colt, Gilly, and Eliza sat near the back so they could keep an eye on people who boarded.

The train lurched forward in a shower of sparks and swung from where it was connected to the cable above. There were several stops, including one for Vincent Isaac's palace.

After another stop, Eliza escorted them off and led them to a bank of brass and glass elevators. They saw more of the Lyra elves around, tinkering with the mechanisms. Colt would have thought that Bafflestone would be up here doing the work, but the elves were prettier, and Vincent Isaac seemed to like pretty things.

They would find Bafflestone and the other Tomte in the laundry, or at least that was the hope.

The elevators dropped down through the underground city—lamps and lights from a collection of wooden houses winked at them. It really was beautiful. Above, they could see the gold river of the Ley Line sparkling underneath the ghostly traffic of the translucent highway.

Colt had a question. "You said you knew about YouTube. Do you have internet down here?"

Eliza shook her head. "No. I have a clever phone, but it doesn't work down here."

"Smartphone?" Gilly asked.

Eliza winced. "Yes, sorry. I had a smartphone, but I had to go out to make calls. Vincent had me organizing getting donations from blood banks and setting up those who wanted to be bloodbonded. I also worked with hospitals and the medical examiner's office. A lot of unclaimed bodies wound up here."

Of course there was a dark side to the beauty.

At the very bottom, near a water treatment facility, they got off the elevator. They were the only ones who did. A simple concrete walkway edged a dirty canal.

Colt recognized the cave that led to the laundry.

Gilly led the way.

Colt had Eliza go next. They entered the steam-filled room with the big industrial machines whirring and chugging.

One of the Tomte gnomes called out from above. "Hey, Barney. Yer friends have come back. Tell 'em we don't need their clothes back. Already reported 'em missing!"

Bafflestone came sliding down from one of the ironing tables.

He flipped up his goggles. "Well, now, the missy and mister are back. But back with the traitor. What'd ye want with that traitor anyway?"

Colt felt the anger fill him. The cuffs of his shirt glowed red from his runes.

Urgu chuckled in his head. *I am glad to be back in this Gaia Town. There is so much wood. Wooden buildings are very easy to destroy, but the fun is in the burning. I enjoy burning what I destroy. Better still is the scent of sorrowful flesh cooking amidst the carnage.*

Colt took in a deep breath. "The god of rage just said he likes the smell of people cooking, so we're going to stop with the traitor talk. Eliza is helping us. Why don't we talk somewhere more private? You help us, and we can help you."

Gilly lifted the purse. "And I have the Gaia Orb, Barney. That should sweeten the pot."

Bafflestone whipped off his goggles. "Well. Twas just getting off my shift. But fine. Maybe she"—he pointed an accusing finger at Eliza—"can tell me why she wanted to get us all killed.

"Going off shift!" Bafflestone yelled.

The other Tomte gnomes repeated that call down the way. "Bafflestone is off shift!"

The gnome marched passed them, then whirled around. "Well, come on then. Been thinking about ye two. I heard about the trouble in the lobby. No trouble at the party though, other than Vincent Isaac drinking the heart's blood of that poor girl."

They left the laundry cave through the same back passage, but this time they went up stone steps to a wooden walkway that put them back in the main part of Firestone Alley. They were five or six stories up.

Bafflestone lived on the south side, so they had to take a covered bridge, glowing with lamps, to get to his place. He lived off a nice little park. He had a rather big house, with a ton of rooms. The back walls were blank stone.

Bafflestone's main level was a kitchen and his workshop. It seemed every single room was his workshop. All were filled with his tools, parts, and gears. The whole front of the house was a window that looked down on the park.

The house was human-sized, with normal furniture, but everything had stepping stools or booster chairs for someone who was only three feet tall.

Bafflestone caught Colt looking around. "Sold enough gizmos to afford a bigger place with lots of rooms and windows. But twasn't made for Tomte. Aye, twas made for bigger folk, but I make do." He motioned for them to sit at a big table off his kitchen. "Ye sit there. As for the other rooms, ye won't need a tour. I got different projects going in each room. That limits me. I don't clear a room until I finished a project. Ye hungry? I was going to have tea and cookies."

"The Tomte love sweets," Eliza said in a quiet voice.

"The traitor ain't wrong," Bafflestone growled.

"How safe are we here?" Gilly asked.

"Safe as anywhere, missy. No one is gonna come around. Why would they? I do the laundry, and I do it well. Though that doesn't give me any strategic importance." He bustled around the kitchen, filling a pot of water and putting it on an electric stove. Thanks to him, they could turn Gaia into energy.

From out of what looked like an icebox he pulled a metal bowl. After washing his hands, he grabbed dough, rolled balls, and put them on a tray. "Well, I'd like to take a gander at the Gaia Orb first, but no, we probably have to talk about the vampire first so I can trust ye. But garn! I can't believe Walt figured it out! You all can sit."

Colt and the girls took a seat at the long table.

Bafflestone shook dough at the vampire. "Now tell me, Elizabeth Anne Bennett, why'd ye want to tell the humans about us Leyfolk? We're relatively safe down here, sure, but not necessarily so. Brightest Light might come with an army of hunters. They'd kill us all dead. Sure, some of the Monstra can blend in to the human world, but most Leyfolk, like us Tomte, need to stay hidden. As does the whole Leyworld."

"It's a long story," Eliza said softly. "Perhaps we should start with the Gaia Orb."

"Now that makes me happy!" Bafflestone got his cookies into the oven and then rushed past them into another room. He came back with a wooden box with brass handles. He climbed up onto a stool, which sat on a bench next to the dining room table. The gnome put the box on the table. From it, he took a glass globe set in an ornate pewter base. It looked like an empty snow globe. "That's one I made. Let's see yours."

Gilly lifted the Gaia Orb out of the purse and gave it to Colt. It immediately lit up with green snowflakes surrounding the red god with the flaming hair.

Bafflestone came close, his little face full of wonder. "Aye, there he is, Urgu-Uku, and look at those sections of information. Garn! Rune Genesis Status is green. It would have to monitor yer Gaia Core, so it's strong enough to take the magic. Those powerful runes are ancient, and they give ye control, but they'll also give ye the Special Gaia Mutations. If Walt did what I think he did, I just might be able to come up with a way for ye to see what yer options are. It says right there ye can upgrade yer abilities."

Gilly clapped her hands. "This is such good news! Hear that, Colt? We just might be able to hack the system! From what we've seen, the Rune Genesis Status can be red, yellow, or green, and it matches stoplights."

"Do you know about human stoplights?" Colt asked.

Bafflestone rolled his eyes. "Can't hardly not. Ye humans love yer cars. But I'd have to do more study to tell ye anything specific. But, little lady, do ye wanna try out yer Gaia Orb?"

Gilly looked nervous. "Uh, it's experimental, right?"

Colt laughed. "If you can't trust a Tomte gnome in his own workshop, who can you trust?"

Bafflestone grunted. "Come now, if I wanted to hurt ye, I'd have reported ye to Vincent Isaac the minute ye stepped into the Alley. No. Come on and trust ol' Barney."

Gilly raised an eyebrow. "Eliza?"

"You heard what he said," the vampire replied. "Let's trust ol' Barney."

Gilly picked up her globe. "This ought to be interesting."

Inside was a beautiful woman with dark hair and dusky skin. She was naked, with curvy hips and full breasts. She was breathtakingly beautiful. An instant later, she held a bow made of blue light. A blue energy arrow was nocked and ready to be fired.

Bafflestone nodded. "Aye, and there's Zeh-Gaba, the goddess of lust and fertility. Ye two are for real all right, but I want to do more tinkering. Maybe if I—"

There were more flickers of blue light as information tried to appear, matching Colt's, but then the goddess was gone, and the orb was empty.

"Aye, more tinkering," Bafflestone whispered. He cleared his throat. "I'll want to do it right off, while ye're still here. But first, how did all this happen to ye? And why are two gods here with such a disgraced vampire? Notice I didn't refer to her as a garn traitor?"

Colt gave him a brief explanation. Statues shipped to Vincent

Isaac. An accident. Eliza stepping in to stop Vincent from getting them.

"And we're back tonight searching for the Fate Blade. You wouldn't happen to know where it is, do you?" Colt asked.

For being a little blue wrinkled man, Bafflestone turned pale.

A ding sounded from the kitchen.

The gnome slid off his booster stool. "We can talk more over tea and cookies. I want to know yer story, Eliza. I want to know every bit of it. I know about the Fate Blade. And I know ye're the last person in the Leyworld I'd ever want to touch it."

Eliza's eyes dropped to the table.

Colt knew she was scared. He wanted to take away her fear, but they needed Bafflestone's help.

Like it or not, the vampire was going to have to tell them more of her story.

CHAPTER TWENTY-FOUR

Colt noticed that Eliza didn't even bother with the tea. She sat stiffly. Her dyed hair and awkward makeup made her seem sadder. It was paint trying to cover tragedy. The real Eliza was blond and flashy, with red lips and a smirking smile. At the same time, she had the humility of a schoolteacher from a hundred and fifty years ago.

Bafflestone munched cookies and slurped tea. He wasn't saying a word. He had the information they needed. He could wait.

Gilly took a bite of the cookie. Her eyelids fluttered. "Oh, that's good. I mean, that's like the best sugar cookie I've had in a long time. Now for the tea." She sipped the tea and sighed. "Oh, that's some good stuff right there."

Colt decided to tease her a little. "How do you know there's no human blood in that? We are in a city full of vampires."

Gilly's eyes widened. "Oh my gosh. How dare you say that without trying it?"

Bafflestone rolled his eyes. "Please, missy. Mister. Why ruin my tea and cookies with blood? No, ye're fine. We bring in some stuff from the surface—flour, sugar, what not, but I add a little Tomte magic when I cook."

Colt went with the tea. Normally, tea smelled far better than it tasted. But this tea tasted like blueberries drenched in cream and covered in just the right amount of sugar. He then bit into the cookie. It was the perfect combination of crusty, crumbly, and chewy.

Eliza smiled sadly at him and then Gilly. "I'm jealous. I've heard stories of Tomte cookies and tea. You are fortunate." She took in a breath and exhaled slowly. "I won't tell you everything, Mr. Bafflestone. If you want to be a hero in this endeavor, you'll have to trust me. Otherwise, you'll embrace the role of a villain. I know about that. I've been both in my time."

Bafflestone shrugged and didn't speak.

Eliza continued. "I was born in 1865, turned into a vampire in 1885, right after I came to Denver. I didn't even think I could try to blend in, and it was…it was Vincent Isaac who brought me down to Firestone Alley. It was different back then. It was older, without lamps. We burned tallow candles, and there wasn't the train. We added those things to catch up to the humans. But we had blood-bonds back then. Vincent Isaac always saw me more as a daughter than a lover. I should be grateful. I might have needed to end my life if that hadn't been the case. I've thought about doing just that, many a time. But nature abhors suicide. And I do too."

She paused.

Gilly had stopped eating. Colt did as well. He couldn't help but listen carefully.

Bafflestone didn't. "Sure. Vampires and their bloodbonded. Don't get the heart's blood, though. Don't get real power. To get that, ye need to kill. So it's either love or power for yer kind? Aye, it's a damn shame. But ye've not said anything that would make me want to help ye."

"And I probably won't, Mr. Bafflestone." Eliza's eyes went to Colt. "Perhaps it's a waste of time, but I'd like Colt and Gilly to hear it."

Colt nodded for her to continue.

Eliza swallowed. "Forty years later, in 1925, I met Ruth Jones for the first time. She was such a joy, from the minute I met her. She'd grown up rough in Denver, in the worst parts of Denver, and that meant she was...that she was a woman of the night." Eliza clenched her jaw. "That kind of work wearies one's soul. But not Ruth. She rose above it. She learned of the Leyfolk—for that is the way it has always worked. The outcasts, the poor, the misfits—they learn about the Monstra when others don't. Ruth knew that having one lover who pays well is better than having a string of strangers who pay a pittance. She found a life for herself in the Alley, and that life included me. She was a gift from Victor, who knew I would never drink heart's blood. Not after that first time."

Eliza's voice failed her. She seemed to pull into herself. Her eyes were dry, but she seemed to be feeling a grief that was beyond endurance—a sadness too deep for tears. Then she smiled and a little sparkle came back to her eyes. "Ruth was blood-bonded to me, but it was more than that. She was my joy. In all the sorrow, in all the death, she was the light. I had never been with a woman—it wasn't spoken of in my time. And yet, when she gave her...blood...to me, it seemed natural to kiss her. And do more."

Eliza's face grew red with embarrassment. "I'll not say much more of that aspect of our relationship. It wouldn't be proper."

Gilly's eyes flashed a bright blue. She slapped her hands over her mouth while the runes glowed on her arms. Then she blinked and put her hands back on the table.

Eliza looked amused. "I can only guess what Zeh might've wanted to say about that."

"You don't even want to know!" Gilly said a bit loudly. She quieted herself with another cookie.

"Ruth wanted to return to her world. She'd learned of her grandmother, who was sick and dying. She thought we could help her grandmother. I went to Vincent, but he said the blood-bonded have to sever ties with the human world. For our safety."

Eliza swallowed hard. "Ruth begged me to help her. Her grandmother had been lost to her for a decade or more. The circumstances of the poor and desperate are not to be envied by anyone. I saw the savagery of the vampiric world. I'd lived it for forty years, which, compared to the age of gods, is nothing. A brief moment in an endless afternoon. But I'd watched vampires feed on the unwilling, watched them drain humans dry, and I thought if the Brightest Light destroyed all of them, perhaps the world would be better. Or perhaps coming out of the shadows would change the Order of the Night. Then Ruth would be able to return to the human world to be with her grandmother. It wasn't meant to be."

"What of the Tomte, girl?" Bafflestone asked. "What of the Lyra, or the Houdon, or the Goyangi?"

Colt wasn't sure what all the names were.

Eliza must've seen his confusion. "The Houdon are the Order of the Bite, the dog people. The Goyangi are the Order of the Scratch. They are the cats."

Her eyes went back to Bafflestone. "I wasn't thinking clearly. I was as much in love as I was in hate. You grew up Tomte. I grew up human and was turned into a vampire against my wishes. I was bound to be bitter."

Bafflestone's face softened for the first time. "Aye, missy, I ain't never thought of it that way. And this girl, Ruth, even I'd heard of her. She was like underground sunshine, as the saying goes. She disappeared. Or that's the story. One day here, the next gone."

"How old are you, Mr. Bafflestone?" Gilly asked. "If you don't mind me asking."

"Two hundred and thirty-five winters I've seen. I helped in bringing the Alley into the modern age. But go on, Miss Eliza. What's the real story of Ruth's fate? I know what happened to ye. Ye were thrown into Isaac's dungeon. In the deep rock. Where there's little light and bad heat."

"It wasn't all that terrible," Eliza said with a blank look on her face. "It was mostly movies and nothing. It's the vampire in me. I can go long periods just…not in myself. I become no one and nothing. Just the hunger. And when the hunger is satiated, even for a little while, it feels like so much of heaven that you can easily forget the hell."

She blinked. "Vincent Isaac took Ruth away. I can only guess what happened to her. He never told me because if he told me that he'd drank her heart's blood, I would've killed him. Or killed myself. As it was, all of my attempts to expose the Monstra to the outside world came to nothing. I did get a visit from Mr. Gentleman. No, it wasn't a visit. It was a warning."

Bafflestone's shock was so great, he stood up on his stool, put up a finger, then sat back down. "You can't mean that, missy. Not one person in a million, Monstra or not, has seen Mr. Gentleman."

"He's with the Umbra Alliance, right?" Colt asked.

"He just might be older than the gods inside you," Bafflestone sputtered. "He's a legend. Sure, he might've started the Umbra Alliance in his spare time, but he goes way back before that. Some say he was the first of the Leyfolk to ever get dust on his feet."

"He visited me," Colt said. "He needs to update his outfit."

Bafflestone's voice turned deadly serious. "Don't joke about him. Don't even speak his name. Let's move on. I don't want him to even know I exist. It's a shame about Ruth. Aye, it pains me. Souls like that don't come around very often. And, Miss Eliza, I can understand ye more now. Because yer turning twasn't easy. I can see that. By what ye've said, and what ye've not said, ye didn't want this fate. That's clear. We heard a different story. We heard ye wanted to expose us for yer own personal power. People said ye wanted fame and money, and so we wanted yer blood. But Mr. Isaac pretended he twas showing ye mercy. Maybe it was just a mercy for him because he saw ye as his daughter and didn't want to kill ye outright."

"So that's my story," Eliza said. "I spent ninety-five years being fed only enough to keep me alive. It was darkness when it wasn't movies. How I loved the movies. The romance, the love, the excitement. I could pretend to be someone else for a time. It kept me sane. It also sowed the seeds of my eventual rebellion when I left to intercept the statues. And I must've learned something about being an actress—from Greer and Ingrid, Bette and Betty, and of course, Olivia de Havilland and Vivien Leigh. I was the reformed convict for Vincent. I was reborn. Perhaps that was true. But I wanted to become an angel of vengeance. And I have, in my own, quiet way. Now, Mr. Bafflestone, you know my story. Where is the Fate Blade?"

Gilly wiped some tears from her cheek. The way she was looking at Eliza, it was clear that Gilly wanted to throw her arms around her and try to soothe away some of that tragedy.

Colt sat there a bit stunned. He could hardly wrap his head around her story. Eliza had been through a lot, and she'd been vilified when all she'd wanted was to help her love.

Aunt Jewel always said that the best love stories ended in tragedy. She meant it as a joke about her own doomed love affairs, but there was a certain ironic truth to it.

"We'll get to that," Bafflestone said. "But first, I want to see something else as far as it relates to our god and goddess." The gnome stood and rummaged around in the box from which he'd pulled the snow globe.

Bafflestone pulled a contraption out of the box that looked like the world's oldest typewriter. Two metal rods arced over the keyboard. "We don't get all the tech from the outside world, but we get some. Now, I know that Walt liked his video games, and maybe ye two do as well. Do ye?"

Colt couldn't answer for Gilly, but he could answer for himself. "Sure. I like video games. But why are you asking us?"

Bafflestone smiled. "Ye'll see. Walt twasn't the only genius."

CHAPTER TWENTY-FIVE

Colt glanced at his watch. It was well past midnight.
He was expected at work the next morning. If he didn't call in sick or dead, he might get fired, and there went the whole warehouse. Phyllis, Marcy, and Andy would all have to find other jobs and the last vestiges of New Eden Shipping & Receiving would be gone.

Colt glanced around—at all the gears and engines, at the park down below, and at the faces of the people at the table. His life was so different now. And Bafflestone's cookies were probably in the top five of the best things he'd ever tasted.

Gilly squinted. "Why are you asking us about video games?"

The gnome made some adjustments to the keyboard, tweaking the two rods and fiddling with some gears. "Like Walt, I have an interest in them, missy. I've had a phone in the fuel station, and I've seen some amazing things. The Gaia Orbs can track yer Gaia, as it relates to the gods. But what if we could track yer rune progression? Ye're only going to get more powerful. Ye have the old runes on yer arms. Tell me about them."

Eliza leaned in closer.

Gilly shrugged. "I, uh, well, it was Zeh-Gaba's idea. Zeh-Gaba.

She and Urgu haven't possessed anyone before. They were imprisoned in the statues—"

Bafflestone interrupted her. "Two of the statues broke, obviously. Where are the others?"

Colt glanced at the vampire. "Yeah, Eliza. Where are they?"

"Safe for now," Eliza said. "Go on, Gillian."

"Well, it was Zeh's idea. To get control of Urgu. When Colt and I are, uh, intimate, it creates a flow of energy that allows us more control. And I feel stronger. For example, I had pretty bad asthma before, but that seems to be gone. And I think I'm bulletproof now."

Bafflestone nodded. "So ye got powers. And I saw Colt when he had big, red muscles and fire for hair. Now, in yer video games, ye can track yer progression. I did some research on Zeh-Gaba. She did this before, when she was in her true form, and she was able to stop Urgu from destroying the world, but she wasn't enough. This time, I would imagine, the goddess thinks to bring more women into the fold. I won't embarrass ye, Miss Eliza, by asking if ye were intimate with Mr. Colt, here. But that's where it will lead."

Eliza sat stiffly. "Let's not discuss my involvement. It's unclear what will happen. But why are we discussing this?"

"I'll show ye." Bafflestone hit a switch on his typewriter. The machine whined as red sparkling energy flowed between the two rods. "Now, Colt, Gilly, pick up your orbs."

Colt touched his globe. So did Gilly.

Bafflestone typed like mad. "Aye, I see what Walt did. Oh, I can see it. He was real secretive, but he had to be. He was messing with things the Umbra Alliance would kill him and his family for."

Urgu-Uku appeared in Colt's orb. Gilly was holding a miniature version of Zeh-Gaba. Colt's orb had his stats. But Gilly's sphere didn't.

The gnome glanced at them. "Ha. I got the goddess back. But Walt's magic might take me a bit to figure out. Let's see. Body

Progression and abilities. Sure. One possible configuration might look something like this…"

Bafflestone did more tapping, and scarlet energy flowed from the two rods at the top of the typewriter to Colt's globe.

Colt watched as Urgu's body grew wings. Long horns erupted out of his skull. A prehensile tail burst from the end of his spine. His feet became two ebony hooves with knife-like edges.

"That would be one Body Progression configuration," the Tomte gnome said. "It would take a lot of Gaia Unum to get there. But we can track those levels. As for yer other abilities, I think we could come up with different abilities based on rage and fire. Ye could channel yer fury into a scream, maybe, or a clap, or perhaps a stomp. Maybe a charging ability. Or a blast of fire. We should be able to adjust yer heat as well."

Colt watched as the flickering figure's yellow flames turned red and then became blue.

Gilly watched in fascination. "Dang. Or should I say golly?" She smiled at Eliza.

Eliza smiled back. The two shared a moment.

Bafflestone grunted. "Ye should say garn. Now, let's see what the missy might look like if things go well."

The gnome typed more, and the energy between the rods turned blue. The crackling azure energy hit Gilly's orb.

Zeh-Gaba's body grew wings, and a halo of blue light appeared around her head. She rose from the ground, clutching a bow made of blue light. A quiver filled with sparkling azure arrows appeared on her back.

The gnome blinked. "Ye'll get wings, ye'll get speed, but it'll be yer arrows that will be remarkable. Arrows that bring love, that bring hate, and all them pesky emotions in-between. Bring light. Bring darkness. And ye'll be tough, missy, real tough. But again, ye'll have to work on yer Gaia Force levels."

"How can we increase that?" Gilly asked.

"With each rune, ye'll increase how much Gaia yer core can absorb. Most of the Leyfolk stay near the Ley Lines to get the Gaia from 'em." Bafflestone motioned to Eliza. "Vampires are different. They get the Gaia from the blood of their prey. But they're limited in the end. Even an alpha vampire will only get so powerful. I'll bet that was one of the reasons why Vincent Isaac wanted to host a god in the first place. He wanted to increase his power."

Bafflestone tapped more on the typewriter. The two rods powered down. "I'll keep working on seeing if I can help ye with yer progress. Yer cores are still growing, so they're fragile. Ye'll have to be careful not to push yerselves too far, too fast."

Gilly's eyes flashed a bright blue. "Tell us, Tomte, if we can fuck like we want? Or will we have to consult these fucking orbs when we want to come?"

The girl closed her eyes. "That was Zeh. She's very curious about our, uh, sexual activities."

Bafflestone grinned. "Well, now, it is a rather touchy subject. Those first runes came easily enough. As ye progress, ye'll have to concentrate harder to create the runes. That would take some work. Some practice." The gnome grinned. "Sex with new women would make the runes easier to create 'cause of the excitement, and everyone's core is a bit different. Anyway, the more sex ye have, the more ye'll see how yer cores will progress. In the long run, ye might want to consult with the Fae. They have what they call cultivation techniques to refine their Gaia Cores, but the Fae are bad to deal with. Not as foul as the Unseelies, or as tricky, but still it won't be easy."

Zeh was back. "So, Tomte, you are saying we can fuck as much as we like, but creating the runes will take some time, depending on this status business. Well, good. The girl longs for Colt to treat her like the little whore she is. And I like finding new tools to play with. Urgu does as well."

Zeh stared into Colt's eyes. "I see him in you, Colton Holliday. I see my love. He doesn't speak. He doesn't need to. I can feel him. And I long for him."

Colt felt sudden love for both the goddess and Gilly. It was Urgu inside him. The god of rage did love his goddess of lust.

Bafflestone did some typing, and suddenly yellow energy flowed from the rods to both Colt's and Gilly's orbs. "That Rune Genesis Status is gonna be important. Yer cores won't be fragile for much longer, so ye'll be able to have all the kissy time you want. But ye won't be able to create runes when the status is red. Yellow is iffy. Ye'll want to see when it's green, and then have all the fun ye want."

Eliza raised her hand. "What about me? Would you be able to track my progress? If I wanted…if I could." She lowered her hand and shook her head. "Never mind."

Bafflestone tried not to frown. He had a troubled glint in his eye. "Miss Eliza, sorry, but ye haven't made much progress as it is. Like it or not, without drinking the heart's blood, ye are fairly limited in what ye can do. Aye, ye have some of the skills, but to advance, ye'd need to take lives. From talking to ye, I don't reckon that's something ye'd want."

Eliza offered a weak smile. "No. You're right. I might be the villain everyone loathes, but at least I haven't taken a life. Except that first time after my turning." Her voice cracked, and she stopped talking.

Colt didn't say it, but he knew that there was another way for Eliza to increase her power. If she helped Colt create a rune, she'd get one herself, and that would make her stronger. It would also probably change her core, so yes, she could have a progression globe of her own.

"We all have our regrets," Bafflestone said in a quiet voice. He switched off his machine and it whined to a stop. "Now, let's change the subject. I'll do more tinkering, but ye came to me with two issues. Yer Gaia Orb and the Fate Blade. So let's talk about that damn knife. Ye have to understand that the Fate Blade has some powerful magic attached to it. It was forged by one of the old gods, the Dingir is what we call 'em, by the way. It was Yaz-Nammu, the god of light and law—he forged the Fate Blade to try to kill the goddess of chaos, Ziki-Urrudu. It was to kill her by stealing her power. Yaz-Nammu would've then forced everyone on Earth to obey every single law laid down in the oldest laws around, the Code of Ur-Nammu."

Gilly nodded. "It's probably the oldest set of laws that we know. Those Sumerians didn't have much of a sense of humor. But it seems like all this"—she motioned around her—"dated back to the Sumerian civilization."

"I would think we're older," Bafflestone said. "We know about the Sumerians because they wrote things down, missy. But what were yer people doing before ye wrote things down?"

"Hunting and gathering?" Gilly offered with a smile.

"Right." Bafflestone scratched his white beard "So Walt wasn't the first human to ship things to Firestone Alley. About a century ago, back when Silas Church was the alpha vampire, he knew the power of the Fate Blade. He hid it in Old Town. I'd go to the Temple of Blood and Darkness there."

"Sounds like such a *lovely* place," Gilly said sarcastically. "Do you have any hints where to look?"

"Not a clue, missy," Bafflestone said. "But you're going there with a goddess inside ye. Good ol' Zeh-Gaba will help ye if she can. Urgu probably won't be much help, from the little I know. That mister is just rage and destruction personified."

"You're not wrong," Colt said.

Bafflestone went from scratching his beard to scratching the wild white hair on his head. "Ye wouldn't want Vincent Isaac getting the Fate Blade. He'd not just kill Urgu, but he'd want Zeh-Gaba as well. Why settle for one god in yer core when ye could have two?"

"We can't have that!" Eliza erupted. "Anything but that. Anything." She dug her nails into the table. They'd become talons. They left scratches.

"Easy on the furniture, missy," Bafflestone said. "I'll keep working on my end. Ye three go and find the Fate Blade."

Gilly leapt to her feet. "Before we go, Mr. Bafflestone, I don't suppose I could practice with the bow. And for the record, I love the possibility of magic arrows. I knew Zeh is really talented, but

I'd like to see if my archery training in my middle school gym class paid off. Mrs. McGowan really pushed us."

Bafflestone glanced out the window. "We probably don't want ye shooting arrows in the park. The less attention ye draw to yerselves the better. Let's have ye practice right here."

The gnome got up and undid latches in the wall. He was able to roll the walls back to increase the space. He had a couple of straw dummies that he propped up against various gears and machinery.

Colt knew if they won, it would be because Vincent Isaac had squandered the natural talent of the Tomte gnomes, Barnard Bafflestone in particular.

Gilly put on the wrist guards and finger guards. She was able to string the bow. She remembered that much from her middle school gym class. She then fired arrows into the dummies from about twenty feet away. She moved back, while Bafflestone measured the distance.

Colt and Eliza watched her shoot. At fifty feet, her arrows kept missing the dummies. The arrows broke when they hit the back rock wall.

Gilly turned. "Colt, could you come and kiss me? I guess I do need Zeh's help, or this is never going to work. But I can't get too worked up."

Colt drifted over.

Bafflestone looked on with a little too much interest.

Until Eliza turned the gnome around. "Let's give them some privacy."

"You're right, Miss Eliza. I forgot muh-self."

Colt took Gilly in his arms. It felt as if he hadn't held her like that in days. It was more like hours, and yet, it still felt new—feeling her heat and inhaling her scent. He kissed her softly until the runes on her arms lit up.

She backed up with the runes blazing. Her voice came out in a sexy growl. "We have to finish this nonsense with the vampire lord quickly, Colton Holliday, because I need you to fuck me until I can smell our fucking."

Gilly tossed her glasses onto the table. She spun and fired an arrow. It struck the head of one of the dummies. She reached back, easily got another arrow, and fired it into another dummy's head, hitting it perfectly. Missile after missile streaked across the floor, hitting the dummy heads.

"This is a waste of time. I need a longer range, at least thirty-six cubits, or it's not worth doing." Zeh-Gaba dropped the bow and pulled the finger and wrist guards off. She dropped it all and started to undress. "I can't wait. I need your cock now, Colton Holliday."

Colt caught her hand. "No, Zeh. Bring Gilly back. We don't have time. We have to get the Fate Blade before Vincent Isaac gets it."

Slowly, Gilly's eyes grew darker until she was squinting at him. When she spoke, her voice was normal. "The goddess doesn't need glasses, but I certainly do. How did I do?"

"With Zeh's help, you hit every shot. But how long is a cubit?"

"A Sumerian cubit," Gilly corrected. "About twenty inches."

"Golly," Eliza said. "She certainly is the goddess of lust, isn't she?"

"Got my old blue pecker hard," Bafflestone spouted.

Colt didn't need the visual. "On that note, let's just go. I want to see this Temple of Blood and Darkness. Eliza, do you know where it is?"

The vampire nodded. "I do. But, Colt, before we leave, can I talk to you for a minute? Alone?"

Something had changed in the vampire. There was a certain look in her eye that hadn't been there before.

CHAPTER TWENTY-SIX

Colt walked with Eliza through the park. There were strange trees growing in the light of the gas lamps. The trees had dark bark, highlighted with glimmers of yellow and green. Oak-shaped leaves sometimes glowed with a golden light. Stone paths cut through the grass that also glowed with a yellow-green light, catching the light of the lamps.

It was gorgeous, otherworldly, especially the flower garden that surrounded a burbling fountain.

"The light is the Gaia," Eliza explained. "Everything here drinks from the Gaia Unum. We have insects, spiders, strange birds—it's an entire ecosystem, hidden away. I've loathed it for the most part. I think about the sunshine, the real sunshine, and it doesn't help my mood any, Buster. Not one bit."

They stopped to take in the odd flowers—the pollen glowed and drifted around the tender, blood-red petals. They smelled good, but not as good as Eliza. Her scent was heaven itself.

Colt stopped her. "What did you want to talk about?"

"Now that you know a little of my story, I just wanted to see if you think I'm still a swell gal. If you ever thought of me that way." She laughed. It sounded oddly happy. "And look at me, like I'm a schoolgirl. You're what? Thirty?"

"Twenty-five."

"And I'm a hundred and fifty-seven. Quite the age difference." She walked away from him, arms across her chest. "I'm not a lesbian. I just wanted to make that clear. Yes, I had my time with Ruth, but I missed having a man's body in my arms. His body is hard. I didn't mean to insinuate anything else was hard. Now I'm rambling like our sweet Gillian."

"You don't have to be nervous," Colt said. "I need more runes, but I don't expect you to help with that. For now, we both have the same goals."

Eliza wheeled on him. Her eyes turned silver, catching the light from the lamps. "To stop Vincent Isaac. But I can't stop thinking about my outburst in that shack. I can't stop thinking about what we could have if I were different. If I were normal." She looked pained.

Colt wanted to take away that pain, but it was one hundred and fifty-seven years in the making, and he'd only known her for a day.

At first, he didn't know what to say. He did feel the anger hit like a lightning bolt. He was furious that she'd been hurt so much in her life. She hadn't chosen her fate.

Eliza touched her head. "Colt, your hair is smoldering."

Colt could smell it. He stopped, clenched his hands into fists, and could almost hear Aunt Jewel's voice. *When life gives you lemons, trade them in for limes, salt, and some tequila. You'll thank me.*

Colt took a deep breath and counted to ten.

Urgu chuckled. *She is full of sorrow, this one. Teach her anger. Teach her to burn up her sadness in the fires of her fury. We can destroy this Gaia Town together. The screams of the dying shall be our music.*

"That's not music, Urgu," Colt said out loud.

"What?" Eliza asked, uncertainly.

Colt tapped his head. "The Rage King is getting chatty. He does that when I get pissed off. He wants to destroy the city, which is nothing new for him. Except, in this case, random damage isn't going to help our cause any."

Eliza's face fell. "You're angry with me. I know. I'm sorry. It's just…I don't think I can ever love anyone again. Not even you and Gillian who seem so…so perfect."

Colt crossed quickly to her and took her hand. He didn't know what to say.

Tears sparkled in her eyes. "You and Gillian must blame me for destroying your life. I loosened the strap. The boxes fell because of me. And now you won't be human again. I did to you what Vincent Isaac did to me."

"That's fucking bullshit!" Colt took in a deep breath and lowered his voice. "No, Eliza. Vincent knew what he was doing. What happened to Gilly and me was an accident, plain and simple. You can't blame yourself. And maybe it's not so bad." Colt gestured around them. "Look at all this magic. There's a whole world I never would've known about. It's not exactly peaceful and happy, and I don't imagine there are pink fluffy unicorns dancing on rainbows, but it's amazing. And now Gilly and I are a part of it. We're going to find a weapon forged by a forgotten Sumerian god. And we're going to go to war against a fucker who kills people for power. No. Maybe it was unexpected, but that doesn't mean I don't like it. Besides, I get to talk to my Aunt Jewel again. Just that is worth the price of admission."

"But what about the god of rage inside you?"

Colt felt the truth hit him in the face. "I've had a god of rage inside me all my life. I was in anger management therapy when I was in the seventh grade. That was when…when my dad died in prison. Mom had bounced in and out of my life a lot, which was awful. Just when I was getting used to her, when I thought she might love me…she'd fucking leave. Because she always loved her drugs far more than she could ever love me."

Colt so wanted to give in to the rage. He so wanted to rip apart the world. The anger was better than the pain. Both were so bright in his mind, like living flames, hotter than the Rage King could ever hope to be.

Urgu kept silent. Colt had the idea that the Rage King was enjoying Colt's anger with divine patience.

Colt looked down to see the skin on his hands was red. And he knew without even sniffing he'd lost his hair to flames. He was half-changed, in a hybrid state, full of anger, with bright red skin. The runes reddened the cuffs of his shirt.

He grinned and spoke in a growl. "This is what I've felt like my entire life. This anger. So, no, Eliza, it's bullshit to blame yourself. I'll figure this out. We'll figure this out. We can just be friends."

Colt felt Urgu fighting him for control, and without the runes, he would've shredded his disguise and gone off on a destructive rampage.

Colt could control him. He could beat this thing.

Urgu finally spoke. *Your rage goes deep, Colton, but I know the sacred anger of creation itself. You cannot control me for long. I will eventually break you.*

"You're welcome to try," Colt whispered. "Because you're alone. I'm not."

Eliza clutched Colt's huge red arm. Was she afraid?

She didn't need to be.

Because of Aunt Jewel. She had helped Colt get through his mother's painful visits and exiles. Jewel often said that you didn't get to choose your family, but most of the time you could choose your donuts. And if you were lucky, you'd love at least one person in your family as much as Jewel loved raised donuts with chocolate frosting, which according to Jewel was the ultimate donut.

Colt didn't think so. He'd go with a cake donut, topped with chocolate and nuts, every time.

Eliza's hands were cool and soft, so different from his own angry red skin. "I understand about the difficulties of mothers and family, Colt. My parents are long dead, and yet, there's rarely a day goes by that I don't think about them. Their blessings, their curses, as well as their sins, for isn't that family in the end? Blessings, curses, and sins?"

She gazed into his eyes. She wasn't afraid after all. Not one bit.

But then, what could scare Eliza? *There comes a point where life tortures the fear right the fuck out of you.* That wasn't from Aunt Jewel. That was from Colt's mother, a Candace Comozzi original. It was one of the last things she'd ever said to Colt, when he was still in elementary school.

"Come back to me, Colt. I don't find this Urgu fella very handsome."

Colt felt himself laughing. That was another tool to deal with his anger. If he could laugh at something, most of the time he wouldn't want to rip it apart.

Closing his eyes, Colt focused on his breathing. In and out. He smelled the strange trees of the park. He smelled Eliza's unbelievably sexy scent. He settled himself down.

Then he inhaled deeply and opened his eyes.

He was back to being just Colt Holliday. "Hey."

"Hey. Are you going to make it?" Eliza stared at him, a little smile on her face.

He nodded. "Yeah. But where is everyone? It's night, right? Shouldn't we be surrounded by vampires?"

Eliza shrugged. "A lot of the vampires do leave at night and are back by dawn. But do we need to sleep? Not really. Most of us do it because we like the dreams. But if we stay fed, we don't need to sleep. Plus, it's hard to be with your own thoughts all that time. Sleep is a break."

They stood there, looking into each other's faces.

Eliza was the first to smile. "You and Gilly are both young. If we did fool around, I'd feel like I was robbing the cradle."

Colt tilted his head. "You keep bringing up sex, Eliza. There's no pressure from us. It sounds like you're pressuring yourself."

The vampire laughed half-heartedly. "Well, now, you two are so cute, you make buttons jealous. Get it?"

Colt felt a tingle go through him. "Yeah, cute as buttons. You don't need to be jealous. You're just as cute."

Eliza let out a sigh. She crossed to him and held him tightly. She rested her head against his chest, and he found himself caressing her hair, still soft, but he did miss that golden color. Well, she'd get it back.

He could feel her breathing. He inhaled her sexy scent.

Colt wasn't sure what the long hug meant.

But he held her for a long time until something passed from her, a darkness, a sadness. When she finally stepped back, she smiled. "I haven't been held like that in a long, long time."

"I'm here if you ever need to be held again," he said. And he meant it.

Colt remembered what Bafflestone had said—sex with new women would be an easy way to get new runes. That meant that he might end up with a harem of women. What would Gilly think of that? She'd done the one threesome, but that had ended in disaster. Would she want to try again?

Maybe. But it probably wouldn't be with Eliza—she'd made that clear. At the same time, she kept bringing up sex, and she'd hugged him for a long, long time. She was sending him mixed signals. Normal women were hard enough to understand, but she was a vampire. Who knew what was going through her mind?

They walked back to Bafflestone's house in silence.

When they pushed open the door, Gilly was eating more cookies. She looked a bit guilty there, with crumbs on her lips. She still wore her archery gear, and it fit her really well. She raised a hand. "Hi, guys. Everything okay?"

Eliza nervously pushed hair behind her ear. "Right as rain, Gillian. The cat's meow."

Gilly had a questioning look at Colt. Was that jealousy or concern?

"We're good, Gilly," Colt said. "We're good."

The little blue man was rifling through drawers. "I just remembered something, Colt. Remember when I said that Walt sent me something, but I hadn't looked at it in a good long while? Well, I remember now. It was an envelope with a letter and a key inside it. He said I'd know what to do with it when the time came, and well, the time has come. I'll look for it. And now that I have some data on your condition, I'll work on perfecting the Gaia Orbs. You all should go look for the Fate Blade in Old Town's temple."

Colt was excited. The key would probably open Grandpa Walt's filing cabinet. It would be nice to see what was inside there.

But first, they had to find the Fate Blade.

CHAPTER TWENTY-SEVEN

Colt, Gilly, and Eliza had to hike through the Tomte section of town, which would lead them to the west side of Firestone Alley. That was where Old Town was, and that included the Temple of Blood and Darkness.

Gilly looked good in the old-fashioned dress and the bow and arrows. She walked with a certain confidence he'd not seen outside in the human world. Eliza led the way.

The Tomte's houses were small, and they were piled on top of each other. Between them were narrow alleyways that branched off from the main cobblestone street. While streetlamps gave them light, most of the houses were dark because unlike the vampires, who didn't need to sleep, the gnomes did. The houses were all closed up and dark.

There were a couple vampire constables that eyed them—both with stubbled heads and silver eyes. They carried pistols and nightsticks.

Eliza flashed her fangs and said they were heading to the temple in Old Town so she could pray. The police didn't ask any more questions.

Besides, the important parts of the city were far above them. This part was for gnomes and ruins.

And Colt came to the ruins. The gnomes' houses ended, and old stone structures started. They might've had roofs at one point, but now they were just foundations. A few lamps were here and there, though most were dark.

A thought occurred to Colt. "So, Firestone Alley was here back before Colorado was even a territory, right?"

"That's the story," Eliza said. "But I don't know much of the pre-history of the place. I've heard about the improvements that Bafflestone made when Silas Church ruled Firestone Alley, but I've only known it as Vincent Isaac's kingdom."

They moved through the shadows, creeping up to a park where the plants hadn't been clipped. Grass grew waist-high. The roots of the trees broke through cobblestones. Green and yellow light glistened across the plant life. It was like the park near Bafflestone's house, only far wilder.

The temple looked like something out of a movie. It was built into the rock at the very edge of town.

The three stood in front of the massive columns. One had crumbled. Inside, though, there was a flickering light.

Eliza stood with her hands on her hips. "At one point, pilgrims might've travelled here to worship, but most of the vampires moved away from worshipping the Dingir. For whatever reason." She laughed bitterly. "I know one. Vincent would rather they all worship him and not Mudd-Ganzer—that's the god of vampires, or the god of blood and darkness, really. Don't know if he's still in one of the statues or not. Maybe Zeh or Urgu knows."

"Urgu doesn't talk much," Colt said.

Gilly laughed. "Lucky Zeh does. I'm really hoping she's in a chatty mood today. Let's get inside. I have class in the morning. If there's a god of coffee, I'd like him to take a turn inside me. That came out wrong. Let's just go."

Colt realized he'd be at work in just a few hours. How weird would that be? Vampire temple at night. Big warehouse in the morning.

Eliza tried to push forward, but she was stopped by an invisible force. "I can't. I can't go any further."

Gilly tried, and she too was stopped. She gritted her teeth and tried to go forward, but she was unable to.

Colt joined them. It was like walking right into an invisible wall. The surface was smooth and cold and impenetrable.

Eliza frowned. "Well, ladies and gents, welcome to a piece of magic that is as unlucky for us as it is lucky. It looks like there might be a bloodwax candle inside. Which means someone doesn't want us going in there."

"What's a bloodwax candle?" Colt asked. "And how do we get past it?"

Eliza shrugged. "We'd have to put it out somehow."

Gilly walked across the shattered stones with one hand on the invisible wall. "If I can see it, I can shoot it with an arrow."

She let out a happy yell. "Yes, between the columns. I can just make it out."

She nocked an aluminum arrow with a rounded tip. "Come out and play, Zeh. I need your archery abilities."

Colt walked up to her and grabbed her ass. "Let's get this Fate Blade, Gilly, so you and I can be together back at my place."

That did it. Gilly's eyes flashed blue. Her voice was a sexy growl. "And Eliza doesn't have to fuck us, but the dirty bitch can watch." She let loose the shaft. It struck the candle flickering on the altar deep inside the temple.

The invisible force field in front of them shimmered away.

Gilly winced. "Sorry, Eliza. I really didn't mean to call you a dirty bitch."

Eliza laughed a little. "Oh, well, you know. I've been called worse." She walked over to a glowing lamp and broke it off an old wooden post, gray with age. "This will give us a little light."

They walked with the lamp into the temple. Mostly, it was open space. At the center was a series of steps that rose up to a central dais. At the top was the altar where the bloodwax candle sat in a bronze candlestick.

The rest of the vast structure was lost in shadows.

"So where do we start looking for the Fate Blade?" Colt asked.

Gilly handed her bow to Eliza. "Come and kiss me, Colt. Let's see what Zeh-Gaba knows."

Eliza took the bow, but she also took Gilly's hand. She stared right into Gilly's face. "Maybe I could help. I gave Colt a long hug, and it felt so good. Maybe I could embrace you, in a...similar manner. You know, what's good for the goose is good for the gander." There was nervous hope on the vampire's face.

Gilly got a goofy look on her face. "Uh, I'd be the gander in this situation, but I'm more of a silly goose." Her eyes dropped to Eliza's chest before returning to the vampire's face.

Colt knew exactly what would happen.

Gilly's eyes flashed blue, and the runes on her arms glowed with a blue light. "So I was right to call you a dirty bitch. Come, creature of the night, come and press your tits up against me, and let me grab your little ass."

Eliza stepped into the hug, and Gilly's hands dropped to Eliza's slender butt.

Eyes blazing, Gilly went to kiss the vampire.

Eliza stepped back. "Zeh-Gaba. What do you know of the temple?"

Gilly suddenly had an evil grin on her face. Her words came out in Zeh-Gaba's growl. "And what do you know of your own heart? You tell them 'no,' while you hide your secret longings."

Eliza stood up straight and tall. "Listen, cookie, my longings are secret, so let's not talk about them. Otherwise, they wouldn't be a secret, would they?"

"Did you have a bad turning, girl? I've seen it before, in my life before my imprisonment. Before I was reduced to this virginal cage."

"Secret. Longings." Eliza emphasized both words.

Zeh-Gaba laughed. "Very well."

Colt did have to wonder how Zeh and Urgu had been imprisoned at all. There was a long story there. He figured he'd hear it at some point.

The goddess of lust tossed her glasses to Colt. "Hold these, lover." She walked with the bow through the vast temple. "This place is new. Can you smell how new the dust is? Perhaps it's seen a millennium or two. Perhaps not. Regardless, it has the stink of Mudd-Ganzer in it. He is the father of the night. He is the father of thirst."

Zeh put her foot upon the first step. "We've come to seek the Fate Blade. But is it here? It was. I can feel it. The Fate Blade. A weapon to sever one's fate. Thus, Yaz-Nammu, the god of law, would've purified Ziki-Urrudu, the goddess of chaos, on it—a weapon forged to slay gods."

Eliza turned and frowned. "Why would Silas Church, a vampire lord, put the weapon here?"

Zeh-Gaba's eyes shone an even brighter blue. Gilly must've really been letting the goddess off her leash. "This is a new place. This is the new world. When we ruled the place between the rivers, far away in other dusty lands, we knew of other gods and other peoples across the world. Drinking in the Gaia Unum on Ley Lines unknown to us. The Order of the Night, and the Order of the Moon, both come from an infection that the powerful can spread to humans. Where there are humans, there are the Leyfolk."

The goddess girl climbed to the top of the dais to stand next to the altar.

Colt gave Eliza a questioning look. The vampire shrugged. "Werewolves. The Order of the Moon. Vampires and werewolves are rather similar." Eliza walked up the steps to join Gilly at the top.

Colt stayed at the bottom of the dais just in case he needed to protect the women.

"The Fate Blade was here," Zeh-Gaba said. "A vampire prince, keeping a weapon close, to use it on another god, perhaps? Mudd-Ganzer and I have always seen eye to eye, for what is lust if not a thirst? But there was hate, always, with Yaz-Nammu, for many confuse light and law. But the darkness has laws of its own, does it not, vampire bitch?"

Eliza stiffened. "You better smile when you say that, Zeh-Gaba."

Zeh was smiling when the bright blue light faded from her eyes, leaving a stunned Gilly behind.

The girl squinted and held out a hand. "Could I have my glasses back? And how much pervy stuff did I say? I'm hoping it's relatively low on the pervy scale."

"Very low, dollface," Eliza said. "I won't talk about you groping me."

Gilly winced. "Top or bottom?"

"Bottom."

Gilly closed one eye. "Is that better or worse? Let's just move on. Zeh doesn't think the blade is here. It was, granted, but it's not here now."

An accented voice cut through the shadows. "Of course, it's not, liebling. If it were, Herr Isaac would have it." Otto, the bald German, was back. He came out of the shadows on the side of the temple. His face had healed from when Colt had punched it before.

Suddenly, he vanished into smoke.

Colt glanced at Eliza at the top of the dais with the bloodwax candle in her hand.

"Can you do that?" he asked her.

Eliza slipped the bloodwax candle into a pocket in her outfit.

"I did it to get in your house, buster. I'd do it again, but I haven't eaten in three days, and such a trick requires a fair amount of blood."

Gilly had an arrow ready. "I have a couple of wooden arrows, but I think they're mostly aluminum and fiberglass."

"Use the wooden ones," Eliza said. "One through the heart will do the trick."

"Does decapitation work?" Colt asked.

"You know it does. We need blood for our brains, and I might've grown back a finger a time or two, but there's no growing back a head."

Smoke coalesced in front of the two women.

Colt raced up the steps to grab the vampire about to appear, but the second Colt got there, the vampire was smoke once more. Finally, Mr. Sodd, the stubby guy with long hair took shape to the left of the girls. He had a pistol in his fist. He fired.

Colt jumped in front of the women.

These fuckers had spied on them. They'd attacked them. Stubby and the thin man had tried to drain Gilly. Given the chance, Colt knew they'd do it again.

The anger was easy to access. The temple might be a couple thousand years old, sure, but it might not survive the Rage King.

Bullets bounced off Colt's chest. He ripped through his clothes and exploded out of his shoes. Colt clung to control—his runes were burning hot—but he didn't know how long he had.

He charged forward to tear the short vampire apart.

But Stubby Sodd turned back into smoke, taking his clothes and weapons with him. That was a neat trick.

A second later, another man leapt on him. It was Warren, the tall, thin vampire. His fangs ripped into Colt's shoulder. Okay, vampire fangs could pierce his skin. Good to know. But the vamp's claws slid off Colt's thick red skin. Well, Colt only had Invulnerability I. He'd have to upgrade that skill. Hopefully Bafflestone could figure out how to do that.

Colt whirled, took hold of the thin man's head, and pulled it off. The results was immediate. Instead of gore, a bright yellow fire burst from the neck of the man's body and the throat of the man's head. A second later, the fire devoured all of the flesh, leaving behind dust and bits of the thin man's burned clothing.

No more healing for that guy. Colt felt the kill in some deep part of himself, the same part that could feel the Ley Lines underneath the highway. He didn't drink in the Gaia Force liberated from the body of the vampire, but he felt the change in the air around him.

Colt, Gilly. and Eliza were all at the top of the dais.

Gilly was down on arrows. She'd been firing, but not hitting a thing. "Kiss me, Eliza! I can't hit a thing on my own!"

Colt saw Eliza grab Gilly and kiss her, right on the lips. It was enough to get Zeh-Gaba's interest. The goddess girl's eyes, runes, and fingernails exploded with blue light.

Another vampire—one of the constables they'd seen in Tomte Town—darted forward with a shotgun. There was gunfire and Eliza screamed, grabbing her leg.

Colt stomped forward, grabbed shotgun constable, and tore him in half. The shotgun fell to the stone as did the asshole's legs. The constable screamed. He wasn't dead yet. So Colt had to tear off his head.

There was more fire and smoke, but by that time, Colt had tossed away the distinegrating body. He then turned to see Mr. Sodd appearing behind Eliza. The poor wounded vampire was an easy target.

Sodd never had the chance to hurt her.

Gilly had her glasses pushed to the tip of her nose. She unloosed an arrow, and it streaked into Mr. Sodd's heart. He flung his hands out to the side and let out a yell. Fire burst from his chest, and as with the thin man, Sodd soon became flame and dust and then nothing at all.

Gilly grabbed another arrow and sent a shaft spinning into Otto the German giant, who appeared out of the smoke with his long fingernails and fangs bared.

This wasn't a wooden arrow, only an aluminum shaft, and it hit his body. He immediately vanished into smoke. Would he come back? His two henchmen were dead.

Eliza was gasping, holding her thigh. Smoke boiled out of the wound.

Another smoky figure took shape—the other constable with a

nightstick. Only, he hit a button and a silver blade appeared on one end.

Wood and silver—those could hurt Eliza.

Colt was too far away to help. And that simple fact pissed him off more than anything. He could use that anger. He was the Rage King.

Colt let go of a bit of his control, which was a mistake.

Urgu leapt at the chance to take over.

Colt found himself vaguely aware of what happened next. He made an impossible jump over both Gilly and Eliza and landed right on top of the nightstick constable. One foot snapped the fucker's thigh. Another huge foot came down on the constable's skull. There was a crunch. No more skull. Golden flames consumed the body until nothing but dust was left.

Glancing around, Urgu saw an entire temple he could demolish.

Colt knew that Urgu liked destroying temples. It was one of his most favorite things, besides killing other gods. But not his Zeh-Gaba. Not the goddess of lust and fertility.

Colt was dimly aware of Urgu turning to see his Zeh, staring up at him with such nice blue eyes. Urgu had some strange questions that Colt didn't understand. Why did she have a human weapon in her hands? Why did she not have her bow made of Gaia Unum itself? With her magical weapon, she could fire arrows of emotion and destruction. Such fun. It had been so much fun to murder with his goddess.

Zeh went to him and caressed Urgu's arm. Colt felt the touch. She'd done this before, to calm him. She was saying something about the other vampires fleeing.

Was the fight over? Colt could still feel Urgu's rage.

The pretty vampire was weeping over her wounds. She'd been hit by silver. That was why smoke was pouring out of her leg.

Who had hurt such a pretty vampire? Urgu would hurt them back. So would Colt.

Only, Zeh was there. Eyes so blue. Eyes so pretty.

Urgu would never hurt her. And Urgu liked the pretty vampire, though he liked her with blond hair and bright red lips more.

So much beauty there.

So much beauty.

Colt had lost himself to Urgu, even as the god of rage allowed himself to be soothed. Colt knew that he needed more runes because both he and Urgu liked the power of their rage a bit too much.

They could have so much fun destroying things together. Maybe even kill a god or two. Why not?

CHAPTER TWENTY-EIGHT

Colt had fuzzy memories of leaving the temple and making their way back to Bafflestone's house. He had to carry Eliza despite the throbbing pain of the vampire bite on his shoulder. It was from a beta, so it wouldn't turn him, but still, it hurt. That helped to fuel his fury.

As did the smell of the silver shot in Eliza's leg—it was pungent, terrible really. She was huffing and sweating.

Gilly was pale as she ran with them. Luckily, the streets of Tomte Town were even more deserted than they had been just an hour earlier.

Colt was fully back to himself, half-naked, with bloodstained feet, by the time they walked through Bafflestone's door.

The gnome's house had been ransacked. Machinery had been smashed. A few things had been thrown out the window. There were scattered tea bags on the floor.

Against the wall, between the straw dummies, Bafflestone himself sat on the floor. His eyes were closed. Blood was drying on his face. He looked dead.

Eliza sank into a chair. She lifted her hurt leg and rested it on the table.

Gilly and Colt rushed over to the gnome. They squatted next to him.

Colt patted his cheeks. "Come on, Barney. Don't die on us. We need your help."

He blinked his eyes. "It's Mr. Bafflestone to ye." He grinned. He was missing several teeth. "Just joking. Barney is fine. Aye, we're comrades in arms now, I'll tell ye what."

"What happened?" Colt asked.

The gnome winced. "Sorry, mister. They beat me awful. They tortured me." He lifted a hand with several broken fingers. "I told 'em most everything. They opened the letter, and like I thought, there was a key and a note inside. Saw the key. Don't know what the note says. Vincent took it."

"Why would Vincent come here?" Gilly asked.

"Spies. Outside my house. Down here." Colt felt his heart die in his chest. "I bet you that my grandfather had the Fate Blade the entire time. It was in his filing cabinet, the one we couldn't open."

"Might be so," Bafflestone agreed. "Vincent Isaac came here himself. He knew his other lackeys were at the temple, but he didn't have much faith that they'd take ye in. Naw, not really. He got down to it. I said I didn't know where the other statues were. And I didn't. I offered up the envelope in hopes they wouldn't cut off my fingers. I need my fingers." Tears mixed with the blood on his face. "So sorry."

Eliza called from the table. "I don't mean to be a nuisance, but I need help. The silver shot hurts me. It hurts me so much." She was close to weeping.

Gilly stood. "First things first, we need to help Eliza. And then we need to get to your house, Colt. We still might beat them there."

"Not likely," Bafflestone whispered. "Vincent is an alpha vampire, turned to smoke, racing the dawn. He's probably already there. I'm so, so sorry."

Colt realized he was holding his breath. His heart was pounding in his ears. When he breathed in, it was like he was breathing in raw rage. He was shirtless, so the runes on his forearms were blindingly red.

Urgu sighed. *Destruction and murder would help you feel better. Trust me. Shedding blood soothes like nothing else.*

Colt was too pissed off to laugh.

Gilly saw it. She bent down next to him. "Don't rage out on me, Colt. Let's just gather our wits. We need to help Eliza. Please."

Colt couldn't talk. It was taking every bit of his control to not completely destroy everything around him. Vincent Isaac might've smashed up a lot of Bafflestone's house, but Colt would wipe it and Firestone Alley off the map. The fires would be glorious. Punching through walls and snapping load-bearing beams would be so satisfying. He wanted to pop the heads off other vampires because the light show was so very pretty.

The runes burned brighter. The smell of burning hair was suffocating.

Gilly pushed her forehead against his.

She kissed his lips softly. "Please, Colt. I need you to be strong."

And that was the truth. He had to be strong. He nodded. "I have to get back home."

But did he? What did he really own there? All that stuff, all those boxes, most of it wasn't his. What if he lost the house? He'd still have his memories. He'd still be able to talk with Aunt Jewel. The only reason to go home was to kill Vincent Isaac and stop him from getting the Fate Blade.

Colt realized that he didn't much care about all this supernatural bullshit. He was more curious about the note that Grandpa Walt had left for him. And what else was in the filing cabinet?

Bafflestone struggled to stand. He grabbed a pair of needle-nose pliers, but his fingers were too smashed for him to use the tool.

Colt let Gilly pull him to his feet. She took the pliers from Bafflestone's hand.

They all went to help Eliza. Her face was pinched in pain.

"Not the swell night I wanted." The vampire gasped as a wave of pain seized her.

"Can we get you some kind of anesthesia?" Gilly asked.

Eliza shook her head. "No, just take them out, quick. They'd probably come out on their own. Bullets would. I've seen it happen."

"We have to get you out of those clothes," Gilly said.

"What a complete hussy," Eliza whispered even as she smiled. "Zeh-Gaba might be a bit of a lesbian."

Gilly's eyes flashed blue. "I'm not the only one, bitch."

Colt helped Eliza out of her slacks. She sat back down in lacy white underwear. There was blood on her skin, red but drying. There were at least five holes from the shot, and that silver had gone deep. Smoke continued to rise from the wounds.

Eliza looked away. "Golly. I've never been so hurt. But I should heal. I hope I heal. Though…"

"She'll need blood," Bafflestone said. "And she'll need to rest. I don't expect Vincent Isaac will return, though he might have eyes on my house even now."

Eliza winced as Gilly touched her leg. "I would imagine we'd be up to our rear ends in vampires if that was the case. Hurry, Gilly. I might cry out, but it will be worth it."

Gilly was sweating and pale. "Things I never expected. Taylor Swift rerecording her songs. And performing surgery on my vampire friend."

"I'm glad we're friends," Eliza murmured. "Just hurry."

Gilly looked at the smoking holes and then shook her head. "I don't think I can. Colt, can you?"

Colt didn't pause. He pulled the silver shot out of each of the wounds.

Eliza twisted in pain and at one point seemed to pass out, but soon the wounds were closing on their own.

Eliza's skin was turning gray. Her veins appeared black. She'd been thin before, but now she seemed withered. When she opened her mouth, her canines had lengthened into fangs. Her eyes, normally such a nice brown color, had turned black. She looked like a creature of the night. "I can't ask you for what I need. But I have to have it. You know what I'm saying."

Gilly exchanged glances with Colt. The girl was afraid.

Colt wasn't. "Fuck it."

He turned Eliza to face him.

Eliza's black eyes were laser-focused on his neck.

Colt's muscles flexed as he balanced himself on the chair. He slid his neck right in Eliza's face. It was the same shoulder that the vampire had already bitten him on.

She latched onto him.

The fangs slid into his skin, and she was licking his neck, sucking on it, and it felt good. No, it felt great. He'd liked kissing, necking, making out before, but this was like sex, it was so blissful. He was rock hard in a second.

Part of it was the sensation of Eliza licking and sucking on his neck. Another was the noises she was making, moaning, groaning, full of lust and passion. Eliza was shy—she was a literal schoolmarm from another century—but this woman writhing underneath him was anything but reserved.

Colt found himself between her legs, pushing his cock against those lacy white panties. He wanted to rip off her underwear and stick his shaft into her slit.

Colt was getting light-headed. Part of him didn't care.

Was she turning him into a vampire? Well, he was already home to the god of rage and destruction. What was a little more supernatural weirdness in the end?

No, she wasn't going to turn him. She couldn't. She wasn't the god of blood and darkness, and she wasn't an alpha vampire, so he'd be fine.

As long as she didn't take his heart's blood.

He knew she wouldn't. She'd sworn not to kill.

She pushed him gently back. But then she gripped his ass and pressed her yearning sex against his.

She gazed up into his face. She was open and vulnerable. Her eyes were big and brown again, so wide and trusting. They were innocent in a way. But the rest of her face was smeared with his blood, which was the very opposite of innocent. That corrupted soul, mixed with those bright, trusting eyes, made him fall in love with her a little.

In a lot of ways, Eliza and Gilly were so alike.

He watched as her hair went from the dyed brown back to its bright blond color. Her lips grew red and plump. She smiled sadly, showing her bright, white teeth—back to being human.

This fucking girl was the master of the sad smile. "Thank you, Colt. You're a swell fella."

Colt didn't make the joke about him being swole. She wouldn't get it.

Gilly stood back, eyes wide, nipples hard. The runes on her forearm were as bright as the blush on her face. "Wow. That was. That was hot. I kinda want a turn. I mean, next time. What did it feel like, Colt?"

Colt stared into Eliza's eyes. "It felt like one of the best kisses of my life, and we didn't even kiss."

"I definitely want to try it," Gilly whispered.

Colt reached for his throat, expecting to feel wounds there. All he felt was skin, dry and intact. Even the wound on his shoulder was gone.

Eliza saw his confusion. "My spit heals wounds like that."

Bafflestone cleared his throat. "Yes, uh, well. I don't mean to ruin the moment, but I doubt you want me leering at you. Us Tomte have been known to rub noses every now and again, but we certainly don't do it in public, and we don't do it groups. So…"

"Oh, yes, I'm so very sorry." Eliza rose but faltered, and Colt had to catch her. Her skin was warm, she looked pink and healthy, and those big, brown eyes fixed on him. This wasn't her hypnotic ability. This was something else.

Gilly kept her bow. "Thanks so much, Mr. Bafflestone."

"Barney," the gnome said. "We both are up to our knees in this business. Might as well be on a first-name basis."

Bafflestone found Colt another set of clothes. Some vampire guy was going to be missing another outfit. The Tomte engineer babied the hand with the broken fingers. "Don't worry about my hand. I have a doctor I'll call. But take the Gaia Orbs. Before I got attacked, I was able to make some adjustments." The gnome tucked both orbs into a leather satchel.

Colt didn't like the idea of leaving the little guy. "Are you sure you'll be okay?"

Bafflestone waved him on. "Yes, mister. This wasn't my first beating."

"But it will be your last," Colt said forcefully.

Bafflestone grinned. "Let's hope so. Now, ye and missies need to get out of here."

Eliza lifted out the bloodwax candle. "Do you need this?"

"No, missy. Ye take it. Mr. Isaac is done with me. But I would imagine he's just started with ye."

Eliza kissed his cheek. "I wish I could heal your fingers. I wouldn't know where to start."

"I'll heal them on my own," Bafflestone said with a weary smile.

Eliza stowed the candle in the satchel and slung it over a shoulder.

Then Gilly kissed the little guy's other cheek. "Thank you, Barney, for everything."

Colt waved goodbye.

"Sorry about the note, Colt," the gnome said.

"Don't feel bad." Colt said the words, but he felt terrible about losing some last words from his grandfather. "If I'm meant to read it, it'll happen."

"I hope it does." Bafflestone said.

Colt and the two women hurried out of Bafflestone's house and raced through the park. Taking the back ways, they were able to make it out of Firestone Alley, dodging constables and anyone else that might mark them.

Colt still felt eyes on him. He figured that Isaac's people were letting them go. For one, they didn't have a weapon that was going to stop Colt. Yes, vampires might be able to bite him, but if a bloodsucker got close, he'd pull off their heads.

No, Vincent Isaac would wait to attack Colt once he had the Fate Blade. The vampire lord was probably already on his way back.

Outside, under the stars, Colt found his truck next to the shack. He'd expected to find the vehicle destroyed, but that wasn't the case. The stars above seemed as frigid as the snowbanks on the ground. The freeway was full of roaring traffic.

Colt started his truck with Gilly riding shotgun. Eliza was in the jump seat behind her. Eliza glanced fearfully at the eastern horizon.

"There's a blanket back there," Colt said."

Eliza grabbed it and threw it over her head, just in case.

They didn't talk much the entire way home.

Colt pulled into the driveway.

The sunrise was only a few minutes away. Everything inside his house looked in order. There were no broken windows, the door was closed, the windows were dark.

The only thing out of the ordinary was the FoodWheel woman, who was parked in front of his house.

She got out. "Hey, Colt, uh, I have a box of Voodoo Donuts for you. I got paid extra to wait because I have a message for you from Aunt Jewel. Wanna hear it?"

CHAPTER TWENTY-NINE

Colt slammed his truck door. He inhaled the cold night air. The Sir Car-A-Lot's neon sign buzzed off. The early morning train, on its way to the airport, clattered past the back of his house.

Gilly and Eliza waited in the car. Colt didn't want them going inside, just in case Vincent Isaac and more of his vampires were in there.

Colt crunched through the snow to get to the FoodWheel woman.

Mrs. MILF handed him a box of donuts. She read off her phone. "You can leave a note on orders, and this one was a doozy. It said to tell Colt that the bastard emptied out the cabinet and got the thing but left everything else alone. The bastard has a note, but she couldn't read it. She would've done something but couldn't. Because she can order food but can't do much else. She'll talk to you tonight."

Colt nodded. "Thanks."

Mrs. MILF put her hand on her hip. "Aren't you going to tell me anything? I mean, it was quite the message. Do you have any idea what's in the note?"

"I don't," Colt said.

The FoodWheel woman nodded. "Okay. I just wanna know if everyone is okay."

"Everyone is okay," Colt said. "For now. What are you doing up so early?"

She smiled. "I'm a terrible sleeper, and my insomnia doesn't pay me a cent. So I drive for FoodWheel. And I like how mysterious your house is."

"Why is my house so mysterious?" he asked.

She nodded. "I'm surprised this is zoned for residential. It's mostly machines shops, warehouses, and storage facilities. And the Sons of Italy. I love that place."

"So you've been to the Sons?" Colt asked.

She flashed a grin. "Sometimes. Funny that I haven't seen you there. Anyway, I have to run. But enjoy the donuts."

Mrs. MILF got in her car and drove off.

Colt had to wonder about the FoodWheel driver. Now that he knew there was this whole secret world, how many times had he encountered the Monstra without knowing it?

"Okay, girls, it's safe to go inside." He motioned to the door.

Eliza and Gilly got out of the car, both a little spooked.

Colt led the way inside.

Eliza rushed past him, the leather satchel hanging off a shoulder. "I'll be in the basement. Can you throw me down some matches? I'll light the bloodwax candle. It will keep us safe."

Colt knew that was the truth. He'd experienced the force field firsthand.

"I'll help." Gilly grabbed some matches off the counter.

Both girls clomped down the steps.

Colt put the box of donuts on the kitchen table. He couldn't stop himself from grabbing a Fruit Loops donut and taking a bite. He ate while he texted Ernie about the old guy's Aunt Sophia. She'd had heart surgery over the weekend. She was doing well. As for Ernie's pets, they were being taken care of by people from the Sons of Italy. For now, things were okay with Ernie.

He marched upstairs into his grandfather's room, which was

still a disaster, but the filing cabinet was open. Bouncing across the bed, he looked inside. It was empty. Fucking Victor Isaac had taken everything.

Colt couldn't believe their luck. He went back to the kitchen.

Gilly came walking up the steps from the basement. "Well, we have the bloodwax candle keeping us safe. Thank goodness. Eliza said that it will burn for months, if not years. We're not sure who lit the candle in the temple in the first place. Eliza doesn't know, and neither does Zeh. Kind of a mystery."

"Just one of many," Colt said.

Gilly nodded. "You're not wrong. Eliza doesn't think Vincent Isaac is going to come after us. Not during the day. He might have the Fate Blade, but it's going to be a bright, sunshiny Colorado day."

Gilly walked into his arms, and he held her. He'd just finished his donut, but he was going to need another one.

She leaned back to look up into his face. "So, uh, I have work and classes today. At this point, it's not even worth trying to sleep. In fact, it's probably a bad idea."

Colt grinned. "It is. If you can't get at least three hours, it's better to go without. We sleep in ninety-minute cycles. You need two cycles to do anything."

Gilly's eyes brightened. "That's right! I thought I was the only person to ever go sleepless rather than sleep a little."

"Nope. Aunt Jewel talked about that all the time." He paused. "It's weird. I would've been so worried about her if she hadn't been a ghost. But now she can't be hurt anymore. I would hope that she'd get better at her Gaia Unum so she could be around more. She's so great."

"I'm sorry you lost her." Gilly sighed. "I just hope we make it. This Fate Blade sounds bad."

Colt shrugged. "At least it's not the Fate Bullet. Vincent is going to have to get close to me. If he does, I'll kill him."

"What about that smoke thing?" Gilly asked.

Colt shrugged. "You and Eliza will just have to watch my

back." He glanced at the microwave clock. "I have to go work soon. Want to have some coffee and a couple of donuts with me? They're Voodoo Donuts."

Gilly got a dizzy smile on her face. "That's the sexiest thing I've ever heard in my life. Yes to the Voodoo Donuts. Yes to everything."

"That's what I like to hear," Colt laughed. "Yes to everything."

Gilly pushed her glasses up her nose. "We have to talk about that." Her eyes weren't flashing blue. Nor were the runes on her forearms. This was serious, and she wasn't feeling sexy. Colt could feel the weight in the air.

She got the coffee started.

He sat down at the table and surveyed the donut explosion in the pink box. He was going to have to go with the chocolate éclair-looking thing.

Gilly poured them coffee and sat across from him. Less than a week of having her around, and it felt so natural. She filled up his house with such love and laughter. That morning, though, she seemed nervous.

"What's up?" Colt asked.

Gilly sipped her coffee. She wasn't grabbing a donut. She was frowning, and there was a furrow in her brow.

"What happened to 'yes to everything?'" Colt asked.

"I'm hoping you'll say yes." Gilly set her coffee on the table. "So, I've been calling my parents, you know, to let them know I'm okay. I still live with them, which isn't ideal. But until all of this trouble passes, this is the only place I'm going to feel safe. They asked about you, and I had to tell them that yes, I have a boyfriend. But are we boyfriend-slash-girlfriend?" Gilly cast her eyes down. "You don't have to answer that. We don't need to have the big 'relationship' talk."

She used air quotes. Normally, Colt might've found that annoying. With her, he found it cute.

"I get it," he said. "We have the bloodwax candle. This place is a sanctuary. And we won't be truly safe until we fucking kill

Vincent Isaac or snap the Fate Blade or both. You can stay here, Gilly. You can move in. I love having you here. More than that…" He found himself dangerously close to saying he loved her. It was probably too soon.

But she'd heard the next part, whether he wanted her to or not. "More than what?"

Colt felt the anger burn. This time, it was anger toward himself. He was being a coward. Grandpa Walt and Aunt Jewel hadn't raised him to be a coward. "More than that, Gilly, I love you."

She didn't move. She didn't say a word. Colt's heart fell. Being pissed off was a lot easier than being vulnerable. He wasn't a coward, but he might've just made a critical mistake. Saying "I love you" too soon in a relationship was death. And five days into a relationship was far too soon.

At the same time, he and Gilly had been through some shit together.

Gilly slowly took off her glasses.

Colt squinted against the incoming pain. He figured Gilly would tell him that he was moving too fast, or she would back away awkwardly, or she'd take off in a rush.

Instead, her voice cracked as she said, "And I love you too, Colt. You're handsome, sure, and I like how strong you are, both inside and out. You stay at a job you hate just so other people will have work. You helped out your friend Ernie with his animals. You made it through so much hardship and death without losing your spark. And hey, if Aunt Jewel loves you, I kinda have to love you back." Tears trickled down her cheeks.

Colt felt his heart soar. He felt like he might explode with happiness. He found himself laughing. "Jewel would say I was family. She had to love me a little."

Gilly dried her eyes with a napkin. "Yeah, you have to love family, but you don't have to like them. I know that from my parents and how they deal with our relatives. But your aunt both likes and loves you. Present tense."

Colt went over and knelt beside her. He took her hand. "We're in this crazy adventure together, Gilly. You can stay as long as you want. And let's be boyfriend and girlfriend."

She smiled impishly. "Or are we god-friend and goddess-friend? I think that's probably closer to the truth. And I'm just fine with that. This is me talking. Zeh-Gaba didn't try to get control of the reins even once. It's me here."

"Hello, me," Colt said.

"Hello, you," Gilly whispered. Then she knelt on the floor with him. Her arms went around his neck. Her lips found his.

She had a little coffee breath, but that would never stop him from kissing Gillian Hermione Croft. Never.

Their kiss deepened. At that moment, Colt didn't care about work, or the fact that if he was late, he might get fired. All he cared about was kissing this woman.

But it wasn't just one woman. It was two.

Zeh-Gaba went to push him back, but Colt simply picked her up and set her down on the chair. Zeh smiled, blue eyes blazing. "Your Gaia Cores will be ready for the next rune soon. You have done well, Colt Holliday, in this fight. You couldn't have known the Fate Blade was here. No one knew. In this, Vincent Isaac got lucky. But luck is a fickle whore who eventually eats those she fucks. Do not fear. The vampire lord will not attack during the day. He will wait for night. Even then, you have the bloodwax candle to keep you safe."

"I'm not afraid," Colt said.

Zeh appraised him. "The vampire in the basement—I watched you give her your blood. She wants you, even though she can't admit that to herself. She would gain in power, as would you. This path you are on will require more than one woman. You do understand that, don't you?"

"I understand. I know you are up for anything. Luck isn't the only whore around here. But I wonder about Gilly."

Zeh smiled. "Oh, this little virgin? She won't be a virgin long. You need not fear. The depths of her lust and imagination are staggering. But she wouldn't want me to say more, and while this is strange, and while my hold on her wanes, I don't mind. For me to enjoy the fucking, she must enjoy the fucking. Just as Urgu enjoys your rage and destruction. You will be victorious, Colton Holliday."

The bright blue eyes faded until it was Gilly, squinting at him. She found her glasses. "I would've taken control, but I do like a chatty goddess. I caught most of what she said. Some of it was a little fuzzy."

"Did you hear the part about the harem?" Colt asked gently.

Gilly rolled her eyes. "She didn't say harem exactly. But yeah, I did. I also get the feeling that Urgu is far more powerful than Zeh, like exponentially more powerful. You'll need more runes as you grow in power."

"I need more runes just so I can stay in control longer," Colt said. "But you're fine with this situation?"

Gilly picked up a big maple bar with bacon bits on it. "Yeah." She took a huge bite.

"You're fine with me having sex with other women?"

Gilly chewed and swallowed. "Uh, yeah. And I'll be right there with you. Remember how I said I wasn't a lesbian? I'm not. But I'm super bisexual. And let me tell you, watching you grind on Eliza? That was one of the hottest moments of my life. Like I said, I want a turn. We can be bloodbonded, or whatever."

Colt smiled, remembering how it felt to be pressing himself against Eliza while she sucked on his neck.

Gilly pointed at him. "Now that is a goofy smile."

Colt picked up a chocolate glazed donut, raised and yeasty. It was Jewel's favorite. "You caught me. Are you sure? Are you just not the jealous type?"

"It's more…" Gilly paused. "It's more that I'm curious about everything when it comes to sex. Zeh wasn't wrong about any of that. And I trust that you'll not hurt me. We'll talk things through. And I have to say, I really like having Eliza around." Gilly opened her mouth, then closed it.

"What?" Colt asked.

"It's like the threesome I had with Maddy and Jack. I liked it. I must be polyamorous. Until it went to shit, I really thought a threesome would've worked for me." Gilly licked her fingers clean. "Maybe not with Eliza. She seems like she's pretty troubled still about losing her girlfriend from so long ago."

"I think it was something before that. Something happened when she turned that really hurt her." Colt recalled that she had killed only once—she'd drunk someone's heart blood only one time. And she was never going to do it again.

Colt gave the clock another glance. "I can't believe I'm saying this, but I have to go to work. I'm going to text you every hour, okay?"

Gilly nodded. "Yes. Every hour. I'll respond, and I have Eliza's phone number, and so we can do a group chat. I'm going to stay away from shadowy places, and I'm going to keep the bow and arrow in the car. We can get through the day, I think. But what about tonight?"

"The sun sets around five," Colt said. "Let's meet back here as close to five as possible. I'll get off work early. Can you get here by then?"

"I can."

Gilly stood, and they kissed one last time.

Colt opened the door to the basement. He saw the flickering light. "Eliza, we're going to text you today to make sure you're all right."

"Golly, Colt, but I don't know how to text."

Just like Ernie. Colt winced. "You can answer your phone, right? If I call?"

"I believe so. Would you call me?"

Gilly laughed. "I'll go down there and give her a lesson."

It was going to be a tense day regardless. But they had the bloodwax candle. His house was now a fortress.

After Gilly gave Eliza her texting lesson, one that Ernie might need at some point, the goddess girl and Colt left the house and got into their cars. They pulled away at the same time.

Colt and Gilly took off at the same time.

Colt kept glancing in his rearview mirror. That little blue house meant the world to him.

When he parked in front of the United Shipping & Post building, he saw a black limo with tinted windows out front. It put a bad feeling in his belly.

Colt had the surprise of his life when he walked through the doors of the warehouse. The district manager, Jameson Astor, stood in the shadows near the corner. Next to him was a man in a black suit and a huge black coat. He had gray hair and a perfectly unlined face. In his black leather gloves, he gripped a black hat with a wide brim as well as a black scarf.

Vincent Isaac's eyes glowed silver.

Jameson waved him over. "Hello, Colt. There's an old friend of the family here to talk to you. Take as long as you want."

Colt approached the pair cautiously.

Isaac smiled, eyes glowing silver. "Yes, Colt. I knew your grandfather. You and I have a lot to talk about."

CHAPTER THIRTY

It was easy for Colt to get angry. All he had to do was focus on Vincent Isaac's sneer. This fucking guy had drunk the heart's blood of some woman at his party just to parade around his power. Isaac had beaten and tortured Bafflestone. Isaac had turned Eliza into a vampire, ruined her life, then imprisoned her. He'd kill her in two seconds if he had the chance.

Isaac would also kill him and Gilly to get at the gods possessing them.

He was a piece of shit.

The only thing keeping Colt from letting Urgu-Uku out of his cage was that he didn't want to kill anyone, and he didn't want to piss off the Umbra Alliance. However much of a badass the Rage King was, Mr. Gentleman seemed up to the task of fighting him.

Colt was glad he was wearing his coat. His sleeves covered the runes. He kept a fair bit of distance between them. If Isaac leapt out to stab his chest, Colt wanted room to maneuver.

Urgu grumbled. *Why are you always worrying about property damage? The world longs to burn. Here is your enemy! I promise I will only kill him and leave your precious warehouse alone.*

That was a lie. Urgu was still longing to hurl cars into trains. Colt could get behind that idea. But he needed to stay strong.

Jameson sniffed the air. "Does anyone else smell burning hair?"

"It's fine. You can go, Mr. Astor." Isaac waved the man away.

Jameson wandered off.

Isaac tried to catch Colt in his hypnotic gaze.

But Colt was channeling the power of a god right then. "Your tricks aren't going to work on me, asshole."

"But you did know I had to try." Isaac lifted his chin. "You know, Colt Holliday, I knew your grandfather. I knew he was collector. His house is very shabby given his connections to the Leyfolk. I am surprised at the state of his affairs."

"He's dead. I'm alive. Don't fuck with me." Colt's hands were fists. Could he trust that the video cameras around the warehouse would malfunction like they had last time? He couldn't risk it. Besides, Phyllis, Marcy, and Andy were watching him out of the corner of their eyes.

"You do know I have a weapon that will free you, do you not?" Isaac asked.

"The Fate Blade. Yes, I know."

"Such luck that I found it. According to the note he left for you, your grandfather had a unique connection to both Firestone Alley and the Fate Blade. How that can be is a mystery. But you aren't a mystery, Mr. Holliday. You must know your life can't go on like normal. Here you are, at your place of employment, when someone is actively trying to kill you. That shows a lack of imagination."

"Or a keen sense of responsibility." Colt was relaxing. He could feel Urgu wanting to take control, but Colt could still crack jokes.

"Would you want to be free of Urgu-Uku?" Isaac asked. "I can do that for you. I can purify you on the Fate Blade, and you can return to your normal life. As can your little friend Gillian."

This was a bluff. Colt knew it to his core. He trusted Eliza far more than this bloodsucker. "You have to stab me in the heart.

While I've been called heartless before, I do have one. And I've grown attached to it."

Isaac nodded. "I can hear your heart beating. It's strong, and you have so much blood. I would think my dear Eliza must've fed off you or Miss Croft by now. You know her spittle has healing properties, however weak she is. Poor Eliza has always been such a wretched creature. I blame myself for that. She shouldn't have been turned at all, but what's done is done. You should've seen her when the blessing took hold. She was so very bloodthirsty. Has she told you of her one and only kill?"

"Sure," Colt lied.

Isaac grinned, showing fangs. "No, she hasn't. She hasn't told anyone. It's her great shame. I saw it, though. I know exactly what happened. It was glorious. But let's not get off track. I am an alpha, I am at the very top of the Order of the Night, save one, the one who blessed me. I could use my own spittle to heal your heart. I could release you from your fate. For the fate of Urgu-Uku will be tragic in the end. As it was before."

"So why do you want the Rage King riding shotgun in your soul?" Colt asked.

"I have resources you do not. And perhaps I don't mind tragedy, for I have had my share, and I have a taste for it. No, silly little human, you can't imagine the destruction that lies in store for you. For me? For someone like me? I have my plans. Oh, yes, I have my plans. As does the one who sent me." Isaac paused. "You don't happen to know where Eliza put those other crates? I would like very much to have them."

"I bet you would." Colt stared into those weird silver eyes. "If you're smart, you'll leave me alone. But you won't, will you?"

Isaac's eyes went from silver to a light gray, nearly colorless. "I can't. You have something that belongs to me. You can either give it back willingly, and I'll not bother you again, or you can die. Because if I have to take it, I will heal your heart, and then I will drain it dry."

Colt couldn't help but smile grimly. "Let's pretend you don't think I'm an idiot. You'd stab me in the heart, steal Urgu-Uku, and then try to guzzle me like a mojito."

Isaac lost his cool demeanor. "And a mojito is what?"

"It's a big glass of lime and fuck you." Colt squinted. "Are we done here? I don't think you'd risk attacking me here, and you can't hypnotize me, so there's not much else we need to discuss."

Isaac put on his hat. "I do miss a world with hats in it. For a long time, we had hats. And for a long time, it was easy to move among the humans of the world. True, the Monstra spent most of the time in the Gaia Towns spread out across the lands. And yet, we would leave our dens. We would go out to hunt at night, in the darkness of a moonless night, in the midnight streets of the Holy Roman Empire. The menfolk would huddle behind wooden walls that couldn't protect them. We ate our fill. They spoke of us with awe in their voices. Hiding was less important. For man's numbers were kept down by their wars and diseases."

Isaac's face lost all emotion. "It wasn't just the light of reason that pushed the Order of the Night back into Gaia Towns. It was the lights of whale oil lamps throwing a glow on rain-slick cobblestone London, where the air was black with coal dust from the factories. Man's numbers increased, their weapons increased, their science brought the elderly longer lives and took the young in rainstorms of machine-gun bullets. And now, with the power of the atom, they have ways of annihilating the Monstra. So we hide from the Brightest Light. And the Umbra Alliance will ensure that we will outlive the human filth. We won't wipe them out completely, we can't, for the Order of the Night must feed."

It was a long speech.

Colt couldn't say he got bored. Listening to someone a thousand years old, at least, was kind of captivating. He'd mentioned the Holy Roman Empire. What the hell?

But in the end, it didn't change shit. "So you want the Rage King to help you even out the human population. It's not going to happen. So don't fuck with me, Vince. It won't end well for you."

The vampire shrugged. "We shall see. Your days are yours.

When the sun shines, we will not go after you or your friend Gilly. And you have the bloodwax candle to keep Eliza safe in your little blue house. When night falls, however, when the sun leaves, we will come for you. We will kill you. I gave you a chance to save your own life, but you are too stupid to take it."

Isaac vanished into smoke. The black fog crept along the floor and then leaked through a heating duct. In seconds, he was gone.

Phyllis and Marcy drifted over. "Who was that guy, Colt?"

Colt's mind went blank for a second. What could he say? A creature of the night? A bloodsucker? A murderous bastard who wanted to jab a magic sword through Colt's heart? There was no good way to get out of this. So he went with the lie Isaac had hypnotized Jameson with in the first place. "He's a friend of my grandfather's. Old customer. Like, really old."

"He was kind of sexy." Marcy waggled her eyebrows.

"A little old for you, Marcy," Phyllis teased.

"You have no idea," Colt muttered.

Phyllis smiled at him. "There's something different about you, Colt. I can't quite put my finger on it. Ever since the accident last week, there's just something different."

Marcy rolled her eyes. "It's because we don't have those assholes making our lives difficult. I don't mean to speak ill of the dead, but those guys were assholes."

Phyllis winced. "You are speaking ill of the dead, Marcy."

"I am, aren't I?" the other said, batting her eyelashes.

Colt laughed. "Let's just get to work."

The day started, and it was a flurry of everyday bullshit. After his weekend of exploring hidden worlds and fighting vampires, ordinary felt strangely good.

Jameson didn't say another word to Colt. The district manager just worked in his office.

Colt could focus on work because he believed Isaac—the vampires wouldn't attack them during the day.

But once the sun set? Colt didn't think Isaac would wait long to come after him, now that he had the Fate Blade. That gave Colt some power. If he could set up an ambush, lure Isaac in, he could end things that night.

Colt didn't want the threat of murder hanging over his head every single night. Not for him and not for Gilly.

All that day, he, Gilly, and Eliza texted to make sure they were all safe. Colt didn't mention Isaac's visit. There was no way to summarize it easily.

When Colt punched out of work that night, the sun was just disappearing down behind the Rocky Mountains to the west. The world was still full of light, and would be for a little while longer. Colt was relieved to see Gilly's car parked in front of his house.

He pulled into the driveway and saw Gilly and Eliza in his kitchen, talking. Both were out of direct sunlight.

He wasn't coming home to an empty house. He would walk in there and be greeted by two gorgeous women, one who loved him, and one who wanted to love him.

Eliza needed time, maybe a lot of time, and Colt would give it to her.

He banged out of his truck and walked around the back. He pushed through the back door.

Gilly smiled. "Made it here safe, I see. Hi, Colt." She was in jeans and a blouse.

Colt stood by the door, drinking in his blue-eyed beauty. "Hi, Gilly."

She stared back, a dizzy smile on her face.

The bloodwax candle flickered on the table. Every so often, a rune would appear on the wall, caught in the dance of flame. Bafflestone's leather satchel containing the two orbs sat next to Eliza's chair.

The vampire sighed. It sounded heartbroken. "Golly, you two. Just get a room already." She'd changed from Jewels old clothes to the green wool jacket and skirt he'd first met her in.

Colt put his stuff down and took off his jacket. "We can't leave to get a hotel room. Or to get dinner. We'll have to order in Food-Wheel. Denver Biscuit Company."

Gilly came over to him and grabbed his hand. "You just think Mrs. MILF is cute."

Colt squeezed her hand. "I believe the word is sexy. Cute is for a younger woman. But you, Gillian Hermione Croft, you're more in the dangerously beautiful category."

Gilly kissed his hand. "It's the ancient goddess of lust in me."

Eliza gasped.

At first, Colt thought it was Vincent Isaac, coming to attack them.

Then he saw the tears. Eliza was sobbing quietly in her chair. She looked up with tear-stained cheeks. "Seeing your love, it makes me want to be a part of it. But I can't…not until I tell you the truth about me. Not until I confess all my sins."

The timing wasn't perfect, but Colt wasn't about to stop their vampire from unburdening her heart.

CHAPTER THIRTY-ONE

Colt and Gilly sat down at the table with Eliza. They were on one side, and Eliza was on the other. It felt like a job interview or a courtroom tribunal. That wasn't the vibe Colt wanted.

The leather satchel holding the Gaia Orbs lay against the wall. The flap was open, and Colt saw a green light glowing there. Even from a distance, he knew his Rune Genesis Status was set to "go." That was very good news indeed.

Still, he didn't want to stay in the kitchen. "Let's go into the living room. We can bring the candle. We can talk. We want to hear about your life, Eliza."

Gilly gave Colt a nervous glance.

Colt found himself feeling anxious as well. He thought this confession would be about her turning, but what if it wasn't? What if her sins went deeper?

They got up from the table and moved into the living room. The candle flickered on the coffee table. If things had been different, Colt would've built a fire in the fireplace. But Eliza couldn't wait that long.

"What's going on, Eliza?" Gilly asked. She was on the couch next to Colt. The vampire sat in the easy chair.

The vampire held a lacy handkerchief in her hand. She dabbed at her nose. "All day long, I've been thinking about things. Being intimate with…with Colt." She shuddered. "It wasn't intimacy. It was feeding. I fed on him. I hoped he liked it." She caught Colt up in her gaze. "I liked it, too, to be honest. I liked feeling you on me. It's been so long since I've been with a man. Before, with Ruth…" Eliza closed her eyes. She looked so anguished.

"I'm so sorry about her," Gilly whispered.

"We've talked about Ruth." Eliza raised her eyes. "You look like her, Gilly. I probably didn't say that before. It might come off odd. I'm old enough to be your grandmother several times over."

Gilly squeezed her eyes shut. Her arms glowed. "You don't want to know what Zeh thinks about that. Sure, you're a hundred and fifty-seven years old, but you don't look a day over twenty."

"That was when I was turned."

Colt got angry. "I saw Vincent Isaac today. He used the word 'blessed.' He's an asshole."

"What?" Gilly slapped Colt's leg. "You saw Isaac? Why didn't you tell us?"

Colt shrugged. "It didn't come up. And there was no way to really tell you over texting without freaking you out. Let me tell you now." He quickly summarized his conversation.

Eliza looked even more devastated. "It wasn't a blessing. It killed me without killing me. It gave me a living death. Not like in the stories or the movies, I'm not a walking corpse, but what happened later, what happened with John, murdered whatever soul I had left."

"Who was John?" Gilly asked.

"He was…he was the friend of a distant cousin I had in Denver. It's all so different now. You wouldn't believe the change." Eliza motioned to the window at the dark streets. It was night. There might be vampires out there, watching them, waiting for them to leave.

"I can believe it. When did you come out from Kansas?" Gilly asked.

"In 1885. I was twenty years old. It was late in the summer, early autumn, and I'll never forget those warm days and cool nights."

Colt realized that Bafflestone had a similar story. He'd come to Denver from Kansas, but their experiences couldn't be more different.

Eliza continued. "It was so very exciting. In Denver, I lived with my distant cousin, and we went to dances held by local halls as I prepared to teach. That was where I met John Bennett. We fell in love. We were married at the end of November. Our Thanksgiving had been jolly, and we were already decorating for Christmas. I avoid the holiday season now. The festivity and decorations only bring me pain. We hadn't been married even a month before I was attacked. We had a small house. We were walking home from a party. The streets were so dark back then. The smell of warm horses was in the air. This was before cars, you see, and we were out in the country, outside the city proper."

Eliza went quiet for several long moments. "Forgive me. This is difficult, more difficult than you can ever imagine. I told Ruth this story, but only the one time, and she told me to forget it. But I can't. I'll never forget."

"Take all the time you need," Gilly said.

Colt nodded. "Yeah. We have the bloodwax candle. We're safe."

"Safety is an illusion," Eliza said in a dull voice. "I thought I was safe. I was with John. But he was knocked unconscious. A figure appeared out of the darkness, and it took me. Right there in the ditch beside the road, full of snow and ice. I smelled the dried mud and the cold. I smelled the thing on me. It was horrible, pinning my arms down with such strength. It wanted me, you see, because John and I had just been…intimate. Prey tastes best—has the most power—after coitus."

Gilly smiled at the old-fashioned word.

Colt was too pissed off.

"I liked it," Eliza whispered. "He smelled so good. He felt so good between my legs, at my throat, like you this morning, Colt. But not like that at all. Because he was taking everything from me. Everything at all. He nearly drained me. Then he bit into his wrist, and he gave me his blood to drink. He said that I was special. He said he'd met me at a dance, and right away he knew I had a grand destiny as his greatest daughter. I didn't know what any of that meant. I still don't. All I knew, I had blood in my mouth, and that I had been violated to my core. Not sexually. But in every other way possible."

Colt had to stand up. He couldn't sit there. He smelled his hair smoldering. He walked to the edge of the living room and thought about punching walls. Because he knew where this was heading.

Urgu's voice was quiet. *It is the way of the Order of the Night. It is a destruction of the soul rather than the flesh, and I find it boring. All will pass away in the end. Might as well die in fire and carnage.*

Colt couldn't argue there. Perhaps dying would've been better for Eliza than what had happened to her.

"What's wrong, Colt?" Eliza asked breathlessly.

"I'm so fucking angry. John took you home. You were sick after that. You'd lost most of your blood. You were on your way to becoming a vampire, but you couldn't have known that. You called the doctor, didn't you?"

Colt turned to face her.

Eliza's lips quivered. She couldn't answer. She dropped her head to weep.

Gilly's eyes begged Colt for help. But he couldn't do a thing. He might have the god of rage inside of him, but he couldn't time travel. All he could do was avenge Eliza for what Vincent Isaac had done to her.

Eliza didn't hide her sorrow. She spoke through her grief. "I woke up on the third day, when the sun went down. I could feel the sunset. I could feel the buzzing of the Ley Lines where I-70 and I-25 cross now, but back then, they were little country roads. My husband came to me. I remember hearing his heart thudding.

I could smell it. I could smell his blood. The vampire was gone, but I could feel him as well. Vincent Isaac was outside, skulking in the shadows. He could've stopped me, but that wasn't his plan. He waited for me to…"

Colt could've finished that story. But part of him knew that it was important for Eliza to finish the tale for herself. To say the words.

Eliza stared into the past. Her brown eyes were blank. "I was too hungry. This instinct to feed came over me. The first time is always the most intense, or I learned that later at any rate. I didn't even see John as John right then. He was just…prey. I didn't know what I was doing. I ripped open his throat. I drank him, every bit of him. I drank his heart's blood. I remember waking up…hours later…against the wall, with him lying there in front of me. He looked like he was sleeping. But he was dead. And I killed him."

She cried out, tortured by the memory. She fell to the floor and knelt there. Gilly went to hold her, and then Colt held them both. He knew that the moment would bind them together forever. They would beat Vincent Isaac. Colt would break the Fate Blade. And then they would all live in the house together. This wasn't just about sex. This was about love. It was about fate.

Vincent Isaac thought he could sever their destinies with the Fate Blade, but Colt wasn't going to let that happen. The very thought of anyone hurting those two women made him change forms. He burst out of his clothes. His arms thickened into unstoppable muscles. The runes on his forearms gleamed like two red suns. Now he could easily hold both women.

Gilly clung to one arm. Eliza clung to the other.

Colt didn't trust himself to keep that form for too long because Urgu wanted to go rip apart the Monstra world and tear Vincent Isaac's intestines out of his fucking thrashing body.

His shape-shifting had surprised Eliza so much that she stopped crying.

Colt slowly turned human. His fire had heated up the room.

They all wound up sitting on the floor. Colt and Gilly had their back to the couch. Eliza sat across from them. "Vincent Isaac gathered me up before dawn. He said that he had tried to get to me before I did the horrible thing. He's a lying sack of shit."

In her crisp accent, those last words sounded so funny that Colt had to smile.

Gilly laughed. "Yes. He's terrible. But you were vulnerable, Eliza. You were traumatized. He took advantage of that, he engineered that, so fuck him. And forgive yourself."

A specter of doubt flashed across her face. "That's the trick of it, isn't it? Letting the past go and forgiving oneself."

"It's like that for me," Gilly said. "Colt knows about my story. I lost control one night and did some things I loved, but then stuff happened. I had to forgive some other stupid people, but I also had to forgive myself."

Colt nodded. "Me too. I've done things I'm not proud of." His anger had hurt people before. And he'd had to forgive stupid people as well.

Eliza blinked. "Thank you. Just. Thank you."

Colt got to his feet and started picking up pieces of his ruined clothing. "Let me get dressed a bit. This raging out is going to cost me a fortune in clothes."

He put on a shirt and some socks.

When he came back out, Gilly and Eliza were drinking wine and talking.

Colt stopped to take them in. Eliza was feeling better, and Gilly's eyes sparkled. She put down her wineglass and stood up.

"Colt, if we're going to fight Vincent Isaac tonight, we need another rune. I want us to be together. I've never felt closer to anyone in my life. To you. And to Eliza." She gave the vampire a long look.

Colt realized his life was about to change forever. Sex, actual sex with Gillian Hermione Croft, was going to bind him to her permanently. Knowing her, knowing her character, the idea didn't bother him one bit.

He could understand Gilly's desire. But Eliza wasn't leaving.

CHAPTER THIRTY-TWO

After the tears that Eliza cried there, Colt's living room felt sacred.

"We should close the curtains," Eliza mumbled.

"I don't care about the curtains." Gilly started to unbutton her blouse with trembling fingers. "I don't care about anything. I want this, Colt. I want to feel you inside me."

Eliza still stood and closed the curtains.

And Colt suddenly had Gilly in his arms. His hands fell to the soft skin of the goddess girl's back. He could feel muscles there. Lower down, though, there were her squeezably soft hips and ass.

Gilly's mouth was hungry on him. This wasn't Zeh-Gaba. This was the girl herself. She smelled a little musky after her long day of work and classes, but her perfume was still sweet.

Colt wanted to feel the bare skin of her ass, but her jeans were too tight.

Gilly knew what he wanted. With her lips on his, she unzipped her jeans and pushed them down.

Colt grabbed her hard and cupped one of her big, soft butt cheeks. He pushed his hard cock up against her body.

Her little hands went to his shirt to tug it off him.

Colt took it off himself. He felt her bare skin on his, except for that damn bra. He got it unclipped and Gilly shouldered it off.

Colt knelt down and took one of her nipples into his mouth. It hardened as she gasped. His hand found her other tit, which fit his hand perfectly.

They heard a gasp.

He turned to see Eliza there in her wool suit and skirt. The coat was unbuttoned some, as was her shirt, to reveal a lacy bra. Her big, brown eyes were bright. Her red lips were hanging open. Colt wasn't sure he'd ever seen such a horny woman, except maybe for Gilly. He could hardly remember the name of his old girlfriend. What was it? Pam something?

Gilly caressed Colt's head. "Is it okay if we do this in front of you, Eliza? You can watch. I think it would be hot if you watched."

"You two are so beautiful together," Eliza whispered. "Will you think ill of me if I stay?"

Gilly laughed. "I was worried you'd think I was a slut if I wanted you to stay."

"Never, Gilly." Eliza looked like she might explode at any minute. "Can I maybe kiss you? And afterwards, after you climax, maybe I could…maybe." The shy vampire couldn't ask.

"You can drink from me," Gilly said softly. "I know I'll taste good."

Colt stood. "You taste good now." He gave the goddess girl a long, wet kiss, turning his head so Eliza could see them French kiss. He found the little bit of exhibitionism exciting.

Gilly still had jeans on, unbuttoned and hanging off her. She stripped them off, leaning on Colt while she did.

Colt thought about going back to his room, but he knew that wasn't going to happen. He was going to have sex in his living room. There was a first time for everything. Speaking of first times, he remembered that Gilly was a virgin. He'd have to be gentle with her.

Gilly sank to her knees. "I'm going to show you Colt's cock,

Eliza. It's really wonderful. I love how big it is. I love how it tastes. And I love his cum."

Gilly freed Colt from his pants. She pushed his jeans down his thigh so his sex was exposed to Eliza's gaze.

She put her hand on her chest. "Oh, my. He is big. It's only the second one I've ever seen."

Gilly wrapped her slender fingers around his thick shaft. She squeezed, and a dollop of pre-cum burst from the tip. She licked it off and then licked all around the head. "Do I look good licking his dick, Eliza? Do I look like a little cock-sucking slut?"

Eliza nodded, breathless.

Gilly was talking so dirty. She must've really embraced Zeh's lust.

Eliza pulled her jacket and shirt open more. More bra showed. Colt so wanted to see her tits. He wondered what her nipples looked like. Would she let him look at them?

Then Colt couldn't think because Gilly had his cock in her mouth. She sucked hard, and Colt had to close his eyes because of the intensity of the feeling. She was doing something with her tongue that made him want to explode.

And she knew it. Gilly stopped sucking and pulled his cock into the back of her throat. She made a slight choking sound before backing off. Her face was red. Spit hung from her chin.

Her hand made obscene sounds as she stroked him. "Zeh loves to help me with Colt. She offers suggestions because, if anything, the goddess of lust loved to suck cock. How do I look, Eliza? Do I look pretty on my knees?"

Again, Eliza nodded. Speechless.

Gilly got to her feet. She walked over to the vampire in only her white panties. "Can I kiss you, Eliza? You'll taste Colt's cock on my mouth, and you'll get your face all wet. But I think you're dirtier than you first let on. Zeh thinks so too. Zeh thinks you're a slut like me."

"Yes, you can kiss me, but I'm not a—"

The vampire's words were cut off. Because Gilly was kissing

her, nipping at Eliza's lips and then tonguing Eliza's surprised mouth. The vampire's face was soon as wet as Gilly's.

Gilly broke the kiss. "You kissed me, Eliza. Do you want to kiss Colt now? I think he'd like that."

Eliza nodded. Her cheeks were red with lust. "I'd like it too. I think I'm ready now."

Gilly motioned for Colt to come over.

He stripped off his pants and underwear. He was the only naked person in the room. He came in close to Eliza, and then took her gently into his arms. He felt her hips through her wool skirt.

He didn't break eye contact as he came in close. When she closed her eyes, he closed his. Eliza smelled perfect.

Then he was tasting her. And tasting Gilly.

Eliza sobbed.

At first, he didn't know why. Then he realized he was the first man she'd kissed since her husband over a century ago. She moaned into his mouth. She was breathing hard, and her skin was hot, sweaty even.

Gilly drew back, and Colt had the idea she was stripping out of her panties.

But he couldn't look to see what she was doing. He was too involved in Eliza, feeling her body against him. And inhaling her scent. When he offered her his tongue, she accepted it, and she made a sexy growling sound that made his cock even harder. There was just something magical about her, inhibited but sexy.

He felt her tongue exploring his mouth.

She gasped and fell against him. "It's too intense. It's too much." Then she gasped again. "Look."

Colt turned to see Gilly on the couch, her legs spread, with a finger gently sweeping across her clit. Her pussy was so much bigger at the top than it was at the bottom. Her thick lips shone with her juices.

Gilly was also playing with one of her nipples. "Watching you two kiss is so hot. But I like you watching me. Do you know what

I'd like more? Colt. Here." She pushed a finger into her pussy. She then took it and smeared her girl cum around her clit. Then she pushed two fingers into her horny hole. "Yes, I want Colt inside me. Can you help him, Eliza?"

"Golly," Eliza whispered. Sweat trickled down the side of her face. Her dress and blouse were even more undone, unbuttoned all the way. And yet, she still had that bra on. "Yes, I think so. I think I can help."

Eliza gently guided Colt over to the goddess girl on the couch.

It was strange—every guy fantasized about having sex with two women, but generally, it was together. Having Eliza there, and mostly dressed, was somehow hotter than if she'd been naked. Her wide eyes and heavy breathing made it better.

Colt knelt on the floor between Gilly's legs. "Are you sure?"

"Yes. Don't tease me. I'm close to coming, and I just want to feel you inside me. As deep as you can. I can't explain it. I just want it, Colt. I just want you to fuck me."

Colt brushed his big helmet up and down her lips, getting the tip all wet with her juices. Then he watched himself go into her. She was so warm. She felt so good. He was inside Gilly's pussy. He pushed in more until her lips were around his shaft. He climbed on top of her to really feel the depths of her.

Gilly let out a yelp. "Oh. Oh, Colt. You're so big in me. You're so big in my pussy. I'm gonna come. I'm gonna come on you."

Colt knew. In his Gaia Core, he could feel her getting closer and closer to coming. He could feel her pleasure, and it increased his own. He withdrew and thrust into her. That single thrust was all it took.

She arched up into him. Her sweaty tits were against his chest. He felt her pussy contracting around his manhood.

Waves of energy radiated out of her. The runes on her arms were glowing a bright blue. But there was a new light.

He looked down. There was a new rune on her chest, above her breast, over her heart. Her orgasm had created a new rune on her. But where was his rune?

"It feels so good, Colt," Gilly wept. "You on me. You in me. I love fucking more than anything."

"I'm glad. Because I love it too." He kissed her.

They felt the couch sink. He turned. Eliza was there, watching. Her brown eyes looked huge in her face. "I felt that. I don't know how, but I felt Gilly's climax."

"You felt me coming?" Gilly asked, surprised.

Eliza nodded.

"I might come again," Gilly said. "If you showed me your tits."

Colt's heart was in his throat.

Eliza's bra opened in the front. She unsnapped the clip. "I'm surprised you want to see my breasts. They aren't that big. But if it will bring you pleasure…maybe you'll be kind enough to give me some pleasure in return."

Colt could easily guess what that meant.

Eliza slowly opened her clothes to reveal two tiny titties with long, pink nipples—so cute, so perfect, that Colt immediately wanted to suck on them both.

He started working his cock in and out of Gilly again.

He nearly came when Eliza pulled on her nipples, getting them even harder. He was fucking Gilly, but he was looking at Eliza. And she seemed to be getting as turned on as they were from just watching.

Was Eliza a voyeur or an exhibitionist? Or was she just horny? Her eyes were so bright.

Colt thrust into Gilly, over and over, fucking her. He hadn't had sex in a long, long time. He needed to do this every day. The wet, warm bliss was this perfect feeling that he would never get bored of.

Eliza abruptly stood up and removed her panties. She sat back down in her skirt, but she wasn't about to just start masturbating in front of them. She was far too reserved for that. But she did get on her knees and brought her head close enough so the goddess girl could kiss her. But then, it wasn't going to be enough. "Can I drink from you, Gilly? I know you just climaxed, and I want to taste it."

Gilly leaned her neck back.

Eliza didn't pause. She latched onto it. And Colt couldn't see her throat, but he could see the look of ecstasy on Gilly's face. Her eyes sparkled. "Oh, I can feel her sucking. It feels…it feels amazing. Keep fucking me, Colt."

"Touch me," Eliza growled. "Rub me, Gilly. It's okay. I need it. I need to be touched so much."

Gilly reached out with her right hand, pawing through Eliza's clothes until she must've found the vampire's sex because Eliza inhaled violently. She was moving her slim ass, matching the rhythm of Gilly rubbing her.

Colt knew that with the energy in the air, there was no way he was going to be able to hold back. He was right. He slammed into Gilly one final time.

Then he felt the vampire with them. It was three souls on that couch, three bodies alive with Gaia Unum, drinking from the world.

Colt let out a single bark. Then his skin was on fire. His soul was on fire. His arms glowed red, but as with Gilly, the new rune appeared over his heart. He looked down to see the burning red lines forming, and he felt the increase in his Gaia. But a second later, something odd happened.

Eliza started grunting softly. Her left hand was on the back of the couch to give her some support while she fed off Gilly.

Eliza's orgasmic grunts matched the pulsating shine of a white rune appearing on the back of her left hand.

Colt felt an orgasm rush out of him, matching Eliza's blissful climax. And on his own left hand, another rune was appearing, as red as his other markings. It was too much. It felt so good, but it was also taxing his Gaia Core. It was too much.

Urgu laughed. *Perhaps there is something I enjoy more than murder, mutilation, and mayhem. Let us do this often, Colton.*

Colt didn't have time to respond. He was too busy passing

out. The last thing he remembered was slumping down onto the two women.

He woke up several minutes later with the two women bending over him. He was on the floor between the sofa and coffee table.

He blinked and raised his left hand. "Well, what doesn't kill you makes you stronger."

Eliza bent close and kissed him. She still had some blood on her face from feeding on Gilly.

Colt didn't care. Nor did the god of rage and destruction.

He kissed the vampire, and then Gilly was kissing them, and they all collapsed into giggles.

Colt was alive. He recalled what Bafflestone said—the more he had sex, the more his Gaia Core would be strengthened, but it would be harder to craft runes. He should enjoy the easy stuff while he could. Nevertheless, he couldn't wait to grab one of Bafflestone's globes to see the results.

First, they needed some dinner. Eliza might've feasted, but Colt and Gilly were still hungry. They would need the strength. They were probably going to face off with Vincent Isaac that very night.

Ready or not, Colt needed to finish things.

CHAPTER THIRTY-THREE

Colt decided not to order from FoodWheel. He didn't want Mrs. MILf to be caught up in the violence. Colt ended up in the kitchen with the vampire and the goddess girl. He and Gilly needed something to eat before they went to fight Vincent Isaac. Colt also wondered what Bafflestone's Gaia Orbs might reveal. He'd added two more runes, and the gnome had said he'd done some tweaking to the settings.

Colt stood in front of an open kitchen cabinet. "We have pasta. And I think we have spaghetti sauce. Maybe there's some ground beef in the freezer."

"That should be enough, right?" Gilly asked.

Colt pulled out his phone and looked up a recipe for quick spaghetti with meat sauce. He just had to hope those noodles weren't too old. Aunt Jewel would've bought them, so they were at least a year old.

A second later, a voice came from the living room. "Oh my God, two gods and a vampire cooking. It's kind of embarrassing. Just follow the instructions on the package for the noodles. Brown the meat and then add the spaghetti sauce. This isn't rocket science. It's pasta science."

Colt had to laugh. "Thanks for having our back, Jewel. You,

uh, didn't watch us from the great beyond, did you? We have to have some boundaries."

Jewel walked out into the dim light of the hallway. "I'm dead, kiddo. No interest in sex. And you're still my nephew, so, ew."

Eliza blushed. She was full of blood and power from feeding from Gilly and from the rune on her left hand. "Golly, but I'm afraid I won't be of any use at all. You two clever people should be able to handle it. I'll just watch."

Gilly's eyes glowed blue as she growled, "Like you did in the living room, you dirty, dirty girl?" She winced. "Sorry. Zeh had to tease you a little bit. It was wonderful. Really.

Eliza looked at the back of her left hand. "I forgot I could feel things like that. It's been a long time, toots. A very long time." She smiled.

Colt loved the look of hope on her face. Telling them her secret, and then the sex, had really helped Eliza relax into their little family. It was sweet.

Colt felt stronger than ever. Creating the two runes had knocked him out, but he was back and ready for a fight.

Gilly got a pot of water boiling while Colt browned the meat. Eliza leaned against the sink, gazing at the stove. "I've seen kitchens like this in the movies. But I never thought I'd be standing in one."

Gilly wrinkled her nose. "Do you mind cooking, Eliza? I'd really like to check out the globes with Colt."

"That sounds bully," Eliza said.

"That means cool in old-timey slang," Aunt Jewel called from the living room. "If you dim the lights, I can help the vampire cook."

Colt's life had become so very weird.

They dimmed the lights and Jewel appeared in the shadows in the corner. "Remember, Eliza, a watched pot never boils. But you should stir the meat."

"Yes. Stirring the meat, ma'am."

"Jewel is fine."

Colt and Gilly retrieved the orbs from the bag and set them on the kitchen table.

Gilly swallowed hard. "Do you want to go first? I'm feeling kind of nervous."

Colt picked up his orb, which was glowing red. That wasn't a surprise.

Urgu-Uku stood there in the crimson snow, a great muscled red man with yellow fire flickering on his head. There were four runes glowing—two on his forearms and one on his left hand. The brightest of the runes was the one over his heart.

Like before, text appeared on the outside of the glass, but it was different this time. Certain words glowed brighter than others.

<<<>>>

Gaia Orb for Urgu-Uku
Gaia Force Level: 4 (**Four New Updates Available. Update Abilities**?)
Rune Genesis Status: Red (Stop)
Body Progression:

- Unknown

Gaia Abilities:

- Strength I
- Invulnerability I
- **Update/Add New Ability**

Special Gaia Mutations:

- **Update/Add New Mutation**

<<<>>>

Colt touched the first bolded words. A new dialogue box appeared on the right, and it was written how Bafflestone spoke. He must've had some kind of speech-to-text technology.

<<<>>>

Colt, I was able to find a way for ye to have some choices when it comes to upgrading or adding abilities. It wasn't easy, not a garn bit, but like I said, Walt wasn't the only genius. Ye max out yer Strength, Invulnerability, and Endurance at Level III. Basically, Strength is gonna make ye bigger. Invulnerability will thicken yer skin. Then there's Endurance, which will allow ye to keep on destroying when others get tired of the destruction.

I did some research and found two Special Gaia Mutations you might like:

- Fury Burst – Turn yer raw rage into a burst of destructive energy that will damage anyone within fifteen feet of ye. Be careful to avoid friendly fire, though, 'cause friends and foes alike will take the raw Gaia Force thrashing. Bring yer fists together to knock yer enemies on their butts.
- Rage Fists – Fill yer fists with Gaia Force destruction. This will make your punches about a thousand times more deadly. There will probably be glowing. Garn, but I'd be disappointed if there wasn't some glowing. Ye wanna go through a wall? Create yer own doors through solid rock with punches that pack power!

So it's up to ye, friendo, make yerself stronger or get new mutations. I still haven't figured out how the Body Progression works yet. But I'll keep working.

<<<>>>

Gilly looked at the orb in wonder. "Wow, Bafflestone must've worked fast! So, Colt, what are you going to do?"

Colt could answer that easily. "I'm going to definitely upgrade my Invulnerability. I'm going to max that out because I don't want anything, nothing, to be able to hurt me. I've been hurt enough." That was probably a bit too much information.

But Colt hit the Upgrade/New Ability, and was given the option to either add a new skill or upgrade an existing one. He upgraded Invulnerability twice, so he only had two more upgrades to use.

This time, Colt chose a New Ability. He was given only one option: Endurance.

Gilly wrinkled her nose. "Well, that doesn't seem fair. Only one?"

"Only one." Colt thought for a second. "It doesn't exactly tell me what Endurance might mean. It could keep my Rune Genesis Status green longer, but it's probably for fighting."

Gilly's eyes blazed blue as she snarled, "Or fucking." Gilly blinked. "Or fighting. Probably fighting."

Colt wasn't going to choose Endurance until he understood more about what it might mean. So he clicked on the Special Gaia Mutations section. Once again, he only had the two options—Fury Burst I and Rage Fists I. He wasn't going to pass up any new abilities, especially with the fight coming up.

He chose them both before taking a look at his newly updated Gaia Orb:

<<<>>>

Gaia Orb for Urgu-Uku
Gaia Force Level: 4
Rune Genesis Status: Red (Stop)
Body Progression:

- Unknown

Gaia Abilities:

- Strength I
- Invulnerability III

Special Gaia Mutations:

- Fury Burst I
- Rage Fists I

<<<>>>

Colt glanced at Gilly. "Are you ready to take a look at your Gaia Orb?"

Before the goddess girl could answer, Eliza drifted in from the kitchen. "The pasta is boiling, and the hamburger is nearly blackened."

"Hopefully it will just be browned," Jewel corrected from her position in the corner shadow.

"Browned." Eliza gazed at his orb. She read through the readout quickly. "Golly, but that's helpful. I wonder if Bafflestone can make one for me. I do feel...different. I'm not sure how to put it."

"Mutations," Gilly whispered. "Bafflestone said something about mutations from how the Gaia Force is interacting with our bodies and the souls of the gods. You are a part of this now, Eliza. If you want to be."

Eliza looked into the goddess girl's eyes, bravely now, and without shame. "I want to be. You both have given me something I thought I'd lost."

Gilly glanced away, getting a little shy. "I'm glad that Zeh-Gaba hasn't frightened you off. Before we eat, I want to try my orb."

Colt put his orb down. The base was plastic, blue and orange because of the Broncos.

Gilly's orb was far more ornate, with a silver base. She picked it up. There was a flash, and inside the orb the goddess appeared, completely naked. In her left hand was a bow of crackling blue energy. The runes on her arms and her chest gleamed with an azure radiance. Around her spun scarlet snowflakes.

Gilly had a readout just like Colt's.

<<<>>>

Gaia Orb for Zeh-Gaba

Gaia Force Level: 3 (**Three New Updates Available. Update Abilities?**)

Rune Genesis Status: Red (Stop)

Body Progression:

- Unknown

Gaia Abilities:

- Limited Invulnerability I
- Enhanced Aim I
- **Update/Add New Ability**

Special Gaia Mutations:

- **Update/Add New Mutation**

<<<>>>

They were reading over the information when Aunt Jewel called from the kitchen corner. "Hey, fangs. You have to stir the meat. I think we should add the spaghetti sauce."

"Golly. Sorry." The vampire hurried back to the stove.

"She might not like fangs as a nickname," Colt said. "Be nice, Jewel."

"I'll try. I'm sorry, Eliza. Being a ghost hasn't helped me with my filter. I'll be nicer."

Eliza smoothed her blond hair. "Thank you, Miss Jewel. I really am rather ashamed of being a vampire. And does anyone else find it ironic that I'm the one doing the cooking?"

Colt got up from the table. They could finish talking about the Gaia Orbs over dinner.

Gilly still stared at her options. "I hope the spaghetti is as delicious as the irony. Okay, so I seemed to have started out with two abilities, which isn't surprising. I'm bulletproof, and I have archery skills that I was never taught in middle school. I'm a little disappointed I have Limited Invulnerability and not just Invulnerability. I still like being bulletproof, though."

Colt checked a piece of pasta, but it was still too chewy.

Gilly called over from the table. "I'm going to choose Limited Strength I, which again, isn't all fancy like your Strength I, Colt. That gives me two more choices. I only have two options for Special Gaia Mutations—Summoned Bow and Energy Arrows. The question of the day? Will Energy Arrows hurt vampires?"

"Wood and silver only," Eliza said. "As far as I know."

Gilly sat back. "Thanks, Eliza. Not to change the subject, though I am, but I was a little surprised that you joined us in the living room. Weren't you just going to watch?"

Aunt Jewel laughed. "Well, now, I'm kind of sorry I didn't stay to watch. Other than the fact that it's my nephew. Colt, do you want me to leave while you three talk about your sex lives?"

Colt winced. "If you could, Jewel. This is really kind of uncomfortable."

"Are you sure?" Jewel asked. "I'm a ghost. No body. And you wouldn't really know if I were watching or not."

Colt pinched the bridge of his nose. "This is not helping me."

"Dead aunts tell no tales. Just teasing. You'll have your privacy. I'll go check outside. I'm getting better at this ghost business." Jewel vanished from the corner.

Colt helped Eliza drain the grease off the meat and then added the spaghetti sauce.

Eliza started stirring. "A lot of it was the Gaia coming off you, Colt. It drew me to you and to Gilly. We were connected. I could feel that. Not just connected—bonded. And then when Gilly, uh, what's the word?" The vampire was pink from embarrassment.

"Came like a slut?" Gilly growled with her eyes shining like blue fire.

"Yes. Uh. That." Eliza stirred the mixture vigorously. "I had to ask if I could drink from you. By that time, I was dying to be touched. Dying."

Colt moved to drain the spaghetti noodles. "And that's another piece of irony. A vampire dying. As for me, you know it's good sex when you lose consciousness. No worries, though. With four runes, my Gaia Core is stronger than ever."

"It was scary, buster." Eliza gave him a troubled look. "Seeing you lying there, unconscious, I nearly had a heart attack. Colt. Look." She pointed at Gilly.

The goddess girl's runes were blazing. She put her globe down and then reached out a hand. The blue light coalesced around her fist to create a thick bow made entirely of light.

Gilly's glowing blue eyes narrowed. It was Zeh's voice that spoke. "Oh, yes, my weapon has returned to me, but in such a surprising way. Perhaps one of you would bring me an arrow. I have a bow, but I still need arrows. The little slut decided to enhance her strength and my aiming. I find that satisfactory. I am saddened, however, that she is no longer a virgin. I did enjoy being a virgin again after so many millennia."

Colt hurried into the living room and returned with the quiver, which was full. Gilly must've hit the sporting goods store before coming home.

He returned and tossed the goddess girl an arrow. She caught it and fit the arrow to a string of blue energy. She fired the shaft past Colt's head. The arrow hit the door, right where she'd hit it before, but this time it sunk in twice as deep.

Zeh-Gaba nodded. "Yes. My weapon is returned."

"What about Fury Burst and Rage Fists? How do I access that power?" Colt asked.

Zeh frowned. "As if I could help you with the intricacies of being the god of rage and destruction. It is not something I know. But I have seen Urgu reduce walls to dust with a single strike of his fist. And I have seen him explode with energy, knocking his opponents down with his fury alone."

She wasn't saying anything that wasn't already in Bafflestone's description, much to Colt's disappointment.

The bow disappeared, and Zeh brought her fists together in front of her. "With that motion, he was able to channel his fury into a burst. You could try that."

That was new. Colt nodded. "I'll try."

The goddess looked around. "But perhaps not in this little house. I have to say, Gilly now sees this as her home. Though she probably wouldn't want me telling you that. I shall leave. But I will be with you during the battle tonight. I will be watching." The blue eyes returned to normal.

"Zeh definitely has boundary issues." The goddess girl blinked. "Okay, I can see how my bow works. That's my special mutation—I can summon the bow from my Gaia Core."

"You have the one special mutation," Colt said. "And you're level three. I'm level four. That's why I have both Fury Burst and Rage Fists. I bet that given enough time, Bafflestone will be able to give us more choices when it comes to our abilities. We might even be able to create our own."

Gilly threw up her hands and let out a squeal. "That would be so awesome! Do you want to try your new powers outside, Colt?"

"Not until we fight. Let's see your updated Gaia Orb."

Gilly showed him.

<<<>>>

Gaia Orb for Zeh-Gaba

Gaia Force Level: 3
Rune Genesis Status: Red (Stop)
Body Progression:

- Unknown

Gaia Abilities:

- Limited Strength I
- Limited Invulnerability I
- Enhanced Aim II

Special Gaia Mutations:

- Summoned Bow I

<<<>>>

Colt figured Gilly could also add Endurance to her Gaia Abilities since he had that option. He was simply happy that they could use their upgrades. And he was confident that Eliza could get her own Gaia Orb now that she had a rune.

Jewel appeared in the kitchen corner. "I'm seeing people in the Sir Car-A-Lot. I think they're your friends, Eliza."

"I can assure you, Miss Jewel, that they are *not* my friends." Eliza grabbed plates out of the cupboard. "I shall set the table for us. I'll include myself, though I won't eat." She stood with the plates in her hands, not moving. "But before we eat, or before this fight, I want to tell you both how…how grateful I am. Something has awakened in me, something that's been asleep for a long, long time."

Colt held a bowl of pasta and stood with her in the kitchen. "What is it, Eliza?"

She smiled even as her big, brown eyes filled with tears. "Hope." She set the plates on the counter.

Gilly rushed over and gave the vampire a big hug. Gilly pressed her cheek against Eliza's. Both had their eyes closed, enjoying the closeness and warmth.

Then it was time for dinner.

Colt ate two helpings of spaghetti and used up the last of his cheap parmesan cheese.

Jewel went out to do more recon, but soon returned. "A big limo showed up down the street. If that ain't Vincent Isaac, I'd eat some of that vampire spaghetti there."

Eliza sighed.

"Sorry, fangs."

More sighing.

Colt knew that the spaghetti might be the last meal he'd ever eat. He also knew he wasn't going to spend the long winter nights huddled in the safety of his house.

It was time for them to rush headlong into a trap.

Only it wasn't a trap for them. This was Colt's part of town. He knew every inch. And he knew exactly how to fight creatures of the night who could become smoke at will.

He wasn't going to be trapped out there in the darkness with them.

They were going to be trapped in the night with him.

After dinner, Colt told the women his plan to defeat the vampires. They would wait. They would plan and prepare. And then they would strike without mercy.

CHAPTER THIRTY-FOUR

At midnight, Colt left his house.
He walked down the back porch and across the snow. A good portion of it had melted—he could smell the mud, frozen solid.

The lamps over the light rail tracks shone in the cold darkness. The stars above were pinpricks in the curtain of night.

Colt could feel the eyes of the vampires locked onto him.

Going through the middle of the cars parked at the back of the Sir Car-A-Lot would've been suicide. You didn't fight monsters that could become smoke where there were a lot of places for them to hide. However, Colt had plans for those cars.

The best thing about the battlefield he'd chosen? He could try out some of his new powers without worrying about destroying property in large quantities. He'd have to be careful to stay off of Franklin D. Schmidt's security cameras. The city also had cameras near the light rail tracks. He'd have to remain hidden so Mr. Gentleman wouldn't come calling.

Colt was barefoot and shirtless. What was the point? He hardly felt the cold because of the adrenaline. It was like he could see every blade of yellow grass in the field. He could smell mouse farts. He was vibrating with energy.

He leapt over the fence.

"I'm out here, Vincent! Let's not fuck around!"

Smoke poured out of several cars about ten feet away. They swirled around Colt, slowly taking shape.

Colt accessed his anger easily. All he had to do was remember chasing after his mother's car as she drove away. Again. In seconds, Colt was completely enraged.

The Gaia in his core exploded through his body. His four runes lit up the field. His hair was burning brightly, and his hands were now big red hammers, ready to pound vampires into butcher shop smoothies.

Colt felt Urgu's thrill at being unleashed. The god inside him really only cared about smashing things. Urgu wasn't too concerned about who died and how, as long as there was murder and destruction. But damn. Colt and Urgu agreed on one thing—breaking things just felt good.

Colt hoped the Rage King would help him use his new mutations—Fury Burst and Rage Fists.

He suddenly had five vampires standing there in cloaks around him. No sign of the bald German or Vincent Isaac.

The vampires came at him with fangs and claws bared. With Invulnerability III, Colt hoped that those fangs wouldn't pierce his skin.

The vampires had also come with other weapons. Each had silver knives attached to their right hands, kind of like a Freddy Krueger glove. Those knives gleamed as if with magic. This must've been Vincent Isaac's elite guard. But why in the fuck were they wearing cloaks over their black three-piece suits?

They moved with vampire speed. They thought they could chop him into pieces.

It was the perfect time to try Fury Burst.

Colt slammed his fists together like Zeh-Gaba had showed him. Thumbs hitting thumbs. The knuckles of his index fingers slamming together.

The results were immediate.

A wave of pure energy exploded out of Colt's Gaia Core. The pure power swept out to about fifteen feet in every direction. Those vampires were swept off their feet. They fell into the weeds.

Colt felt a good portion of his Gaia Unum leave him. That was a mighty blow, but it was expensive. He'd have to be careful or he'd run out of energy. He and the god had a long way to go until they were the city-killing murder machine Urgu had been back in Sumer five thousand years earlier.

The vampires were stunned, but they wouldn't be for long. Colt stampeded one, snapping his leg bones under his feet. Colt then jumped on his spine. It might not kill him, but those nerves weren't going to heal anytime soon.

Colt then stepped on the head of the next guy. He liked that popping feeling—it was like bursting bubble wrap back at the warehouse.

Colt grabbed the third vampire and used him to beat the holy fuck and blood out of the other two vampires. Again, they might heal, but it was buying him some time until he could murder the shit out of them.

Colt finished off his vampire club by yanking off his skull and throwing it into the head of another vampire. Those two bloodsuckers immediately burst into flame and dust. In seconds, they were just yellow scorches on the black mud.

More smoke swirled around Colt, and it was like he was in a London fog. There was going to be a fuck-ton of vampires on him in a second.

He raced across the ground on his powerful leg muscles. He grabbed a Kia Soul, a stupid-looking boxy car and probably not the best weapon, but it was the car closest to him. It might work okay. He punched his hand through the hood, grabbed the engine, and whirled, just as Otto turned from smoke to flesh.

Colt smacked him with the car.

Otto went flying across the ground.

Colt whirled and turned another vampire with the *Nightmare on Elm Street* gloves into a stain on the bumper of his car club.

The bald German was back in a flash. Otto tried to sink his fangs into the ridge of muscles across Colt's shoulders. That was where Colt had been bitten before, but not this time. Otto couldn't even break the skin.

Colt dropped the car and grabbed the German, but then he was smoke once more.

Still no sign of Isaac.

Colt saw a flash behind him. He felt one of the silver blades try to sever his skin, but no, Invulnerability III wasn't going to let that happen.

Then the vampire paid for his mistake.

Gilly's Enhanced Aim II sent an arrow through the villain's chest. A wooden arrow. Fire burst out as the vamp was dusted. That was Zeh-Gaba, in the darkness, taking out the bad guys with her arrows. He saw her bow—it wasn't a great weapon to fight with in the dark since it glowed blue. But she was standing under a lamp. A security camera sizzled and sparked behind her. She'd already taken out at least one of Schmidt's eyes. But it wouldn't be long before cops came to check out the carnage behind the Sir Car-A-Lot. Schmidt was paranoid about his property. He'd always blame Grandpa Walt, or one of his kids, or even his grandson, Colt, for any shit that went on. Schmidt was a grade-A asshole, and had been for decades.

It was just more fuel for the Rage King's fury.

Gilly dusted another vampire with an arrow.

Still no sign of Vincent Isaac.

Otto appeared above Colt, dropping down onto him.

A woman in a green wool suit leapt out of nowhere and tackled him to the ground. That was Elizabeth Ann Bennett, taking her revenge. Her fingers were long talons now, clawing wounds into Otto's face and neck.

Though it was clear she was far more a schoolmarm than a scrapper.

After the initial surprise, Otto tossed Eliza to the ground. He leapt on her to rip out her throat.

He never had the chance.

Colt grabbed him around his neck and squeezed. Otto's head popped off like a champagne bottle cork. But instead of bubbly, there was just a great deal of blood and then fire as the bald German turned to dust.

Colt felt the presence behind him. He spun just in time to take a knife blade in his right arm—but not in his chest.

What could fucking possibly cut him?

The answer was Vincent Isaac and the Fate Blade. Isaac had appeared, gray-haired, smooth-faced, in a three-piece suit. He had an overcoat instead of a cloak. In his hand was a long dagger. That blade was at least twenty inches long and gleamed in the starlight. The hilt was ornate, beaten iron, with engravings, but Colt was too far away to see them in detail.

Before Colt could get to him, the guy was gone—smoke once more. The mist was lost in the night.

Colt saw another vampire racing toward Gilly from behind the lamppost. She was still firing but was running out of arrows.

Colt picked up the Kia and threw it. His aim was good, and it crashed into the vampire. But Colt was bleeding badly, and his arm was killing him. He grew dizzy, his eyes blurring, which pissed him off further.

His runes were glowing brightly, but he could feel Urgu trying to take control.

Colt knew he didn't have forever, not with how much Gaia Unum he'd used for the Fury Burst.

Eliza rose and then was slashed up her back by Vincent, who vanished again.

Eliza fell, her skin smoking.

Colt ran to her. He wasn't sure where to touch her because she'd been cut up pretty badly.

Eliza's eyes were squeezed shut. The pain had to be intense. "It burns. It burns so bad. Watch out, Colt!"

Colt spun and swiped a big hand through smoke. Isaac solidified and drove the dagger into Colt's side before disappearing again.

Colt fell to his knee, gripping his side as blood poured out. He loved Eliza, but he couldn't stay with her. He had to keep moving.

Colt ran through another vampire, trampling him under his big red feet. Colt ran to the cars and started tossing them at vampires and smoke, though it was so hard to see. He couldn't linger near the cars or else a security camera—one that Gilly hadn't shot—might catch him. And it gave Vincent Isaac another place to hide.

Colt grabbed a Buick and hauled it over his head.

He retreated from the edge and swung it around himself.

A voice laughed at him. "Urgu-Uku must be so ashamed of the vessel he's found himself in. What a fucking idiot you are, boy. You're in a world you can't understand. You're a poor pathetic beast, enslaved to your own anger."

Colt was losing blood. He was also losing control.

He punched a vampire's head off, and more fire spouted out of the neck stump, but it wasn't Vincent Isaac. Colt kicked a leg off another vampire, and then stomped his huge feet down on the body. The crunch of the bone was so satisfying, but he couldn't focus on that. He had to get to the alpha vampire. He had to destroy the man who wielded the Fate Blade.

The vampire lord continued to taunt him. "Poor Colt Holliday. Your grandfather lied to you your entire life before he died. Before his daughter died, leaving you alone in the world. Friendless. Without a family. Clinging to your little blue house. I'll bulldoze it. I'll kill your little girlfriends, Gilly and Eliza. You won't miss them because you'll be dead, purified by the Fate Blade."

"No!" Eliza screamed. Her face melted as she became smoke. She swept up into the air, mixing with other mist there, until she appeared, dragging Vincent Isaac to the ground.

He was there, with the Fate Blade, and he plunged it into Eliza's chest.

She dropped to her knees. Blood poured from her mouth.

Colt flung the Buick across the light rail tracks. He was seeing red. Urgu was seconds away from taking control of him.

Vincent Isaac grinned. "Eliza couldn't be purified, no matter how hard I tried. I always wanted to possess her soul, but she fought me every step of the way. And now she'll die thinking I turned her. She'll never know the truth."

He was laughing. Vincent was becoming smoke.

Colt was pretty sure if the alpha vampire disappeared, his next strike would be in Colt's chest.

Seeing Eliza, on the ground, eyes open and lifeless, was the final straw. Urgu rose inside Colt, but Colt thought of something that calmed the rage monster inside of him. It wasn't something funny that Aunt Jewel had said. It was a memory of Gillian Hermione Croft rambling outside his warehouse because she'd been nervous. She'd dropped off the book, forgotten to pick up the notes, and gone on a nervous ramble.

Colt remembered every detail. Her beautiful blue eyes. Her dark hair. Her impish smile.

Colt couldn't let Urgu take control. Colt himself had to finish the fight.

An arrow struck Vincent in the throat. He laughed as he sputtered out words, garbled because a good portion of his voice box had been destroyed. "What a horrible fucking shot. Aim for the heart, bitch. Aim for the heart."

Colt took three big steps, and he clenched his right fist and felt the power going from his Gaia Core to his knuckles. This was the Rage Fist. This was him using his other Special Gaia Mutation.

Colt drove his fist through Vincent Isaac's chest, easily cracking through his ribs, and reaching around his heart.

Colt ripped out the pumping organ, but he didn't stop.

With the slimy heart in his hand, dripping blood, Colt reared back his fist and filled it full of fury—another Rage Fist.

Vincent Isaac's eyes widened. "You can't be serious."

And then Colt punched his fucking head off.

A geyser of blood and flames erupted from the stump of the alpha vampire's neck. More fire licked out of the hole in his chest. And then Vincent Isaac was just the outline of dust, standing there. A gust of wind came and blew him into countless pieces of nothing.

He was gone.

Then Colt realized that Isaac probably had Grandpa Walt's note in his pocket. Now he might never get to read it. Colt felt sad, but there was nothing he could do about it.

The Fate Blade fell to the ground.

Colt didn't pause. He picked it up and broke the blade off the hilt. He then hurled that length of steel away from him before dropping the hilt.

Urgu laughed. *Yes! Yes! Though our enemy is dead, let us embrace this moment for destruction. True destruction. Let us play.*

Colt thought that sounded like fun. He stormed across the field, picked up a Ford Explorer, and threw it into the back of the used car lot building. If there had been a camera in the wall, it was gone now.

He then decided to beat the holy shit out of a white Mercedes van. He punched through the metal, and it was like punching through paper. He ripped out the seats and flung them behind him, and then picked up the entire van and dropped it onto its back. Grabbing the drive shaft, he used it as a club, smashing in the metal until he could leap onto it. He jumped up and down until he'd completely flattened the vehicle. He wasn't sure what Strength II would give him, because damn, Strength I did plenty of damage.

Maybe Strength II would let him do to the Denver skyscrapers what he'd just done to the car.

After so long trying to rein in the Rage King, it felt so good to just unload, and Colt realized that Urgu wasn't trying to take control. No, because Colt was doing what Urgu wanted. Well, fuck it. It was fun.

He thought he saw a camera, so Colt grabbed another car and hurled it into the building.

"Colt!" Gilly cried out.

Colt turned.

The goddess girl was kneeling beside Eliza's body. Gilly's bow was gone, and her runes weren't glowing blue. "Colt, I need you."

He'd forgotten the blond vampire had been stabbed through the heart. He'd forgotten everything except for wanting to kill Vincent Isaac and then give in to the rage.

Colt knew that if Eliza was dead that he wouldn't have the will to resist Urgu. He hoped—he prayed—she wasn't dead.

He lumbered over.

Gilly held Eliza's hand. The goddess girl whispered, "Don't give me a sad ending, Miss Bennett. Don't do this to your old pal Gilly."

The flames on Colt's head cast flickering light on Eliza's face.

The blond vampire's eyes opened. She smiled. "I'm not a damn god. I'm a mother-loving vampire, don't you know? And it's either silver or wood to the heart. Iron, not even magical iron, can hurt me."

"Or a fist," Colt said with a grin.

Urgu chuckled. *Murder and destruction, Colton, are what we were built for. Love and sex are mere distractions. Enjoy them while you can, but our main meal is and will always be fury in all forms.*

Then the Rage King retreated, and Colt kept the god's form without anything trying to wrestle control from him. He bent and kissed Eliza.

She sighed even as her hair smoldered from his heat.

He went to kiss Gilly, but she put a hand on his huge chest. "Easy there, Rage King. I like to kiss gods without being barbecued."

Colt concentrated and returned to his human form. He then kissed Gilly with the sound of police car sirens filling the air.

They had to get going.

Vincent Isaac was dead. The Fate Blade was broken. And Colt and Gilly were in no danger of losing the gods inside them.

For the first time in days, they were free to enjoy their new lives.

But if Vincent Isaac hadn't turned Eliza into a vampire, then who did?

CHAPTER THIRTY-FIVE

The nicest thing about fighting an epic battle so close to home?

Colt and the two girls were back in his house five minutes later.

Gilly had listened to enough true crime podcasts to hide their tracks up to his house. Gilly and Eliza pulled off their wet and muddy shoes and left them on the back porch.

The three of them were soon sitting in the living room with the lights turned off. The bloodwax candle flickered, throwing runes on the wall. In the flickering light, they watched the police cars race down the street. Colt had put on an old Broncos sweatshirt and his good sweatpants. He also pulled on wool socks. He was comfy and cozy, sitting with the two women.

The hilt of the Fate Blade sat on the table. There were runes on it, like the runes they had on their bodies, but they couldn't read them. Colt figured he'd have Bafflestone take a look. He probably shouldn't have thrown the blade away, but he could look for it in the morning.

Eliza's face was peaceful in the light of the police sirens. "I can't believe he's gone. I've lived with him for so long that, golly, I believed he'd always be a part of my life. Not anymore, buster, that's for sure."

"Not anymore," Gilly agreed. "Who wants hot chocolate? We should celebrate. Hot chocolate is probably a dumb idea, but I want some. Do you have any, Colt?"

Colt winced. "Hey, Jewel, do we have hot chocolate?"

No one answered him. His aunt had probably tired herself out.

"Let me go check." Colt went into the cupboard and started shuffling through gravy packages, instant coffee, and other relics in the back corners of his cabinets. He didn't turn on the overhead lights. The microwave light was on, and that was enough for a start, but he was soon forced to use his phone's flashlight to search. He found very old Swiss Miss packets shoved behind some cans of tuna. They had little marshmallows. There were three packages.

Something moved out on the back porch.

"Motherfucker." Colt clenched his hands into fists. He smelled burning hair.

Another battle so soon? Can we throw more automobiles? I enjoy destroying automobiles. Your world has so many of them.

"Don't get so excited, Urgu," Colt muttered.

There was someone standing right in front of the back door. Someone in a hat.

Glowing green eyes peered out from underneath the fedora. His smile showed white fangs. He had a goatee streaked with white.

It was Mr. Gentleman.

"Are you okay in there, Colt?" Gilly called from the other room.

Colt opened the door, but as it swung open, the figure standing on the porch vanished. Like he'd never been there at all.

But someone had been there.

Colt bent and drew a finger through the wet mud on the wood. Those footsteps weren't dry, and they weren't frozen, so that meant they were new. Gilly's and Eliza's shoes lay in a pile under the back porch swing.

Colt looked around, but there was only the old hulking shape of his father's truck and nothing else. Police with flashlights walked the light rail tracks. Other bright lights came from the field behind the Sir Car-A-Lot, but that was because the police were checking out the battlefield. They'd find arrows, sure, but Colt could just say he messed around with an old bow. It probably wouldn't come to that. The tossed cars and property damage would be harder to explain, though the cops weren't going to come looking at him for that. They'd be on the lookout for a crane. Or a superhero.

Schmidt, though, might come asking questions. But fuck Franklin D. Schmidt. Colt was far more worried about Mr. Gentleman.

Urgu had a definite opinion. *This mysterious entity seems like a worthy foe. He is smug. I like dismembering smug people.*

Colt thought that sounded reasonable, but he wasn't about to go searching around in the dark for the smug bastard. Instead, Colt went back into his house and locked the back door. He was so glad they had the bloodwax candle. It should keep out any supernatural creatures, and that should include the mysterious leader of the Umbra Alliance.

Gilly and Eliza slipped into the kitchen. Both were wearing fuzzy socks pulled from Aunt Jewel's dresser.

Gilly's eyes went to the back door. "You saw something. Out with it, Colt Holliday. You're scaring me."

Eliza nodded. "Give us the straight poop, buster."

Gilly wrinkled her nose. "Uh, not sure I would phrase it exactly like that. But yeah."

Colt went to put a kettle on the stove.

Gilly grimaced. "No, buster, hot chocolate is better with milk. But you have to stir it. Do you mind if I, uh, take over this operation?"

"Help yourself." Colt set the packages on the counter.

Eliza looked them over. "I don't think I would digest the marshmallows very well. You two enjoy yourselves. I'll be drinking with you in spirit."

Colt backed up and stood leaning against the sink. "Sure you're scared, Gilly, and so am I. Losing sleep is scary, and it's going to be another night without sleep. You have no idea how boring my job is."

Gilly fluttered her eyes at him. "Whatever." She found a pot easily, like she'd been living with him for months instead of just a few days. She set the pot on the stove and then poured milk in. "Out with it."

Colt shrugged. "I saw Mr. Gentleman on the back porch. It could be he was there to congratulate us on our victory. Or he might've thought to come inside, but the bloodwax candle had other ideas."

Eliza sighed loudly. "This is terrible. I met him once, and it wasn't pleasant, but in the end, I don't know a thing about Mr. Gentleman, only that he gives me and every Monstra I've ever met the willies. He is quite the bogeyman, and I don't relish the idea of him taking an interest in you. Or us."

Colt liked the sound of that last word. Us. Eliza was thinking of them as a family.

"Is he a vampire?" Colt asked.

Eliza shook her head. "I don't think so. People wouldn't be afraid of a vampire, except if he were a god maybe. It makes me wonder if this Mr. Gentleman didn't turn me. Maybe he was here looking for me. I've lost my vampiric father. Perhaps he thought he could take Vincent's place."

Gilly laughed. "Colt is your daddy now, girlfriend."

Eliza blushed. "Oh, I know what that means. Not from personal experience, mind you, though I have been curious." She let that hang in the air awkwardly. "Let's change the subject, shall we?"

Colt felt himself get a little stiff from the idea of being Eliza's daddy. That seemed like it would be a long way off. She wasn't ready to join them in bed. Still, he'd felt her orgasm, and he had the rune to prove it.

Gilly stirred the milk on the stove. "It's important not to let the milk scorch. But in other news, it's really messed up that Vincent Isaac let you believe he turned you when he didn't."

"Or he might be lying," Eliza said, a little breathlessly. "Either way, I am through with him. I do wonder what will happen to Firestone Alley now. Vincent ruled there with an iron fist. It was one of the reasons why he demoted Bafflestone and enslaved the Tomte. He wanted total control. He removed other factions through murder and extortion. There will be a power vacuum."

"Maybe you could fill it," Gilly suggested.

Eliza cast her eyes down. "Never. People despise me, sweetheart. No, but there's a newcomer on the scene." Her eyes went up to take in Colt. "Maybe Firestone Alley doesn't need a vampire lord. Perhaps it needs a god."

Colt put a hand to his chest. "Me? I've only known about the Monstra for like five days. No, I'm the wrong guy. And I have to finish off this job. I have a year left of working at the warehouse."

"Why?" Eliza asked.

"Long story." Colt didn't want to go into the terrible deal that his Uncle Elam had made. It was all ugly family business.

Gilly turned off the stove and dumped the hot chocolate mix into the mugs. She had to bang them against the tile counter because they were old and the sugar had crystalized. Then she poured in the milk and stirred the contents.

She licked the spoon clean. "That's so good!"

She stirred his and offered him the spoon.

Colt slurped the sweet off it. He liked the idea of sharing the spoon with his goddess girl.

Eliza watched them with an odd look on her face. "Let's go back to the living room. I'm far more comfortable there."

Colt checked to make sure the back door was locked and then walked with the girls back to the sofa and easy chair.

There was less action outside.

Colt did see Schmidt's Cadillac out there. He was yelling at some cops.

Gilly sat on the sofa with her feet on Colt. He massaged her toes while he sipped from his mug.

Eliza leaned forward on her chair, looking at them. "So, what happens now?"

Gilly giggled. "We all move in here. We help Colt clean out all the boxes. And we have a home." She laughed more. "Of course, I'm joking. We can't just invite ourselves to live with Colt."

"Why not?" Colt asked.

Gilly's mouth fell open. "You don't want us living with you. I mean, there's the PMS issue." She winced. "I can't believe I said that out loud. And I can't even blame Zeh-Gaba. Don't worry, Eliza, I'm not going to ask you about your, uh, womanly cycles."

Eliza put up a hand. "If we're going to talk about such inappropriate things, I'd rather talk about sex, frankly, but yes, I still have my monthlies." She rolled her eyes in complete embarrassment.

Colt gripped Gilly's foot. "I love having you both here. If it doesn't work out, you can go back to living at your parents', Gilly. And Eliza…"

The vampire put her hands in her face and dropped them. "I don't have anywhere else to go. Bafflestone might help me. He seems to have warmed up to me. But perhaps not. I find myself orphaned and alone. I've never had to…had to rely on the kindness of strangers, as it were."

"It's fine, Eliza," Colt said. "I want you to stay here. Since we're fixing up the house, we can clear out the basement and give you a room. I hate the idea of you spending your days sitting in a chair."

Eliza's eyes filled with tears. "Well, here's more waterworks, right on schedule. And I always considered myself a rather tough dame. It seems you have caught me at my most emotional."

Gilly shot the vampire an understanding smile. "You've had a lot of things to work through. Trauma with a capital 'T.' We're glad we can help. Really. We are."

"We are," Colt agreed.

Eliza got up and motioned for Colt and Gilly to join her in a hug. They all embraced, and Colt kissed each of their cheeks, inhaling first Gilly's sweet perfume and then Eliza's unmistakably alluring musk.

Colt liked the hot chocolate, but so much had happened that he needed something stronger. He went into the kitchen and grabbed an old bottle of Wild Turkey from the cabinet above the stove. He spiked his and Gilly's mugs, and they finished off the evening, toasting each other.

It was decided. Gilly would be moving in, and Eliza would as well.

Just like that, Colt had roommates. But they were going to be more than just roommates. Far more.

That night, Eliza didn't want to be away from them. She sat in a little chair in his room, next to their bed, as Colt wrapped Gilly up in his arms. Seeing the vampire girl in her chair, smiling at him with her silver eyes, might've been scary for normal humans, but Colt found it completely comforting.

He'd been so alone after Aunt Jewel died. Now? His life had never felt fuller. And he couldn't wait to see what the future held.

He drifted off to sleep.

He heard Gilly moan when the alarm went off. "So tired! Tonight, we're going to bed early!"

Colt left her bed and escorted Eliza to the door of the basement. The sun had broken over the horizon, but none of the rays were shining into the house.

Eliza threw her arms around him. "Thank you, Colt. Thank you for taking me in. I might have to move slowly, but I want to give you another rune. I do. I do!"

Colt held her, stunned by her outburst. He gripped her shoulders and looked into her wide, brown eyes. "We'll go as slowly as you like. We don't have anyone attacking us. The Fate Blade is gone. Vincent Isaac is gone. And I don't know what kind of game Mr. Gentleman is playing, but I don't care. If he messes with me, I'll literally punch his head off."

Eliza grinned. "You did it once."

Colt nodded. "And I can do it again."

Eliza held him tightly and gazed into his eyes. Then she slowly brought her lips to his.

She inhaled sharply and moaned as the kiss deepened.

Colt had one arm around her hot, supple body, and the other cradled her head. He felt her strength as she clung to him, as she offered him her tongue and he accepted it. Lips, tongue, moaning —the more they kissed, the harder Colt became.

Eliza finally stepped back. "I love that, Colton. And I love you."

Colt smiled at her. "I love you too."

Eliza gave him one last hug, one last kiss, and then walked down the steep stairs into the tiny basement under the little house.

Colt closed the door. He could hear Gilly marching up the steps toward the shower on the second floor.

For the first time in a long time, Colt was looking forward to a normal day, and that included his soul-crushing job. But he'd get to come home and heal that soul with the two best women in the world.

Life was good.

CHAPTER THIRTY-SIX

The rest of the week passed without any major supernatural incidents.

There was one minor one, though.

Colt and Gilly, on Tuesday night, were there when Amanda Buckman and her three horrible friends went to get into Amanda's Escalade. It was turned upside down, with the wheels yanked off and stuffed inside.

Amanda stood there, mouth hanging open, until she burst into tears.

The police were baffled by all the ruined cars at Sir-Car-A-Lot. They added this mystery to the pile.

Colt and Gilly thought that might bring the Umbra Alliance down upon them, but in the end, it was worth it. A bit of revenge was always a tasty treat. And it wasn't like Urgu and Zeh were going to argue that. Divine wrath was part of the ancient god deal.

Later that night, a policeman did show up to Colt's door, asking if he'd seen anything weird the night before. Colt had shrugged.

The cop had grinned at Gilly and Eliza, back in the kitchen, waving at him. He'd said something about Colt being a lucky so-and-so before taking his leave.

As for Franklin D. Schmidt, the owner of the car lot just glared at Colt whenever their paths crossed that week. It was going to be an expensive week for Sir Car-A-Lot, but Schmidt could more than afford it.

Colt searched for the twenty inches of iron he'd snapped off the Fate Blade. He'd not been able to find it, and he'd looked everywhere. He checked with the cop who'd visited, an Office Dennis Polanski, but the friendly Polish cop hadn't seen anything like it. Polanski ended up giving Colt his card, saying if he saw anything strange, he could contact him.

Colt didn't mention that his whole life had become strange. He put the card aside, though, just in case he needed information from the police.

All that week, Ernie Corlino spent his days and nights at the hospital, taking care of Aunt Sophia, who was going to make a full recovery. Ernie said the doctors told her to cut back on pasta. Aunt Sophia said that was never, ever going to happen.

With Ernie at the hospital, Colt had to take some shifts taking care of his friend's animals.

Of course, he took Gilly with him.

Thursday night, both he and the goddess girl returned to Ernie's house in Globeville. The cats, Bluto and Olive, came out of hiding to get scratches from Gilly. They avoided Colt.

Luckily, Bugs and Daffy loved Colt. He petted the two pit bulls until it felt like his hands might fall off. He brought in Ernie's mail, watered his plants, and checked to make sure the heater would kick on during the cold at night. It would be terrible if Ernie came home to find his pipes busted.

While they were taking care of the animals, Colt grinned at Gilly. "How about celebrating our one-week anniversary by visiting Aunt Sophia in the hospital and then taking a trip to Firestone Alley?"

Gilly petted one cat, then the other. They were purr factories around the goddess girl. "Well, returning to Firestone Alley seems really dangerous, but I'm a woman of adventure. First, though, I have two questions for you, buster."

"I thought it was only Eliza who called me buster."

Gilly took Olive's paw and shook it at Colt. "I like how it sounds. Do you want to hear my two questions?"

"I'd love to." Colt had to push Bugs back or he'd get licked to death.

"For one, why don't you have any pets? You clearly love them."

Colt looked into Gilly's eyes. "Do you want the truth?"

She nodded. "Yeah, give me the truth."

Colt sighed. "I've lost a lot of people in my life. I didn't want to lose a pet as well. Besides, with my hoarder family, I could easily see one cat turning into thirty."

Gilly laughed. "Okay. Wanna hear my second question?"

"Hit me." Daffy was whining. He wasn't being petted enough, so Colt switched pooches.

"What is our anniversary date?" Gilly asked. "Was it when you and I got possessed by an ancient god and goddess? That's kinda how our relationship started. And I don't count that first kiss where I, um, pleasured myself on you." Gilly laughed a little with embarrassment.

"I think it's the shack," Colt said. "That's when I knew I'd want to spend the rest of my life with you."

"Oh, so one little blow job, and I'm yours forever. Such a man."

"Guilty as charged." Colt turned serious. "But really, I knew I wanted to get to know you the first time I met you in our statistics class. The first time I saw you. I'll never forget it."

"What was the date?"

Colt winced. "Septemberish. Maybe late Augustish. Not Octoberish."

Again, Gilly pointed Olive's paw at him. "Let's go with the night in the shack. That was January 7, and it was our first night in Firestone Alley. And it was our first night together. So this Friday it will be a week. Aunt Sophia and Firestone Alley seem like a good way to celebrate it." She paused. "What's going to be our anniversary date with Eliza?"

"Our?" Colt asked.

Gilly rolled her eyes. "Don't be dense. Eliza is with us. She needs to take it slow, but I've felt the connection with her, and I think you have too. Zeh-Gaba doesn't think she'll be the last girl to join us. Like it or not, Colt, you need a harem."

Colt looked down at his arm. "To get more runes."

She nodded. "To get more runes. Not sure what Bafflestone meant when he said the first runes were easy but the next ones will be harder to come by. And there are fairies who cultivate magic? That I find awesome."

"At least we can still have sex when our Rune Genesis Statuses are red. It would suck if we had to consult our orbs every time we got horny."

Gilly giggled. "Not sure that would stop us. We might die, but it would be worth it."

Colt expected her eyes and arms to glow and for Zeh-Gaba to say something filthy, but Gilly just smiled. She was integrating the goddess of lust nicely.

"So, Colt, I'll ask you again. What's our anniversary date with Eliza?"

Colt hugged Daffy and petted Bugs. "The truth is, I don't think we've had it yet. Part of me could see her running away. I hope that's not the case, but like you said before, she has a long journey ahead of her."

Gilly got a sad expression on her face. "She's been through a lot, but she's strong, Colt. Like you are. I sometimes get afraid I'm the weak one."

Colt left the dogs to kiss Gilly and hold her. They only had a second before they were swamped in puppies. The cats scattered.

"No," Colt whispered into her ear. "You're a goddess. The

worst years of your life are behind you. We get to be gods together."

Gilly didn't argue one bit with that.

That Friday, Colt finished off another week of working for USP. He only had fifty more weeks before he was free. Actually, without Jimbo and his fucking henchmen, work wasn't so bad. Jameson didn't get in their way. Phyllis and Marcy kept him entertained, and the best part about them was that they were funny and capable. They were not—in the words of Aunt Jewel—useless motherfuckers. Even Andy was stepping up to make sure things ran smoothly.

And leaving for work meant Colt could come home. It was one of the best parts of his new life.

After the sun set, Eliza would clamber up the steps, and Aunt Jewel would appear out of the shadows. Gilly would pull up in front of their house, singing the song that was just on the radio as she walked up the path.

Aunt Jewel loved the new arrangement, and she didn't ask too many questions. As in, was Colt banging both Gilly and Eliza? It was a question of don't ask, don't tell at the moment.

At night, while Colt and Gilly slept, Jewel and Eliza would go through boxes. The ghost and the vampire were making amazing progress. Most of the stuff went to Goodwill or the trash. But there were always special objects that Jewel insisted on putting aside for Colt to go through.

Colt was still sad that Grandpa Walt's letter was probably gone.

They were doing Jewel's stuff first to clear out the room for Gilly. In the meantime, she had her stuff in the living room, and she was sleeping in Colt's bed.

Colt had wanted to meet Gilly's parents, but she said it was too soon. In her words, Colt really needed to love her before she inflicted her parents on him.

Colt said he already loved her enough, but Gilly was still a bit scared. Her parents were hitting the roof at their little girl running off to North Denver to live with some older guy. Gilly was pretty sure they were going to come after him. Hard.

Colt probably needed more runes before he faced them.

For the most part, when Colt got frustrated at work, which was a daily occurrence, or driving around in Denver's insane traffic, he'd have to think about some joke Aunt Jewel had made. Or just thinking about Gilly calmed him. She was so heartbreakingly beautiful.

However, the longer he went without destroying something or murdering someone, the more the god of rage fought to break out of him. It was a problem. Again, more runes would help. As would giving the Rage King a bit of leash. Demolishing the cars and part of the Sir Car-A-Lot had really satisfied Urgu. Colt could get behind some mindless destruction. Maybe he could find a demolition team and help them out.

Friday night, Colt came home from work and pushed open the door. Gilly's boxes filled the hallway.

Colt called out. "Honey, I'm home!"

"We're in the kitchen!" Aunt Jewel's voice came to him.

That was why all the lights were off. Colt walked through the wreckage and found the table full of little knick-knacks from Jewel's life. He saw that she had a snow globe of downtown Denver with her name on it. Unlike the Mile High Stadium snow globe, this one wasn't magical.

Colt's heart melted.

Eliza saw it. "Golly, Colt. We don't have to throw away everything. We can keep what you like."

He picked up the globe. "This we keep." He surveyed the rest of it. Concert ticket stubs, some old dried roses from high school sweethearts, a broken Lite-Brite, and some other toys.

Jewel grinned at him from the corner. "That's the last of it."

Gilly came rushing out of his room. "Come on, buster. Wait until you see Jewel's room. It's perfect. This is so fun!"

Colt allowed himself to be dragged up the stairs. Eliza came up behind him. Jewel, being the good ghost she was, was already in the room. It had been completely cleared out. Gilly's stuff was all over because she was moving up into Jewel's old room.

Gilly wrinkled her cute nose, which pushed up her glasses. "Are you sure it's okay I move in here, Jewel?"

Aunt Jewel just laughed. "Of course. Who am I to say no to a goddess? I'd love to have you here. Seriously. I don't need it. I spend most of my time, if you wanna call it time, just in the Gaia, chillin'."

Gilly sighed in relief. "Okay. Do you guys want to help me bring up my stuff?"

Colt and Eliza jumped to it. They cleared the living room.

At one point, Gilly bumped him with her hip. "Don't worry, Colt. I still want to sleep in your bed. But maybe we can move Jewel's queen bed into your room."

"Just buy a new bed already!" Jewel called from the darkness. "You don't want to sleep on some old lady's mattress!"

Colt wasn't going to argue that. For now, Gilly would keep her stuff in Jewel's room, but she'd sleep in his bed. And they would work on getting Eliza's room set up in the basement. Best of all, their house would be protected from any supernatural intruders because of the bloodwax candle. It truly was a safe haven for them.

Jewel had ordered FoodWheel for them, and once again, it was Mrs. MILF who showed up with Denver Biscuit Company.

The older woman couldn't help but glance inside. She saw the two girls. Like Officer Polanski, she grinned. "Looks like a party in there."

Colt could only shrug. "We have fun."

Mrs. MILF raised her eyebrows. "I bet you do. Thank Jewel for me. For the good tips. I like a good tip."

Colt didn't know how to respond to that. He just nodded and laughed.

There was something about Mrs. MILF that he couldn't put his finger on. How come she was always the FoodWheel driver who delivered to them? There had to be something else going on.

After dinner, Colt rode with Gilly and Eliza over to Denver Health.

Ernie met them in the lobby. He looked like a mafia guy in a suit with no tie, his hair receding, and a big Italian smile on his face. "Buddy! Thanks so much. Aunt Sophia is kinda tired of relatives at this point. Fresh faces will do wonders for her."

"Glad to help," Colt said. He introduced the two women with him. Gillian Hermione Croft and Elizabeth Anne Bennett.

Ernie's eyes went from Colt to Gilly to Eliza. Those two were so beautiful you couldn't help but stare.

Ernie put a hand over his heart. "Colt? I think I had the heart attack. Tell me I'm dead. Tell me you brought me two angels." He then laughed that old laugh.

"Hello, Mr. Corlino," Eliza said. "It is a pleasure to make your acquaintance."

Ernie blinked. "I don't mean to be disrespectful, but you sound like an old movie. That's a Mid-Atlantic accent."

Eliza blushed. "I'm from the east. Would you believe Kansas City?"

"Atlantic City maybe," Ernie said with a chuckle. His eyes went to Gilly.

Gilly raised an awkward hand. "I'm, uh, a native. And Eliza has all the class. I'm kind of nervous, meeting you, since you're kind of famous."

Colt and Ernie both squinted at that.

"Famous how?" Ernie asked.

Gilly rolled her eyes. "Uh, you're friends with Bluto and Olive. Anyone who can have such nice cats must be famous in some way."

Ernie melted right there. "I love my kitties like I love my dogs. You're so kind, Gillian."

Gilly didn't correct him. She liked it when Eliza called her that.

They chatted for a minute and then visited Aunt Sophia, who was already demanding cigarettes, red wine, and lasagna. In that order. Like Ernie, the old Italian woman was immediately won over by Colt and his girlfriends. They chatted and laughed, but Colt had plans to return to Firestone Alley that night.

On the way out, Ernie asked to speak to Colt alone.

The blond vampire had a strange look on her face. Standing in the lobby, Eliza grabbed Gilly's hand. "That's bully, Colt. I have something I need to check. Would you come with me, Gillian?"

Gilly looked confused. "Uh, yeah, but where are we going, Eliza?"

"To the morgue," Eliza said mysteriously.

Colt wondered if it involved blood. He wasn't sure. The two women marched down a hallway, and Eliza seemed to know exactly where she was going. The hospital seemed like a second home.

Ernie didn't seem to notice. His smile was downright goofy. "Level with me, Colt. Are you dating both of them?"

Colt patted his buddy's arm. "Not yet, but it looks like it's heading in that direction. I'd tell you more, but a man in your condition might not be able to handle it. Didn't you say you had a heart attack?"

"That was my aunt." Ernie sighed. "You and I got lucky when it came to aunts. I still can't believe Jewel is gone."

"Gone but never forgotten," Colt said, so grateful he still had Jewel's ghost around.

Colt thought about what he'd said to Gilly. Yes, he wanted the bad years behind him. He only wanted to have happy times from here on out. But then, that's what everyone wanted, right?

A short time later, Eliza and Gilly returned. Eliza was pale, and Gilly frowned.

Colt would get their story on the way up to Firestone Alley.

He said goodbye to Ernie, and soon he and the two women were back on I-25, heading north toward Firestone Alley. Gilly was riding shotgun. Eliza was in the back, eyes glowing silver. She held Bafflestone's leather satchel. Inside was the hilt of the Fate Blade as well as the two Gaia Orbs. They wanted to see if he had any more information on how the system worked.

"What happened in the morgue?" Colt asked.

Gilly sighed. "Well, at first it was super creepy and kind of cool. You know, having a friend who's super popular at the local morgue."

"And why were you popular, Eliza?" Colt asked. Then he remembered. "Oh, that's right. You worked with Denver Health and other hospitals to get blood for the vampires in Firestone Alley."

"That's right," Eliza said from the back seat. "And the hospital was where I hid the crates full of Mesopotamian artifacts. They were in a locked drawer in the morgue."

"Yeah. Like where bodies are," Gilly said. "But someone busted the lock and grabbed them."

Colt felt his heart drop. "Do you have any idea where they might be?"

"None," Eliza said sullenly. "Golly, but I should've been more careful."

"Could they be in Firestone Alley?" Colt asked.

It was a question they couldn't answer.

Colt drove faster. They had no idea what they would find in Firestone Alley, but now they had a definite reason for going there. To find the missing statues. There could be other gods locked away.

Even if they didn't find the missing crates, Colt wanted to check on his friend Bafflestone. After all the gnome had done for them, it was the least they could do.

Besides, if they were attacked, Colt knew that Urgu would love the chance to rage and destroy. Colt found himself almost looking forward to fighting another god. Vampires were just too easy to kill.

CHAPTER THIRTY-SEVEN

The two big front doors of Firestone Alley's lobby were wide open.

Eliza pointed at them. "Well, that's concerning. Those should be closed."

The lobby itself had been cleaned, though, and there were new couches as well as new bottles of both blood and booze on the glass shelves of the bar.

Colt walked out onto the welcome platform with the two women trailing him. The big metal gates to the right were open as well, and the constable station on the left was empty.

Eliza frowned. "Golly. I thought Edward would die at his post. Vincent had him running the Firestone Constabulary."

Gilly had her quiver of arrows, just no bow, not one that you could see at any rate. She closed one eye. "Edward. A vampire named Edward. You're joshing me, right?"

"Why?" Eliza asked, confused. "Edward Mason. He was turned in 1901. He was another one of Vincent Isaac's victims, or so we all thought. Who knows now? But why shouldn't a vampire be named Edward?"

Colt wasn't going to go into the whole *Twilight* thing. "Let's just see who is in charge of Vincent Isaac's mansion."

They walked down the walkways and stairs to get the gates on the east side of the manor house. At those gates were two Tomte gnomes, one male and one female. Their eyes lit up. "Come on, come on," the boy gnome said excitedly.

Colt and the girls were led through the front doors and into a huge dining room. It was covered in different gears, machines, and straw dummies that looked familiar.

In the center was Barnard Bafflestone himself. He was itching his scalp with a Phillips-head screwdriver. He was currently talking to a stately elven woman in a sparkly green dress.

"Mellia, I know, I know, we have a lot to consider." Then Bafflestone saw them. "Friends!"

He rushed over to them. "Colt, Eliza, Gilly, yer here! We were wondering when ye'd show up! Mellia used a little soothsaying to let us know Vincent Isaac is one garn-awful dead dog. No one knew what to do. There are factions, and Edward Mason thought he should do martial law, but none of the elves liked that idea, and a fair number of vamps were killed along with Isaac. Long story short, since I've been here the longest, they put me in charge! See? It pays to be smart and friendly!"

Bafflestone's face was positively glowing. He didn't look like any laundry guy. But he also didn't look very kingly. He wore grease-stained clothes, and he was a bit sweaty. Both his white hair and beard were wild and bristly. His broken fingers had fresh splints and bandages on them. Other than a few scrapes and bruises on his face, he looked like he was healing nicely.

Mellia bowed to Colt. "Hello, Mr. Holliday. We knew your grandfather to be a friend of the Leyfolk. It is a pleasure to meet his grandson. And Bafflestone told us about your special friend, Gillian Croft."

The elf woman didn't give Eliza a second look.

Colt hated that the Monstra couldn't forgive Eliza, even after she'd spent nearly a hundred years in prison. He wasn't sure how to change that, but he could stand up for her.

"This is Elizabeth Bennet," Colt said with some force. The

scent of burning hair hung in the air. "She's with me and Gilly. And if it hadn't been for Eliza, we probably wouldn't have been able to kill Vincent Isaac."

Elves, Urgu growled. *I like to kill elves.*

Colt didn't flinch at the murderous thought. He was getting used to having the Rage King whisper atrocities. Just because he heard the evil voice didn't mean he had to do what it said.

Mellia gave Eliza a curtsy. "Of course I know Eliza. I was in charge of the Lyran staff of this mansion when Mr. Isaac was alive. Now that he is gone, I will be helping Bafflestone with his regency duties. He will be the regent until another leader is chosen."

"I'm hoping it will be that civil," Bafflestone said with a sigh. "All the other times, there was killing. I'm so tired of all the garn killing."

Mellia snapped her fingers. "Can I bring you refreshments?" She shot Eliza a cruel look. "I can bring blood for you, if you can't control yourself."

"I'm fine," Eliza said politely. "But thank you."

Mellia turned from them and went to join other elves in the kitchen. There were also Tomte gnomes here and there, but no sign of vampires.

Eliza noticed. "Where are the vampire factions? I can't believe that Alexander Bryant wouldn't be chomping at the bit to take over."

Bafflestone shrugged. "Alexander was killed by Edward right when we heard the news. There had been bad blood between the vampires for quite a while. It's chaos down here. I have to admit. But ye two are kind of celebrities." He motioned to Colt and Gilly. "Word of the gods returning spread quickly, but they don't exactly know the whole story, and I haven't told anyone a thing. But I have been wondering how the upgrades to the Gaia Orbs worked."

Eliza pulled the spheres out of the gnome's leather satchel. "Here they are."

"Oh, good. I've been dying to know some things." Bafflestone hurried up a little stepping stool to get to the tabletop. "My working theory is that yer levels are gonna match yer runes. Like I said, it's gonna get harder to get the runes, but all that sex magic is beyond my paygrade. Ye'll have to do some experimenting." He grinned. "But I suspect ye might enjoy that."

Colt smiled. "We'll figure it out. We were wondering if you could make a Gaia Orb for Eliza. She has a rune now. The first of many, hopefully."

"Don't see why I shouldn't be able to," the gnome said. "As long as ye have a Gaia Core, I can track it. Most Leyfolk have limits to their power. Gods, and their loves, however, are bound to work differently."

Mellia's elven butlers returned and handed out beers and big, soft pretzels. They brought a goblet full of blood for Eliza.

The butlers didn't treat her any more politely than Mellia had.

Colt swore he'd change that. Everyone needed to know how instrumental Eliza had been in bringing down Vincent Isaac.

Colt loved the pretzels, and the beer was perfect. "Who do you think is going to take over, Barney?"

The Tomte quaffed down a good portion of his brew. "Well, now, the vote turned to me as regent. That might be permanent, though I can't say I really want the job. I like machines more than people. But, garn, am I glad to be out of that laundry room! As are my friends. There's some dog folk who would love to work the laundries for some good gold. The Houdon are always up for working."

Eliza sipped the blood from her goblet with some delicacy. Her red lips didn't get any redder. She was still as beautiful and flawless as ever. She handled all of the hate toward her far better than Colt would've.

"Where's Edward right now?" Gilly asked. "And what's with the front gates being wide open? Is that a good thing?"

"No, it's not ideal," Bafflestone agreed. "I locked down the manor house for the Tomte. As for everyone else, we're still trying to figure things out. Edward was pretty displeased when not everyone voted for him, especially after he killed Alexander Bryant. There's a rumor Edward is gonna bring in a werewolf army to take over. The Order of the Moon has a lot of territory up north. They pretty much have the entire I-80 corridor. More likely, I'd think the Fae would come trying to claim this for themselves. I-70 is important, but it ain't that big."

Eliza set her goblet on the table. "Mr. Bafflestone, I stole crates containing other Mesopotamian artifacts from Mr. Isaac. I had them hidden away, but they seem to have been stolen. Have you heard anything about them?"

Bafflestone shook his head. "No, and I'm sorry about that, missy. And I'm sorry that the Leyfolk still hate ye. I'll keep my ears open." He chuckled sadly. "I would imagine if any more gods turn up, we'd know about it."

"I hope so," Gilly said. "But it looks like we have a little mystery on our hands. I kind of love mysteries, to be honest."

Eliza didn't appear to agree. She was clearly upset.

"We'll deal with whatever comes," Colt assured her. "Let's just be happy for Bafflestone. And that we survived."

"You're right," Eliza said. "Golly, you're a swell fella, Colt."

Colt didn't know how to respond to that. He chewed on his pretzel and enjoyed the doughy texture and the salt.

Gilly tilted her head. "Okay, so I have a question I've been pondering. Human civilizations built their freeways over Ley Lines, probably drawn to the natural power flowing there. And here and there are Gaia Towns, built on nodes that are an important source of the Gaia Force. Am I getting that right?"

"Aye, missy," Bafflestone agreed. "Why do you ask?"

"Do all the Gaia Towns look like Firestone Alley?" Gilly asked.

The gnome smiled. "No, Miss Gillian. They don't. Someday, ye should see the parks and fountains of the mountain villages of the Fae. Why, even Plainsong City, the home of a big pack of werewolves, has its charms. And ye should visit the Tomte towns over in what ye would call Kansas. All are special. All are beautiful. We have to hide from the humans, aye, but our hidden cities are special."

Colt could well believe it. The mysterious world he'd stumbled upon was so full of amazing creatures and places, and he wanted to see every one of them.

Bafflestone then knocked his head. "Wait. Mr. Colt, I found something for ye. It was while I was clearing out Mr. Isaac's room that I found Walt's note."

Colt's heart leapt into his throat.

A second later, he was holding the envelope that Grandpa Walt had kept in that locked filing cabinet along with the Fate Blade. What else had been in there? They might never be sure, but at least Colt had his grandfather's note. He couldn't wait to read it. And he wanted Bafflestone to translate the runes on the hilt of the Fate Blade.

A second later, the front window broke into a thousand pieces. A huge creature came bounding through the broken glass.

It was a dark red wolf creature, standing seven feet tall on powerful wolfish legs. The ten fingers of its gigantic hands ended in gleaming metal talons. The thing's face was a wolf's muzzle, but in its ears were glittering diamond earrings. It was a female werewolf.

She laughed and let out a howl. "A Gaia Town without a leader. We can't have that! We've come to replace you, Barney Bafflestone. Firestone Alley is gonna belong to the Order of the Moon now. We're taking over this joint!"

Another dozen werewolves burst in through the ruined windows. They were all different colors, but the biggest one had bright red fur and a scar down its right eye. His belly was nearly white. He pointed a shining metal claw at Colt. "That one is mine. I want to see what a god's heart tastes like."

Colt easily drew forth Urgu, and the Rage King was so happy to be let out of his cage. Colt ripped out of his clothes. Again, his shoes were toast. Damn, he liked those shoes.

That made him even angrier. And Colt was already pretty

pissed off that another new enemy was attacking when they'd just gotten rid of Vincent Isaac. However, he didn't think killing a werewolf could be that tough. Besides, they didn't have the Fate Blade.

Gilly had already manifested her energy bow. The runes on her arms were a bright blue. "Darn, guys, I don't have any silver arrows, just wood and aluminum. But I do have a little bit of Strength I and a little bit of Invulnerability I. Let's put 'em to the test!"

Eliza flicked out the fingers of her right hand. Each finger ended in a silver knife. She must've grabbed one of the gloves from their battle with Vincent. "I have silver, toots. Come here, puppies. Come to Mama." She was smiling.

The werewolves roared in response.

"Why are you smiling?" Colt asked the blond vampire.

Eliza didn't stop grinning for a second. "Because I'm with the Rage King. And he can do everything."

Bafflestone grabbed what looked like an old-fashioned blunderbuss musket. He pulled back on the action, and it made a very shotgun sound. "Then let's teach these pups how we do things in Firestone Alley."

The werewolves attacked.

And the god of rage and destruction, along with the two women he loved, attacked right back.

THE END
Rage King
Book 1

To be continued…
Colt, Gilly, and Eliza will return in RAGE KING #2!

AARON CRASH

RAGE KING
BOOK TWO

THE ADVENTURE CONTINUES...

… in *Rage King Book 2*.

It's a god-eat-god world and the RAGE KING is hungry!

Colt Holliday has the power of a god, and he's learning to control it. But that means gathering women to forge runes of power that give both him and his wives power undreamed of by mortal men.

Colt conquered the vampires, but now a pack of werewolves has moved into his territory. Accompanying the pack is a heart-breakingly beautiful wolf girl who has clawed her way into Colt's life and bed, but taking in the stray has also turned his little blue house upside-down. Can he tame this wild creature of lust before the God of the Moon and the Hunt destroys everything Colt holds dear?

BOOKS AND REVIEWS

If you loved *Rage King* and would like stay in the loop about the latest book releases, deals, and giveaways, be sure to subscribe to the Black Forge Books Mailing List.

BlackForgeBooks.com

Sign up now and get a free copy of *The Five Widows: An American Dragons Short Story*! Your email address will never be shared and you can unsubscribe at any time.

Word-of-mouth and book reviews are beyond helpful for the success of any writer, so please consider leaving a rating or a short, honest review on Amazon—just a couple of lines about your overall reading experience. Thank you in advance!

You can also connect with us on our Facebook Page where we do even more giveaways: facebook.com/blackforgebooks

MORE BOOKS BY BLACK FORGE BOOKS

BLACK FORGE BOOKS

ENTER THE BLACK FORGE LIBRARY to take a peek at all of our amazing gamelit/harem books! American Dragons, Dungeon Bringer, Creature Girl Creations, and more... Your next favorite book is waiting for you inside!

BlackForgeBooks.com

LIST OF THE LEYFOLK ORDERS

Vampires – Order of the Night

- Leyfolk with magical abilities that need to drink human blood to survive

Werewolves – Order of the Moon

- Lycanthrope shifters who prowl the Gaia Towns on the plains

Fae – Order of the Dew

- An ambitious, if delicate, winged people who prefer mountain Gaia Towns, but can shift to appear human if they need to

Houdon – Order of the Bite

- An ancient race of dog people known to be friendly and hard-working

LIST OF THE LEYFOLK ORDERS

Goyangi – Order of the Scratch

- Cat people who are found in Gaia Towns across the globe

Kobolds – Order of the Scales

- Greedy, sneaky, scaled people who hoard gold, jewels, and all manner of money

Tomte – Order of the Forge

- Small blue gnomes who excel in engineering as well as magical crafting

Lyra – Order of the Song

- Tall, slender elves who are good artists and engineers

Unseelies – Order of the Laugh

- Small, winged creatures who like to play tricks on humans and Leyfolk alike

Kelpie – Order of the Waves

- Ocean shifters who rule the waves and Gaia Towns close to the coastline

Uttuku – Order of the Damned

- Demonic creatures who worship the goddess of chaos, Ziki-Urrudu

Annukai – Order of the Adored

LIST OF THE LEYFOLK ORDERS

- Angelic forces who worship Yaz-Nammu, the god of light and law

ACKNOWLEDGMENTS

The RAGE KING started as an idea that James Hunter and I kicked around, driving around in Lexington, Kentucky, pondering what I should write after wrapping up THE PRINCESSES OF THE IRONBOUND series. I wanted to get back to urban fantasy, and James agreed, and hence, the RAGE KING was born. He and Jess worked on several iterations of the cover, so I hope you like it.

This time, I went and talked out the ideas with the alpha team at Black Forge Books, a collection of readers, writers, and fans that helped me with world-building, names, character motivation, and mechanics. Thanks to DJ, Jess, Cameron, Ken, and a bunch of other people. Love your ideas! Love the RAGE KING!

Special thanks to my Lord-Level Patrons: Bruce Johnson, Colt McIntosh, Daniel, Robert Crowder, and Tygah Shawk. You guys make this whole deal possible.

Thanks to my amazing editors, DJ and Kelly and Bethany, who help me not to look too stupid. Final thanks to everyone at Black Forge Press. We're writing books and kicking ass.

PATREON

Thanks so much for reading *Rage King* (Rage King Book 1)!

Be sure to check out my Patreon page. I'm posting cover art and chapters, and giving away free ebooks when they come out. Yes, being my patron gets you the chapters and the ebook before anyone else! It's a deal.

Also, if you have an idea for a story, or a suggestion, my Patreon page is the perfect place to reach out. That's the thing with Patreon—if the fans want a specific story, I'll write one, however spicy, in any of my worlds.

It's been my lifelong dream to become a professional novelist, and I hope to share more of my journey with you as I continue to write books people love.

Sign up here at www.patreon.com/aaroncrashbooks.

Thanks again!

Aaron Crash

ABOUT THE AUTHOR

Aaron Crash writes adrenaline-fueled odysseys into the extreme regions of speculative fiction. If you're looking for cyborg vampires or jellyfish centaurs, you've come to the right place. He is the co-author of the War God's Mantle series (Shadow Alley Press) and other over-the-top sci-fi/fantasy novels. He's been an Amazon All-Star and his books have broken into Amazon's Top 100. When he's not wrestling the word dragons, he mountain bikes, kills pixels dead, and has been known to watch a movie or three. He lives in Colorado where he does devilish things.